VINDICTA

VINDICTA

ROGER HUNT

Cover illustration by Rob Page

Troubador Publishing Ltd
Unit E2 Airfield Business Park,
Harrison Road, Market Harborough,
Leicestershire LE16 7UL
Tel: 0116 279 2299
Email: books@troubador.co.uk
Web: www.troubador.co.uk

ISBN 978 1 83628 271 6

British Library Cataloguing in Publication Data.
A catalogue record for this book is available from the British Library.

The manufacturer's authorised representative in the EU for product
safety is Authorised Rep Compliance Ltd, 71 Lower Baggot Street,
Dublin D02 P593 Ireland (www.arccompliance.com).

Printed and bound by CPI Group (UK) Ltd, Croydon, CR0 4YY
Typeset in 11pt Minion Pro by Troubador Publishing Ltd, Leicester, UK

For Anthea and all the encouragers

Vindicta, ae, *f,* the ceremonial act of claiming as a free man one who contends he is wrongly held in slavery; vengeance; punishment.

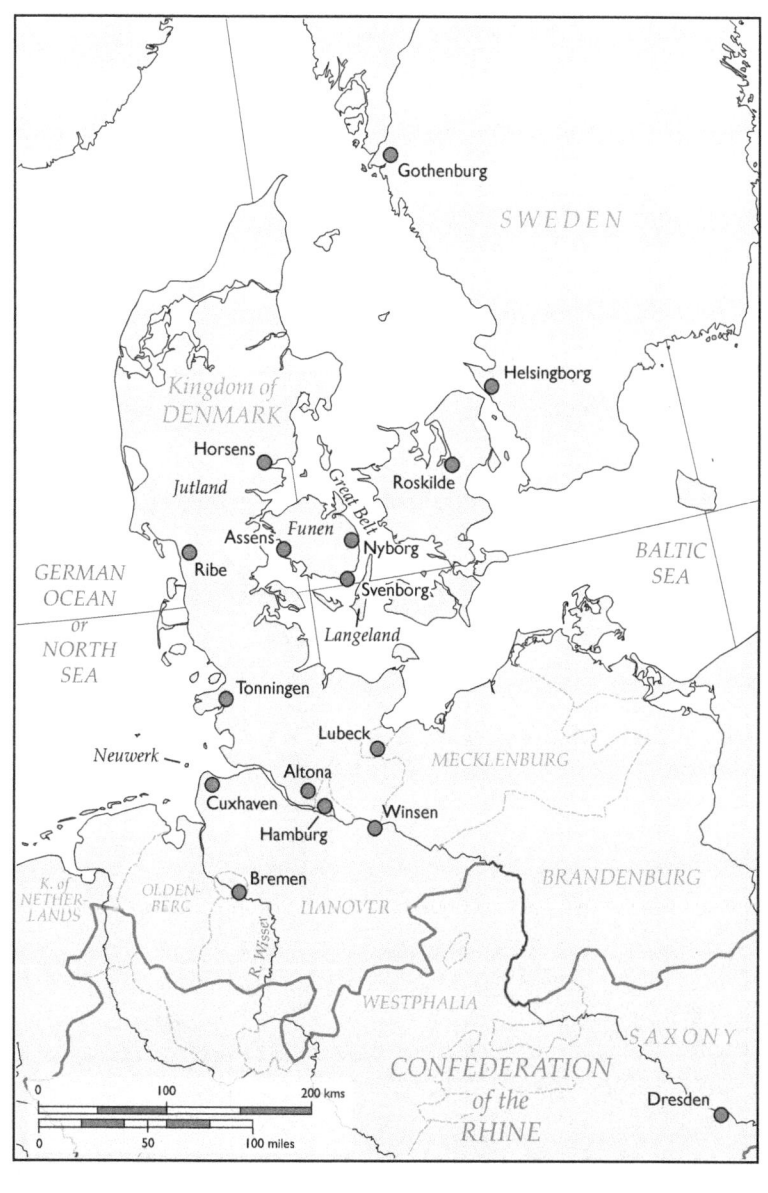

Gothenburg

SWEDEN

Helsingborg

Kingdom of
DENMARK

Horsens

Jutland

Roskilde

Great Belt

Funen

Assens

Nyborg

Ribe

Svenborg

GERMAN
OCEAN
or
NORTH
SEA

Langeland

BALTIC
SEA

Tonningen

Neuwerk

Lubeck

MECKLENBURG

Altona

Cuxhaven

Winsen

Hamburg

K. of
NETHER-
LANDS

OLDEN-
BERG

R. Weser

HANOVER

BRANDENBURG

Bremen

WESTPHALIA

SAXONY

CONFEDERATION
of the
RHINE

Dresden

| 0 | 100 | 200 kms |
| 0 | 50 | 100 miles |

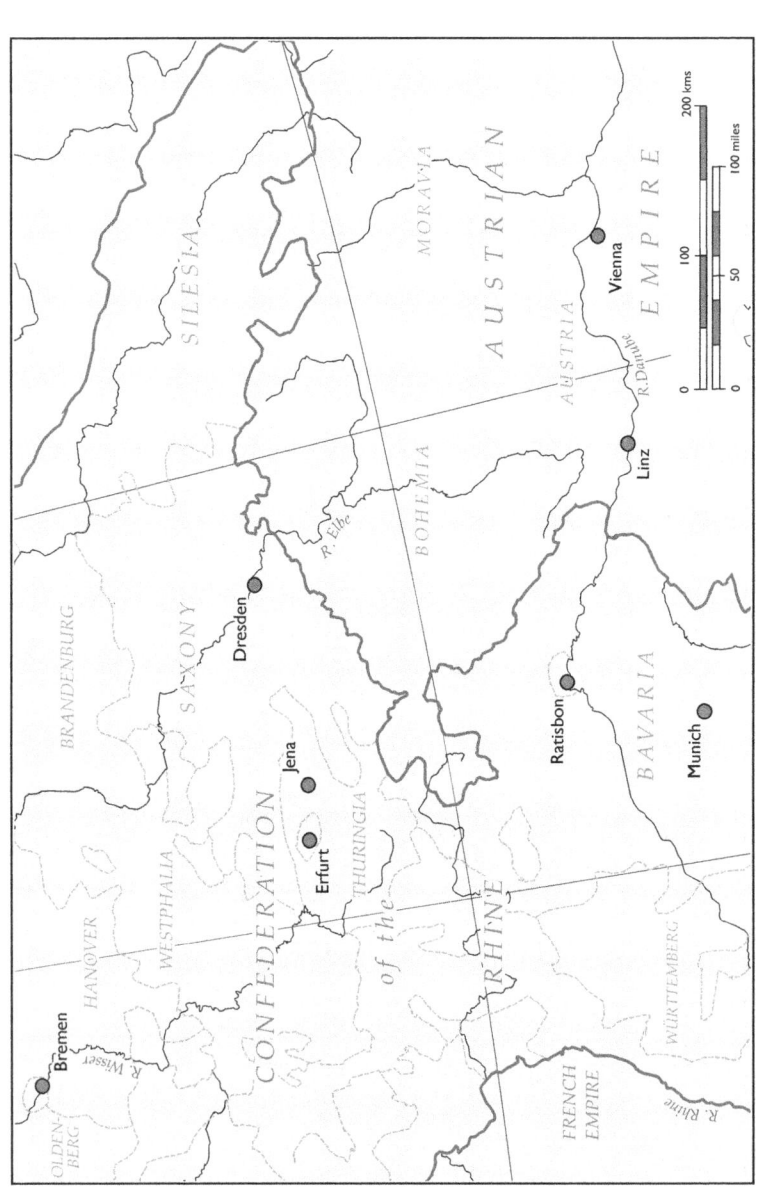

1
Dawn Ritzebuttel Castle, Cuxhaven, Hanover, March 1808

Wrapped in his greatcoat against the biting northerly wind, Jacques Marquet de Montbreton watched as the guard of six gendarmes escorted the blood-spattered man into the walled garden. Hands tied behind his back. The man tripped and fell. The corporal spat.

'Huchet and Mortemart, pick him up.'

Two gendarmes transferred their muskets to their other hands, grabbed the man under each shoulder and dragged him to the post. Propping him up against the post, they untied the man's hands and retied them behind the post. The man's knees buckled. His chin collapsed onto his chest. The corporal ordered the gendarmes into line facing the man and walked up to him.

'Blindfold?' No answer. The corporal returned to the side of the line.

'Load.' Each gendarme reached into his pouch, took out a paper cartridge and bit off the end containing the ball, retaining the ball in his mouth, opened the pan of the musket, poured in the priming charge, closed the pan, and ordered arms. Each tipped the remainder of the charge down the barrel, spat the musket ball after it, folded the paper into a wad and then forced ball and wad down the barrel with his ramrod.

'Present… aim… fire!'

The six Charleville "1777" model muskets roared with flame and dense white smoke. Once the smoke had cleared, Marquet looked at what was left of the man. Great blotches of red appeared on his chest. Marquet also saw a steel pin in the dead man's shoulder.

'Is that a ramrod?' he asked the corporal.

The corporal spat again. 'Which one of you idiots left his ramrod in the barrel? You are supposed to all be veterans!' The six gendarmes looked down at their belts. Huchet's chest sank.

'Get it out of the spy's shoulder. My god, you have fought at Austerlitz and Jena and should know better! Cut the body down and dig the grave.'

The corporal turned to Marquet and saluted. 'I am sorry, Captain.' Marquet acknowledged the salute, turned and walked back to the warmth of the castle.

Taking off his shako and greatcoat, Marquet made his way to the Great Hall. The gendarme guarding the entrance demanded his name, knocked on the door and at the sound of 'come', opened the double doors.

Marquet followed the gendarme.

Colonel Pierre Henry Joseph Maupont was warming his back against the roaring fire. He turned and nodded his response to Marquet's salute. Looking Marquet up and down, Maupont opened: 'What a pretty uniform! Look at it: white button jacket with collar, green tipped siding, scarlet waistcoat, silver knots to the trousers and black boots in the Hungarian style. But of course, that is to be expected of an officer of the Ordinance Gendarmerie of the Imperial Guard!'

Marquet's face coloured.

The colonel went on: 'What would one expect when the unit was composed solely of wealthy gentlemen from the great families of the *Ancien Régime*? Some of us have had to make our way without a silver spoon stuffed in our mouths from birth!'

Marquet sighed internally. How many times had he been ribbed as a member of the nobility and had to defend himself. Now this, coming from a veteran late of the 17th Legion of Gendarmes based in Liège, what was it? Jealousy?

'Colonel, I was arrested after the *coup d'état* of the 17th Fructidor and jailed in La Force eleven years ago. I was tried by the War Council and permanently released after the 18th Brumaire. I was cabinet secretary to General Leclerc and spent three years in Santo Domingo. Three attacks of yellow fever forced me to return to France. I served in the Ordinance Gendarmerie for two years in Prussia, but you know that.'

The colonel smiled. 'Of course, my dear Marquet, and you received the *Légion d'honneur* following the

Marienwerder affair. What was it like tangling with the Cossacks?'

'Brutal.'

'I can imagine. Tell me later. Now let's have a cognac, breakfast and discuss your appointment to Marshal Bernadotte's staff.'

After breakfast, they moved to the small salon.

Marquet asked, 'Why was the man executed?'

'Not your first execution?'

'Indeed not. There were many spies operating in eastern Prussia.'

'I'll explain, but first, some background.'

Colonel Maupont began: 'Reporting to me, you will be responsible for counter-intelligence in the Hamburg region and will work with our new allies, the Danes, to counter British activities in the area. The Emperor has instructed the foreign minister to write to Marshal Bernadotte and the chief consul in Hamburg, Monsieur Bourrienne. He reminds them both that they should most rigorously apply the conditions of the Berlin Decree and now that the Tsar has agreed to join the Continental System, prevent England from distilling her poison on the continent. Are you aware of the Berlin Decree?'

'Yes, Colonel, to strangle England's economy and to prevent her exports reaching the continent.'

'Correct, and now after the glorious victory at Friedland and the Emperor's meeting with the Tsar at Tilsit, we now have the Russian empire as allies and will close the Baltic to English shipping.'

'But what about the British Navy? Does it not have large

fleets operating in the North Sea and Baltic? And isn't their navy even more powerful since they bombarded Copenhagen last year and stole the Danish Navy's major ships?'

'The Emperor regards that unprovoked attack as a major strategic blunder by the British Government. It has driven all the governments of the world to our side and left the English even more isolated. In particular, the Danish Government signed the Treaty of Fontainbleau with us last October that leaves just Sweden as allies of the British in the region. Remember as well that Norway is part of Denmark. We are also building new ships in Antwerp. It won't be long before we are able to sweep the British from the sea. Even the King of Spain offered a division of his best troops to help the marshal suppress the Swedish stronghold of Stralsund.'

'I had heard that there were Spanish troops wintering around Lübeck. They are quite a novelty and the butt of many a joke among our troops.'

'Don't be too dismissive of our Spanish friends. They performed well at the siege of Stralsund and in the Marquis de La Romana, they have a fine commander. The Spaniards are a powerful force of 14,000 and, as we speak, are moving into Denmark to help protect the Danes from any further British incursions and to prepare for a possible invasion of Sweden.'

'Will they be billeted with the Danish populace? And at Danish expense?'

'Of course, as all our troops are across the German states, Prussia, Poland and the other states who have joined the Empire.'

Hardly popular with the Danes, thought Marquet.

Maupont continued. 'That is enough of the bigger picture for now, let's look at the local situation in more detail. Have you heard of the island of Heligoland?'

'Is it somewhere in the North Sea?'

'It is sixty kilometres north-west of here. That's around six or seven hours' sailing from Cuxhaven. The English captured the island from the Danes last September. Since then, many English merchants have established trading offices and warehouses. In just these few months, smuggling operations have increased dramatically.

'But more relevant to your mission, the British now have both military and diplomatic staff on the island. It did not take them long to find ways around both ours and the Danes' gunboats which patrol the mouth of the River Weser and the harbours in Holstein.

'Thanks to the persuasive methods of the corporal you met earlier this morning, the man you saw executed told us that the English foreign minister, Canning, has appointed an experienced diplomat to head the mission on the island. The man did not know his name but he told us that the diplomat arrived on Heligoland in January. Nor was he able to tell us what his role is but if Canning was involved in his appointment, he must be important.

'I suspect that the diplomat could be an important link in the English attempts to spread their poison across the continent. The marshal wants you to find out who this man is, what he is up to and then do what is necessary to prevent and disrupt his operations. You are to prepare a plan which you will present to the marshal and the consul. How long do you need to prepare?'

Marquet thought. 'Two weeks?'

'One.'

'If it must be. Can I ask what else the spy revealed?'

Maupont looked disappointed. 'He was a local from Hamburg and was acting simply as a courier delivering letters that he had collected from the main post office. His name was Johannes Schmidt, aged twenty-eight, married with two children. We have yet to interrogate his wife. Schmidt told us that he worked as clerk in the fish market and had been persuaded to act as a courier by his brother who had traitorously joined the British Army. We know that there is an active network of pro-British Hanoverians who recruit young men for the British, to serve in a unit called the King's German Legion. This network may also be run from Heligoland.'

'Quite a web of intrigue,' noted Marquet.

'Indeed, that is why the marshal and Monsieur Bourrienne require action to counter this threat.'

Marquet asked: 'What happened to the letters Schmidt was carrying?'

'The incompetents from customs were full of themselves when they found letters hidden in Schmidt's cravat but somehow allowed him to swallow the letters before they handed him over to us.'

'That is disappointing. The letters would have been very revealing. Presumably they would have been in code – do we know what ciphers the English use?'

Maupont looked at Marquet. 'I am waiting to hear from Paris. Gendarmerie Inspector General Moncey will talk with both General Desmaret and General

Landrieux of the Security Police. We may have been reading their ciphers. There may also be information locally left over from the disastrous British expedition to Hanover in December '06. They landed 26,000 troops here in Cuxhaven and ran away home in February, having achieved nothing!'

'Perhaps the English use something similar to our *Petit Chiffre*?'

'That's possible but it is unlikely that they have been able to deliver sets of coding tables to all their agents. No, if they use ciphers, it will be something simpler and therefore easier to crack.'

Marquet asked, 'How come there is so much support for the English in this region?'

'My dear Marquet, do you know where King George comes from? He's a Hanoverian. His father was born in Hanover. To add to that, all merchants in the Hanseatic ports have close ties with England, none more so than Hamburg and Bremen. A week, then. I look forward to hearing from you.'

Both men stood. Marquet saluted and watched Maupont leave the room. It grated that whatever he did, it was impossible to disguise his noble background. However, apart from the jibe – Maupont's idea of a joke, maybe – the colonel had been professional. Someone he could work for? Probably. In any case, he would need all the friends he could cultivate when it came to stepping into the backstabbing nest of vipers; a delightful phrase he had heard used to describe the staff based at Marshal Bernadotte's headquarters. Only seven days to prepare; that meant not much sleep if he was to impress Maupont. To start, some geography. Where exactly was Heligoland?

2

Heythrop Park, Oxfordshire,
March 1808

The Reverend James Robertson picked up his cut-throat and sighed. Here he was now just a simple chaplain. Yes, a chaplain to a leading member of the aristocracy – the Earl of Shrewsbury and Waterford no less – and ensconced in a magnificent baroque mansion. But still merely a chaplain.

He pulled the towel round his ample girth. He looked down. He could not see his toes. Short and stout he had overheard him being described. In the mirror he saw the full face, the sideburns either side of a balding pate and fat neck with sadly more than a hint of double chin. He ran his thumb across the blade of the cut-throat – sharp enough – and pulled the skin around his jawbone tight.

As if he was about to change his mind, he put down the blade. Placing both hands palm down on the table either side of the bowl, he locked his elbows so that his arms were rigid. Robertson stared into the mirror once again. Not normally morose, on this particular March day, he was in a reflective mood.

He would be fifty in October, regarded by most people as old. What had he achieved? The promise and enthusiasm of youth had faded. Now all these years later, here he was, Father Gallus, still simply a Benedictine monk. What were the words that Abbot Arbuthnot had used? "You may be extroverted, energetic, talented, fearless and determined, but you are less well endowed with prudence and patience. You are uncomfortable as a subordinate."

Was that why he had never achieved positions of authority? He looked down from the mirror and now saw his face in the water. Sadly, Arbuthnot was probably right. Yes, there had been successes: persuading Consul Napoleon not to close the seminary in Ratisbon while all the other monasteries in Germany were forced to shut their doors, was certainly an achievement. His work in Ireland had been admired by Secretary Arthur Wellesley and even the lord-lieutenant himself, His Grace the Duke of Richmond. But those highlights had been interspersed by mundane work as a priest, teacher and tutor. Here he was now a chaplain. Comfortable, easy work at the highest levels of society but hardly exhilarating. Robertson could envisage a period five years hence when his girth had widened further and gout had set in. He looked up at the mirror again. Was that really what life had in store for him?

He should really count his blessings. Remember, he was a Roman Catholic and a Scottish Catholic and from an English gutter-press perspective, worse still, a Scottish Catholic from the Highlands. It would not take any journalist looking for a sensational story long to connect Clan Robertson to the '15 and '45 rebellions and therefore question his loyalties. How far from the truth that was. Even ten years ago, he had been thanked by the lord advocate for warning of the efforts of the Robespirists to infiltrate masonic lodges and the army. The French Government's goal was to break the Catholic Church throughout Europe. Britain had been at war with France for fifteen years. While the country's goals were aligned with his, he would do all he could to help defeat Napoleon. And if the goals diverged at some later date, where would his final loyalties lie? Mother Church and the Rule of Saint Benedict, of course.

Hopes for a change in status with political pressure for emancipation had come up against the bulwark of the King who believed that any relaxation would break his coronation vows. Despite his position at Heythrop, could he see any change in his lifetime? Probably not: he had to resign himself to being a second-class citizen as he had been for most of his life. Settle for the status quo, that was the sensible option. But the gnawing feeling would not leave him. Surely there was something more to life? But, more likely, perhaps there wasn't.

Robertson picked up the cut-throat again, pulled his skin tight across his jawbone and felt the blade begin to do its work.

Hammering on the door of his garret room made him jump. The blade slipped. He could feel his blood oozing from the cut. He picked up a hand towel, held it to the cut to staunch the flow.

'Yes? Come in.' A footman appeared. Robertson turned.

'Look what you have made me do. I was shaving.'

The footman ignored him. 'His Lordship has been summoned to Court and wishes to hold Mass early.'

'When, may I ask?'

'In fifteen minutes.'

'Let me finish my ablutions. Is there time for breakfast?'

'No, breakfast after mass.' As the footman left, Robertson rubbed a mixture of salt and St John's wort into the cut. The bleeding would soon stop. So the start of another day. At least the routine would be slightly different today, but not much. He had better get used to it. He felt a twinge in his foot. Was that gout coming on already?

3

The Foreign Office, Downing Street, London
March 1808

Two months earlier, Richard Belgrave Hoppner and the senior clerk, Stephen Rolleston, were shown into George Hammond's office. The Under-Secretary of State for Foreign Affairs indicated that both should sit.

Hammond turned to Hoppner: 'Before we begin, I believe that your father has not been well. How is he?'

'Rather frail, I'm afraid. That's why he is unlikely to exhibit in this year's Royal Society's summer exhibition.'

'I'm sorry to hear that. I admired the portrait of Admiral Hood that he finished last year – a fine likeness, I understand. And his talent has rubbed off on you, I see. You exhibited some watercolours in last year's exhibition, did you not?'

'That is very kind of you, Mr Hammond. My father is indeed fortunate to have had the patronage of His Royal Highness, the Prince of Wales.'

'Fortunate indeed. But on to business: You have been with this department for seven years now and yet you are still only twenty-two. Mr Rolleston and Mr Bidwell report that you have made good progress. Agreed, Mr Rolleston?'

'Yes, Mr Hammond, we concur.'

'Thank you.'

Hammond continued: 'You have fluency in German, Spanish as well as French. This and your record to date have persuaded us that, of the clerks of the department, you are the one who should prepare an important report for the Secretary of State. If it reads well, it will no doubt be circulated to the First Lord of the Treasury, Lord Portland, and to the other King's ministers. Viscount Castlereagh in the War Office will also be an important correspondent.'

Hoppner's stomach tightened. This could make or break his career.

'Following the success of our operations in Denmark last September, the Secretary of State is determined to look for other opportunities to damage the Corsican and to spread unrest in the states he, Napoleon, has occupied. You are tasked with writing an appreciation of the current state of affairs in northern Germany and the Baltic and then to suggest what actions we can take to damage the Corsican's regime. Mr Canning is looking for subtle approaches. With planned operations elsewhere, we do not have the resources to launch major expeditions and certainly cannot match the size and strength of the *Grande Armée*.'

Hoppner thought: 'Should the appreciation begin with the Corsican's meeting with Tsar Alexander at Tilsit last

June, the fallout from their agreement and the impact it has had on His Majesty's government?'

'Yes, a good starting point. But be aware that your readers are only too aware of recent events. We are effectively fighting France alone. I'm afraid that we will not be able to count on Sweden or Portugal for active support.'

Hammond's eyes seemed to bore into the back of Hoppner's head.

'A challenge for you?'

'Yes. Thank you, sir, I will do my best.'

'You had better.'

'Mr Rolleston, please give Hoppner whatever resources he needs.' Hammond looked down at the papers on his desk, waving his arm to dismiss the two subordinates.

Back in the clerk's hall, as the other senior clerks and his peers wondered why he had been summoned to the senior under-secretary, Hoppner felt chastened by the responsibility of the task he had been given.

Rolleston put an arm around his shoulder. 'I believe that what the under-secretary and Mr Canning really want is ideas. Yes, of course summarise the current position but keep that brief. Have your Etonian-trained brain focused on where we can do damage to the Corsican with the minimum of risk and cost.' Hoppner let the Eton jibe pass as he had many times before. Perhaps one day Rolleston and the others would give up attempting to provoke him. Just ignore them, he had been told years ago.

He sat, elbows on his desk and rested his chin on the heels of his hands. It had been a long, long time since the glorious news of Trafalgar. Since then, there had been one disaster after another. The Austrians defeated at Austerlitz, the supposedly invincible Prussian Army, that magnificent creation of Frederick the Great, crushed at Jena and Auerstadt. And then, despite the promise of the bloody nose that the Russians had given him at Eylau, Napoleon had recovered to smash a much larger Russian Army at Friedland last June. It was indeed a gloomy picture.

Then Tilsit, that meeting between the Corsican and Tsar Alexander on a raft moored in the middle of the River Niemen. It was bad enough that the treaty allied Russia to France, forced Prussia to become a puppet state and gave Napoleon control of central Europe. Once British agents had discovered the secret clauses of the treaty, the Tsar had agreed to close Russian ports to British shipping and forced Austria, Sweden and Denmark to do the same. Once implemented, Napoleon would achieve his aim of closing the whole of mainland Europe to Britain's trade.

Hoppner remembered a paper he had read about the trade with Russia through the Baltic ports. Over 17,000 of the Navy's masts came from Russia with similar quantities of hemp and flax. How would the Royal Navy replace this critical source?

By action: to prevent the powerful Danish Navy falling into Napoleon's hands, the British launched a pre-emptive strike against Denmark. The Danes were still neutral but, under intense pressure from the Corsican, were unlikely to remain so. In August a task force under Admiral Gambier landed troops commanded by Lord Cathcart and Sir Arthur Wellesley. The army besieged Copenhagen. The civilian loss of life and the destruction of much of the city by fire were to be regretted. There was outrage from across Europe and even protests from the opposition in the House of Commons. However, the bulk of the Danish fleet including seventeen men of war, were towed or sailed back to England – a triumph of British arms.

What of Britain's remaining allies in Europe? The oldest, Portugal had succumbed to Marshal Junot's Army in December. At least the Portuguese royal family, much of the nobility and government had escaped on Royal Navy ships to Brazil. It seemed though that another ally had fallen into the Corsican's clutches.

That left Sweden. With the surrender of her fortress at Stralsund in August, she had lost Pomerania, her last territory on the mainland. Now the Tsar had launched offensive operations in her territory in Finland. To end a turbulent year, on 26 December, Russia had declared war against England.

Hoppner took sheets of paper from the drawer of his desk and began to map out the headings of his report. He just hoped that the writing process would trigger ideas, because at this stage there was nothing.

4

Cesar Rainville's Hotel, Altona,
North of Hamburg

Exactly one week after the execution and his interview with Colonel Maupont, Jacques Marquet de Montbreton rode up to the gates of the hotel that the Prince of Ponte Corvo used as his headquarters when he was in the Hamburg region. His eyes were sore from lack of sleep. His neck and shoulders ached; too much time hunched over his desk working in poor candlelight. When he had finally flopped into bed and had fallen asleep, to be woken by the night soil man emptying the cesspit was the last straw.

He had attempted to discuss his research with the colonel but Maupont was away in the east and would not return until today. Not having the colonel's approval left him feeling exposed especially when all he had had from the colonel was a note informing him that he was to present his report to the Prince of Ponte Corvo himself. Despite his exhaustion, when he read through the final draft, he was reasonably satisfied with the result.

Looking up the drive to the elegant Palladian house, Marquet admired the verandas, a feature on both the ground and first floors. It was no surprise that the marshal had chosen this as his base in the Hamburg area despite it being just over the border in Denmark. Now that the Danish King had signed the Treaty of Fontainbleu allying Denmark to France, Marquet supposed that the Prince was able to choose any house or palace that took his fancy.

Rainville's was owned by a Frenchman who had bought the property in 1799 and had developed it as the region's premier hotel. The guest rooms were the ultimate in luxury while the dinners, state receptions and garden parties were based on the French model for wealthy guests. Such were Rainville's events marked by exclusivity, it was no surprise that he became known as the "God of Innkeepers" – an obvious choice for Bernadotte.

Should he be summoned into the "presence", he must remember to refer to Bernadotte as Prince not as Marshal Bernadotte. His wife's sister was married to the Emperor's brother, Joseph. A faux pas of that magnitude could easily lead to prison or, worse, Madame La Guillotine. "Prince" it was.

Marquet presented his pass to the sergeant of the guard. He noticed that some of the guards wore uniforms that he did not recognise and asked the sergeant who these troops were.

'Ah, they are Spaniards, part of the Marquis de La

Romana's Division del Norte. The Prince commanded that the marquis provide him some of his best soldiers to join his personal guard.'

Marquet was surprised but then remembered that the marshal had been born in Pau in the foothills of the Pyrenees and might well have an affinity with his Basque neighbours over the border.

He made his way up the drive, showed his pass again to another sergeant of the guard, walked up the steps and knocked on the front door. A corporal of the Imperial Guard opened the door and ushered Marquet into the hall. The room was full of staff officers. The corporal lead him to the adjutant's office and asked him to sit. The wait then began. He was offered coffee and took the opportunity to stretch his legs. He made his way through the double doors and out onto another large veranda. The view over the gardens across to the River Elbe was glorious. Marquet returned to his seat. Coffee arrived. The wait continued.

Finally, the adjutant showed Marquet into the large salon. There, sitting behind an elegant desk in the latest imperial style, was the man Marquet recognised as Marshal Jean-Baptiste Bernadotte, Prince of Ponte Corvo. Standing to one side was Colonel Maupont and sitting was another man he did not recognise. Marquet saluted.

'Prince,' Maupont began, 'may I present Captain Jacques Marquet de Montbreton?'

Bernadotte nodded. Tapping the file on the desk, he said, 'You have served the Emperor well despite your parentage.'

Marquet saluted again. 'Thank you, Your Royal

Highness.' Inside he was seething. It was not his fault that his parents had been members of the minor aristocracy. But he supposed that was the sort of jibe to come from the son of a tailor.

Maupont indicated to the other person sitting. 'And this is Monsieur Bourrienne, the Emperor's consul in Hamburg.'

Marquet bowed. So, this was the famous Bourrienne, Bonaparte's personal secretary for five years. Rumour had it that Napoleon had finally been so fed up with Bourrienne's rapacious greed that he had him sacked. After a period of disgrace, Bourrienne had ended up here.

Marquet turned back to the marshal. The reports were true. Bernadotte was indeed impressive. He could see why Napoleon's one-time fiancée, Desiree Clary, had fallen for the marshal. It was common knowledge that Bernadotte had earned his reputation as a fine commander in the early days of the Revolutionary wars. The fact that he was "family" persuaded Napoleon to tear up the order to court-marshal Bernadotte after his failure to engage his 1st Corps at either Jena or Auerstadt. A musket ball to the neck in the action at Spanden necessitated rest, hence the posting as governor of the Hanseatic towns and northern Germany.

The Prince looked up: 'So, Marquet, what do you suggest we do to disrupt this irritating English activity emanating from Heligoland?'

Marquet took a deep breath. 'Your Royal Highness, I propose interlinked courses of action. Now that we have closed Tonningen to the English, they have switched to smuggling through the rivers Weser and Elbe. We must increase the presence of the gendarmerie around the mouths of each river coordinating with our gunboats. The offshore islands, in particular Neuwerk, should be regularly inspected. And finally, before I move on to Heligoland itself, I understand that many of the banks in Hamburg still have close ties to English merchants warranting most careful investigation.'

'Very commendable, Marquet,' interrupted Bourrienne, 'but what would Director of Imperial Customs, Monsieur Pyonnier, feel about you gendarmes treading all over his turf?'

Marquet was ready for this. 'We would cooperate with and support the Imperial Customs, not take over from them.'

'I think you'll find that Pyonnier is very protective of his patch,' retorted Bourrienne.

'With all due respect, Monsieur Consul, my research of the past week has shown that the whole coastline leaks like a sieve – large quantities of contraband find their way into Hamburg and the other major towns of the region.'

Bourrienne's face darkened. 'Your research?' He spat the words out. 'And which Hamburg banks do you propose investigating?'

'Well, Parish & Company for a start.'

Bourrienne glowered, ready to explode.

What had he said to offend the Consul? Marquet realised he had unknowingly dug a hole for himself. He turned to Maupont, eyes pleading.

Maupont responded. 'Captain, your brief was to put

23

forward ideas to counter the English intelligence activity emanating from Heligoland. Other suggestions are laudable but outside your remit.'

'Of course, Colonel, my apologies.'

Bernadotte smiled at the consul. 'It seems the captain realises that he has blundered into areas outside his capability.'

Bourrienne turned to Marquet, smiled but with pure hatred in his eyes. 'He has indeed, my Prince.'

Bernadotte slapped the edge of the desk. 'The brief.'

Time to climb out of the hole. 'Yes, Your Royal Highness.' Another deep breath; 'Since the English captured Heligoland six months ago, there has been a significant build-up of military, diplomatic and merchant personnel. It appears that the British wish to make Heligoland the linchpin of their smuggling efforts. An English diplomat arrived on the island in January. We don't know his name but it seems he is known as "Der Consul".'

'So, what do you propose?' interjected Bourrienne.

'With the British Navy dominant, there is no prospect of us launching an attack on the island without significant loss of life. More subtle means should be used to disrupt English operations.'

Bourrienne, again condescendingly, said, 'Well then, let's have it.'

'We should put our own agents on the island.'

'If I may, Your Royal Highness?' asked Maupont.

'Of course.'

Maupont turned to Marquet. 'How will you recruit these agents and how will you get them onto the island and the intelligence back to us?'

'Ideally, they'll be French who speak fluent German. We will equip them with ciphers so that they can encode their information and we will use the same smugglers that the English employ to transport them to the island and receive their reports.'

'But that's ridiculous!' shouted Bourrienne. 'Those villains will inform the English as soon as they have the chance!'

Marquet stood his ground. 'If they know what will happen to their families if they betray us, I doubt it. And besides, Monsieur Le Consul, we'll pay them double the rate they receive from the English. That way they are paid twice for each trip they make.'

The Prince stood up. 'Proceed. Colonel, I will leave you to work up the details of the plan with Marquet. Report back once you are ready to put the operation into action.'

Maupont and Marquet saluted and were waved from the room. Maupont took Marquet's arm and led him out of the house and into the garden. Marquet let out a sigh of relief. He felt he had been put through a mangle. As they reached the garden, he realised he was drenched in sweat.

Maupont released Marquet's arm and turned to him. 'A word – be careful of crossing swords with Monsieur Bourrienne. He is very well connected and has powerful friends. We do not want you back in the La Force prison as you were after the *coup d'état* ten years ago.'

Marquet looked at Maupont. 'But why was Bourrienne so worked up about my comments on the sieve-like nature of our coastal patrols?'

'Because maybe he likes them that way?'

'And the bank?'

Before he had any time to ask Maupont what he meant, the colonel put his index finger to his lips.

5

Heythrop Park, Oxfordshire, March 1808

Mass over, the Reverend James Robertson waited at the door of Heythrop's lavish private chapel. He bowed as Charles Talbot, 15th Earl of Shrewsbury, came towards him. The earl extended his hand.

'An excellent service, Father Gallus, and a thought-provoking homily.'

'Thank you, my lord.'

'I trust that you are settling into life here at Heythrop.'

'I am indeed, my lord.'

'We haven't had the opportunity to have a proper talk. Once you have cleared up, come to my study. The weather looks well set, we'll take a stroll round the garden.'

'I shall look forward to it, thank you.'

Robertson watched as the earl made his way through the Great Hall. As soon as the earl was out of sight, he returned to the chapel and tidied the hymn and prayer books. At the altar, he finished the small amount of bread and the holy wine left over from the sacrament. He took the gold chalice and plate to the vestibule, washed and locked both away. Then he peeled off and carefully hung up his holy vestments and put on his Benedictine habit. Checking that all was in order, he closed the door of the chapel and made his way to the earl's study. As he was about to knock, the butler opened the door to leave the study. The butler turned back towards the earl who was sitting at his desk bent over what looked like a manuscript. The butler coughed.

'Father Gallus, my lord.'

Charles Talbot looked up. 'Ah, Father, good. Will you be warm enough for our stroll?'

'I'm sure I will be, my lord.'

Grabbing a cloak, the earl led the way to the formal garden in front of the Palladian facade of the house. It was one of those delightful early spring days, breezy with a few scudding clouds only occasionally hiding the sun. Daffodils poked their heads about the privet.

'I'm glad to hear that you have settled in. I expect you are glad to be away from the dampness of Ireland.'

'Yes, my lord, though during my travels, some of the scenery reminded me of home.'

'I didn't know that the Irish countryside resembled the rolling hills and pine forests of Bavaria?'

Robertson laughed. 'No, my lord, I meant home in Perthshire, near Blair Atholl, on the edge of the Cairngorms.'

'Splendid clan country, hence your faith.'

Robertson shot the earl a glance, worried the direction of the conversation could lead to awkward questions about his ancestors' involvement with the Jacobite uprisings. He kept his reply as bland as he could.

'The Clan Donnachaidl has strong Catholic roots.'

'Do you still have family in Scotland?'

'My mother is still with us, thank the Lord, as are my two sisters, though it has been quite some time since I last saw them.' Time to move the conversation away from Scotland.

'I was only thirteen when I left for my schooling in the Scots College in the Low Countries.'

'And then on to the Scottish seminary at Ratisbon. Remind me, how long ago did you take your vows?'

Robertson had to pause. This was rather like an interview but he couldn't see any harm in answering fully.

'Gosh, I've just realised. It was thirty years ago.'

'*Tempus Fugit.*'

'Time does indeed fly.' Both men laughed.

'So, I assume you know Father Maurus well?'

Robertson stole a glance at the earl. How did he know of his friend and colleague, Alexander Horn? This could be another potentially sensitive line of questions. Time to answer a question with another.

'Indeed, I do, my lord. May I ask how you know Father Maurus?'

'I have not met the man. I recently visited the Earl Spencer at his Althorp Estate to view his magnificent library. His Lordship told me how useful Father Maurus had been in helping him to acquire rare books and manuscripts.'

Robertson breathed a sigh of relief. It appeared that the earl was not aware that Horn had been a British government agent for the past eighteen years.

Talbot continued. 'Spencer told me that Maurus's connections enabled him to be first to inspect and acquire the best and rarest books from the libraries that were being forced to close by Napoleon. And that, my dear father, is where your name came up!'

'Gracious.'

By now they had reached the end of the formal garden. Talbot led the way down the curved stone staircase on to the roughcut grass marking the start of the parkland that stretched into the distance.

The earl smiled. 'Extraordinary how these coincidences come about, isn't it? We were lunching. The earl told me of the monastery closures. I asked him how come the monastery at Ratisbon did not meet a similar fate. Because, he told me, one of Maurus's colleagues had travelled to Paris and persuaded the then Consul Bonaparte to exempt the Scottish seminary from closure. I must say I was astonished when my host told me who had brought off this coup – a Father Gallus. I must say we roared with laughter when I told the earl that Father Gallus was about to enter my employ. Extraordinary! Now tell me how you managed to change the mind of the man who rules Europe?'

'With some reasoned arguments and the help of two Scottish generals working for the French Army.'

'Come, come, Father. There must have been more to it than that.' Before the earl could press further, a footman appeared out of breath, having run from the house.

'There you are, my lord. The butler asks me to remind you that your guests will arrive in fifteen minutes.' Talbot pulled his half hunter from the pocket in his waistcoat and glanced at the dial.

'Oh dear. I had better prepare. I will have to make time to hear more and of your recent exploits in Ireland. You worked for Sir Arthur Wellesley, did you not?'

'Yes, my lord.' But by then the earl was already walking fast back towards the steps up to the formal garden and the house.

Robertson decided to carry on the walk. He'd be happy to expand on his meeting with Bonaparte. After all, that was years ago. Ireland was a subject that was more tricky to talk about, particularly some elements of the intelligence that Sir Arthur had asked for. As he walked, he began to frame suitably general and bland answers to the questions that the earl might ask.

6

The Foreign Office, Downing Street, London, April 1808

Hoppner stood in front of Mr Rolleston's desk waiting for the chief clerk to finish re-reading the fair copy of his report. He had lost count of the number of times he had written, crossed out, changed, deleted and rewritten the paper. The wait reminded him of his schooldays, that sweaty silence before a dreaded cross-examination.

It was his suggestions for offensive action that had given Hoppner so many sleepless nights. Stalemate had seemed to sum up the situation: the Royal Navy omnipotent at sea while Napoleon all-conquering across Europe. Was it possible to utilise the navy's strength as had been done last September at Copenhagen? If so, what was the target? Hoppner had scoured the maps of northern Europe looking for openings and ideas. Nothing, absolutely nothing came to him. He had even followed his father's suggestion that he should clear his mind by concentrating on something completely different. He forced himself to pack his sketchbook, charcoal and pencils and take a cab to Deptford where he immersed himself in the bustle and hubbub of shipbuilding. That did no good. To make matters worse, his sketches were poor. He tore the pages from the sketchbook and threw them on the fire.

One evening, he had been persuaded by his colleagues, James Bidwell and young Henry Rolleston to put down his pen and adjourn to the Red Lion in Parliament Street. Only when they threatened to drag him out of his chair did he succumb. At the inn, there had been plenty of office gossip. It was when the conversation turned to the events of the moment in Spain that Hoppner had an inkling of an idea. War with Spain continued. Despite the ejection of the ambassador, Mr Hookham Frere and the closing of the Madrid embassy three years before, there were still many sources across Spain providing reliable intelligence. The embellished and biased reports from Pars in *Le Moniteur* and the other government-run newspapers could be taken with an amused pinch of salt. The news had come thick and fast. From the moment in February that the Corsican had accused King Carlos of breaking the terms of the treaty of alliance that had only been signed last October, it seemed obvious that Napoleon meant to force Spain to accept French domination.

Marshal Murat's troops had captured the fortress of San Sebastian on 6 March. On the eighteenth, the residents of Aranjuez rose up. Godoy, the first minister and royal favourite, had a lucky escape from the mob.

The next day, the King abdicated in favour of his son, the popular Ferdinand. It was no surprise to hear that Murat had occupied Madrid. How long would Ferdinand remain on the throne with French troops occupying his capital? Another European kingdom had, it seemed, fallen to the all-powerful emperor.

Walking home that evening, Hoppner wracked his brain. What was that report he had read last year? It had come from Bavaria, he thought, something about Spanish troops. After a fitful night's rest, he was in the office early. He went straight to see Mr Ancell, the librarian and keeper of the papers. Mr Ancell summoned one of his clerks. After a short wait, Hoppner had the file of despatches from Bavaria from Spring 1807.

He was right: In the file was the letter from Alexander Horn. Now it came back to Hoppner, Mr Horn had been a Benedictine monk at the Scottish seminary in Ratisbon. Under the auspices of the Abbot Arbuthnot and with the encouragement of the Duke of Richmond, he had acted as the British agent at the Imperial Diet.

Hoppner returned to the despatch. The monastery's church was one of the few Catholic churches that had escaped Napoleon's secularisation. The abbot had conducted Mass for the senior officers of a division of Spanish troops who were marching to northern Germany to join Marshal Bernadotte's corps. After mass, Mr Horn met the general commanding the division – Pedro Carro Y Sureda, 3rd Marquis de La Romana. He and the marquis had a common interest. La Romana had created one of the largest private libraries in Spain. Horn reported that in earlier years the marquis had travelled extensively through Europe, Russia and in America. His command, the Division del Norte, comprised fourteen battalions of infantry and five of cavalry, some 14,000 troops. Most had marched from Spain, the remainder from Etruria.

Hoppner returned the file to Mr Ancell and asked if there had been other reports of the Spanish division. There had: the British aide-de-camp to Hans Henric von Essen, the Swedish general commanding the defence of Stralsund in Swedish Pomerania, reported that the marquis and his troops formed part of the successful attacking force that compelled von Essen to surrender the town on 24 August.

Further despatches from the agent code-named Pimpernel reported that Spaniards had spent the past winter billeted around Hamburg. It was presumed that the marquis and his division were still in the region on guarding duties as part of Bernadotte's army of occupation.

Hoppner wondered how much the marquis knew of the recent events in Spain. How would La Romana, a man of noble birth, take the news of King Carlos's abdication and Murat's occupation of Madrid? He decided to ask for another interview with Mr Hammond.

Two days later, Mr Rolleston and Hoppner were shown into Mr Hammond's office. Hoppner summarised his work to date. Mr Hammond nodded.

'And the future action you propose?'

Hoppner took a deep breath. 'As we know, Napoleon has a deep hatred of the Bourbons whether they be French, Spanish or from the Kingdom of the Two Sicilies. With Marshal Murat in control of Madrid, it cannot be long before he decides that he has had enough of Carlos and Ferdinand. And the next step: to put one of his brothers on the throne as he's done in Holland, Westphalia and Naples.'

'An interesting scenario, Hoppner, much in line with Mr Canning's thinking. Go on.'

'We will have to await events but surely the deeply Catholic Spanish will rise against an imposed king. From what we know, La Romana is a royalist and patriot. He will surely be deeply troubled by such a *coup d'état* as will most of his troops. If a rebellion against French rule takes place in Spain, the British Government would do what it could to support and foment the rebellion. One way we could support the rebellion would be to provide the rebels with 14,000 experienced troops.'

Hammond interjected. 'You mean that the Royal Navy should transport La Romana's troops from northern Germany back home to Spain?'

'Exactly, sir.'

Hammond sat back in his chair, interlocked his hands behind his head and stared at the stuccoed ceiling. Silence. Hoppner felt a dribble of sweat run down from his armpits. After what seemed to Hoppner to be an age, Mr Hammond leant forward.

'Well, with the success at Copenhagen in September, the navy has necessary recent experience. But how do you propose we communicate with La Romana and, more importantly, persuade him to take action?'

'I would like help to consider the various options, but my initial thought is to send an agent to meet the marquis.'

'That would require a man with particular skills.'

'Yes, sir. This has the additional advantage that, to be brutal, if things went wrong, we would only lose one man and, even if he was caught and interrogated, everything would be deniable.'

'I am glad to see that you appreciate the nuances of diplomacy.' George Hammond stood. 'There is merit. I will discuss your ideas with Mr Canning.'

Rolleston and Hoppner left the office. 'Well done, young Hoppner.'

Three days later, they were summoned into George Hammond's office once again.

Hammond began. 'The Foreign Secretary instructs you to prepare a detailed plan of operations. He will speak with Lord Mulgrave at the Admiralty about the navy's role. This will most likely involve Admiral Saumarez's Baltic fleet and for Captain George in the Transport Office to source the vessels to carry La Romana's troops. Check the marquis's background. We must have a good understanding of motivations and his commitment to the Spanish king whether it be Carlos or Ferdinand. What will be his likely reaction to hearing that a Bonaparte has been placed on the throne? You should then plan how to communicate with La Romana and how best to persuade him to take up our offer of repatriation. Finally, if the best way to brief the marquis is to employ an agent, you should make a list of qualified people. Mr Rolleston, please ensure that Hoppner receives the assistance he requires.'

'Yes, sir,' replied Rolleston. 'May I suggest that someone who has served in our embassy in Madrid may well know the marquis or at least know of him?'

'Very good and why not start with our former ambassador, Mr Hookham Frere?'

'The very man I had in mind, sir. I believe that he is well acquainted with Mr Canning, indeed, I understand that they were friends at Eton. I wonder if the Foreign Secretary could make an introduction for Hoppner?'

'I'm sure Mr Canning will be pleased to effect a meeting. You were at Eton as well, were you not? A useful way to break the ice.'

'Thank you, sir,' replied Hoppner, 'though I was at Eton a number of years after Mr Frere.'

'You'll have plenty to reminisce about despite the gap in years. Now, to the choice of agent. Mr Rolleston will brief you on the people we have working for us. I will also obtain introductions for you to meet Sir Charles Flint, the superintendent of aliens and secretary to Sir Arthur Wellesley at the Irish Office. Sir Charles operates a separate network of agents and may well be able to suggest suitable people. Is that clear?'

'Yes, sir. Can I ask how the chosen agent will report his progress?'

'Mr Rolleston will advise you on the best methods, probably invisible writing or cipher.'

Days later, Hoppner was reading through the notes he had taken at his interview with John Hookham Frere. What a pleasure the discussion had been. He had even come away with the gift of one of Mr Frere's humorous poems. Mr Frere had indeed met the Marquis de La Romana and was able to give Hoppner a thumbnail sketch of him.

Pedro Caro Y Sureda was a nobleman and was born in 1761 into a family with many generations of service to the Crown. He finished his education at the Seminario de Nobles where the sons of the nobility were trained before occupying the highest positions in Spanish society. After time in the navy, the King sent him on a diplomatic mission. Travelling across Europe, La Romana spent time in Berlin and Vienna. At the start of the war with France, he transferred to the army. At the peace of 1795, he retired as a lieutenant-general but returned to the colours in 1802 and became Captain-General of Catalonia, effectively head of both military and civil government of the region.

Mr Frere had met the marquis at Court in Madrid on a number of occasions and had enjoyed wide-ranging conversations with La Romana. He found the marquis well read and travelled. He was intellectual and a keen student of foreign languages. La Romana was immensely proud of the library he had created at his home in Valencia, by all repute one of the finest in Spain. Mr Frere portrayed the marquis as a Spanish patriot whose loyalty to the Crown was, he believed, unshakeable.

Without divulging the direct reason for his question, Hoppner had asked Mr Frere what he considered the marquis's reaction would be to the current events in Spain. There was no doubt, La Romana would be horrified that the King or more likely Godoy, the manipulative first minister, had allowed a French Army to march across Spain to invade Portugal. And now San Sebastian had fallen to the French, if he knew of these events, he would surely wish to return to Spain to do what he could to support the King.

As the interview drew to a close, Mr Frere had told Hoppner not to be misled into believing that all Spaniards would object to regime change. There was a strong pro-French faction in Court that supported the modernisation of Spain. This faction included some senior army officers and in particular, those of Irish descent who were fiercely anti-British and would stop at nothing to promote an Ireland free from the British yoke.

So, Hoppner reflected, the marquis could well be susceptible to an approach, but how was this approach to be made? He took a sheet of paper and listed possible options. A letter smuggled or even posted was out of the question. The risks of interception were too high. If the letter was in cipher, how would the encoding cipher be delivered to the marquis? Even if La Romana managed to receive and de-code the letter, would he believe it? Surely he would be suspicious that the letter was a French plant aimed at testing his loyalty.

Could the navy land a party to make contact with the marquis? With Britain still at war with Spain, it was likely that the party would be arrested or even shot before reaching La Romana. Hoppner kept on returning to the idea of an agent who would somehow obtain a private interview with the marquis. Who and how?

7

Number 12 Krayenkamp, Central Hamburg, April 1808

Jacques Marquet de Montbreton reflected on the progress or lack of it that had been made in the past weeks. He was pleased with the quality of the squadron of twenty-four gendarmes he now commanded. All were veterans. He had despatched one lieutenant with a troop of six to Cuxhaven, another to Bremen, keeping the third in Hamburg. In accordance with gendarmerie practice, to maintain their aloofness from the local populous, unlike most soldiers, none of the gendarmes was billeted with locals. The men were tall, their uniforms of blue tunics with red cross bands and tall shakoes adding to the impression of power. All were equipped with the best weapons including the latest carbines.

The meetings with the local customs officers had reinforced his initial findings. Despite there being over

500 *douaniers* in the region, smuggling was rife. Since the British had captured Heligoland the previous September, contraband, whether it be coffee, sugar or any other luxury, was even more readily accessible. Marquet looked at the empty cup on his desk. The coffee had been excellent but had he contributed in a small way to the British exchequer by drinking contraband coffee shipped from Heligoland?

His thoughts returned to the officials. Excuse followed excuse: prevention of smuggling at sea was extremely hazardous, they said. The Royal Navy escorted the smugglers to within a few kilometres of the coast. French gunboats were blown out of the water as soon as they encountered British warships. Even if one of the larger French ships outgunned a small British vessel, it would soon be despatched by the escort frigates protecting its smaller brethren. But once the goods had been landed and the British no longer had control, Marquet had argued surely with 500 *douaniers* patrolling it was possible to put an end to the smuggling? The wringing of hands was nearly palpable. In theory, he was told, it should indeed be possible. In practice, however, things were different.

The Emperor's Berlin Decree forbidding trade with Britain and the retaliatory British "Orders in Council" had a catastrophic effect on trade in the Hanseatic cities. Large numbers working in shipping and warehousing had been thrown out of work. How would these citizens support their families? The officials estimated that there might be as many as 10,000 who had turned to smuggling to survive.

One of the officials described one of the *douanier*'s

successes. It had been noted that there was a steep rise in the number of funerals passing between Altona in Denmark and Hamburg. One officer became suspicious. An intensive search of the funeral cortege revealed large quantities of coffee and sugar hidden in secret compartments under the coffins. The culprits had been imprisoned.

He had come away from these meetings frustrated and furious. So that was what Maupont had meant when he raised his finger to his lips after the meeting with Bernadotte and Bourrienne. It was obvious that the smugglers greased the palms of the *douaniers* to look the other way and that those at the very top were taking a juicy cut. It was just as if things had turned full circle. The worst of the excesses of the *Ancien Régime* were now mirrored by a dictatorship riddled with corruption – *plus ça change!*

There was at least one positive: with so much activity between Heligoland and the mainland, it should be possible to transport the agent he needed to the island.

The quest for a suitable agent had been easier than Marquet expected. Marquet had envisaged that he would have to scour the Hamburg jails for sad cases who could be persuaded by the promise of freedom, money and coercion to make the hazardous journey to Heligoland. After all, he had had some success in similar ways in eastern Prussia. He had found that the most willing cases were those who knew that the gendarmerie had already had conversations with the candidate's wife and family. That knowledge tended to ensure compliance.

However, during one of his conversations with

Maupont, the colonel asked if he had heard the name Charles Schulmeister. While serving in Prussia, Marquet had heard whispers of a secretive individual nicknamed "The Schoolmaster". The Schoolmaster had made his name by providing the Emperor vital intelligence before the Battle of Ulm by persuading the Austrian General Mack not to withdraw his army. Mack was then surrounded and forced to surrender with hardly a shot being fired. During the campaigns against Prussia and Russia, the Schoolmaster has built a network of agents across northern Germany and into Poland.

After Friedland and the Treaty of Tilsit, these agents had become redundant. A fellow Alsatian, Frans Colville, was a close associate of the Schoolmaster. Colville had been operating across the Hanseatic towns and was now at a loose end. An obvious candidate.

Colville replied to Marquet's letter and suggested that they meet on the Lime Tree Terrace at the Louis Jacob Hotel on Elbchaussee, some eight kilometres to the west of the city walls. Colville insisted that Marquet arrive in civilian dress. An obvious precaution, though why would he have to journey outside the city walls?

His disguise was blown when the guard at the Millenthor gates brusquely asked for his pass. As soon as Marquet showed it, the guard snapped to attention. He swore at the man. The guard had no idea what he had done wrong. There was no point in creating a scene. Marquet's carriage charged through the gates passing Bernhard Strasse and Pinnasthor along the banks of the Elbe and on to the hotel. Marquet instructed the driver to return in an hour. He climbed the steps and into the entrance of the elegant hotel. A doorman ushered him through the lobby onto Lime Tree Terrace with its delightful views over the river. Not quite Paris but pleasant enough.

A man sitting at a corner table waved at him. Marquet made his way to the table and asked quietly: 'Monsieur Colville?'

'Correct, Captain,' and began to stand. Marquet waved that Colville should sit.

'How did you know who I was?'

'I kept watch on your house on Krayenkamp. In your flamboyant uniform you were not difficult to spot!'

Marquet hid his surprise. 'I see. May I ask why you suggested this hotel for our meeting?'

'It is a quiet and delightful location. More important is the fact that the owner, Jacob, is actually David Louis Jacques, a Huguenot. He changed his name when he married the widow of the founder of the hotel. We can therefore be assured of privacy.'

Marquet was impressed.

Colville sat back. 'How may I be of service to the illustrious Ordinance Gendarmerie of the Imperial Guard?'

Another barb to be ignored. 'Colonel Maupont tells me that you have carried out many missions for the "Schoolmaster".'

'Indeed and learnt from the master of his trade. I was proud to be with him when we fooled the Prussians into surrendering Wismar. I carried the false messages to the garrison commander persuading him to believe that we had a full brigade only a few hours' march away. Once he had ordered the surrender of the town, he was amazed when he saw that we were only a small contingent of cavalry. What a coup that was!'

Let him blow his own trumpet, he's putting on a show because he wants work.

They paused as coffee arrived. Once the waiter had moved away, Marquet leaned forward.

'I suppose you know that this is probably contraband coffee smuggled into Hamburg?'

'Everyone knows that and the sugar in the pot beside it.'

'Yes, but where does it come from and how does it get here?'

Colville looked at Marquet. 'I've never thought about the detail.'

'Large quantities are shipped from England to Heligoland then smuggled across to landing places up and down the coast. But this is not directly what I wish to discuss. Since the English captured the island, they have established a mission headed by a governor. Now it seems they have appointed another diplomat whose remit is more challenging. Since his arrival in January, we have noticed a significant increase in English covert operations and the orchestrating of pro-British propaganda. These operations work hand in glove with the smugglers. We need you to discover who this diplomat is and what his objectives are. We can then disrupt his operations.'

Colville was silent for some time. 'If I am going to spend time on the island, I'll need a new identity which will blend in with the locals. What do we know about the island and its inhabitants?'

'There are actually two islands and they are about seventy kilometres from Cuxhaven. The main island is small, only about one square kilometre. But it has a population of around 3,300 which has grown since the arrival of the British. Most of the people are involved with fishing, hence the ease to which some turn to smuggling.'

'I see, and what are your ideas about an identity and cover?'

Marquet smiled. 'We captured one of the smugglers who lives on the island with his parents. He is in prison but could well be persuaded to help on the promise of a stay of execution and possible early release. He pleaded that his parents are both very frail and need looking after. My thought is that you could be a cousin who comes to the island to help the parents. Staying with the elderly would give you a roof over your head and the cover you need to carry out the mission. What do you think?'

Colville again sat back. 'Yes, that would seem to work. How do you propose that we engage with the parents to accept me?'

'The smuggler will write to the island's priest explaining that he is in prison and has begged for your help. As he has bailed you out in the past, you have agreed to help. On arrival, you will introduce yourself to the priest who can make the introduction to the parents. I am sure that the priest will have their trust. It should be straightforward.'

Colville interjected. 'Good, I can use one of my German cover names and my Westphalian accent will not be a problem as I have been living there for many years. As the parents have not seen me since I was a child, they should accept who I am.'

'What name will you use?'

'Herling. I have the passport but will also take another in the name of Lauda in case I have to make an escape. Now to report my findings. I will write to you as soon as I have useful information. Are you aware of the code called the Vigenère Cipher?'

'I have heard of it but have not used it.'

'It's quite simple but very effective. Let me show you.' Colville pulled a sheet of paper and a pencil from his pocket. 'We agree a keyword and apply this to the alphabet. Let's agree a keyword; say Jena, that famous victory. To encode the message write out the letters of the alphabet and below that the numbers from zero to twenty-five. Then we apply the code Jena. So, to encode your name, we take J which is the ninth letter, E is the fourth, N the thirteenth, and A is zero. Now we add these to the letters of your name. So M + 9 becomes V, A + 4 becomes E, R + 13 becomes E (carry on counting past Z on to zero, 1, 2, 3 and so on), Q is + zero so stays as Q, and then repeating again U + 9 is D, E + 4 is I and T is +13 and so becomes G. This would give your coded name as VEEQDIG. To decode the message, simply use the keyword but subtract rather than add. You'll need to practise but I'm sure you'll soon be proficient.'

'Practise indeed. And how do you suggest that we send the letters between the two of us?'

'I imagine that the English control the post to and from the island, therefore we will have to pay one of the fishermen to carry the letters. We can make it worth his while and apply the usual warnings if he is tempted to betray us. Someone with a wife and family would be ideal. We can agree a dead letter drop on the island and use something like a simple chalk mark when there is a letter to be collected. You can leave the details to me.'

'That should not be difficult.'

'And now, Captain, we should discuss my remuneration. After all, I am the one taking all the risks.'

As am I, thought Marquet. He inwardly shuddered at the consequences of failure. No doubt reduced to the ranks and placed in one of the punishment battalions. How long would he survive the next battle?

'What did you have in mind, Monsieur Colville?'

'1,250 francs per month plus an allowance of 300 per month, all payable in advance.'

'How much!? That's over five times my pay and probably what a divisional general is paid.'

'Exactly and worth every sous for the information I will provide you.'

Marquet stared at Colville. 'I will have to have approval.'

'Of course, but I doubt you will have much difficulty.' From Colville's confident tone, Marquet assumed that was the standard rate for the job. Would he want such a sum for the risks involved? Probably.

More coffee arrived. They discussed the details of the mission, how Colville would get to Heligoland, refinements of his cover, emergency procedures in the event of discovery, weaponry and finally, Colville sprung another surprise.

'I shall also need 500 francs in gold in case I need to bribe my way off the island, returnable of course if it is not needed.'

'I will ask. If there is nothing else, let's meet here again in two weeks. That should give both of us time to put the plan in place.'

Both men rose and shook hands. 'In two weeks.' Colville smiled and turned, leaving Marquet thinking how he was to persuade the colonel to part with such vast sums. As he summoned the waiter to pay for the coffee, Colville re-emerged.

'I forgot to mention, Mr Captain Spy-catcher, in my circles, word is that there is a French royalist agent operating in these parts. I thought you might like to know. Oh, and he seems to use some sort of flower as a code name. Just a rumour, you understand, probably nothing in it.'

With that, he turned and was gone.

8

The Foreign Office, April 1808

Hoppner made notes in preparation for his meeting with Sir Charles Flint, the Under-Secretary-of-State at the Irish Office. Rolleston had briefed Hoppner that Sir Charles had previously been the superintendent of the Aliens Office succeeding Sir William Wickham. Their roles had expanded over the years at war. As well as responsibilities to detect enemy activity and agents in England, they had been given the tasks of running agents on the Continent. Fourteen years previously Sir William had been based in Berne in Switzerland liaising with royalist opponents of the French Revolution.

Sir Charles was now secretary to Sir Arthur Wellesley, chief secretary of the Irish Office. Hoppner knew that Sir Arthur's reputation, built on his successes in India, had been enhanced by his actions as one of Lord Cathcart's major-generals in the siege of Copenhagen the previous

September. Sir Charles was obviously well regarded at the highest levels of government. Possibly, some of this regard would filter down to him.

According to Rolleston, Sir Charles was still closely associated with the Alien Office and its chief clerk, Henry Brooke. Sir Charles had agreed to meet Hoppner in the Alien Office, located only a few yards away from the Foreign Office in Crown Street. Hoppner hoped that Sir Charles would be able to suggest how to find a suitable agent for the mission and, more importantly, how this approach should be made. However much he prepared, he felt way out of his depth.

Hoppner left the Foreign Office, walked past the entrance to Downing Street and into King Charles Street where he had been told he would find the entrance to the Alien Office. The doorman informed him that he was expected and showed him into the waiting room. Rolleston had told him that the Alien Office had in the past been used as a prison for arrested agents before they were sent to the Tower. Hoppner wondered if the building was still a temporary prison. That a building so close to the heart of government could be an interrogation centre and who knows maybe worse, made him feel distinctly queasy, adding to his apprehension.

The door opened and he was ushered along a corridor. The doorman knocked and Hoppner entered a large office. Two men were sitting.

'Ah, you must be Hoppner of the FO. I am Sir Charles Flint and this is Henry Brook, chief clerk. Mr Hammond tells me that you are planning a mission to the Continent.

You had better explain what you have in mind. We will then be able to advise if we can help.'

Hoppner bowed. 'Thank you, Sir Charles.' He took a deep breath outlining the plan and the options that had been discussed.

'We consider the best chance of success will be for an agent to be smuggled into Hamburg, locate the marquis and persuade him to take his division back to Spain or wherever he wishes to go. We hope that you can suggest a suitable man to undertake this mission?'

Sir Charles turned to Mr Brook raising his eyebrows. From the knowing look, Hoppner realised he was about to be told unwelcome news. He waited for the axe to fall.

Sir Charles's eyes bored into his. 'Do you know that three, maybe four agents have already attempted to contact the marquis? None has been heard of since.'

The colour drained from Hoppner's face. He grabbed the edge of the table in front of him and tried to catch his breath.

'I had no idea. No one told me that this has already been tried.' He felt sick.

Mr Brook rose and pulled over a chair. 'Sit down.' Brook went over to a table and poured brandy from a decanter. Handing it to Hoppner, he said, 'Two were our people and the others were possibly commissioned by the War Office. One of ours was already in Lübeck and the other had made his way into the area during the siege of Stralsund. Our networks lost track of both. We concluded that they must have been captured. Of the other two, I know nothing.'

After a gulp of the brandy, Hoppner felt better. The intense shock of the news subsided. He turned to Brook and asked, 'When was this?'

'The first was despatched on 20 August just before Stralsund surrendered. The second was instructed to infiltrate the Spaniards' headquarters to test out what sympathies there were to our cause within the Spanish officer elite. We heard nothing more from either of them. The other two, if there were two, were probably sent by the War Office. You would have to ask them.'

Typical, Hoppner thought, *turf wars, all for departmental glory, but of course, the Foreign Office was one of the worst offenders.*

He regained some poise, asking, 'As at that stage the Spaniards were fighting with the French at Stralsund, why was it imagined that they might welcome feelers from us?'

'Remember, my dear Hoppner, that the Treaty of Tilsit had not long been signed. The Russians had gone over to Napoleon. We were desperate for any crumb after the reverses we had during the past year. But now there are just a few signs, a very few that our fortunes may be improving. The news from Spain may well make the timing of your proposed mission more propitious. However, the danger and risk is extreme. Whoever undertakes this mission will have to be able to move in Germany without attracting attention. Do you know where the marquis's troops are now?'

'Our information is some weeks old, but we have reports that the Spaniards are on garrison duty in Lübeck and other nearby towns.'

'Presumably the Marquis de La Romana is in Lübeck, correct?'

'We believe so, Sir Charles.'

'So, once our agent locates the marquis, how do you propose that he obtains an interview, an interview that will surely need to be conducted in private?'

'I thought that the chosen agent would be able to provide suggestions.'

Sir Charles Flint looked at Henry Brook. A hint of a smile appeared.

'We predicted that you would struggle to answer that question. Maybe we can help. The marquis is a devout Catholic, is he not?'

'So Mr Frere assures me, sir.'

'Then what would be more natural than if a Catholic priest or monk presents himself to the Spaniards and suggests an interview with the marquis?'

A degree of confidence returned. Time for a little gentle pushing back.

'That's very good, Sir Charles, but the priest will have to speak excellent German to progress safely through Germany. Then, if and when he is able to meet La Romana, he will need to speak with him in Spanish or, as the marquis is both well educated and well travelled, in French. That was how Mr Hookham Frere spoke with the marquis when he met him in Madrid.'

Sir Charles Flint sat back.

'A fair point. Mr Brook and I have discussed your proposal and feel that we should support Mr Canning's adventure.'

'Thank you, Sir Charles.'

'We also may know of someone who fits the profile and could be recommended to undertake the mission. Have you heard of the Reverend James Robertson?'

'No, sir.'

'The Reverend Robertson is a Benedictine monk. He has recently provided excellent intelligence in Ireland for Sir Arthur. But of more relevance, he took his monastic vows in the Scottish seminary in Ratisbon and was ordained as a priest there in 1782. His religious name is Gallus. Six years ago, Robertson was instructed by his abbot, Father Arbuthnot, to travel to Paris and present a petition to the first consul asking that the seminary should not be one of those closed after the passing of the anti-religious laws. With the help of General Lauriston, the distinguished Franco-Scottish general, he was successful. A fine demonstration of what a persuasive individual he is.'

Hoppner was amazed. 'But the first consul was Napoleon! Robertson has met with the Emperor?'

'Indeed he has.'

Hoppner couldn't restrain himself. 'So he will know Alexander Horn whose reports from Bavaria I have read. Robertson must have taken vows at a similar time to Father Maurus.'

'I expect he does and, more importantly, he is known to His Grace, the Duke of Richmond, the viceroy of Ireland to whom Sir Arthur reports. His Grace spent time in Ratisbon during his travels some twenty years ago. Powerful contacts do help and would be useful in Cabinet should that be necessary.'

Mr Brooke put his hand up. 'A question, Hoppner. Wouldn't Mr Horn be an ideal candidate?'

'I did suggest that to Mr Rolleston. I was told very firmly that Mr Horn was far too valuable in Bavaria and Austria to be risked.'

Sir Charles continued. 'Reverend Robertson speaks German and French fluently as he does Latin. He may well have some Spanish given the excellence of his education. He should be able to travel through Germany without arousing suspicion and converse easily with the marquis.'

Hoppner asked, 'Is there any doubt of his loyalty? He is after all a Scottish Catholic.'

Sir Charles looked at Hoppner. 'I have no reason to doubt his loyalty. Just consider the dire relations between the Emperor and the Pope and the actions Napoleon has taken to break Catholic power across Europe. Remember as well that Napoleon humiliated the Pope at his coronation, seizing the crown from the Pope and placing it on his own head. I'm sure that Reverend Robertson will do everything he can to support anyone who resists Napoleon. As I said before, his Catholic faith will surely be a real advantage when he meets La Romana.

'And in the past months, on the instruction of Sir Arthur Wellesley, Robertson has been travelling across Ireland to assess the conditions of the poor and the educational opportunities that the Church provides to them. His published reports have been most instructive. However, Sir Arthur had an ulterior and more important motive. You will be aware that ever since General Hoche's expedition of 1796 supporting Wolf Tone and the Society of United Irishmen, the French have had designs on Ireland to create instability and to foster rebellion. The government in London had no idea of this invasion despite the fact that the French fleet was forty-four ships strong with transports containing 14,000 troops. Luckily, and it was luck, the December gales in Bantry Bay prevented a landing. That was a wake-up call for the government in Dublin and London. Further attempts two years later luckily failed. As did Emmet's rebellion, again French backed, just five years ago.

'In his travels across Ireland, as well as his published remit, the Reverend Robertson was instructed to covertly gauge the sentiment of the populace and test out the support for the United Irishmen and other rebellious societies. As a Catholic priest, he was accepted across all levels of society and his confidential reports to Sir Arthur and to me were of immense value. He is a man of proven ability.'

Sir Charles looked at his pocket watch. 'I suggest that you discuss the Reverend Robertson with your colleagues. Our view is that you will not find anyone better. Should you need any further assistance, let Mr Brook know. Good luck, young Hoppner.'

Hoppner thanked them both. 'One more question, if I may, Sir Charles? If the Reverend Robertson has finished his work for Sir Arthur, can you tell me where I can find him?'

Mr Brooke replied, 'He has written to tell us that he has taken a position as priest and tutor in the household of one of our leading Catholics, Charles Talbot, the Earl of Shrewsbury and Waterford. Robertson is based at the family seat at Heythrop, Oxfordshire, and the earl's London house. He will continue the Catholic education of the earl's heir, John, who has received a Benedictine education at Vernon Hall, Stonyhurst, and St Edmund's College in Ware.'

'Thank you, sir. But how will the earl take it if we ask him to release the Reverend Robertson just as he has begun his new role?'

Sir Charles looked at his watch again. 'I am sure the Foreign Secretary or one of his Cabinet colleagues can speak to the earl and explain that Robertson is required for service of national importance. Now, I have a pressing engagement.'

As he left, the Alien Office seemed to have lost some of its intimidation. Hoppner was elated.

9

Cesar Rainville's Hotel, Altona, North of Hamburg

Marquet had been summoned by Colonel Maupont. One of his gendarmes had driven him the nine kilometres to the Prince of Ponte Corvo's headquarters. He was shown to the colonel's office and after a few pleasantries with coffee served, reported his discussion with Colville. With some trepidation, he explained Colville's monetary demands. It was a surprise and relief that the colonel nodded his agreement. It seemed to Marquet that these huge amounts were nothing out of the ordinary to Maupont.

Once Marquet had finished, the colonel smiled at him. 'Good, Captain. Let me know when Colville is ready to travel to Heligoland. Now, I have another task for you. Have you heard of the recent developments in Spain?'

'No more than what I have read in the newspapers. *The Moniteur* reported that our troops had occupied

Madrid and that King Carlos had abdicated in favour of his son, Fernando.'

Maupont sipped his coffee. 'Matters have moved on since last month. The Emperor has summoned both Carlos and Fernando to a conference in Bayonne. Both will be accompanied by their wives and immediate households. If my reading of the Emperor's intentions are right, following what he has done in Holland and elsewhere, there will be a Bonaparte on the throne of Spain in the near future.'

'Who will that be?'

'I don't know but I overheard Bernadotte and Bourrienne talking about Joseph. He is, after all, the Emperor's older brother and as such deserves one of the large prizes on the conquered nations. If Joseph becomes the King of Spain, there is likely to be considerable disquiet among our Spanish friends now stationed in Denmark. The Marquis de La Romana and his fellow officers have been fine allies and acquitted themselves well in the operations around Stralsund. But most are loyal to Carlos and Fernando. Who knows what they will do if they hear that their king has been usurped, as they would surely see it.'

Marquet interjected. 'I understood that they had been moved into Denmark to be part of the invasion force for Sweden. Is this still the Emperor's plan?'

'I doubt it. For one, we have missed the opportunity to make a winter crossing of the Oresund or the Sound as the English call it, when the ice prevents the English Navy operating. Now that spring has arrived, the English have moved a powerful fleet into the Baltic with as many as twelve ships of the line and many supporting frigates and gunboats. Even though we have over 40,000 French, Danish, Spanish and Dutch troops stationed in Denmark, the chances of making a successful crossing and avoiding the Royal Navy are minimal. Besides, the Emperor seems to be concentrating on the much bigger prize that is Spain. As the Russians have already invaded Finland, he'll let them keep the pressure on Sweden.'

Maupont paused, took another sip of coffee and continued: 'The Prince of Ponte Corvo has wisely spread the Spanish troops across Denmark and has interspersed the various units with our own troops and our Danish allies. The marquis is based on the island of Funen in the town of Nyborg. The other troops are stationed on Zealand, Jutland and Langeland. With the situation in Spain being so fluid, we have blocked the post from Spain to La Romana and his fellow officers. Their letters to family and friends that we have read show the early signs of disquiet. They complain that there has been no news from home. On top of this, the Danes have intercepted English propaganda leaflets which give news of the events in Spain. We don't know if these have been read by La Romana's troops but it doesn't help. There is, therefore, an urgent need to understand the marquis's mind and intentions. Luckily, we have had an offer of service from one of La Romana's French valets. You are to travel to Nyborg, meet with the valet, assess his credibility and agree methods of communication and remuneration. You will instruct the valet to report anything of interest that transpires between the marquis and his senior officers. We should then be able to take pre-emptive action if La Romana's intentions change for the worse.'

Marquet asked, 'What do we know about this valet?'

'Very little, but I am sure that you can impress on him the importance of his watching and reporting. It is after all for the security and glory of France!'

'Yes, sir.' He rose. Maupont returned his salute with the peremptory wave, returning to the papers on his desk. As Marquet got to the door, he turned.

'A question Colville put to me: did I know of a royalist spy who uses some sort of flower as a code name? He is rumoured to be in this area.' Maupont lifted his head.

'If it is the same man, he has been plotting against France ever since the start of the Revolution. Let me know immediately if you hear more.' Marquet wanted to ask more but was waved away.

During the journey back to his quarters, he pondered how he was to run this source as well as Colville in Heligoland and his extensive counter-intelligence duties. He could not afford to spend much time in Nyborg, some fifteen hours' coach journey from Hamburg. He would therefore have to delegate contact duties for the valet to one of his gendarmes. He would ask Maupont to instruct the captain of the gendarme unit based in Funen to add one of his men to the unit. One of his sergeants would recommend the best man for the task, probably a corporal. The corporal would then be close enough to the valet to set up clandestine meetings, take the valet's report and forward it on to Marquet.

His report despatched to the colonel, he summoned

the duty sergeant and explained what he wanted. Marquet then requested to the staff officer on the liaison team with the local Danish forces to ask for passes and an escort for the journey to Nyborg.

Maupont's approval came the next day. The sergeant introduced a young Corporal Lejeune. Within a few minutes, Marquet was impressed with Lejeune's grasp of what he had been told and the perceptiveness of the questions he asked. The sergeant had made a good choice.

A day later, Marquet and Lejeune rode out through Hamburg's western gate and on to Altona to meet their Danish escort. After two days hard riding, two nights in inns en route and the ferry to Funen, by the time he arrived in Odense, Marquet was thoroughly saddle-sore. He still ached the next morning. Perhaps laudanum would help but he dismissed the temptation.

After breakfast, the local gendarme captain briefed Marquet on conditions on Funen. The 4,500 Spanish troops were spread across the island in small detachments watched over by a force of 3,000 Danish troops based in and around Odense. The remainder of the Division del Norte was similarly spread in Zealand, Langeland, and on the Jutland mainland intermingled with French, Danish and Dutch troops.

On his arrival, the marquis had seen the magnificent Holckenhaven Castle and ordered that this be requisitioned as his headquarters. The owner, Frederik Conrad Holck, protested to the newly crowned Danish King. To avoid a diplomatic incident, Bernadotte told La Romana firmly that he should look elsewhere. Nyborg Castle, occupied by the local governor and used as an arsenal, was found to be too small. La Romana eventually settled on the Hotel Postgarten. The owner along with the other residents of the town resigned themselves to the reality of the alliance with Napoleon. The loss of the use of the hotel paled when compared to the funds needed and taxes to be raised to pay for food for 4,500 Spanish soldiers.

As well as two valets and liverymen, La Romana employed two cooks and a full kitchen staff. It soon became known that the marquis and his staff enjoyed a "good table".

It seemed that the valet, Martin, was sincere. The next meeting was arranged for the next day at the Church of our Lady in Nyborg at ten thirty, and Marquet thanked the captain, complimenting him on the arrangements so far.

The next morning, breakfasted and dressed in civilian clothes, Marquet and Lejeune rode to Nyborg. At least the stiffness was easing. In the church they sat on one of the pews in the nave. A man entered through a side door. He looked around nervously and then spotted the two seated men. Marquet waved at the man indicating that he should follow them as they rose and left the church.

Outside, Marquet and Lejeune made their way to a quiet area of the churchyard. The man followed. Marquet turned and looked at the face of the middle-aged man. One eye returned Marquet's stare, the other seemed to be looking well to the left towards the corner of the churchyard. It was as if there were two different beings inhabiting the same skull. It was most disconcerting.

'You are Martin?'

'Yes, sir.' Anticipating the next question, Martin pointed to his left eye. 'From birth.'

'Ah.' A pause. 'I am Captain Marquet and this is Corporal Lejeune. You wish to serve your country?'

'Yes, sir.'

'Why?'

'I am a passionate supporter of the Revolution and the Emperor. I became a servant to the Prince of Henin who was found guilty of counter-revolutionary activities and was guillotined in '94. I provided the Revolutionary Tribunal with some of the evidence that convicted him.'

With one eye looking in a different direction, it was unsettling to interrogate Martin. He concentrated on the eye looking at him.

'Did you, indeed? But why fourteen years later do you suddenly wish to serve your country again?'

Martin's shoulders slumped. It was as if he felt he had been found out. Tears welled up in his eyes. 'Sir, I am a widower. I have one child, a son, Jean-Luc, who is a constant reminder of my late wife. Jean-Luc is just nineteen, he is small and looks very young for his age. He was conscripted last year and is now in Spain serving in the 2nd Legion of Reserve in General Frere's 3rd Division, part of General Dupont's 2nd Corps of Observation of the Gironde.'

Irritated, still looking at the good eye, Marquet asked, 'Why do we need all this detail?'

'Please, sir, hear me out. Jean-Luc has become the butt of teasing by his fellow soldiers. His corporal dislikes him and gives him all the dirtiest jobs. Some weeks ago, he was cleaning his musket when it inexplicably went off and shot him through the side of his foot. It was luckily only a flesh wound but the corporal accused Jean-Luc of being a conscript "*mutiles volontaires*" – guilty of self-mutilation to escape duty. He tried his best to plead that it was just an accident, but the tribunal believed the corporal. He was found guilty. He has been sentenced to five years in a punishment pioneer company. He is now in a military prison awaiting transfer. He has written to me to explain his predicament and to protest his innocence.'

'And what do you expect me to do?' snapped Marquet, irritated that this little man was probably wasting his time.

'I hope, sir, that if I offer my services to spy on the Spanish general and provide you with useful information that I might be rewarded by a pardon for my beloved son.'

Marquet paused. Looking hard at the good eye, his exasperation subsided and began to change into some small admiration for him. He looked at Lejeune who nodded.

Marquet turned to Martin. 'Very well, let's see what you can provide. I am detailing Corporal Lejeune to be attached to the gendarmerie unit based in Odense. He will become your contact and will make regular visits to Nyborg and to this church. Do you know the plaque on the wall of the south transept in memory of the Holck family?'

'Yes, sir.'

'Here is a piece of chalk. When you have something to tell us, go to the church and draw a vertical line on the right-hand side of the plaque. When Lejeune comes to Nyborg, he will check for your mark and will put a horizontal line across your line. That will be the sign for you to meet him twenty-four hours later. Put a circle on top of your line if you can make a meeting in the morning – as we have today – and a circle on the bottom of your line if the meeting is to be in the afternoon. Lejeune will already have located a safe place for the two of you to meet in private and for you to give him your report. Is that clear?'

'Yes, sir. But what about my son?'

'I can make no promises. However, if your information proves useful, there may be something that can be done.'

'Thank you, sir. I will do my absolute best.'

'For the sake of France and your son, I hope you do. Remember complete secrecy is mandatory, understand?'

Martin blanched. 'From what I have heard, Jean-Luc would not survive six months in a pioneer company building roads or fortifications.'

'His life is in your hands.' The little man visibly shuddered. One eye looked down, the other off to the left.

On the ride back to Odense, Marquet expressed quiet satisfaction. He told Lejeune that as soon as he had received information from Martin, he was to make notes and ride immediately to report to Marquet in person. Lejeune saluted. 'Yes, Captain.' Two agents in place, now back to Hamburg.

10
The Foreign Office, May 1808

Returning to the Foreign Office from his meeting with Sir Charles Flint and Mr Brook, Hoppner touched his hat as he entered. William Dakin, the door-keeper, bade him good afternoon and noted Hoppner's arrival in his daybook.

Hoppner returned to his desk, responding to the waves of welcome from his peers. He made notes about his meeting with Sir Charles. He then made his way to the library and asked if he could make an appointment to see the head librarian and keeper of the papers, Mr Richard Ancell. Hoppner hoped that Mr Ancell could provide more background on the Reverend Robertson to expand on what he had been told by Sir Charles. Ancell had been a clerk in the library for many years before succeeding Mr John Bruce as the head librarian and keeper of the papers. Mr Ancell's reputation of having encyclopaedic knowledge of the papers in his care was well deserved. Among his many works, he had produced an alphabetical index of all the British ministers resident at foreign courts from the fifth year of Charles II's reign in1665 until 1780.

It was not long after Hoppner had returned to his desk that one of the junior clerks from the library came to his desk and told him that Mr Ancell would see him now. Hoppner followed the clerk back to the library and was shown into Mr Ancell's office.

He told Mr Ancell that the Reverend Robertson was being considered for a mission in Germany and explained that Robertson had been recommended by Sir Charles Flint. If Mr Ancell had more background that would indeed help him in writing a convincing report for Mr Hammond and hopefully, if it passed Mr Hammond's scrutiny, to Mr Canning himself.

Mr Ancell asked Hoppner what he had been told about the Reverend Robertson. Once he had told the keeper what he knew, Mr Ancell summoned the clerk.

'Please bring me the recent papers that we have concerning German affairs, Bavaria and the Imperial Diet.'

The clerk did not take long to return with a thick folder of papers tied together with a wide ribbon. He placed them on the desk and left the office. Mr Ancell put on his tortoise-framed eyeglasses and began shuffling through the papers. Hoppner waited. Mr Ancell muttered, 'Now let me see', and, 'Ah yes', and 'Of course, I remember now'. Hoppner waited patiently. Finally, Mr Ancell looked up.

'We are indebted to His Grace the Duke of Richmond who first made contact with the Scottish Benedictine monastery at Ratisbon. Do you know that the monastery was originally founded in the eleventh century by the Irish and later by Scottish monks?'

Hoppner shook his head, wondered what this had to do with the Reverend Robertson but did not dare to interrupt Mr Ancell.

'In his travels over twenty years ago, His Grace was introduced to the abbot, Charles Arbuthnot. The abbot has a formidable reputation as a polymath. Both he and his brother monks had developed good contacts with the Bavarian nobility and the members of the Imperial Diet. His Grace asked Arbuthnot if he could suggest members of his community who might be willing to keep HM's Government informed of events and personalities. The abbot suggested Robertson and Horn. On his return to London, His Grace briefed the Duke of Leeds, then Foreign Secretary. From there, we at the Foreign Office made contact with the two. Both have provided useful intelligence.'

Hoppner couldn't prevent himself from butting in.

'You mean to say they were recruited as agents, spies, even?'

Ancell removed his eyeglasses and rubbed the bridge of his nose.

'Nothing as dramatic. As with most of our informants, no, let's call them correspondents, we have an informal arrangement with our embassies, Horn developed a network over the years. His closeness to the Thurn and Taxis family, for example, has given us valuable insight into diplomatic thinking at the highest levels. As a result, the agreement with Mr Horn has become more formal. He is now our chargé d'affaires in the area.'

'And they are rewarded for the information provided.'

'Precisely.'

Hoppner nodded. 'I remember seeing reports from our chargé d'affaires in Berlin, Sir George Jackson, referring to the Reverend Horn.'

'But now to move on to the Reverend Robertson, Dom Gallus.' Mr Ancell shuffled more papers. 'Good, here is a letter and notes from Sir George written two years ago after a meeting with Robertson. Born 1758.'

Hoppner's enthusiasm was immediately cooled. *How could someone so old take on such a mission?* Mr Ancell continued reading the notes.

'Excellent education at the Jesuit seminary in Dinant. Forced to move to Ratisbon after the suppression of the Jesuits. Vows in 1778, ordained five years later. Brought Scottish Catholic boys to Ratisbon to join the monastery. Successful petitioning Napoleon – an indication of the calibre of the man. Fluent French, German, Greek and Latin.'

Ancell looked up. 'From Sir George's comments, his recent employment by Sir Arthur Wellesley in Ireland and what we know from Sir Charles Flint, it seems that you have a very accomplished man.'

'But he is fifty!'

'Some of us are older than that, young man.' Hoppner immediately apologised. Ancell raised his hands in acceptance of the faux pas.

'Consider what he will be asked to do. This mission is

much more cloak and, one hopes, no dagger. He will have to travel incognito through French-occupied Germany, find a way into La Romana's headquarters and engineer a private meeting with the marquis, probably more than one. Would a young cut-throat succeed? Not a chance. This calls for subtlety, finesse and a proven ability to put and argue a persuasive case. Who better than a well-travelled Benedictine monk? One other thought, how old is the marquis?'

Hoppner had to drag his memory. When was he born? 1760, no 1761. 'Forty-seven.'

Ancell smiled. 'So just three years younger than Robertson. A man of a similar age to La Romana is more likely to be heard. I rest my case.'

'Indeed.' Hoppner thanked Mr Ancell and made for the door. Ancell had a parting shot.

'You do realise that whoever you send will almost certainly be going to his death.' Hoppner could not reply. He felt a cold sweat rising as the implications of those words hit home.

It took him time to recover. He began to outline in his mind the substance of his report. One question would not go away. Did he think that he had found the right man for the mission?

Before he could answer the question, Mr Rolleston came to his desk.

'I don't suppose you have heard the latest news from Spain?' Hoppner shook his head. 'You will know that in March, King Carlos abdicated in favour of his popular son, Fernando. Reports advise that the Emperor has summoned both the new and old kings and their families to a conference in Bayonne. The new King Fernando and his party had been staying in Vittoria. When the populace heard that he was travelling into France, there was uproar and some people even attempted to cut the traces of the King's coach. The King was not prevented from leaving Spain and arrived in Bayonne on 20 April. His father arrived ten days later. Meanwhile, the Emperor has moved 100,000 troops into Spain.'

'What do you think this means?' asked Hoppner.

'Given Bonaparte's hatred of the Bourbons, I think it can only spell trouble for both the new and old kings. Whatever, this means that the mission to do mischief to Boney in Germany becomes even more of a priority for the Foreign Secretary. Mr Hammond requires your report first thing tomorrow morning.'

Hoppner knew that he would be writing until the small hours, something he was by now well used to. Mr Ancell's parting words still reverberated around his head.

11

The Walk from St Nicolas's Church, Heythrop

The attempt to mend fences with the rector of St Nicolas's had not been a success. As Robertson walked back to the house, he could at least enjoy the early summer sunshine and the bright emerald green of the leaves. The Cotswold countryside was looking at its best. The soirée last evening had been a delight until the rector had made it clear that he objected to what he saw as Robertson's usurping of his rightful place in local society.

He had woken early. The May sunshine streamed through the oriel window of his room in the top of the house. It was more spacious than his cell in the seminary, but he had no feeling of home. His mother's letter, dated March, had finally been delivered the day before. She pleaded for him to "come home" to see her "before her time came". It would give her and his two sisters so much comfort. There had been may similar letters over the years but now it could not be too long before God called her. He regularly sent money home to Perthshire topped up when he had received extra payments from work such as that recently carried out in Ireland. But then he mused, where was home? In Lude near Blair Atholl or among the community in Ratisbon? Whenever this debate came to the fore, he remembered what he, aged thirteen, and his older brother had been told when they first arrived at the Jesuit College in Dinant: "You are here to serve God." Seven years later, the night before he took his vows, Abbot Arbuthnot had told him that if he had any doubts, he could walk away but once he had sworn before God and the congregation, there was no turning back. His life would be totally committed to His service in whatever way He directed. Robertson looked round his room. This was "home" for the time being. In his heart, he still missed his families whether in Lude or Ratisbon.

What to say to his mother? As he wrote, he knew she would understand. It was she who had sent him away all those years ago. She had gone through the pain of childbirth and brought him up to serve. Her faith was stronger than his.

He folded and sealed the letter. Now, how to approach the rector?

Since his walk those weeks ago with the earl, Robertson had become something of a local celebrity. His Lordship must have told his wife about the meeting with Napoleon. Now it seemed that all society knew. On a visit to nearby Chipping Norton, he felt sure that elegant ladies were whispering to each other behind their fans, pointing at him.

Last night, as he was announced, a hush came over the gathered throng; more whispering and pointing. He bowed to the earl and then to the countess. As he bowed to Lady Elizabeth, she leant forward whispering, 'Don't go too far, there are many friends who wish to meet you.'

He moved to the side of the ballroom. As the earl and countess began mingling, he saw her beckon. He bowed again. Within seconds he was surrounded by the countess's lady friends. All were wearing the latest in fashion, the high-waisted empire-style gowns. Some of the younger ladies' dresses were so low cut that he found it difficult to drag his eyes away from the revealing décolletage. Introductions came too fast for him to remember all the names. He bowed and smiled at the sea of beaming faces. Then the bombardment of questions began;

'What was he like?'

'Is he handsome?'

'Is his French coarse Corsican?'

'Does he really wear a bicorne hat?'

Robertson tried his best to field the volley. He raised his hands to quieten his audience, turning on his natural charm. Within minutes, the ladies were gasping and laughing as he regaled them with his impressions of Napoleon. As he finished, another guest asked, 'Father, is it true that you recently have carried out duties for Sir Arthur Wellesley? Does the hero of Assaye really have a hooked nose?'

'Rather more L-shaped,' he replied. The next bombardment commenced. Finally, the earl came to the rescue.

'My dear, I'm sure Father Gallus is in need of refreshment. May I take him away and introduce him to other guests?' Disappointment shone through on the faces of circled ladies.

'Of course, my dear.' Turning to Robertson: 'Father, I shall expect you at my next afternoon tea. You will be able to charm other friends.' Relieved, Robertson bowed and follow His Lordship.

It was later in the evening. Robertson had stepped outside for much needed air. Hands on the veranda balustrade, he took in the delight of the May evening air. The spell was broken as he smelt foul breath on his shoulder, a mix of port and tobacco. He turned, the rector's red face up against his.

'I want a word with you,' he said, stabbing Robertson in the chest with his forefinger. The effort caused the rector to lose his balance. He grabbed the balustrade. Straightening himself again, he took a deep breath. The words that tumbled out were unintelligible. The man was drunk – paralytic. Robertson stepped back, out of range of the rector's halitosis and any swinging fist.

'Sir, I don't know what I have done to offend you. Now is not the time to find out. I will call at your church in the morning. I bid you goodnight.' He beckoned a nearby footman, explained the rector's condition who at that moment was fiddling for his trouser buttons. It seemed that the fresh air had brought on a desperate need to relieve himself.

Back in the ballroom, he found the earl and countess, thanked them for such an enjoyable party and asked to be excused. He made his way up the back stairs to his room, entered, made ready, said his prayers and climbed into bed. The rector's antics had taken the gloss off what had been a good evening. He was not looking forward to the morning's meeting. As he drifted off, he was left with a picture of the lovely ladies and their revealing décolletage. What might have been if he had not taken his vows all those years ago?

The next morning the rector was waiting at the entrance to the vestry. He looked terrible. A vein pulsing across his forehead contrasted with the whiteness of his face. Robertson realised he had made a mistake. Now was not the time to have a sensible conversation.

'May I suggest, sir, that we agree another time to talk?' The rector nodded. As he walked back down the nave, the stark white interior of St Nicolas's church reminded him of the few Lutheran churches he had visited in Germany – what a contrast to the glories of Catholic churches he loved.

Halfway back to the house, a pony and trap cantered up to him and a groom, whip in hand, shouted down. 'There you are, Father, we have been looking everywhere for you.'

'Well, now you have found me, what do you want?'

'I am to take you back to the house immediately. The butler has an urgent message for you.' The groom reached down his hand to help Robertson up. He wheeled the trap round, whipping the pony into a canter. The butler was waiting in the stable yard. Robertson opened the proffered letter. He was summoned to Sir Arthur Wellesley's house in Harley Street.

'Does His Lordship know about this?'

'Yes, Father. You are to leave in one of the earl's coaches without delay. Your clothes have already been packed. Cook has prepared a cold lunch for you to eat on the journey.'

12

Number 12 Krayenkamp, Central Hamburg,
May 1808

Some days after his return from Nyborg, Marquet was working at his desk. There was a knock on the door. One of his corporals entered, saluted and gave Marquet a packet explaining that it had been delivered from the quayside by a courier. He thanked the corporal. Once he was alone, he untied the packet. Opening the letter inside, Marquet saw that it was written in code. Colville!

BIGT UIQO WXUE RWYA WH

Marquet had been practising coding and decoding using the JENA keyword – J corresponded to the number 9, E corresponded to the number 4, etc… and A, although the first letter of the alphabet, corresponded to zero. Writing the sequence against each letter of Colville's code

9, 4, 13, 0, 9, 4,13, 0 he began B + 9 = K, I + 4 = M… *Idiot*, he said to himself, *you're supposed to be decoding so it's minus not plus – plus is to encode*. He started again: B – 9 = S, I – 4 = E, G – 13 = T and T – 0 = T. But why was the code in blocks of four letters? He was sure that Colville hadn't told him anything about blocks of four. He continued to the end of the letters:

BIGT UIQO WXUE RWYA WH
SETT LEDO NTHE ISLA ND

He stared at the letters again. Had he made a mistake? Of course, Colville had written "SETTLED ON THE ISLAND". Thank goodness he had managed the first line. Colville had presumably used four-letter blocks to further confuse those who might try and crack the code. Without the key, that would surely be impossible.

He carried on. Surely, this would get easier? It did, but Marquet worked for the rest of the day before he made it to the end of the letter. The decoding was worth the wait.

Colville reported that his journey to Heligoland on one of the many fishing boats that landed their catches on the mainland had been without incident. On arrival, he made his way to the church of St Michael and introduced himself to the priest as Franz Herling. The priest had received the letter from the imprisoned smuggler and showed him to the smuggler's parents' house. The parents were welcoming and Herling soon made himself indispensable to the elderly couple. The many errands he ran for them enabled him to explore the island and to become known to the local residents and also to the British military police, who, after some suspicion and vigorous questioning, seemed to accept him. His cover of being the cousin of a smuggler imprisoned by the French helped allay further investigation into his background.

Colville continued. Since the British had captured the island in October last year, military and diplomatic staff had been sent to Heligoland followed by ever increasing numbers of merchants keen to smuggle their goods onto the Continent across the short sea journey and down the Elbe and Weser rivers and into the ports in Holstein. Herling listened in to the gossip in the local taverns. It seemed that the smugglers had not taken long to find ways around the French and Danish gunboats guarding the rivers and posts. The local fishermen were only too pleased to spend even more time smuggling than they used to, given the rewards which were spectacular compared to mere fishing. They, of course, knew the waters intimately. Their vessels ranged in size from just five to fifty tons and were flat-bottomed with drafts of only four or five feet enabling them to navigate through the many islands and mudflats in the estuaries of the Elbe and Weser. Now that the Royal Navy had a powerful presence around the island, the French and Danish gunboats were confined to the immediate coastal waters.

Colville estimated that there were nearly 200 different merchant businesses operating on the island and new firms were arriving every week. They smuggled produce from across the British colonies: coffee, sugar, tobacco, cotton wool, pimento, cocoa, ginger – the list went on. The profits from the trade were immense.

It was not just colonial produce that was being shipped. There was also a thriving trade in British manufactured goods. Colville had heard rumours that a high official in the French administration had even placed an order for 10,000 greatcoats for the *Grande Armée*. This caused much amusement in the tavern. Napoleon buying from his sworn enemy. What a scandal that would make if it ever became known! Without being too inquisitive, Colville had asked of those gathered who was the high official: Monsieur Bourrienne who had also done very nicely from the fat commission that went with the purchase.

Marquet was amazed by this report and wondered if there was any truth in it. Almost certainly not, but he would mention it to Colonel Maupont when they next met. He returned to Colville's letter.

Colville had then asked how all this contraband was paid for. Again, the gathering was unanimous; this was all made possible by transactions managed by a number of Hamburg-based banks.

Marquet made a mental note to discuss this valuable information with Colonel Maupont. If the banks could be prevented from operating, that could be an easy way to stamp out this trade. The banks were on the doorstep. Surely pressure could be applied?

Colville's letter continued. The trade between Germany and Heligoland was not simply one way. It appeared that the British had developed a covert operation to recruit young Hanoverians to join the British King's new German division. There were plenty of young men who were opposed to French rule and wished to fight against it. The smugglers were able to return to the island laden making the journeys even more profitable.

Another note for Marquet's next discussion with Maupont.

Colville had not forgotten the main purpose of the mission. It had become clear that his initial understanding of who controlled British intelligence and propaganda activity was misplaced. He imagined that the governor, Charles Hamilton, who had taken up his duties in February was responsible. However, in his travels, he kept on hearing of a person called "der Konsul".

Colville assumed that this was Hamilton. However, he was told firmly that "der Konsul" was a different man and it was he who was the controlling power on the island.

Colville finished the letter by promising to investigate "der Konsul" further. In a footnote, he also asked if his remuneration had been approved and had been paid.

Marquet sat back in his chair. He smiled to himself. Good, progress. Now to report to Colonel Maupont and then write back to Colville.

13

Number 11 Harley Street

Robertson was relieved that the journey on the lanes from Heythrop to the turnpike was short. Even in His Lordship's new single-horse cabriolet, he bounced across the carriage. The coachman, standing high up on the footboard behind the covered seats, shouted his apologies. He had been told to drive as quickly as possible. Once on the turnpike to London, progress was smoother and rapid. Stopping only for tolls, changes of horse and the mail coach, they reached London by the evening. Even at that hour, the hubbub and, of course, smell assaulted Robertson's senses. It was too late to call on Sir Arthur. He found a room in the Barley Mow Inn in Dorset Street and sent the coachman to Harley Street with a note saying that he would call at 10 a.m. After a quick supper, he returned to his room. There was barely time to run through all the scenarios he had imagined on the journey. Why had he been summoned? Exhausted sleep came too quickly to answer.

The next day started badly. Whoever had packed at Heythrop had simply thrown his clothes into the case. The suit he planned to wear was crumpled. The clothes he had travelled in were covered in dust. Hardly the right impression for a meeting with the chief secretary of the Irish Office. The innkeeper was no help. He could not iron. The laundry maid was off sick. Robertson smoothed his suit with his hands. Once he had dressed, he looked in the mirror – shambolic; worse, embarrassing. By the time he had breakfasted, his mood was foul. On the walk to Harley Street, he began to find a degree of equilibrium. But then while admiring the greenery of Paddington Street Gardens, he stepped in dog mess. No amount of cleaning on a nearby boot scrape could properly clear the mess.

By the time he arrived at Sir Arthur's imposing four-storey townhouse, his mood was volcanic. The footman opened the door before he had time to knock, and looked at Robertson raising an eyebrow. In the hall, he was shown a chair. The butler emerged.

'Reverend Robertson?'

'It is.'

'Sir Arthur is just finishing breakfast.' He looked Robertson up and down. 'I cannot do anything about your suit but if you give me your boots, we can at least ensure that *those* are presentable.'

'Thank you.' He undid the filthy boots.

'Take them and clean them, Jones.' The footman

looked at Robertson then at the butler with daggers drawn in his eyes.

'And before you say anything about cleaning not being part of your job, your job is to do as I tell you. Get on with it.'

Both men left. Robertson wondered what he had done to deserve such a start to the day. At least the butler's prescience helped to quell the volcano. The butler returned.

'Please follow me.'

He was shown into the morning room. Sir Arthur Wellesley was sipping coffee. Putting the cup down, he rose, smiling, shook Robertson's hand and waved him to a chair.

'Well, Reverend, it has been some time. Thank you for coming so promptly. You are well, I trust?'

'Well, thank you, Sir Arthur, though I have had rather a trying morning, domestically.' He looked down at the suit and his shoeless feet encased in black hose.

'I gather. But now to business. Tell me, would you be prepared to undertake, how shall I put it, an "opportunity" that will test both your loyalty and your courage?'

Robertson paused briefly. The words came out somewhat pompously. 'There is no danger that I would not cheerfully accept in the cause of my country as long as it did not discredit my clerical profession.'

'So, Mr Robertson, you tell me that you are a man of courage.'

'Try me, Sir Arthur.'

'Will you assist in rescuing a division of Spanish troops now in northern Germany by taking our government's proposals to the troops' commander, the Marquis de La Romana?'

So that was it. A mission to Germany. The cares, doubts and worries of subsiding into early gout-ridden old age faded as the adrenalin pumped through his veins. This was what he was made for. Forget climbing the clerical ladder, what he really craved was the opium of danger and to use his wits to defeat it.

'Will I? Of course. With fluent German and as a Catholic monk, I believe I am more likely than anyone else to gain the marquis's confidence. This may be my last such opportunity before old age hobbles me. Please tell me more, Sir Arthur.'

Wellesley put his hand up. 'All in good time.' He scribbled a note then rang the bell pull. The butler entered with Robertson's gleaming boots. 'Ah, Davis, have this note taken to Mr Canning's private secretary at the Foreign Office.' Turning to Robertson, he said, 'Mr Canning expects us.'

***

An hour later, Sir Arthur and Robertson followed the private secretary up the back stairs of the Foreign Office, through a private door and into the Secretary of State's apartment. A knock on another door produced a 'Come.'

'Sir Arthur Wellesley and the Reverend James Robertson, Foreign Secretary.'

George Canning rose. Robertson had seen a reproduced Hoppner picture of Canning in the press.

But now his head was bald. The slim figure was elegantly dressed in black. His white silk cravat covered Canning's long neck.

'Sir Arthur, good of you to come so promptly.' Wellesley gave a short nod of the head.

'This is the man we spoke about, Foreign Secretary, the Reverend Robertson.'

Robertson bowed. Canning looked him up and down. Robertson saw the contempt with which the second most powerful man in Britain regarded him. Embarrassment was written all over Robertson's face.

Wellesley read the situation immediately. 'Mr Robertson was summoned from the country yesterday. He has had no time to prepare for this meeting.'

'That is obvious.'

How to retrieve faulty first impressions? The fact that he was here with the Foreign Secretary himself surely meant that the decision to employ him had already been made. It just needed Canning's blessing. Time to be at his most persuasive. He would ram home what they must have already discussed.

'Sir, from what Sir Arthur has told me of the mission, I believe that I am uniquely well qualified to succeed. I have over thirty years' experience travelling in Germany. I speak the language as a native. I have some Spanish but La Romana will converse in French. My discussions with Napoleon are perfect evidence of my fluency. Finally, the marquis is a man of Catholic faith, as am I. My religious qualifications will surely give the best opportunity to gain access to the marquis, however well he is protected.'

Silence. Canning put his knuckles on the top of his desk, looking down at them. Robertson turned to look at Wellesley. Sir Arthur nodded and smiled. It seemed as if minutes had passed. Canning looked up at Robertson.

'Very well. Proceed. Mr Hammond will lead the detailed planning. One thing more: my good friend Mr Frere knows La Romana. Speak with him.'

'I will, sir.'

'Well, unless there is anything else, I must prepare for the Commons. I wish good luck and Godspeed. Ensure you succeed.' He looked down at his papers.

'There is one matter.'

Irritated, Canning said, 'Well?'

'The matter of my remuneration and what happens to my aged mother and two sisters in the event of my death?'

'Sir Arthur and I have discussed that subject.' Canning pushed a sheet of paper over the desk. Robertson read it. One hundred pounds for life for his three relatives would keep them comfortable. His reward was much more than he was about to ask for.

'Satisfied?'

'Yes, sir. Thank you.'

Canning rang a handbell. The private secretary returned.

'Please inform Mr Hammond that I have decided to proceed.' He turned to Robertson. 'Return to the main entrance of this office at 2 p.m. sharp tomorrow. At the reception, ask for Mr Hammond. Now, Sir Arthur, Portugal.'

Robertson was shown out. A full day to prepare with time to list all the questions that he would need to have answered. But first to find spiritual guidance. He walked out of Downing Street onto Whitehall. Minutes later he was at the entrance of Westminster Abbey. A verger was able to tell him where the nearest Catholic church was to his inn on Dorset Street. The chapel of St James's was close to the now-closed Spanish Embassy. The half-an-hour walk would do him good.

Entering, he made the sign of the cross. A chaplain told him that Mass was not held until six in the evening. Robertson asked, as the chapel was so close to the embassy, if there was a Spanish connection. He identified himself. The chaplain had spent time in Madrid. For the next two hours Robertson questioned and listened until he had a reasonable understanding of recent Spanish history and personalities.

'And have you heard the latest news from Spain?'

Robertson shook his head. 'No more than I have read in *The Times*, that King Carlos and his son had been summoned to Bayonne by Napoleon. You have something more recent?'

'From my seminarian friend, Robert Brindle, who is in Madrid. Marshal Murat's troops have occupied the city. Murat has quartered his men in the locals' houses. Brindle has spoken with many *Madrileños*. Their guests take what they want. If the *Madrileños* protest, they must complain to French officers. You can imagine the result.'

'It's the same in Bavaria. They're no respecters of their hosts' property.'

'According to Brindle, there was trouble outside the royal palace in Aranjuez. One of Murat's aides was attacked.

The French shot into the crowd. Ten of the protesters were killed, sending the already pent-up populace into a frenzy. The next day, 2 May, armed with whatever came to hand, swords, pikes, bricks and roof tiles, the crowd set upon any Frenchman they could find. The French response was savage. Those rioters who had not melted away were brutally suppressed. Even then the fighting did not cease. A small group of Spaniards seized the main artillery depot. After a brave rear-guard action, they too were subdued.'

Robertson saw that the chaplain was close to tears.

'It gets worse. Over 400 Spaniards were killed and wounded and another 300 were taken prisoner and executed. Among the dead were a number of women; it seemed that even possessing a pair of scissors was enough to be sentenced to death. Those sentenced were not even offered a priest to administer the Last Rites. News of the events of "*Dos de Mayo*" spread like wildfire. Rumour fed on rumour. You can imagine the outrage.'

'Especially in such a Catholic country. Hardly the way to win over the local populous.'

'Brindle enclosed a cutting from *Le Moniteur* informing that at the meeting in Bayonne, both Carlos and Ferdinand had agreed to abdicate.'

Robertson interjected. 'Agreed or forced?'

The chaplain smiled. 'Synonymous, don't you agree? *Le Moniteur* delights in relating the family falling out during the negotiations. When Ferdinand initially refused to agree, the old King tried to strike his son with his cane. He missed – he could hardly move because of his rheumatism. The Queen, meanwhile, screamed abuse at

Fernando in tones worthy of a fishwife. You can imagine Paris readers' laughter. Anyway, it seems that both will retire with fat pensions. Carlos to Italy and Fernando to Valençay in the Loire region. I wonder who will be the new king?'

Robertson had already guessed the likely candidates. In a matter of days, Napoleon had achieved the overthrow of another Bourbon kingdom and was now free to nominate his chosen leader of Spain.

He smiled. 'Father, I believe that another Bonaparte will be the new king.'

The chaplain laughed. 'To add to the growing list!' He took out his fob watch from a pocket.

'Will you excuse me? I must prepare for Mass.'

Robertson thanked him. He found a side chapel and knelt. Before prayer, he pondered. How would La Romana react if he heard this news? And what about his troops? Would this make his task easier? Probably. He put these temporal thoughts out of his mind and prayed. By the time he returned to the Barley Mow, he felt rested in mind and body. The day had improved.

14
The Foreign Office, May 1808

The next day, Robertson woke early, dressed and returned to St James's. He found the chapel's solace reassuring. After breakfast, he retired to his room. Preparations for the day ahead complete, he changed into his suit, now cleaned and pressed. Leaving plenty of time, he strolled down to Piccadilly, took the air in St James's Park before lunch in an inn in Whitehall. At 1.45 p.m. he walked up the stairs of the Foreign Office, his mind a mixture of anticipation, excitement and apprehension.

Through the imposing doors, he announced himself to the hall porter.

'Yes, Mr Robertson, you are expected. I will let Mr Hammond know that you have arrived. Please take a seat.'

A few minutes later, a young, slim man rushed in and up to the hall porter's desk.

'Hello, Dakin.'

'Good afternoon, Mr Hoppner.' Dakin noted Hoppner's arrival in the register.

'I'm late. Must dash.'

'Not so fast, young sir. You can escort Mr Hammond's guest to his room.'

This was the perfect excuse for his lateness back from lunch.

'Of course, delighted to.'

'Mr Robertson, may I introduce Mr Hoppner, one of the clerks. He will take you to Mr Hammond.'

Robertson stood and extended his hand. 'A pleasure. How do you do?'

Hoppner was motionless, simply staring at Robertson. He shook his head. 'I'm sorry but are you the Reverend James Robertson, the Benedictine monk.'

'I am indeed. I don't believe we have met. How do you know of me?'

Hoppner shook Robertson's hand. 'I rather think that Mr Hammond should explain.'

Both men were in quandaries about what to say to the other. Was this purely coincidence or something more sinister? Robertson decided that small talk would be the best policy as he followed the young man up the marble stairs. As Hoppner took the stairs two at a time, Robertson had to raise his voice.

'Are you related to the painter John Hoppner? I admired his portrait of the Foreign Secretary.'

Hoppner stopped, waiting for the guest to catch up. Was this man fit enough to take on such a hazardous mission?

'He is my father.'

'An admirable artist.' Robertson, Hoppner noted, was blowing.

They reached the door to Mr Hammond's office. Hoppner knocked.

'Come.' As they entered, Robertson's eyes scanned the large high-ceilinged office. Portraits of the no-doubt illustrious predecessors crammed the walls.

'Dakin asked me to show Mr Robertson to your room. May I present the Reverend James Robertson?'

George Hammond, the senior Under-Secretary of State, rose, made his way around his large desk, and walked across the room to shake Robertson's hand.

'Delighted. I have heard a lot about you, sir. Please do sit.' He turned to Hoppner. 'And you, please return to your desk and return with your report. We will proceed with the detailed planning on the lines you have suggested.' Hoppner was relieved and elated. It would appear his work had been approved.

Robertson watched Hoppner leave the office and Hammond as he returned to his chair.

'He seems a bright young man.'

Hammond smiled. 'Hoppner shows some promise. Moving on, thank you for agreeing to take on this mission. Our political masters and in particular Mr Canning, keep us on our toes. His policy is to keep prodding the Corsican's empire looking for weak points where we can cause damage.'

'As I understand. Where are the Spanish troops located now?'

'Our most recent intelligence is that La Romana and

his troops have moved from the Lübeck area and are now garrisoning the region around Glückstadt, a Danish town on the River Elbe about twenty-five miles north of Altona. Since our capture of Copenhagen pushed Denmark into the arms of the French, you will be operating in true enemy territory. Let me show you.'

They moved to the map cabinet. Hammond pulled out a map of northern Germany and Schleswig-Holstein.

'Here.'

Robertson followed the pointing finger. 'This part of Schleswig-Holstein is German-speaking, is it not?'

Hammond nodded.

'That at least mitigates some of the risk operating in Denmark. Though it is a shame that the Danish ports are now closed to us. What do we know of the marquis?'

There was a knock on the door. Hoppner returned.

'Hoppner, you have talked with our former Spanish ambassador, Mr Frere. What did he tell you about La Romana?'

'Mr Frere has met the marquis on many occasions. La Romana is a patriot and a royalist, a firm supporter of the Bourbons. Mr Frere believes that he would be outraged by the enforced abdication of both the King and his son. La Romana is probably the ablest general in Spain. The troops he commands are some of the best that Spain has.' Hoppner decided not to add that Frere was a close friend of the Foreign Secretary; that might compromise the objectivity of his report.

Mr Robertson raised his hand. 'What about the general's officers and the make-up of his troops?'

Hammond looked at Hoppner. 'Do we have any more information?'

'Our military attaché attached to the besieged Swedish force defending Stralsund reported that La Romana's division was part of the attacking French forces. The marquis commanded around 15,000 troops – his deputy was Juan Kindelan y O'Regan and his senior aide-de-camp was a Colonel Jose O'Donnell.'

The names brought back unpleasant memories of his recent work in Ireland for Robertson. How many so-called Irish patriots had threatened him? He raised his hand again.

'As both of these gentlemen are of Irish Catholic descent whose families were driven out of Ireland by their hatred of British rule, are you sure that their loyalty to the Bourbons will remain firm? Will they not be persuaded to transfer their loyalties to a French-appointed ruler?'

Mr Hammond looked at the monk. 'You make a very fair point. Surely that will be a question you will wish to ask the marquis when you have the opportunity?'

'Touché!' replied Robertson, and raised an eyebrow, a twinkle in his eye.

Hammond ignored the gesture and took a sheet of paper from his coat pocket. 'When you speak to the marquis, Mr Canning has given these instructions.' He now read: '"*You will inform the Marquis de La Romana that our transport fleet shall be at his disposal and at his orders to convey him and his troops to any place or country he chooses. We ask nothing in return. We do not ask that they fight with us. We simply desire to give him the power to withdraw from their present situation. We offer to carry them free of cost to South America, to Minorca, to England or to Spain, whatever is their option.*

'Tell him that if Spain is resolved to resist the usurper, we are ready to cooperate with her by every means at our disposal. Our cavalry has never been better mounted, our artillery never better served and our soldiers of every rank long for the opportunity to measure themselves with the French on land. We consider Spain as the fairest field of action."'

Typical diplomatic pomposity Robertson was tempted to say but didn't. Instead he asked, 'Do we have the transports to carry such a large force of men, horses and equipment from Glückstadt?'

'The Admiralty assures me that Captain George of the Transport Office can secure all the shipping required. Once the Spaniards have taken control of the town, port and the surrounding area, the navy has control of the North Sea and will prevent any enemy ships from interfering with the transports berthing at the quayside to load the troops. And well before any of Bernadotte's troops can assemble in strength enough to prevent a smooth embarkation.'

'Can we now move on to the detail?'

Robertson nodded and Hammond looked down at the map, pointing to a speck well out in the North Sea.

'We captured Heligoland from the Danes last year. The island is now a thriving smuggling centre. The excellent Mr Nicholas has established a centre for intelligence gathering and propaganda. A German officer is actively recruiting disaffected Hanoverians to make the journey to the island. From there, they move to England for training to become soldiers in the King's German Legion. All is made possible by the fishermen who transport men and goods. They have an intimate knowledge of the coast, tides and currents and are expert at evading French and Danish gunboats.

'Given its proximity to Hamburg and Glückstadt, we will use the island as the base for the mission. Mr Robertson, you will sail on one of the regular packet boats from Harwich to Heligoland. You will be accompanied by another agent, Mr MacKenzie, who will be with us shortly. Mr MacKenzie will act as the pivot for the mission. You will report to him on the island. He will then coordinate with Mr Nicholas and us. Mr Nicholas will engage one of the smugglers to take you direct to Glückstadt or another town or village on the coast. You will then make your way to La Romana. We will establish safe methods for you to communicate from the mainland to Mr MacKenzie on Heligoland.'

Hammond was in full flow, about to continue his monologue. Robertson thought that the man liked the sound of his own voice. He put his hand up again. Hammond's opened mouth snapped shut, his eyes flashing anger at Robertson.

'Is this MacKenzie proven? I'd prefer not to put my life in the hands of a novice.'

Hammond retorted, 'You should know that he has already provided most valuable service to His Majesty's Government.'

'In what way?' Robertson was beginning to enjoy

winding Hammond up: a reaction to pomposity or a way to release the fear pressure valve?

'Mr MacKenzie has toured northern, eastern and central Europe extensively. In 1804 he volunteered to serve with the Russian Army and fought against the Persians in the Caucasus.' Hammond was about to start again.

Robertson put his hand up once more. Hammond stopped.

'My dear Mr Hammond, please be brief. I will have plenty of time to hear an autobiography from MacKenzie when we are en route.'

'You may have read the Parliamentary debates on the Tilsit Treaty's secret clauses. Suffice to say then, it was Mr MacKenzie who brought back this intelligence. He is well connected with the French royalists still opposing Napoleon. More on the latter shortly.'

A knock on the door. 'Enter.'

The door opened. Dakin, the door porter, entered followed by a tall, immaculately dressed man of about thirty. 'Mr MacKenzie, sir.'

Colin Alexander MacKenzie entered the room, bowed and was introduced by Mr Hammond. MacKenzie nodded to Hoppner. Robertson returned the bow. MacKenzie looked composed and confident.

'Mr Canning has told me all about you, Mr Robertson. You are a brave man. I do hope that we will work well together.'

'I am sure that we will. Do I detect a Highland accent?'

'You do indeed. I was raised in Dingwall. And you?'

'Near Blair Atholl.'

'Fellow Highlanders together, we will make a fine team.'

It was Hammond's turn to cut the talk short.

'Gentlemen, we have a lot of ground to cover. You will have plenty of time to get to know one another in the coming days when you discuss the minutiae of the mission. To complete the communication link, letters from Mr Robertson will be delivered to Mr MacKenzie on Heligoland by our smuggler friends. He will then send reports by King's Messenger on the fastest packet to Harwich and on to the Foreign Office. We will ask the Admiralty to inform us of the arrival of the report by shutter-speed telegraph on the roof of Admiralty House. Mr Hoppner here will be responsible for receiving the reports and distributing them to Mr Canning and to me. You understand, young Hoppner, that, for the duration of the mission you will have to be available at any time, night or day.'

'I do, sir.'

'Now we come to the matters of encryption of your letters, Mr Robertson. Have you used ciphers in the past?'

'I have, but using cipher would require me to carry tables or such. These would possibly incriminate me should I be stopped and searched by someone who knew what they were looking for. Perhaps I should use sympathetic ink which could be interspersed by innocent religious text as presumably I shall be travelling as a monk?'

'Agreed.'

'Thank you. I will not carry any letter from His Majesty's Government. It is just too risky should I be stopped. I will convey Mr Canning's message to the marquis verbally and use Mr Frere's name and friendship with La Romana as evidence of my credibility.'

'Again agreed.'

Hammond turned to MacKenzie. 'Mr Canning also confirms that should the marquis require that we make a formal treaty with him, you are empowered by His Majesty's Government to conclude such an arrangement with La Romana. Understood?'

MacKenzie nodded.

Turning back to Robertson, Hammond continued. 'We will leave the final detail of how best to transport you to Glückstadt to Mr Nicholas. He has the local knowledge and is better informed of the up-to-date situation in the area. Now, it is probable that, once you land on the mainland, you will be met by another of our agents or one of his men. Monsieur Louis Bayard is known to his friends as the Chevalier or simply "B". He and his friends use the monograph of a small flower, the scarlet pimpernel. M Bayard is a committed royalist and has provided intelligence to us for over twelve years at great risk to himself.'

Robertson had heard that even fifteen years after the King's execution, there still an active royalist opposition.

Hammond continued. 'And, finally to the matter of funds, my colleague Mr Rolleston will provide you both with sufficient coin to cover your expenses. Mr Nicholas will provide you, Mr Robertson, with both French and Hanoverian coin for your needs once you are in Germany.

It is unlikely, but should you require additional funds, Mr Nicholas will provide you with an introduction to Messrs Parish & Co, a most reliable firm of bankers based in Hamburg. Mr John Parish will attend to your needs. I suggest that the three of you spend time discussing the mission and become better acquainted.'

The meeting was over.

Hoppner led Robertson and MacKenzie down the main stairs to the atrium. As it was past six, perhaps it was appropriate to suggest that they should adjourn to the Red Lion? He asked. Robertson enthusiastically agreed.

MacKenzie looked at Hoppner with a degree of disdain.

'Perhaps my club, Boodles, would be quieter? I could do with the walk to St James's.'

Robertson glanced at Hoppner: he looked like someone who had firmly been put in his place.

At Boodles, MacKenzie signed his guests in. They were shown to the visitors' salon. They sat. MacKenzie ordered drinks and looked at Robertson.

'I am intrigued, Mr Robertson – why does a man who, if I may put it, is in the later stages of life, want to take on such a risky assignment?'

Hoppner leant forward. It looked as though that was exactly the question he wanted answered. Robertson smiled.

'Perhaps, Mr MacKenzie, for the same reason that you do? To pit your wits against an implacable enemy. The more the challenge, the more the excitement, the more the reward. Am I correct?'

'Yes, exactly.'

'And the financial rewards can also be rather tempting!'

Robertson and MacKenzie laughed. Hoppner realised that behind the joke, both men were deadly serious. Hoppner couldn't stop the next question.

'But you haven't said why.'

'Napoleon wants to crush the Church. I will do everything in my power to resist him. And if the work aligns with my country's goals, so much the better.' Robertson paused and smiled. 'And I enjoy it!'

15
Number 12 Krayenkamp, Central Hamburg,
May 1808

Marquet was at his desk deciphering the latest letter from Colville. He was improving but it still took time and concentration to complete the process. He was also tight for time. His next meeting with the colonel was only in just over two hours and he needed time to prepare. There was a knock on the door. An interruption was the last thing he needed. He angrily shouted, 'Come in.'

It was Lejeune who entered and saluted. He and his gendarme breeches were spattered with mud.

'I have come straight from Nyborg. I had a meeting with Martin.'

Good timing thought Marquet. *I'll be able to give Maupont more intelligence.*

'And what did he have to say?'

'I met him as arranged. Martin's Spanish is poor

but when he was attending to the general he was able to pick up some of the meaning of a conversation that the marquis was having with his senior aide-de-camp, Colonel O'Donnell. It appears that the general was most concerned that he had had no mail from Spain for over two months. There had been no responses to his letters. The colonel also told the general that there was disquiet among the troops who also had had no communication from their families at home. Martin went on to tell me that he has made friends with one of La Romana's chefs – the marquis likes to eat well. The chef comes from the Basque country and speaks passable French. Martin asked if the report of no mail was correct. It was and the lack of news from home was the subject of much concern. The chef also told Martin that some of the soldiers guarding the coastline had picked up leaflets from the beaches. These leaflets were worded in Spanish but appeared to be printed in England.'

'And what did they say?'

'They reported the events of 2 May and of the abdication of the King of Spain! Is that true?'

'From what I have read in *Le Moniteur*, it appears that some of it may be, but in the main it is English propaganda no doubt delivered by their navy to confuse our poor Spanish allies. Is there anything else?'

'No, sir.'

'Then get cleaned up and go to the NCOs' mess, have a good meal and rest then return to Nyborg. Arrange to meet Martin again and tell him to keep up the good work. Well done.'

'Thank you, sir.'

Marquet sat back. That the Spaniards were becoming restless was news that the colonel would value. He leant back over Colville's letter and completed the deciphering. Colville had discovered the identity of "Der Konsul". He was Edward Nicholas who had been appointed as minister plenipotentiary for Heligoland in February. His appointment came from someone at the very top of the British Government. He had been given extensive powers. Colville went on: It seemed that Nicholas signed passports for all vessels arriving and leaving the island. All residents had to have identification cards authorised by him and most importantly all mail had to go through him. Colville would do what he could to find out more about Nicholas's activities but warned that he had to operate with extreme care. There was an increasing police presence. He had heard that another traveller from Hamburg had been arrested on suspicion of working for the French.

He also reported that he had discovered the name of the commander of the King's German Legion's base on the island, a Major Kentzinger. Kentzinger had agents who brought volunteers from the mainland to join the legion. While the volunteers mainly came from northern Germany, some came from as far afield as Austria and the Tyrol. They were a mixed bunch: deserters, draft dodgers and escaped prisoners of war.

Colville also wrote that even more merchants had arrived on the island and were establishing covert supply routes with the German and Danish traders.

Marquet looked at the clock. Time to go. Two spies in place. Maupont should be pleased with his progress so far.

16

Cesar Rainville's Hotel, Altona, North of Hamburg

As soon as he arrived at Bernadotte's headquarters, he was shown into Colonel Maupont's room. The colonel accused him of being late but was more sympathetic when Marquet explained the arrival of Lejeune with Martin the valet's news.

Once Marquet had told Maupont of the Spaniards' disquiet, Maupont explained that Monsieur Fouche, the minster of police, General Landrieux, chief of the military secret bureau and General Moncey, the inspector general of the gendarmerie had been instructed by the Emperor to put measures in place to intercept all correspondence from Spain to La Romana and his troops and vice versa. Maupont said that he would alert Moncey to the Spaniards' concerns. He also told Marquet that he would brief Marshal Bernadotte and his staff. He was surprised however that the marshal's staff had not informed him of any disquiet, particularly as the marshal now had a troop of Spanish cavalry among his personal escort.

Was Marquet aware that the Prince of Ponte Corvo had been born in Pau in the Basque country, spoke reasonable Spanish and had a strong affinity with the Spanish? Marquet admitted he was not but suggested that the intelligence from the valet was taken seriously.

They discussed Colville's reports. Maupont summoned one of his clerks and instructed him to search the files to see if there was any further information on the consul Nicholas. It was not long before the clerk returned. Until the French occupation of Hamburg in 1806, Nicholas had been the assistant to the British Consul in Hamburg, Edward Thornton. He had been identified as the coordinator of British intelligence across northern Germany. Maupont instructed Marquet to check what information was available linking Nicholas to suspected agents operating in the region. Action could then be coordinated to eradicate them.

'Let me know how you get on.' It was clear to Marquet that the interview was at an end. He could not let Colville's other intelligence go unquestioned.

'But, Colonel, what about the report of the purchase of army greatcoats from the British in May last year? Surely we cannot be seen to be doing business with our sworn enemies? And what about the Hamburg bankers who are making possible all the smuggling from Heligoland? Should we not be taking firm action to stamp on them?'

The colonel rose from his chair, his face flushed, and said very quietly, 'Captain, you are instructed not to stray from your remit. These matters should not concern you. Do not pursue them.'

Maupont paused and continued in no more than a whisper, 'Remember what you saw at Ritzebuttel Castle two months ago? If you do not want to end up at the wrong end of a firing squad and you value your life, do as I say. There are people far more senior than me who will stop at nothing to prevent prying eyes. I certainly will not be able to help you and indeed, I would most likely be next in line for the firing squad.'

Marquet was shaken. It really hurt not to investigate further. After all, when he became an officer, he had sworn an oath to uphold the law and honour of France. Brushing wrongdoing aside grated. It was just not right.

'Do you understand, Captain?'

'Yes, Colonel, I understand completely.'

'Now come with me.'

Marquet followed the colonel into the garden. Once they were far enough from the house and out of earshot, he turned to Marquet.

'You have to understand that it was necessary for me to warn you. Yes, of course Bourrienne and the other marshals and generals are lining their pockets with nice commissions, bribes and other backhanders. That is regarded as the privilege of rank and is expected. If you investigate and find what might be construed as embarrassing evidence which compromises the elite, then my prediction of a firing squad for you is inevitable. As to the bankers, we have indeed taken action. When we first occupied Hamburg two years ago, we arrested John Parish of Parish & Co. We had evidence that he was involved in the smuggling of British contraband but we were ordered by Paris to release him.'

'For what reason?' asked Marquet incredulously.

'Do you know where Britain obtains a good proportion of its wheat?'

Marquet shook his head.

'From us, shipped mainly from Bordeaux! And the Emperor insists that the English pay for the wheat in gold so to deplete their reserves. How are these payments made? By English banks acting on the orders of the English Government. The banks, therefore, become a necessary evil. I have also heard it said that English banks have organised the shipment of Spanish silver from Mexico to us in payment for outstanding Spanish loans to the French Government. Amazing, isn't it?'

Marquet shook his head in astonishment. Maupont continued.

'When your father was a receiver general of finance, he may well have known M Gabriel-Julien Ouvrard, one of the leading bankers in Paris. It was Ouvrard who negotiated with the Amsterdam bankers, Hope & Co. Hope & Co had moved their offices to London when the war started. Through them, the English bank Barings was used to make the shipment of the Spanish silver. Hope & Co's agents in Hamburg are Parish & Co. So you can see that we cannot come down too heavily on Mr John Parish and his brother, David, without causing much displeasure in Paris.'

'Now I begin to understand, thank you, Colonel.'

Maupont waved his hand in acknowledgement. 'But we can ensure that Parish and his brother know that we are watching them. After all, we can catch their spies, can we not?'

'Yes, we most certainly can, with Colville telling us when the British send agents from Heligoland. I would like to talk with Pyonnier, the commandant of customs. A note from you would carry more weight than one from me. Could you write to him?'

'Of course.'

Marquet saluted, turned and walked away from the colonel in a better frame of mind.

Marquet's carriage reached the city gates. A crowd milled around. His driver had to shout to clear the road. The carriage slowly made its way through the scrum of people. Some of them looked up and seeing Marquet's uniform began hissing. Reaching the gates, Marquet asked the corporal of the guard why the crowd were so angry. He was told that the governor General Dupas had increased the tax to enter the city once again. Dupas had only been appointed by Bernadotte in April but his extravagant lifestyle paid for by the citizens of the city was further alienating the populace. Marquet's men had reported increasing levels of resentment. Questions were met by silence and shrugs. Even the normally willing informers were now reluctant to volunteer information, citing the risk of beatings and then demanding yet more money. Marquet sighed inwardly; driving the locals into still more passive resistance would only make his work harder.

17
The Foreign Office, May 1808

The next morning Robertson announced himself to Dakin, the door porter who greeted him with a 'Good morning, Father'. Shown up to a side office, he was greeted by Mr Rolleston, Hoppner and MacKenzie. It was agreed that the time spent at Boodles should be repeated after the success of the mission. Mr Rolleston ushered them to a large table covered with maps.

'You will sail from Harwich on one of the regular packets to Heligoland. As discussed yesterday, Mr Nicholas will make the detailed arrangements. MacKenzie, you will carry letters of instruction from Mr Canning to Mr Nicholas telling him to provide you with every assistance that you require. Mr Nicholas will organise the necessary vessel to take you, Mr Robertson, the sixty-eight miles to Glückstadt. It may well be that the journey is made in two stages, the first to the island of Neuwerk, which lies off Cuxhaven and then down the River Elbe on to Glückstadt.'

He used dividers to show the route up past Holland, into the German Bight and Heligoland and the journey south-eastwards to Neuwerk, close to the mouth of the Elbe and on upriver to the town.

'Understood?'

Robertson looked at Mr Rolleston. 'Can these guides be relied on?'

'There is always some risk, Mr Robertson. Yes, the coastal waters are patrolled by French and Danish customs cutters. Privateers do operate. However, the Royal Navy has complete control of the waters up to twelve miles to the coast and closer in depending on the tide. The map is deceptive; mudflats extend nearly ten miles out from the coast. Even our cutters draw ten to twelve feet of water and so cannot move closer at low tide.

'The navy will escort your guide close to the shore at high tide – the tides rise and fall by over thirteen feet. He is a local with a lifetime of knowledge of the coast. The guide will take you to Neuwerk where you will rest for the remainder of the night. Then there are a number of alternatives. Either you will be sailed down the mouth of the Elbe and landed in or near Glückstadt. If this is not possible, the guide will use the River Weser as an alternative or as a final option, and once the tide has gone out, he will guide you across the mudflats to Cuxhaven, about a six-mile walk.'

'A six-mile walk across mud carrying my luggage is hardly practical for a man of fifty. I'll be covered in mud and, if spotted, surely arouse suspicion.'

Mr Rolleston looked at the priest. 'Not ideal, I grant you, but it is an option if these others do not work out.'

'Let's hope I can sail direct to Glückstadt!' He bent down again looking at the map. 'If I cannot, I will have to make my way down the Weser to Bremen and then by road to Hamburg, cross the border into Denmark and on to Glückstadt.'

'Correct. Be assured that Monsieur Duval and other friends will be primed to support you.'

'Another question: will the navy be able to force the River Elbe, reach Glückstadt and take the Spaniards off? With at least one bank of the river in enemy hands, that will be a daunting task.'

Hoppner was impressed by the perceptiveness of the question and looked at Rolleston.

'The Admiralty is looking at a number of options. I believe that we can leave that worry to the navy. Just remember how successful the combined operations at Copenhagen were last year. Can we move on?'

'By all means.'

Before Rolleston could continue, MacKenzie raised his hand.

'Mr Rolleston, since our meeting yesterday, I have been thinking about the communication between Mr Robertson on the mainland and me on Heligoland. Do we not run the risk that his letters will be intercepted at the post offices by the French police? Secondly, I also suggest that Mr Robertson should not just rely on sympathetic ink for secrecy. After all, he may well run out of the ink or be separated from it.'

Rolleston smiled. 'A good question. Hoppner has been intimately involved with the establishment of communications from Germany through Heligoland to the Foreign Office here. Hoppner.'

'Thank you, sir. Heligoland has now become the pivot for our intelligence gathering to and from German-speaking lands. Mr Nicholas handles all the correspondence. He is the only person authorised to judge which letters are delivered and which are not. Most of the mail in the region is moved through the main post office in Hamburg. With the help of our friends in the city, we have established links to some of the officials in the post office. With the monetary assistance of Parish & Co, these officials are kept well provided for and ensure that our letters are properly despatched.'

Robertson laughed. 'Well put, Hoppner!'

Rolleston turned back to MacKenzie. 'From the second point you make, are you suggesting that Mr Robertson and you use a code?'

'Yes.'

Robertson interjected. 'As we discussed yesterday, I do not wish to carry papers that might incriminate me, whether they be letters to La Romana or a code book.'

'Therefore can I suggest that we use the Freemason's cipher which can be memorised?'

Robertson looked at MacKenzie, raising an eyebrow.

'My dear sir, I am a staunch Catholic. What would my abbot say if he knew that I was dabbling in the evil art of Freemasonry?' Hoppner was beginning to understand the monk's sense of humour.

MacKenzie smiled and raised both hands in a gesture of surrender. 'The cipher is also known as the Pigpen cipher. Will that assuage your wrath?'

'Indeed it does, sir!'

MacKenzie took a sheet of paper, drew out two blocks of squares as if he was about to play noughts and crosses. Below the squares, he drew two large Xs. Into the first square, he wrote the letters A to I into each block. Into the second square he inserted the letters J to R and placed dots into the corner of each block. The dot below the J was placed to the bottom right, that of the K directly below it and the dot in the L block at the bottom left-hand corner. He proceeded to place the dots with the remaining letters in the block finishing with a dot to the top left of the letter R. He placed the letters S, T, U and V in the first X and the remaining W,X,Y and Z in the second X and finished with the dots, the first under the W and the last above the letter Z.

Robertson grasped the concept instantly. 'And so each letter becomes a symbol? Thus the symbol L represents C and an L with a dot in the bottom left corner is L itself and so on.'

'Very good, Father,' exclaimed MacKenzie. 'The cipher is well known in the right code-breaking circles, but it should preserve our secrecy for the duration of our mission.'

The monk smiled. 'So, Mr MacKenzie, how is your Latin?'

'Rather rusty, but with a little work, I am sure I can bring it back up to speed.'

'Well then, to make it a little more difficult for our enemies, let us converse in Latin.'

'Good,' said Rolleston. 'Let us move on to the matter of your disguise, Mr Robertson. We can provide the necessary papers for your immediate needs. Will you travel as a monk?'

'I think so. I last passed through Hamburg in 1800 conducting boy initiates from Scotland through the city to Ratisbon. I was helped by my good friend, the poet Thomas Campbell. Though the area is mainly Lutheran, the Church has maintained a foothold in the city despite the French occupation. If I was dressed as a priest named Father Gallus, I should still be able to blend in and avoid the attention of the police. Can you provide a passport to allow me to travel in Holstein?'

'Yes, we can and can make the passport appear genuine to all but the most experienced eyes,' replied Rolleston. 'I like the scheme. Any comments, MacKenzie?'

'Mr Robertson, what will be your cover story?'

'It will be best to keep to the truth as closely as possible. I shall be what I am, a Benedictine monk travelling through the area to meet local priests and minster to the faithful.'

'That should work.'

Robertson raised a hand. 'Can I ask how the messages between Mr MacKenzie and me will be delivered?'

'Mr Nicholas will advise you on the detail. But I know he favours the ordinary post. After all, one letter among thousands is much more difficult to intercept than one carried by a courier.'

Robertson nodded his approval.

Rolleston began to tidy his papers.

'Well, gentlemen, if there is nothing else, I shall ask Mr Hammond for instructions to draw funds from the Secret Account and provide the letters of instruction for Mr Nicholas. Here is a note to Mr Brook of the Alien Office.' He handed the note to Hoppner. 'Please ask Mr Brook to write a note that Mr MacKenzie will give to Mr Billingsby, the director of the Alien Office in Harwich. The note will inform him that Mr MacKenzie is escorting a German out of the country and ask him to complete the necessary paperwork. That should keep matters correct for our esteemed Alien Office colleagues. Mr Hoppner, please see the decipherer of letters who will provide the sympathetic ink. You will take my coach to Harwich. Joseph Bigg is my driver and an excellent man. On arrival in Harwich, you will report to Mr Billingsby and then take the packet to Heligoland. Gentlemen, may I wish you fortune and success.'

Hoppner glanced at Robertson. How could the monk look so relaxed? He wondered when they would meet again, if ever.

18

London to Harwich and Heligoland, June 1808

On 4 June, Joseph Bigg collected Robertson from the Barley Mow. He climbed up into Rolleston's carriage and sat beside MacKenzie and they left London to the sound of twenty-one gun salutes ringing out from the Tower of London and across St James's Park. It was the King's seventieth birthday. They hoped it was a good omen.

Reaching Harwich the same evening, MacKenzie took Herr Rorauer as Robertson now masqueraded to the Aliens Office in the town. There, they met Mr Billingsby, the local director. MacKenzie explained that he was escorting Herr Rorauer out of the country and asked Billingsby to provide the correct exit passport. With the documentation in order, they made their way to the quayside.

Robertson sat on a bench watching the packet boat being loaded. He had lost count of the number of times he had sailed to the Continent. The last journey to Hamburg had been escorting boy initiates via Hamburg to Ratisbon. That memory took him back to his first journey. Was that really thirty-seven years ago? Yet he remembered the moment as if it was yesterday: his mother's voice breaking with emotion as she appealed to her husband not to send both her sons away; his firm reply that both were called to serve God; her tears on his cheek as he bent down to say goodbye; his father's handshake, not a comforting hug; being told that at fifteen, he was a man; the walk with his brother to Blair Atholl to catch the coach south; turning around one last time to see his mother's face buried in her husband's chest; trying to hold back the tears; landing in Calais, hearing real French being spoken; the journey to the Scottish college at Dinant and the start of his education. How different the world was then. Louis XV was still on the throne of France and the American colonies were still British.

A shout from MacKenzie pulled him out of his reverie. Time to board. He walked up the gangplank. On board, when he wasn't talking with MacKenzie, he began creating Herr Rorauer in his mind. He would be a Bavarian, hence the southern German accent, but otherwise, his character would mimic Robertson's own to bring natural answers to any awkward questions. With a favourable south-westerly blowing, the 315 miles were covered in forty-eight hours. Sailing past Heligoland's imposing red cliffs, the packet rounded the island and made the port on the south-east corner of the island.

Landing at the quayside of the Unterland, they were

shown directly to the consul's office. Robertson asked why they would be meeting the consul and not the governor. MacKenzie explained that the governor, William Hamilton, reported to the Colonial Office and was, in principle, the senior diplomat on the island. However, it was the minister plenipotentiary, Mr Nicholas, who had real control of the government and of the purse strings. Mr Nicholas reported directly to Mr Canning and, MacKenzie understood, his reports were read avidly by the King himself. It was Mr Nicholas who had a network of not just agents on the mainland but a vast array of contacts and supporters who supplied information and distributed propaganda across north-west Germany. And it was Mr Nicholas, not the governor, who issued passports to all arriving and departing vessels. All mail to and from the island had to be approved by him.

Robertson and MacKenzie were shown into the minister's office. They shook hands with Mr Nicholas and introduced themselves. MacKenzie then handed Nicholas a letter from Mr Canning. Edward Nicholas sat back in his chair and read Mr Canning's letter twice.

'Well, gentlemen, it appears that I am to organise transport to take you, Father, to the mainland. Mr Canning does not tell me the purpose of the visit. May I therefore ask you to explain why you wish to make this hazardous journey?' Nicholas looked at both men seated in front of him.

MacKenzie responded. 'I am afraid, sir, that I am under specific orders not to divulge that information.'

Nicholas paused before answering. 'Well, that makes

matters more difficult but, I trust we will manage. Let us turn to communication. I favour the postal service. It is easy, reasonably efficient and cheap. You will both address your letters to Herr Scheller in Hamburg. He will deliver to and collect your mail from the main post office in the city. We have "friends" in the post office who will ensure that letters from Herr Scheller are directed to the correct people for delivery to Heligoland. Father, you will have to notify Scheller of the delivery address for your mail. Understood?'

Both nodded.

'Father, you may find yourself in Hamburg and in need of assistance. Herr Scheller can help and will be prepared to offer sanctuary if the need arises. Here is his address.' He passed a slip of paper. 'Remember it and destroy the paper. You may also require funds. Scheller will make introductions to Messrs Parish & Co in the city. Parish & Co is a most reputable firm of bankers and agents for Rothschild in northern Germany. John Parish will be your banker under instruction from me.'

Robertson asked, 'Parish & Co sounds as though it is English. Why do the French allow them to continue to operate?'

'Out of necessity. The French Government needs access to alternative sources of banking services. Mr Parish has proved to be an invaluable asset to Paris as well as London. His contacts with America are exceptional.'

Turning to Robertson, he asked in German, 'Father, we manage operations stretching from the Jade Bight and the entrance to the Weser in the west round to the Elbe and northwards to Tonningen and the Holstein ports. It would be helpful if you could give me some idea of your approximate destination?' Did Robertson pick up a little sarcasm in Nicholas's tone? It was understandable that someone of his seniority would be peeved that he was apparently not to be trusted.

Robertson looked at MacKenzie who nodded. 'My destination is Glückstadt.'

'Very well.' Nicholas went to his map chest and pulled out a map showing the mouth of the River Elbe and the towns and villages located close to the river's banks. 'I suggest that you make the journey in two stages. First to the island of Neuwerk,' – he indicated an island in the German Bight, close to the mouth of the River Elbe – 'and the second up the River Elbe to the north of Glückstadt. It would not be safe to land in Glückstadt itself as it is well guarded. I propose a route we have used before. From the Elbe, there is a tributary, the River Stor. A small vessel can navigate up the Stor and land you close to the village of Borsfleth. From there, it is short journey to Glückstadt. You will stay on Neuwerk overnight to wait for the correct tide and to ensure that you can safely evade the patrolling French gunboats and customs cutters.'

'That looks very good, thank you,' replied Robertson.

'Do you have a passport and money?'

'Yes, thank you, sir. Mr Hammond and Mr Rolleston were able to provide me with both.'

'Is the passport accurate?'

MacKenzie responded. 'I am assured that it is.'

'Well then, I shall make the necessary arrangements

and send a signal to the lighthouse keeper on Neuwerk to tell him to expect you and to prepare the second stage of your journey. The keeper is in constant communication with our friends in Cuxhaven.'

'Thank you, sir.'

Nicholas then returned to Mr Canning's letter. 'I read that Mr Canning instructs me to put an embargo on all shipping leaving Heligoland until Father Gallus is safely landed on the mainland.'

'As I understand it,' said MacKenzie. 'To ensure the Father's safety by preventing news of his arrival reaching the enemy before he has safely landed.'

'Quite the opposite; to prevent the normal activities of the island fishermen would only serve to draw attention to the fact that something important was planned. Besides that, while I have control of large vessels leaving the island, it is impossible to prevent the locals in their small boats from leaving.'

MacKenzie smiled. 'I see.' He paused. It was clear that plans made in the comfort of the Foreign Office just did not hold water when confronted with local realities. Here was someone who obviously knew his business.

'Please, sir, make the arrangements.'

Robertson asked, 'It was suggested in London that, once I land, I might have the assistance of a certain D who uses the scarlet pimpernel as a monogram. Is this possible?'

'I regret not without more notice, Father. I believe that D is staying in Bremen. We would have to write to him asking him to meet you outside Glückstadt which is over

VINDICTA

one hundred miles from Bremen. That will take time. I presume you wish to proceed as soon as possible?'

MacKenzie answered. 'It would be for the best.'

'Have something to eat and get some rest. I will make the arrangements.'

After supper, Robertson was shown to a bedroom. He undressed, washed, prayed and clambered into another unfamiliar bed. Since being told that there would be no "friend" to meet him, he felt increasingly apprehensive. He had always hated last-minute changes of plan. Now, he would be a solitary stranger to the locals who had appeared as if out of nowhere. Worse, on his own, a likely person of interest to the authorities. Sleep when it came was fitful, regularly broken by foreboding of what was to come.

19
Neuwerk

The next morning, they were shown to the quayside. Mr Brown, the harbourmaster, introduced the fisherman who had been paid handsomely to ferry Robertson to Neuwerk. They shook hands. Robertson was assisted into the boat. One of the crew cast off and they were soon out of the lee of the island. Robertson was told that the journey would take around six hours. On more than half a dozen occasions, he was comforted to see Royal Navy ships patrolling, some relief from the lack of sleep and the queasiness in his stomach. The skipper found him a cot in a cabin. The gentle roll of the boat rocked him to sleep. He woke sometime later and climbed back on deck, the breeze waking him. A crewman pointed to the south-east. It was the huge brick-built tower above what appeared to be the sea. As they came closer, the island came into view. It looked no more than a mudflat covered with greenery.

The skipper took out his telescope and seemed to look at the tower. Robertson assumed that he must have been given an "all clear" signal as he pulled the tiller to bring the boat towards the jetty. The skipper eased the boat alongside and came to a stop. One of the crew leapt out and made the bow and stern ropes secure. He then helped Robertson up onto the jetty. Another of the crew passed up Robertson's two portmanteaus.

It took the skipper and Robertson ten minutes to walk to the tower. Robertson reckoned that it must be well over one hundred feet tall. They reached the bottom of the external staircase to be met by the watch keeper.

'Welcome, Father, but you cannot stay. The French police have been here on each of the last two days. They will probably come again. Your presence will lead not just to your own arrest and execution but to mine also and prison for many of my fellow islanders.'

Devastating news.

Robertson turned to the skipper. 'Can you not complete the second part of the journey?'

'No, if the French police are suspicious of Neuwerk, the patrols guarding the mouth of the Elbe will be out in force. The risk is just too great.'

Robertson pondered the consequences. They scared him. 'Have the police been here before?'

'No, sir,' replied the watch keeper. 'We have had many visits from customs officers. They can be brushed off by a little...' He rubbed his thumb and forefinger together. 'The gendarmerie are a different proposition. On their first visit, an officer, a captain, was in command. He was suspicious and threatening. We have an understanding with the customs people, if you understand me. These policemen mean business. If they hear that a priest has been here, that will be the excuse they need to interrogate me and the other residents. I have heard from friends in Cuxhaven what form their questioning takes. I have no wish to spend any time with them in the dungeons of Ritzebuttel Castle. We will have to be very careful. You may stay the night but must be gone on the dawn tide.'

Robertson realised he had no choice. He was still shaken by the news that the gendarmes' first visit to the island coincided with his arrival. Had news of his journey leaked out? If so, where from? Or was it simply a matter of chance? Whatever the reasons for the police visit, had it compromised his mission before it had begun?

A shout and another, and they craned their necks looking up to the top of the tower. A man was leaning over the brick parapet, waving his arms.

Robertson asked the skipper, 'What's he saying?'

'Sounds like, "wait".'

In what seemed like no time, the man emerged at the top of the external stairs, tripped, grabbed the handrail, sprinted down the remaining stairs, two, three at a time. Whooping for breath.

'For God's sake, go, now!'

The man caught his breath. 'The French police will be here in minutes. For all our sakes, go!'

Robertson found the man's German unintelligible. He turned to the skipper.

'What's he saying? I can hardly understand a word.'

'The French police are on their way here, right now. He's using a Plattdeutsch dialect.'

It was now the watch keeper's turn. He screamed, 'Go, for Christ's sake, go!'

The skipper wheeled round, grabbed one of Robertson's portmanteaus and began running back to the boat. Robertson took one more look at the men who had begun to run back up the stairs, turned and scuttled as fast as he could after the skipper. Within minutes he was wheezing. He had to stop. He bent over and put his hands on his knees, gasping for air.

A voice in front of him shouted 'No time to stop. Run!'

He looked up. The skipper was fifty yards away, beckoning him, then he turned and ran on. Robertson now heard French voices behind him shouting for the man in the tower. Scrubby bushes hid Robertson's view of the base of the tower. He picked up his portmanteau. The scuttle became more of a gallop. Finally, the quayside came into view. The skipper was already on board. Two of the crew were untying the mooring ropes. Two others ran up to Robertson and picked him up bodily. As they reached the boat, the larger of the two put Robertson over his shoulder and ran up the gangplank. As he reached the gunwale, he threw Robertson down onto the deck. Robertson landed on a coil of rope which helped to cushion his fall.

He must have fainted. When he came to and focused, the boat was already well away from the quay, wind filling the sails. Unsteadily, he began to stand. He looked round to hear shouts from the quay. The French.

'For God's sake, get down!' the skipper screamed at

him. He ducked down below the gunwale and cautiously raised his head to look back at the island. The French had muskets at their shoulders raised to achieve maximum elevation. A musket ball slammed into the timber inches from his head.

'What did I tell you? Get down, you stupid old man.' Robertson ducked down, suddenly feeling very old.

'We'll be out of range in a few minutes. Thank God there's a good breeze.'

The journey back was monotonous. Bruised in body and mind, Robertson felt a deep sense of defeat. He prided himself on his high degree of personal courage. Indeed, there had been many occasions in the past where he had to show bravery but the danger he had experienced on Neuwerk shook him. In times of stress, he always found solace in what he had come to rely on ever since he was a young novice. He reached through the fold of his habit and brought out his small bible. It fell open at one of his favourites. While the words he looked at were in Latin, the language of his faith, he had been devoted to ensuring that congregations understood the words of the Bible. In his mind, he took himself back to the calm of the Schottenkloster, his monastery church in Ratisbon, and chanted the Psalm of David in the wonderful words of the St James's Bible: *The Lord is my shepherd...*

The words calmed him. He read them through again and focused on the fourth verse. He could feel his mental strength returning and reminded himself why he had undertaken the mission. Yes, he had been successful in pleading the case to the Corsican and his monastery had remained open. But for how long? Would Abbot Arbuthnot and his fellow monks also be pitched out of their living as had happened to his colleagues in the monasteries in Erfurt and elsewhere when Napoleon had secularised all Church lands across the Empire? Even in his own seminary, it was forbidden to take on any new novices. The Corsican and his regime meant for the Church to die out, preventing the wonder of God's word from being spread not just among the faithful but to the populace of Europe as a whole. In whatever small way, he had to do what was necessary to bring about the downfall of the tyrant. If that meant working with Protestant Britain, so be it.

His mind was now set. No longer was he ready to accept defeat and return to Heythrop Park under a cloud, he was now determined to see the mission through, whatever the risks in "the valley of the shadow of death". He was a warrior for his Faith. He would do what was necessary. Anxiety dispelled, he curled up in a cloak and slept.

As the fishing boat neared Heligoland, the skipper hoisted the so called "private" recognition signal pennants up the mast. He joked to Robertson that he hoped he had the sequence of flags in the correct order. It transpired that if the sequence was wrong, they were likely to have a shot across the bows from one of the navy's patrolling gun brigs. A brig came into view and hoisted the replying recognition signal allowing the boat to make for the harbour.

Robertson walked to Mr Nicholas's office and found MacKenzie with the consul. He told them of the lucky escape in Neuwerk. Nicholas asked, 'Are you sure that the watch keeper said that the French visitors were gendarmes?'

'That is what he told me. He described the uniforms which were much more elaborate than those worn by customs officers. The officer was apparently dressed in a white jacket with a scarlet waistcoat, nothing like the grey-green of the customs officers who normally visit the island.'

Nicholas stared at the ceiling, deep in thought. He returned his gaze to Robertson.

'Then if the gendarmes are keeping watch on Neuwerk, we had better find other routes on to the Continent for the time being. That is indeed a pity. The Neuwerk route has been very successful. But returning to your mission, Father, will you continue, or have you decided to return to England?'

Before he could reply, Mackenzie spoke. 'After such a close shave, we shall all understand if you have decided to return home. I will take your place.'

'Thank you, MacKenzie, but I am determined to complete the mission. I would like to return to Germany as soon as possible. Are you able to assist once again, Mr Nicholas?'

Edward Nicholas put his hands together and thought. 'Yes, of course, but with Neuwerk being watched and the mouth of the Elbe being too well guarded, I think you had better approach Glückstadt from the landward side. Therefore, a landing in Holstein or to the west with a trip down the Weser to Bremen are the options. After our siege of Copenhagen last year, we have far fewer friends to assist you in Denmark. The Weser and Bremen are a much better option. "D" is probably in Bremen and we have other friends in the city who can provide the necessary passport and help you travel from there to Hamburg and then north to Glückstadt. Let me talk to some of our merchant friends here on the island to see who is running the next contraband operation down the Weser. Many will be desperate to move the cargoes they have sitting in their warehouses on the island. Go and have a good night's rest and come back here in the morning.'

The next morning, Robertson and MacKenzie returned to the consul's office. They were soon joined by another man. Mr Nicholas did not introduce him but said to the man, 'You have two vessels in the harbour and are anxious to get underway, are you not?'

'Very anxious indeed. I am already late returning home and if my absence is observed, I shall, no doubt, be arrested on my return. Please allow me to sail, for heaven's sake!'

'On one condition,' replied the consul.

'Name it.'

'That you will take a friend of mine ashore.'

'Not for any amount of money. It is impossible.'

'Very well,' replied Nicholas, 'since you will not oblige me, do not expect me to oblige you. The sailing embargo will last another two weeks. Do not for a minute think that I do not know your real name, Herr Baumann, and who you work for – the House of Rothschild. Should you not agree, I shall make it very difficult for the House of Rothschild to conduct its business on Heligoland and of course ensure that Mr Nathaniel Rothschild himself knows that you, Herr Baumann, were the cause of this difficulty which will leave him severely out of pocket, as it will you.'

Baumann blanched. He looked at MacKenzie, then at Robertson and at the floor. Finally he looked up at Mr Nicholas.

'You give me no choice. Since it must be done, I agree to take charge of your friend, but he must strictly obey my instructions. Otherwise, I will not answer for the consequences.'

'He shall,' said the consul. 'Now go and get everything ready.' Nicholas rang the bell on his desk. A clerk came into the office. 'Show this man out.' Robertson watched Baumann leave. He put his hands together as if to applaud the consul.

'Nicely done.'

Nicholas turned to Robertson. 'Thank you. Once one knows that all these people all pray at the same altar as King Croesus, they are easy to deal with. I shall send messages to friends telling them to expect you and to give you any assistance that you require once you have landed. They will be able to obtain transport, passports and money to enable you to travel to Hamburg and then into Holstein. Without knowing the purpose of your mission, I cannot advise further. I will, though, see what we can find out about these gendarmes. Wishing you Godspeed and good luck.'

'Thank you,' replied Robertson. *Here I go again*, he thought, *putting myself in the power of a man engaged in illicit trading who might easily be tempted to hand me over to the French for a generous reward.* He had no choice. However, after the scare on Neuwerk, he was in a much stronger frame of mind, ready for the valley.

20

To the River Weser, June 1808

Robertson shook hands with MacKenzie and boarded the smuggler's boat. The apprehension before the journey to Neuwerk had turned to adrenalin. Nicholas had suggested that he took written instructions of how and when to meet "the friends". Robertson refused the paper and committed the instructions to memory.

The small vessel made its way past the guarding frigates and gunboats, steering well to the west of Neuwerk and to the east of another small island, Mellum, and on into Jade Bay and the mouth of the Weser. As they sailed up the river, Robertson watched as green meadows nestling up against mudbanks slid by. The smuggler told the skipper to keep watch for suitable jetties or pontoons. However, at every one of his favourite landing spots, guards were stationed or were too busy with village folk. The smuggler told Robertson that he could disembark and wade through the shallows until he found an unguarded area of the riverbank. Robertson told him firmly that he had neither the energy nor inclination to wade to safety carrying his portmanteaus and being soaked into the bargain. It concerned him that both the smuggler and skipper wished to be rid of their passenger at the first opportunity.

They carried on upstream. Eventually the skipper suggested to the smuggler that he should wade ashore and find a suitable place to land the contraband and their passenger. With some reluctance, the smuggler agreed. A meeting point was decided. The smuggler was helped over the side of the boat into the shallows. As he made his way towards the shore, the boat continued upstream. An hour later, one of the crew stationed in the bows shouted to the skipper standing by the helmsman.

'Revenue cutter!'

'Where?'

'Straight ahead.'

The skipper rushed to join the crewman in the bows, took out his telescope and focused on the cutter. He could see the cutter signalling.

'Run for it! Ready about!' he shouted to the helmsman. 'Lee Ho!'

The helmsman spun the wheel, the crew went through the tack and the boat spun round making its way down river and out to sea and safety.

A puff of smoke came from the cutter followed by the report of a gun.

'Raise all sails,' shouted the skipper. The crew unfurled all the boat's sails and soon the distance between them and the cutter began to increase. It seemed to Robertson that their vessel was faster than the cutter. As the sun began to set, the cutter was no longer visible. They reached the sea. It was clear that they had outrun the cutter. The skipper decided to anchor in the shallows. He would attempt to make contact with the smuggler in the morning.

The unpleasantness of Robertson's evening meal was slightly ameliorated by a large tot of schnapps. He was shown to a small cabin in the bows and wrapped himself in blankets. The gentle rocking motion of the boat at anchor, the effect of the sea air combined with the stress of a long day and the schnapps, worked. He plunged into deep sleep. What seemed like minutes later he was being violently shaken. The skipper was shouting at him.

'Wake up. There are customs men in a boat alongside us. You will have to swim for the shore.'

Robertson was awake in an instant. It was two in the morning. He followed the skipper on deck expecting to be thrown over the side by the crew to save themselves. Two men clambered up from their rowing skiff. An oarsman covered them with a musket. On deck, one announced that they had come from the revenue cutter with instructions to protect the skipper's smack from any French interference. The skipper was amazed. The smuggler was now on board the cutter to ensure that the journey would be completed safely. Robertson wondered how much gold had exchanged hands. He was now not likely to be thrown overboard. The two revenue men were welcomed by the crew. Schnapps was poured. The smack made ready to return to the river and join the revenue cutter.

They made their way towards the mouth of the river and came alongside the cutter. The skipper pulled Robertson aside telling him that both he and the crew had decided that Robertson's presence on board was just too dangerous. He would be put ashore as soon as possible. With a mixture of apprehension and relief, Robertson agreed. He had had enough of the risk-averse skipper. It was time to move on.

A crewman shouted, 'Another boat approaching.'

'Get below.' The skipper shoved Robertson back towards the stuffy bow's cabin. He squeezed in. What else could go wrong on this trip? He listened to the conversation on deck. The words spoken were just too muffled to make out. Once again, the skipper came to the cabin and asked Robertson to come on deck. *Is this when the mission ends and I am turned over to the French for questioning, torture and the firing squad?* he thought as he made his way up and into the fresh air. He was wrong. The newcomers introduced themselves. They were friends of the smuggler. Robertson sighed with relief.

It was now close to dawn. It was clearly too dangerous to make a landing in daylight. The smack anchored off the village of Husum on the west side of the bay and waited for the dark; another day lost. As the sun set, they hauled up the anchor and set sail for the mouth of the Weser.

Two hours later, Robertson saw lights in the distance. The skipper told him it was Lede. More lights above them. Carlsburg Castle glowered over them. Garrisoned by the French was the word. The smack glided quietly underneath the walls of the castle. If there was a sentinel, he must have been asleep or simply not watching. They crossed the mouth of the River Geeste, a tributary of the Weser, and made landfall on the southern side. The smuggler was there to meet them. The cargo was unloaded. Robertson bade farewell to the skipper and followed the smuggler a short distance to the village of Gestendorf. On the edge of the village the outline of a house emerged. The smuggler turned to Robertson.

'Now we have the pleasure of the company of my friend, the local *chef de la douane*!'

Robertson was taken aback. The smuggler smiled. 'What better than a safe house owned by the local customs officer! Don't worry, he is very well looked after. I have been staying here.' Robertson took that to mean that English guineas had worked their magic again. The smuggler knocked on the door. A very bleary-eyed customs officer appeared and showed them to the stables. Two horses were already saddled. The smuggler pressed a bag into the officer's hand. The two men were soon on the road heading south.

They rode for three hours, crossing the Stadtgraben water protecting the northern flank of Bremen. At the Herdentor gate, apart from the torches burning above the gatehouse, it was pitch-black and silent. The smuggler called out for the guard. A soldier emerged sleepily from the guardhouse, looked up at the smuggler's face, smiled, and opened the gates. The two horsemen rode through.

The smuggler turned to Robertson.

'I keep them well supplied in beer and schnapps topped up with regular gifts of marks.'

Robertson hardly heard him. He was virtually asleep in the saddle.

They rode through the Alstadt past the town hall and St Peter's Cathedral and down increasingly narrow lanes to the Schnoor district, to the smuggler's house close to the southern walls overlooking the River Weser. A policeman was talking with a nightwatchman. The smuggler raised a hand. The two men waved in reply.

He was shown to a bedroom. The smuggler wished him a good rest. He would make arrangements for the next stage of Robertson's journey. Exhaustion swept through his body. He barely had time to undress before he was asleep.

21

Number 12 Krayenkamp, Central Hamburg,
June 1808

Marquet was concerned that he had received nothing from Heligoland. He had sent a message to Colville asking for news but had no reply. This was unlike Colville. Marquet hoped there was no trouble. In his last message, Colville had reported much increased military police activity on the island. Merchants and residents alike complained that they were scarcely able to talk to each other without being accused of being a foreign agent. Colville warned that he would have to take extra precautions.

Marquet was interrupted by a knock on the door. A gendarme entered, saluted and gave him a letter. It was from the corporal who reported his visits to Neuwerk. Nothing had been found but the corporal sensed that there was something nefarious going on. *A good man,* thought Marquet, *he has a nose for criminality*. However, with nothing specific, he was reluctant to take action. It was frustrating to have to leave smuggling activity to the customs men. He did not wish to incur Maupont's wrath again. He pondered his next move against the real target, the British agents.

He looked at the map of the region. If Heligoland was the base for these agents, Neuwerk was an obvious rendezvous point. The gendarmerie visits would probably have stopped any activity for the time being. Which other likely points of entry merited his attention? It seemed that the mouth of the Elbe was just too well guarded by both French and Danish gunboats and shore-based troops: possible, maybe even likely, that the British used the myriad of small islands and inlets of the Elbe. He looked to the west. What about the River Weser? From its mouth to that other Hanseatic free town, Bremen, was, he estimated, around sixty kilometres. Like the Elbe, the Weser had many islands and inlets, perfect for smuggling. The towns and villages from the mouth of the river up to Bremen would be his next target. He sent an explanatory report to Maupont and a message to the corporal stationed at Ritzebuttel Castle to meet him at Carlsburg Castle which overlooked the Weser, near its mouth. He sent a note to General Dupas's aide-de-camp asking what troops garrisoned Carlsburg. The prompt reply told him that a detachment of veterans from the 24th Regiment of the Line occupied the fort. A message had been sent to expect Marquet and his men. Carlsburg would act as his base of operations.

Marquet received a brief note of approval from Maupont the next morning. As he made his way to the stables, he was handed a note. It was from the corporal based in Cuxhaven. He and his men had returned to Neuwerk once again. They had been just minutes too late to stop a fishing boat leaving the island. He had used his telescope to read the name on the stern of the boat, but the crew had covered it with canvas. One of his men had fired at the vessel. The range was extreme. The soldier was sure he had seen someone who did not look like a fisherman duck down just as the musket ball had hit the boat's transom. The corporal had interrogated the watch keeper and asked permission to arrest the man. Marquet scribbled a reply: *Approved. Well done.* As Marquet mounted his horse, he was deep in thought, glad that his instincts about the island looked to be correct. Now for the six-hour ride to Carlsburg, escorted by a troop of ten gendarmes.

On his arrival, he surveyed the walls of the castle which were in places in poor condition. Apparently, the castle had been in Swedish control and was subjected to two sieges over a century before. It had never been fully repaired. Marquet entered through the gates and found a corporal lining up the twenty soldiers under his command. The corporal brought his men to attention and asked Marquet to inspect them. Marquet walked up and down the lines. The men were in a dreadful state. It was obvious that they had tried to smarten themselves up for inspection. It was not slovenliness that caused this condition, it was battle wounds and shock.

Marquet ordered the corporal to stand his men down. He asked when they had last fought. The corporal told him that they were proud veterans of the 24th Regiment of the Line. He and some of his men had served since 1799 in Italy and Germany. In the last two years, the regiment had been part of Marshal Lannes's corps. Did the captain know the commander, Colonel Semmelle? Marquet had not had the pleasure. Under the colonel they had fought at Jena and Golymin in '06 and at Eylau, Braunsburg and Friedland last year.

'We lost many fine men,' he told Marquet. 'Friedland was a bloody affair. Those Russians pushed us hard but we pushed harder. *Vive L'Empereur!*' There were tears streaming down the corporal's face.

Marquet shook the corporal's hand. 'Well done, you have served France well.' Sadly it was clear that these men were in no condition to help, except to give background information.

He asked the corporal where the nearest customs officer was based.

'Just to the south of here in Gestendorf. I am not sure how much he will help you. Both he and his men are German.'

Marquet asked how this was so and why there were no French customs officers stationed in the area. The corporal had no idea. In that case, time to rattle the cages of not just the local residents but also the customs officers to see if there was collusion with the villains on Heligoland. He would start by combining his men with the veterans in small groups to patrol the banks of the river.

A gendarme was shown into the room. It was one of his men from Hamburg. He saluted Marquet.

'This letter arrived for you some hours after you left Krayenkamp, Captain. The sergeant thought it was important.'

'Thank you.' He looked at the letter. It was from Colville. At last.

Marquet told his men and the corporal to leave him. He sat and began to decipher Colville's letter. The process was much quicker now that he was well practised. He was soon reading the text.

Colville wrote that soon after a packet ship had arrived from England, Der Konsul had placed an embargo on all shipping leaving Heligoland. It seemed that two of the passengers from the packet had been shown to the consul's office. According to the locals in one of the *bierkellers* Colville used for information, one of the passengers was a man from the Foreign Office in London and the other was a priest. Colville found this information very strange. Then a few days ago he had seen the two men on the quayside. The younger man, presumably the Foreign Office official, was shaking the hand of the priest who then boarded a boat which then left the harbour. From a distance, the priest looked middle-aged and was rather portly.

It seemed to Colville that this was a British plot. However, none of his contacts on the island were able to provide him any further information. Since the priest's departure, security on Heligoland had been tightened even further. Colville had been questioned three times. He was very concerned that his messages to Marquet would be found. Colville asked that Marquet should increase the reward to the fisherman who carried the messages, otherwise their contact might be broken.

Marquet read Colville's letter again. He was very experienced and would not be suggesting British meddling unless he had good reason. But a priest? A priest as an agent? Surely not, unless the plan was for him to travel to southern Germany where the majority of the populace was Catholic. But that assumed that Colville had meant that the priest was Catholic. Perhaps he was Lutheran? How would a Catholic priest stir up trouble in the Protestant north? Or perhaps, he would travel east, into Catholic Poland now occupied by France and Russia. That was surely more likely. Working with the resistance to foment trouble in the occupied areas was much more plausible, and in the areas in which he, Marquet, had fought. He thought of the geography; the east made much more sense. Despite the alliance made with the Russians at Tilsit, the British Navy still controlled the Baltic. It would not be difficult for the British to covertly land weapons and money to arm the rebels. But first, he must find this priest and wring the truth out of him. It was good to have a specific target.

Marquet summoned the infantry corporal. Was he aware of any smuggling activity in the past few days or more particularly at night? The corporal told him that he had a rota of sentinels on the battlements working four-hour shifts covering every one of the twenty-four hours. Nothing suspicious had been seen. One of the night guards reported that a revenue cutter had escorted a smaller vessel, presumably for inspection.

'When was this?' asked Marquet.

'Two, maybe three nights ago,' replied the corporal.

'Exactly which night?' asked Marquet, exasperated.

'I don't remember. I was on leave that day.'

'Summon the guard who was on duty.'

'He is off duty. He'll probably be in the *bierkeller*.'

Marquet was about to explode and then realised that the guard was now likely to be full of beer and schnapps. There was no point questioning him until he'd sobered up.

'Right, we will pay a visit to the *chef de la douane*. He had better have some good answers. Come with me, Corporal, and show me to the chef's house.'

Marquet took five of his gendarmes. The corporal led the way to Gestendorf. At the *chef de la douane*'s house, he was about to tell one of the gendarmes to use the butt of his rifle to hammer on the door, but thought better of it. The *chef* might have connections with Pyonnier, the French customs chief for the whole region. Pyonnier was, he knew, well connected with Bourrienne and thus to Marshal Bernadotte. He remembered what Maupont had told him. No, a gentle approach was wise. However, while he was talking to the *chef*, he would tell his men to see if they could find anything interesting. While one gendarme knocked on the door, he told the remaining four to inspect the outside of the house and the outbuildings.

The door was opened by a maid. Marquet and the gendarme were shown into the hall. The *chef* appeared and introduced himself in faltering French.

'My name is Meyer, how may I assist you, Captain?'

'Captain Marquet, I am the head of counter-intelligence for the region.'

Marquet watched Meyer's face intently to see if this fact caused any concern: none that he could see.

'One of your revenue cutters intercepted a fishing smack two or three nights ago. Correct?'

'Yes, Captain, that was three nights ago. We regularly carry out spot checks. My men inspected the vessel but no contraband was found.'

'Was the smack carrying anything else?'

Meyer flashed a look at Marquet's eyes. 'What do you mean?'

It seemed as if this question had hit a nerve. 'I mean human cargo,' replied Marquet, watching the *chef* intently. If Meyer was off balance, he soon regained his composure.

'The captain of the cutter reported to me personally. He would have told me if he had found illegal cargo, human or otherwise.'

'Then, Herr Meyer, I wish to interview the captain myself.'

'Are you doubting my word, Captain? I have told you that nothing was found during the inspection and that is an end to the matter. If there is nothing else, I will bid you farewell and will return to my family.'

Marquet seethed inside. Just those few seconds convinced him that the *chef* was hiding something, he could sense it. Without evidence, there was nothing to be done, at least for the moment. Time to change tack.

'Thank you, Herr Meyer, goodbye.' He turned and left with the gendarme following. Outside, the four gendarmes were waiting for him. As they made their way back to the castle, he asked: 'Anything?'

The German-speaking gendarme reported that he had spoken with the stable lad. The lad told him that he was to ride to Bremen and return two of the *chef*'s horses. The horses had been used by two men two days ago.

'Did he know who the men were?'

'No, the *chef* had given the lad time off and had also given him money to enjoy himself in the *bierkeller*. And he did!'

The lad was no further help except, as a throwaway line, he remarked that that was most unlike the *chef* who was normally a very strict master.

Bremen, thought Marquet. That made sense. The priest and a guide had been provided with horses by the *chef* and had ridden to the city. He would act against the *chef* later. It was imperative that he travelled to Dresden as soon as possible.

Back at the castle, he wrote a report to Maupont, giving the colonel the background and explaining that he would pursue the priest who was now most likely in Bremen. He asked the colonel to instruct the officer commanding the gendarme detachment in the city to give him whatever assistance he required. Marquet ordered one of his men to deliver the report to the colonel immediately. He and the remaining troops would set out for Bremen at dawn. He sat back and attempted to put himself in the priest's shoes. If he was an agent and was planning mischief, the priest would have to coordinate his activity with other British elements. If so, he would have to communicate with his handlers. Surely, they would be based on Heligoland? Perhaps the man Colville had seen shaking the priest's hand was his handler. That made sense especially if the handler was the same person that Colville had reported was from the Foreign Office in London. He would ask Colville to identify the man from London and to confirm whether the priest was Catholic or a Lutheran minister.

Marquet shouted to the corporal in the adjoining room and told him to stop the messenger riding to Maupont. He should wait until Marquet had coded a note to Colville. Once he had finished coding, he instructed the gendarme where he would find the fisherman who would deliver the note to Colville on Heligoland. He told the gendarme to promise a special bonus payment if he could deliver the note immediately. And it was, of course, obvious how the priest would communicate with his handler: by fishermen, as he did with Colville. Yes, but with the local customs people apparently in the pay of the British and with the connivance of Pyonnier and by extension Bourrienne, how was he to put a stop to these messages? He pondered. Assuming the pro-British networks were as extensive as they seemed, where would he start? The answer was the source – the priest. He was the target. There was no point in wasting resources looking for the messengers. Concentrate on finding the priest.

22
Bremen, June 1808

Robertson woke the next day to find that it was already after nine. He dressed and found his way downstairs where he was greeted by his smuggler host.

'I trust you slept well?'

'Very, thank you.'

His host rang a bell cord and a servant entered.

'Breakfast for our guest.'

'Yes, sir.' The servant left the room.

The host continued. 'The arrangements for your onward journey to Hamburg are not quite in place. You should be there in three days' time. Meanwhile, you will have to stay here another day. Please remain in the house. You can enjoy my library.'

Robertson replied, 'Thank you. I would like to send a message to my friends on the island. Can this be done securely?'

'Yes, again it will take a while to organise.'

'I am most grateful to you. I noted the name "Hoffman" on the wall plate. May I call you Herr Hoffman?'

His host turned and smiled. 'That would be quite appropriate in the circumstances.' Both men laughed. Robertson wondered what Hoffman's real name was – safety in ignorance. Hoffman reached into his pocket. He took out a tiny piece of rolled-up paper. As he unrolled the paper, Robertson saw a picture of three tiny flowerheads on dark green stems. The flowers looked like miniature rosebuds.

Hoffman's smile had gone. 'It is a red pimpernel. If you are ever unsure if the person designated to help you is really who he says he is, he should be able to show one of these.' Robertson remembered the London briefing. Then it dawned on him.

Pointing at his host, he blurted out, 'So you are the agent "B"...

'I am not. How do you know that name?'

'From the London briefing.'

'On pain of death, never mention that name again. Our leader has survived fifteen years fighting the Revolution and intends to continue to do so.'

'Of course, my apologies.' Robertson's face coloured. In his enthusiasm, he realised he had broken a sacred rule. Hoffman left without a further word.

Robertson did his best to enjoy his breakfast and afterwards went into the library and closed the door. First, he used the Pigpen cipher to compose a message to MacKenzie, in the Latin they had agreed.

In Bremen, Hamburg In diebus tribus (in Bremen, Hamburg in three days).

Harmless enough, but at least MacKenzie could keep London informed of his progress. He folded the note and gave it to his host.

Despite his tiredness the night before, he had noted the guards on the entry gates to the city. He was safe while in the company of the smuggler and the other friends. On his own might well be different. The experience on Neuwerk was not to be repeated. If the guards were questioned by the French police, it was likely that they would admit to letting a priest into the city, and why shouldn't they? A priest was a priest, doing no one any harm as far as they were concerned. However, if the police knew that they were looking for a priest, that would surely shorten the odds of capture. The guards stationed on the gates of Hamburg would probably not be so accommodating. Even if he wore civilian clothes, his passport would give him away. It was time to prepare for the Rorauer identity. Hoffman would obtain a local identification to enable him to travel from Hanover into Hamburg, but to reach Glückstadt in Denmark he would require an international passport. He had been meditating about this since his time in London.

Rorauer had been a similar age to Robertson. He had been born and had grown up in a village not far from Ratisbon. All Rorauer's relatives had long since died. An added proof of identity was that Robertson had learnt German at the monastery in Ratisbon and spoke with a distinctive Bavarian accent.

He took out another sheet of paper from the drawer

in the desk. As Adam Rorauer, he wrote to the village parish priest. He explained that, after many years, he had decided to visit his birthplace. He would therefore need an international passport to enable him to travel to Bavaria. He requested that the priest send a certified copy of his certificate of baptism. To save time, Robertson asked that the priest send the documents addressed to the safe house provided by Mr Nicholas. He practised the Rorauer signature, signed the letter *Adam Rorauer*, folded and sealed it and asked the servant to send it by express mail to the priest's parsonage.

At supper that evening, Hoffman explained the travel arrangements for the next day. He had arranged to pass Robertson on to another "friend", a Herr Braun, a merchant based in Rotenburg, a small town fifty kilometres to the east of Bremen. To ensure their safety both leaving and returning to their respective homes, the guards at the gates would need to see that two people left and two returned. Therefore, Hoffman had asked his clerk, as a local, to leave the city by a different gate and make his way to a village just outside the city where his employer would collect him once he had delivered Robertson. His guest would be handed over at an agreed meeting point outside Ottersburg, halfway between Dresden and Rotenburg. The merchant, Braun, would leave Rotenburg accompanied by his clerk. He would deposit his clerk just outside the town. The clerk, another local, would make his way back to the merchant's house using a different gate. When Robertson had joined the merchant, two people would therefore return to the merchant's town as before. Hoffman asked

Robertson to wear a coat over his priest's suit and to put on a local hat. That should suffice to allay any suspicions.

The next morning, Robertson breakfasted early and was shown to his host's carriage. As they made their way to the eastern city gate, Hoffman explained that the merchant Braun had only recently joined the group and was keen to enjoy the exceptional profits that were on offer from smuggling British goods and produce.

The journey to Ottersburg was incident free. Robertson was introduced to his new host. He thanked the smuggler effusively and stepped up into the new carriage. They entered Rotenburg as planned and arrived at Braun's house. That evening, Robertson dined with his new host and his clerk. Braun provided an excellent supper washed down with copious quantities of wine. As the evening wore on, more wine was poured and Robertson began to sense that his host's generosity had a darker intent. It was indeed fortunate he had developed a strong head while working in the monastery vineyards. As his host's face flushed, his questions became more direct and uncomfortable.

'Now, sir, your previous host will have explained that I have recently joined the group and am keen to make the most of my opportunity. Tell me how I can expand my network of connections with the merchants based on Heligoland?'

Robertson replied, 'My dear sir, I cannot help you. I do not have contacts with the merchants.'

'But you are a dealer, are you not? You must be able to make contacts for me.'

'I am not that sort of dealer, sir. I simply do not have the contacts to help you.'

Braun was becoming more agitated. He poured Robertson more wine and topped up his own glass.

Robertson thanked him.

'Then what sort of dealer are you? You landed here with the help of our group and yet deny all knowledge of the network on the island. What then is the object of your mission? I demand to know.'

Robertson looked at the clerk, appealing to him to say something to break the chain of questions. The clerk's face reddened with embarrassment.

Robertson turned back to his host. 'Sir, forgive me, I simply cannot divulge the purpose of my journey.'

The host's face flushed even darker. He pushed back his chair, stood, nearly over-balanced, grabbed the table with one hand and crashed his other fist down on the dining table. Plates bounced and glasses fell.

'Well then, sir, as you do not deign to place your confidence in me, then I need not any longer show hospitality to you. Leave immediately!' He turned, staggered to the door, wrenched it open and exited slamming the door behind him.

The clerk sighed. 'I am afraid that he's like that when he doesn't get what he wants. Let me help you pack, sir, and I will then show you to the hotel.'

They walked the short distance to the hotel overlooking the horse market. The clerk saw to it that Robertson was safely checked in and wished him a good night. Before he left, Robertson asked him to come to the hotel in the morning. He agreed.

As he lay in bed, he debated in his mind if it was now

time to bring the Adam Rorauer identity to life. Whatever, he would need the local identity card validated to continue his journey.

The next morning, Robertson dressed in a modest civilian suit. As Adam Rorauer, he asked the clerk to visit the town hall to sponsor him for a local passport. Robertson would be a friend of his who had travelled from Bavaria en route for Hamburg. It was not long before the clerk returned, telling Robertson that the pass was in order. However, it was essential that he should go to the town hall and sign the pass. The clerk showed the way. Robertson climbed the steps into the hall. He was shown the way to the office where the town's clerk was waiting for him. A straightforward process, he thought.

'Please print your name and sign it here, Herr Rorauer,' the clerk said, indicating the space on the form.

Robertson sat and began to write his name.

J

'Hold on.' The clerk raised his voice. 'Didn't you tell me that your Christian name was Adam?'

Robertson froze. A stupid mistake, caused by being too relaxed. How on earth would he be able to escape this blunder? It was unforgiveable. Speed of thought came to his rescue. He coloured with embarrassment as he looked up at the clerk.

'Sir, in Bavaria where I was born, we are in the habit of writing the baptismal name Johann, shortened to Hans, before every man's Christian name and Maria to every woman's. So, we do not say George, Peter or Adam but Hans George, Hans Peter or Hans Adam.'

The clerk looked at him. 'All right, finish it and leave. But you are not finished yet. You must now take the passport to the French resident's office down the corridor and obtain a French visa as a validation for travel.' He added, 'Frog bastards!'

'You do not enjoy the company of the French, I take it?' asked Robertson.

'None of us does. All those bastards do is take our money, eat our food and drink our wine. And don't get me on to what they would like to do to our young women.'

'As bad as that?'

'As bad as that, bastards!'

Robertson was shown to the resident's office and knocked.

'*Entrée.*'

Robertson walked into a room filled with cigar smoke. At the desk sat an elderly lieutenant sipping a glass of what looked like brandy. It was not yet ten in the morning.

'What do you want?'

Robertson explained.

'Ten thaler.' *Outrageous*, thought Robertson. That was around a third of a labourer's annual salary. He paid and watched the lieutenant pocket the coins. No questions were asked why he needed the visa. Maybe the Frenchman just wanted a quiet life comforted with his brandy? Now he knew why the locals felt so incensed. To have the population on his side would surely help.

Robertson left the town hall with the pass validated. The clerk was waiting and showed him to the coaching station. Robertson thanked him and went to hire an "extra post". He had told MacKenzie that he would travel by the fastest mode possible. The "extra post" was a carriage drawn by two horses. He would travel alone to minimise any interrogations at border posts. In such an expensive carriage, it would be assumed that he was a wealthy and important person. Two more legs of the journey to complete: Hamburg to meet his contacts and finally into Denmark and the three hours to Glückstadt to find the Spanish.

23
Bremen, June 1808

Marquet and his small troop reached Bremen after three hours riding. At the northern gates to the city, he asked the guards where he could find the captain of the gendarmes. A surly corporal made a gesture of a salute and pointed the way. Marquet would wait until he had the reinforcement and local knowledge of Dresden's gendarme detachment before he began to question the guards on duty two nights before.

Arriving at the gendarmerie's billet, he was shown into Lieutenant Robert's office. The young officer leapt to attention.

'Captain Marquet, sir, I have been expecting you. Colonel Maupont has written to explain your search.'

'Thank you, Lieutenant. Have you heard of a priest entering the city in the last three days?'

'No, sir. The guards, like the rest of the inhabitants, resent our presence and will only do the absolute minimum to cooperate with us. My men carry out spot checks on all the gates at varying times of the day or night. While we are not present, who knows what goes on?'

'What about our customs people?'

'Much the same. If we are present, they make a show of being diligent. If we are not – well, I suspect that they are handsomely paid by the contraband runners to look the other way. We have had some success in finding smuggled goods but that's likely to be a drop in the ocean of what actually reaches the city's black markets.'

A familiar story, thought Marquet. *Contraband running makes espionage infiltration easy.*

'Track down this priest and we can open up a whole can of worms. Let's concentrate on him. Find out who was on guard duty three nights ago. They must have seen something. If we are lucky, the priest may still be in the city. He may have been seen walking about. Instruct your men to make enquiries, particularly in the churches. He may, however, already have left. My best guess is that he is headed east. So, let's ask the guards on the eastern gates what they have seen.'

Two hours later, Marquet and Robert were in the yard of the guards' barracks. The lance-corporal and three privates stood in front of them. Robert explained in perfect German what they wanted to know: a British spy disguised as a priest entered the city through the northern gate three nights ago when the four of them were on duty. When and what did they see? Who was with the priest?

The three privates looked at the corporal waiting for him to reply. The man said nothing.

Marquet whispered to Robert who then said to the four men, 'Be in no doubt of the seriousness of your predicament. The captain is on urgent state business. He must have answers now. You have thirty seconds.'

The corporal opened his mouth, swallowed and finally produced some words.

'Sir, no one dressed as a priest came through the gates three nights ago.'

Marquet nodded to his corporal. The corporal reversed his musket, walked up to the corporal of the guard and rammed the butt into the man's crotch. Hardly able to catch his breath, the man crumpled to the ground. The three privates looked at each other, stunned.

'Thirty seconds,' repeated Robert.

Nothing happened. Marquet nodded again. His corporal shouted at two of his men. The gendarmes marched up to the youngest of the guards and ordered him to about face. He turned. Both gendarmes bent down. Grabbing the man's ankles, they pulled in unison. There was no time to put his arms out. The young man crashed onto the cobbled surface, his nose already streaming blood.

The corporal looked at Marquet. 'Bayonet or bullet, Captain?'

'It would be a shame to waste a bullet.'

'Twenty seconds,' repeated Robert.

Silence.

The guard corporal had begun to recover his breath.

'Two men did arrive around nine in the evening. One of them might have been a priest but it was dark. He wore a dark suit but he had a riding cloak over it.'

'What did he look like?'

'It was difficult to see but he seemed stout.'

'Who was the other man?'

'I don't know, sir.'

'Then why did you let them enter the city?'

The guard corporal stopped.

'How much did he pay you?'

The corporal looked at Robert, imploringly.

'How much?'

'Enough!' shouted Marquet. 'Bayonet in the leg, now!'

The corporal shouted, 'No, please, sir. He's got his whole life in front of him.'

'Then your leg will do.'

'No, no, my family.'

'You should have thought about that before you began to take the bribe.'

Marquet pointed to the young private. 'Him, the corporal has to understand that what will happen to him will be much, much worse unless he tells us everything. Understand? Everything.' Marquet nodded.

The young private screamed as the point of a bayonet emerged from the other side of his thigh. He passed out.

'How much?' repeated Robert.

'Thirty thaler,' whispered the guard corporal.

Marquet turned. 'We are wasting time. Take the corporal to the prison and beat him until he tells you who gave him the money. Oh, and take the other two men as well. They can watch. We will now begin the search starting with the east gate.'

As he left the yard, Marquet looked up. There were the

faces of the off-duty guards pressed against the bars of the barracks windows. They had watched it all.

Good thing too, thought Marquet. The word would spread. Cooperation assured.

And it did. The guards on all the gates and the local militia who helped with the search of the city were effusive in their efforts to please. However, the questioning of all the east gate guards on rota duty produced nothing concrete. One guard had waved through a carriage leaving the city. The coach had two men and the driver in it. One of the passengers could have been stout but the carriage had returned a few hours later again with two passengers. As with all incoming traffic, they had made a thorough inspection as had the customs men. Nothing was found. Similarly, no one had seen a stranger priest in the city.

To compound Marquet's frustration, he had received a note from Robert to say that the corporal of the east gate guard had died under questioning. Marquet had told Robert to be vigorous. He needed answers quickly. The two privates who had watched the spectacle were so terrified that Robert had believed their protestations. They had no idea of the identity of the priest's accomplice. It had been a private arrangement. That was why the corporal had been able to live a lifestyle way above his soldier's pay. He never shared his "commissions" as he called them. Marquet believed them as well.

So the priest was still on the loose. In which direction? Marquet studied the alternatives once again. South was certainly possible but the only threat was Austria. She was still licking her wounds from the disasters of Austerlitz and, as far as Marquet knew, was still keeping to the terms of the Treaty of Pressburg that the Emperor had forced on her. East was the favourite. This was where the priest could coordinate activity with the Royal Navy in the Baltic. Again, east it would be.

24
Hamburg, June 1808

Robertson's extra post took him from Rotenburg on to Tostedt where he took a hotel room for the night. The next morning, the carriage drove thirty kilometres to Harburg and then a ferry took him across the southern arm of the River Elbe. It was here that his visa was inspected by both French and Dutch troops. All was in order.

At the ferry across the main river, there was a long queue of traffic. Robertson could see French customs men searching a cart. His driver apologised for the delay. Normally, he said, traffic was waved through on payment of a bribe. There must be a senior officer on duty. The guards were forced to make inspections. The search complete, the cart was waved through. The next vehicle was a hearse. The undertakers were instructed to dismount as the customs men removed the flowers from the top of the coffin and began to unscrew the lid of the coffin. The mourners in the carriage behind leapt out and ran to the hearse, the men shouting and the women screaming. More customs men barred the way to the hearse. A pistol shot rang out and the mourners stopped. An officer appeared.

'Carry on.' The customs officers lifted the lid of the coffin. A young officer burst into tears and made the sign of the cross. The other men shrank back from the coffin.

'Carry on, damn you.'

The men returned to their task. One reached into the coffin and lifted out a small sack.

'Sugar!' The others began to empty the coffin. Once they had finished, a pile of bags and sacks lay on the cobbled street: sugar, indigo, coffee and vanilla.

The customs men rounded up the undertakers and mourners.

'Red-handed,' Robertson's driver remarked. 'I don't fancy their chances.'

'What will happen to them?' asked Robertson.

'Oh, they'll be tortured until they reveal their sources. Then jailed or shot depending on the moods of Consul Bourrienne and General Dupas.'

The traffic jam had cleared. One officer inspected Robertson's passport and visa while another minutely searched his luggage. Finally, they were waved through.

The driver negotiated his way through the crowded streets and took Robertson to his hotel by the Alster lake. Nicholas had suggested this particular hotel. An open reservation had been made for Herr Rorauer. The receptionist told Robertson that the management had given him a room overlooking the lake. He also handed

Robertson a letter and a note. He was shown up to his room. As soon as he was on his own, he opened the letter and note. The first was from Bavaria: it was the attestation from the priest confirming Rorauer's date of birth and baptism. Robertson could now visit the town hall, obtain an international passport and then a Danish visa. The note welcomed him to Hamburg and wished him a good stay. It was signed by the hotel manager. Robertson was initially mystified. He looked at the note again and held it up to the light from the window. In between the lines there seemed to be something. Of course, that was it: sympathetic writing.

He undid one of his portmanteaus and found the small bottle containing the liquid reagent. He brushed the reagent on to the gaps in the note's writing. As the liquid dried, words appeared between the ink.

We are watching the hotel for your arrival. Wait and you will be contacted. At the end of the note there was a sketch of a small flower – the pimpernel. It was a relief that he had allies ready to help. He then destroyed the note.

Sitting on his own in the hotel dining room, Robertson felt that he was being watched, not just by the other guests, French officers among them, but by the staff. Perhaps it was because he was a Bavarian. Outwardly, he appeared the same as other merchants who frequented the city. Was there something that made him stand out? Had he missed something or was he expected by enemies as well as friends?

The next morning, another note was delivered to his room. He examined the note closely before opening it. He could not see any signs of tampering. As before, he used the reagent to reveal the words hidden in the spaces between the lines of the innocent words:

10 a.m. Parish & Co. Again, the note finished with a drawing of a small pimpernel. He then burnt the note.

The bank's offices were only a few minutes' walk from the hotel. Robertson left at nine thirty, walking a circuitous route careful to check if he was being followed. He stood in a doorway across the road from the bank's entrance, looking for watchers. None were obvious. At 10 a.m. he walked quickly across the road, up the stairs and into the bank. He was expected and was immediately ushered upstairs to a back office and was asked to wait. A few minutes later, two men entered.

'I am John Parish. I believe you may have instructions for me to provide you with funds?'

Robertson shook his proffered hand. 'Indeed I do, sir.' He reached into his pocket, retrieved his notebook, took out a penknife, made a slit down the inside cover and produced a plain sheet of paper. He gave it to Parish.

'From Mr Nicholas?'

'Yes, sir.'

'I will take it to apply the reagent. Meanwhile, may I introduce you to the Chevalier?'

They shook hands. Parish left.

'The Pimpernel?' Robertson asked, managing to avoid naming B.

The Chevalier smiled. 'It is a device that my colleagues and I have used ever since 1790. I believe that we have been fighting the same enemy but in different ways. I have been based in these parts for some time. How may I assist you?'

'Mr Nicholas and Mr MacKenzie have told me about you. I must reach the Marquis de La Romana. Can you confirm that he and his troops are still based around Glückstadt?'

'Oh, another one!'

'What do you mean?'

'You are not the first who has tried to outwit Bonaparte. I know of three or four who have tried to reach the Spanish. They were all captured and their papers seized. I dare not think what happened to them.'

'That's hardly very encouraging. Yet try, I must. I can only die once.'

'On your head be it! La Romana now has his headquarters at Nyborg on the island of Funen. That's over 300 kilometres from here.'

Robertson blanched. That was very different to the seventy kilometres he was expecting and a day's sailing to the safety of Heligoland. Where was Funen? Was it possible for the Royal Navy to sail to the island? This called for a complete rethink or even abandonment.

'Are all his troops on Funen?'

'No, we believe that they are spread across the mainland and the other Danish islands and interspersed with French and Danish units. Bonaparte's plan was to use La Romana's troops as part of an army to invade Sweden. That seems to have been moved down his list of priorities.'

'Does Mr Canning know of La Romana's move north?'

'Possibly through his sources based in Sweden or from naval intelligence,' replied the Chevalier. He continued. 'You have to understand that it is an open secret in French circles that La Romana may wish to defect. Bernadotte, as a Basque, may have sympathy with the Spanish but others on his staff think differently. I have spent years building up my networks and cannot risk involving them in your scheme. You can use our communication organisation to converse with Mr MacKenzie but that is as far as I can help.'

Mr Parish returned. 'Mr Nicholas instructs that I am to assist in providing whatever funds you require. You can have as much as you need whenever you need it.' He handed Robertson a handsome sum.

That at least was a relief.

Parish continued. 'It may help you to know that before the Spaniards moved north, they had established a hospital in a Catholic church outside Altona. The hospital is still occupied. The patients are most likely in regular contact with the new headquarters and therefore will have up-to-date information. It is not safe for you to stay at the hotel more than one night. I can organise a safe house for you, but for a maximum of just two nights.'

'Thank you, sir. I need to apply for my international passport and Danish visa.'

'My clerk will accompany you to the town hall and to the Danish consul's office. He will then show you to the safe house once you have checked out of the hotel.'

'Herr Scheller?'

A nod.

By late afternoon, Robertson sat in the room provided in a house to the west of the city centre, passport and visa secured. During the day, he had fleetingly considered abandoning the mission. But he reminded himself of the words he had spoken to the Chevalier and the psalm he had recited on the journey back from Neuwerk. He would see it through whatever the risks.

Using the Pigpen cipher, he wrote to MacKenzie explaining that he was in Hamburg and would shortly leave to travel to Nyborg to meet La Romana. He studied the map he had purchased and began to plan his journey to Nyborg. But first he would acquire what information he could from the patients in the hospital.

The next morning Robertson dressed in his priest's suit. He reasoned that he would be better accepted in this garb than dressed as a merchant. Arriving at St Joseph's church, Robertson stood for a few minutes to admire the baroque facade. He asked an acolyte if he could meet the priest and was shown to the vestry. Asking if there was a Spanish priest present, the German priest took him through the cloisters and introduced Robertson to a Castilian priest. Using Latin, Robertson asked the Spaniard if he could speak privately and was led to a quiet corner of the cloisters.

The Spaniard apologised. 'Brother, I am not used to conversing in Latin. Please speak slowly.'

Speaking in measured Latin, Robertson began. 'Brother, what I am about to tell you is secret. As a fellow brother and priest, can I be assured that the trust I place in you is inviolable?'

'Brother, you can.'

'I have a most important message for the Spanish commander-in-chief. Can you kindly advise the best way to get the message to him in safety?'

The Castilian thought for a moment. 'Brother, I am quite at a loss to suggest how you can send the message. However, there is a wounded officer who is recovering in the hospital. He is a man of honour and a true patriot. He also speaks French. Let me take you to him.'

In the hospital, the priest introduced Robertson as Father Gallus to the Spanish cavalry officer. Robertson extracted the same oath of secrecy and explained his mission.

'Congratulations, Father, on having such a mission entrusted to you. I also note that you carry no papers. Again, congratulations. We regularly have visits from French officers. Any new visitors would certainly be subjected to close inspection. I am only a captain and I am not known to the commander-in-chief. Therefore, I cannot comment what his reaction would be to your proposal. What I can say is that if he wished to take up your government's offer, he would have to have the agreement of his staff and senior officers. I am not recovered to take up my duties as an officer, but I can assure you that your secret is safe with me.'

'At least can you help by asking a fellow officer or even a private soldier to take a letter to the general when he returns to the headquarters?'

'That is a request that I must refuse. Consider if the bearer was intercepted, he would certainly be arrested. I could not ask someone to carry a letter without at least warning him of the content. How could this be done, without risking betrayal of the secret? No, Father, you agreed the mission, it is you who must complete it. I wish you every success but can do nothing to assist you.'

Robertson knew that the officer was correct. It would be too risky to commit the proposal to writing. He would have to journey to Nyborg, there was no alternative.

He thanked the officer and turned to leave when a thought occurred.

'Is there any luxury that the commander-in-chief and his officers are missing?'

'That's easy: cigars and chocolate.'

'Most helpful.' Another part of his planning fell into place.

Robertson returned to the waiting open carriage. He was driven back into the city and paid the driver three streets away from the safe house. He walked for fifteen minutes before turning for the house.

25

Cesar Rainville's Hotel, Altona, North of Hamburg

M arquet was disappointed but not surprised that the searches in Bremen had not produced a positive result. Such a surly and uncooperative populace made that unlikely. He therefore took the road to Hamburg stopping to question each guard post and resident's office on route. Nothing. The French resident at Rotenburg had disgusted him. When Marquet arrived at the resident's office, he was made to wait. The lieutenant finally emerged from his office. Even from well over a metre away, Marquet could smell the cognac on the man's breath. Marquet asked if the man had issued any visas in the past three days. The man flushed, swayed and steadied himself, shook his head and slurred a "no". Marquet didn't believe him. The man was so drunk that even a beating would not produce any coherent answers. Disgusted, he left.

Returning to his quarters, he wrote a note to Colonel

Maupont requesting a meeting. The colonel told him to report to Rainville's at three that afternoon. Time to change, read his correspondence and lunch. Sifting through the pile of letters, Marquet spotted one from Colville. He was now much quicker at deciphering the Vigenère code. Colville reported that there was no more information on the priest apart from reiterating that he was a Catholic. However, the man from London was still on the island. Colville continued: a Prussian had recently landed from the mainland. It was rumoured that he was a member of the clandestine network of Prussian officers who had been fighting a guerrilla campaign ever since the battles of Jena and Auerstadt. The leader of the network could be a Major Ferdinand von Schill. Marquet had some knowledge of the major. Perhaps he was the priest's goal?

Another letter was from Corporal Lejeune on Funen. He had met the valet Martin again. Martin had overheard officers of La Romana's staff complaining that they had not received any correspondence from Spain. There had been no answers to their letters sent to Spain, both official and personal. The officers found it strange that the flow of letters had dried up. There was discussion as to which of the officers should ask the commander-in-chief to formally protest to Marshal Bernadotte.

Marquet arrived at the hotel for the meeting with the colonel with ten minutes to spare. Maupont welcomed him. They talked about the geo-political situation. Napoleon, it seemed, was in complete control of mainland Europe. Yes, Britain remained an irritant but with Russia won over, what threats there were seemed insignificant. Marquet reported on his operations in the past weeks. He skirted around the issues with the customs people but did suggest to Maupont that something should be done about the drunken resident in Rotenburg. They discussed the ever-increasing smuggling and covert operations emanating from Heligoland and specifically the priest. What was his objective? Maupont promised to find out what was currently known of von Schill. As for the Spaniards, La Romana was popular with Bernadotte and his troops had created a favourable impression with the Danes as they had in northern Germany. With their strange ways, many with wives in tow mounted on donkeys, guitars slung over shoulders, the Spaniards were regarded as rather quaint. Apart from one incident in Denmark, discipline had been excellent. Judging by their performance at the siege of Stralsund, they were first-rate soldiers.

Marquet sensed that Maupont had not properly grasped the potential flashpoint of the stopped letters. He had tried to put himself in the Spaniards' position. They had received mail regularly ever since leaving Spain. Now letters had stopped coming. Here they were, camped in an unfamiliar foreign country with suddenly no news from family and friends. Comforting reminders of wives' and mothers' tenderness were suddenly removed. The reaction would first be worry, speculation, fearing the worst. Those sensations would, he could see, soon turn to anger. He turned to Maupont.

'Do you know if there is any other evidence of changing sentiment now that the Emperor has stopped all correspondence reaching the Spaniards?' Maupont shot him a quizzical glance.

'You had better order the valet Martin to report any further rumblings immediately. I have a senior pro-French contact at the heart of La Romana's staff. I'm sure that the contact will brief me if there is any sign of trouble.' A dismissive response, he felt. Marquet was tempted to ask who this contact was but thought better of it. He was dismissed.

His driver made good time until they reached the city's gates. There were queues of carts, carriages and people on foot all pushing their way to the gates. Marquet's driver swore.

'Curfew.' So that was it. Everyone wanted to enter the city before the gates were closed for the night at seven in the evening despite the full daylight. Of course, it was that thug General Dupas who had ordered the early closing some weeks before as retribution for the Hamburg Senate not granting him the allowance of thirty *Friedrich d'or* per day for food and wine for him and his staff. Thirty was the agreed allowance for a marshal. Twenty was the figure for generals. The first day of the early closure had caused chaos. The crowd locked out called for the commandant to come to the gates to order the unlocking. He arrived accompanied by General Dupas himself. Seeing the two, the crowd cheered thinking the gates were about to be opened. Dupas misunderstood the cheer thinking the crowd was about to riot. Ordering his troops to fire into the crowd, some were killed, and others injured. The gates remained closed until the morning. Notices were put up ordering the inhabitants not to cheer or to gather in more than groups of three. So much for fostering good relations.

Marquet stood in the gig to obtain a better view. He looked about for any way round the chaos. As his eyes swept across the heaving mass of people, he saw a man dressed in black with a wide-brimmed hat sitting in the back of a carriage. The carriage was just about to go through the gates. A priest, might it be his priest? He decided to take a chance.

He shouted to his driver.

'That priest is an enemy of the state.' He pointed to the carriage at the gates. 'He must be arrested. Clear a path through.'

'How?'

Marquet pulled one of his pistols out of its holster, cocked the gun, pointed the barrel to the sky and fired. There were shouts and screams as the crowd looked round. So did the priest. The man stood in his carriage. Marquet could see the paunch straining the waistcoat buttons. For an instant their gazes met. Marquet knew and was sure that the priest knew.

He screamed as loud as he could. 'Clear the way.'

The driver pulled his blunderbuss out of its holster and pointed it at the crowd. More screams and pushing to escape this Frenchman. The way parted.

'Drive!' shouted Marquet. The driver whipped the horse. It reared and ploughed its way into the mass. Marquet shouted to the guards on the gate. But his voice did not carry. He reloaded his pistol ready to fire as his gig closed on the gates.

He looked up. The guards had let the priest through the gates. He disappeared from view. At the gates, Marquet swore at the corporal of the guard.

'Which way did the carriage with the priest go?'

The corporal looked blankly up at Marquet. He did not speak French.

'Go!' Marquet shouted to the driver. They burst through the gates. No sign of the priest and there were four different roads. Which to choose?

'Straight on,' Marquet ordered the driver. Standing up in the gig, Marquet hoped he would be able to see the priest's carriage. Nothing.

'Back to my quarters,' he ordered the driver. On arrival, he shouted for the duty corporal. Twenty minutes later, the corporal and six men were saddled ready to commence the search. In pairs, they worked from the gates up each of the four roads.

Two hours later, the driver dropped Marquet at his quarters. The horse was exhausted. They had searched, asking passers-by if they had seen a priest in a carriage. As soon as they had seen gendarmes, fear in their eyes, people shook their heads and slunk away. Again, nothing.

Reaching his room, Marquet slammed a fist on the desk in frustration and poured a consoling cognac. At least he knew that the priest was his quarry.

***

Robertson heard the gunshots as he passed through the gates. He stood in the carriage and turned. A French gendarme officer was standing in an open carriage. It seemed that he was looking straight at Robertson. He was shouting, waving a pistol in the air. For the briefest of moments, the Frenchman seemed to catch Robertson's eye. Any hope that the shots were for just another smuggler being caught vanished. Through the gates, the driver turned left. He was dropped off within a few minutes' walk of the safe house. He was strangely aware, with their eyes coming together, that he and the policeman had made a spiritual connection. Worse, he, Robertson, knew that he was the quarry.

26

Hov, Langeland

Teniente Antonio Fabregues of the 1st Catalonia Regiment was lying on his cot in the annex of the lone farmhouse on the northern tip of Langeland, an island off the south of Funen. From outside the barn, now converted into their quarters, he could hear the men of his platoon and their wives singing to guitars. Feet and castanets accompanied the folk songs from home. Home seemed and was worlds away. How much he would like to join in. He was an officer. He had to be aloof. That was expected and required by both sides of the divide, and divide there was.

As the music drifted into the evening air, he closed his eyes. It had only been three years since he graduated from the military academy in Zaragoza. There had been little discussion with his father about a career. As one of the younger sons of a minor nobleman, the choice was the priesthood or the army. The army was the obvious choice. Postings in Spain were followed by a tour of duty in Italy supporting Queen Maria Teresa of Etruria, the daughter of King Carlos's consort. Then came orders to march north to join Marshal Bernadotte's army of observation in northern Germany. From Florence, he marched 1,000 kilometres to Mainz. There they were joined by other regiments from Spain. After another 500 kilometres, the 15,000 men of the Division of the North arrived in Hamburg. All along their route, they attracted crowds of curious onlookers.

Fabregues found the action he desired at the siege of Stralsund on the Baltic coast. The excitement and elation of victory over the Swedish defenders were marred when Major Quadra had taken him aside. Fabregues had performed well but he should cool that streak of hot-headedness. Calculated risk was to be admired but suicidal risk was just stupid. The criticism stung.

The winter of 1807 was spent in cantonments in Hamburg. The cold: Fabregues had only experienced such penetrating chill once before on exercise in the Pyrenees. The weather went on and on; rain, frost, snow, more bone-numbing rain for weeks on end. At least they received their pay regularly and as auxiliary units of the French Army, the money was better than their Spanish Army pay. In the spring they marched into Denmark. The rumour mill talked of an invasion of Sweden. But nothing came of that gossip. As summer arrived and, thank goodness, some warmth, life fell into a routine: regimental exercises, patrolling, occasional liaison visits to other regiments, delivery of status reports to divisional headquarters in

Nyborg, keeping a note of the British naval ships patrolling the Great Belt between Zealand and Langeland. Mass was held locally in Snode every Sunday and for the whole regiment in the small town of Rudkobing once a month, a seven-hour march each way.

The dark-skinned Spanish soldiers arrived with wives and children in tow, mounted on donkeys. Guitars as well as muskets were often slung over the men's shoulders. Initially, the local populace had regarded the Spaniards with fear and suspicion. Fabregues even heard reports from one village on Jutland that regarded men of the Zamora Regiment as cannibals. The Danes were amazed at how much the Spaniards smoked, some were regarded as perambulating fire hazards. Over the weeks, fear turned to tolerance and, despite the language barrier, affection. The Danes were impressed by the discipline the Spaniards displayed, the military pomp and ceremony, their willingness to help with smithing and the like, their fondness of children. They watched with amazement the strange music and dancing.

While relations with the locals improved, those with the French deteriorated. And then the mail from home dried up. Ever since leaving Spain, Fabregues has taken to reading the letters his men received from their village priests out loud to his illiterate men. The arrival of mail from home became a highlight for all the men of his platoon. They would gather round him in silence as he read of the news from their villages and towns. Over the months the bond between him and his "children" grew stronger. It was his sergeant who asked on their behalf what had happened when the mail stopped. Days later, a French patrol passed through Hov on an inspection visit. After pleasantries had been exchanged, Fabregues asked about the mail. The Frenchman spat, called Fabregues a Spanish "*tas de merde*", wheeled his horse and cantered away.

It was not just Fabregues. In the mess, his colleagues were outraged. News of the events of 2 May, the abdications and imminent crowning of Joseph seeped through. The pamphlets left at night on the island's beaches by the English, initially regarded as propaganda, were, in the hot house, cigar-smoke filled, brandy-fed atmosphere, given credence. The Catalunya was an elite fighting regiment, not a third-rate garrison unit. A growing sense of disenchantment seeped through the platoon. Fabregues found it impossible to hide his disillusionment from his men.

27
The Foreign Office, June 1808

Hoppner read MacKenzie's report once again. The news that the Spanish were no longer stationed around Glückstadt had shocked him. How had the move into the heart of Denmark been missed? Surely all the merchants who were paid to provide exactly this sort of information would have seen something?

He looked at the maps of Denmark and found Funen. The island was in the Baltic accessed from a channel named the Little Belt. The task of transporting the Spanish troops would have to be transferred to Admiral Saumarez's Baltic fleet. Hoppner could just imagine the peals of laughter in the Admiralty when the Foreign Office's error became known. Mr Canning would hardly enjoy the conversation with Lord Mulgrave, the First Lord. Then he thought about his career. There would be a search for a scapegoat. He shuddered. There was nothing to be done. He would

THE FOREIGN OFFICE

have to explain everything to Mr Rolleston. Hoppner was about to rise and go to Mr Rolleston's office, but then sat again. Better to suggest a solution to this mess.

The key remained to contact and persuade the marquis. With the control the navy exercised in the Baltic, Hoppner was confident that this professional force could carry out the embarkation and transport. He looked at the map again. Assuming he was still in Hamburg, Robertson would have to travel close to 200 miles through enemy country to Nyborg. The journey from the friendly territory of Helsingborg, Gothenburg or possibly Malmo, in Sweden, was much shorter. Robertson would need not simply skill but luck to make the journey safely. The answer was surely to double the chances of success. Brief another agent, send him to friendly Sweden and land him covertly in Denmark for the much shorter trip to La Romana's headquarters in Nyborg.

The more he thought about this possible solution, the more he liked it. At least it was something positive and might deflect the criticism that was bound to come his way. He made his way to Mr Rolleston's room and knocked on the door.

'Enter.'

He opened the door and saw that Mr Hammond was also in the room. At least he would not have to go through the explanation process twice.

An hour later, he was back at his desk full of relief. Both the under-secretary and chief clerk had been understanding. It was a case, they both agreed, that these things happen. Hoppner's suggestion that a second agent

191

be sent to the marquis from Sweden had been well received. Mr Rolleston had ideas as to who might carry out this mission and Mr Hammond would talk with Mr William Wellesley-Pole, the secretary to the Board of Admiralty, to smooth the path of Mr Canning's discussions with the First Lord. Hoppner had asked should one of the agents be successful, would General Sir John Moore's 10,000 troops help the Spanish take control of Funen and assist in the embarkation process? Mr Hammond's response was unequivocal. The erratic nature of the Swedish King had made any cooperation with the Swedes impossible. Despite the alliance between Sweden and Britain, King Gustavus had forbidden Sir John to land his troops. They languished on the navy's transports while Sir John attempted to negotiate a settlement. The King lost his temper, arrested Sir John who was forced to escape disguised as a peasant. He arrived back on Admiral Saumarez's flagship in the middle of a ball being given for the ladies of Gothenburg. Sir John had been humiliated and was returning to the Downs, the anchorage off Deal.

Mr Hammond had been in constant communication with his former secretary, Edward Thornton, who was now envoy-extraordinary to the Swedish Court in Stockholm. Thornton advised against using Sweden for any covert action, such was the unreliability of King Gustav. It would therefore be better to land the agent covertly at one of the many ports on the coast of Holstein frequented by the smugglers operating from Heligoland. The agent would make his way north through Jutland and on to Funen.

Two days later, Hoppner was summoned to Mr Rolleston's room. Another man was sitting talking with Mr Rolleston.

'Ah, Hoppner, let me introduce you to Mr Charles McMahon.'

'Delighted, sir.' Hoppner bowed. McMahon acknowledged Hoppner with a nod.

Rolleston continued. 'Mr McMahon has accepted the mission to travel and meet La Romana. He will carry letters from His Majesty's Government for the marquis. McMahon insists on physical proof of his credentials. Word of mouth is not sufficient. We have drafted the contents. Take them to Mr Frere who will check the wording of the Spanish text.'

'Yes, sir. But I thought that it had been decided not to risk carrying letters on enemy territory?'

'It is a risk, but given the urgency that the Foreign Secretary places on this mission, it is a risk worth taking. After you have delivered the draft to Mr Frere, come back here and acquaint Mr McMahon of the background to the Spanish arrival in Denmark.'

'Yes, sir.' Hoppner was dismissed. Leaving Mr Rolleston's room, he thought back to the discussions with the Reverend Robertson and his insistence that he would carry nothing that might incriminate him. As he made his way to Mr Frere's house with the draft letter, he mulled over the change of policy. The more he thought about it, that McMahon would carry government letters, the more it struck him as a strange decision, even foolish. The draft delivered, he returned to his desk to collect maps and files for the briefing. There was a folded note tucked into the top file. It was from Mr Rolleston and read:

No mention of Rev. Rob to McM. Destroy this now. R.

So McMahon would be blissfully unaware of Robertson's quest. As Hoppner walked to Mr Rolleston's room, he reasoned that ignorance of each other's mission was in case of capture and interrogation, probably for the best. He lead McMahon to an annex room, gesturing to a chair. McMahon sat, pushed back the chair, tipping it on to its back legs and rested his feet on a nearby table. Before Hoppner could open his mouth to begin, McMahon blurted out in a southern Irish accent, 'Do be brief, young man. My instructions come from Mr Canning himself. Mr Rolleston has given me as much information as I am likely to need. You should know that I am well acquainted with Marshal Bernadotte.'

Hoppner was already irritated by the man's demeanour and poor manners especially coming from someone only a few years older than he was. This revelation stopped any planned riposte in its tracks.

'Bernadotte. How come?'

McMahon smiled. 'And Foreign Minister Talleyrand.'

'Gracious, perhaps you should explain?' Hoppner's anger at the man's arrogance subsided to inquisitiveness. McMahon sat forward.

'I was just eighteen when I commanded a regiment of the United Irish leading up to the Battle of Ballinamuck. After the surrender to you British, I escaped to America and then to France. One of my relatives introduced me to Talleyrand and then to Bernadotte, who was then minister of war.'

'How did the relative know Bernadotte?'

'He had commanded a regiment of marines in which Bernadotte served. Years later, I travelled to Hanover. It was there that Bernadotte offered me a commission and command of the second battalion of the Irish Legion. But I decided not to accept it. You can read it all in my personal statement which I gave to Mr Canning.'

For the second time, Hoppner was staggered by events. First, that the Spanish were now in Denmark and now it seemed that the government was about to employ an agent who had fought against Britain and had served in the French Army. He made a mental note to read this "personal statement" if it was available to him. Meanwhile, he would do his best not to look or sound surprised.

'Well, if the Foreign Secretary has seen it, what you say must have his blessing.'

'Mr Canning gave me his best wishes on a successful journey. Now. Let's proceed with your brief.'

As McMahon became increasingly fidgety, pacing round the room, looking out of the window, Hoppner's irritation resurfaced. The man was just not listening to what he was being told. What should have been more than two hours, he managed to cut down to thirty minutes. He closed the last folder and folded the map of Funen.

'Finished?'

Hoppner nodded.

'Good.' McMahon marched to the door, pulled it open and disappeared without another word. Hoppner was in a quandary. Surely, if it was true, McMahon's background must cast doubt on his loyalty to the King. But if the

Foreign Secretary had believed the man, then who was he to question the decision to employ him?

A day later, Hoppner watched as McMahon was bid farewell as he followed Robertson's path to Harwich, Heligoland, not into Germany but to Tonnigen in Denmark. He wondered which of the two agents would reach La Romana first if either of them made it. He could not rid himself of the debate raging in his mind. He resolved to have a quiet word with Mr Rolleston. But first he must be more sure of his facts.

Back at his desk the following day, Hoppner sifted through a pile of folders before taking them to Mr Ancell, the librarian, for filing. One folder caught his eye. It was McMahon's personal statement. He scanned the four pages of neat handwriting. Familiar names leapt from the pages: Bernadotte and Talleyrand. He pushed the other folders aside and began to read the statement properly.

McMahon excused his joining the rebel Irish cause as *mine was a momentary act of enthusiasm*. But he then joined the French Army. He protested that he knew nothing of Robert Emmet's planned Irish uprising in 1803. But then, as he had told Hoppner, he travelled to Bernadotte's headquarters in Hanover. He was offered a commission: command of the second battalion of the Irish Legion. He turned the offer down. McMahon *was resolved not to go in the way of being sent on an expedition to subjugate my own country, but I alleged a different one: a wish to improve myself by serving in an army actively employed.*

It was not clear to Hoppner what McMahon meant in the last sentence. He continued to read. The remainder of the statement assured the reader of McMahon's loyalty to the Crown, his abilities and his desire to be of service despite any personal risks.

Hoppner read through the three and a half pages again. Here was a man who had fought for the Irish rebels and who, through relatives and personal connections, had ties with Talleyrand and with Bernadotte, the commander of French troops across northern Europe. These included La Romana's division. McMahon's assurances of his loyalty to His Majesty the King hardly rang true. At the very least, his motivation must surely come into question. Now the man was on his way to meet the marquis carrying letters from the junta's diplomats. What were the chances that he would travel directly to Hamburg and hand the letters over to Bernadotte? Surely there was a possibility that this man was a double agent whose true loyalties lay with the cause of a United Ireland and the French.

Hoppner sat back. He must at least talk through his concerns with Mr Rolleston. Carrying the statement, he walked across the office and knocked on the door of Mr Rolleston's room.

'Enter,' and he did so.

'Is this urgent, Hoppner?'

'I believe so, sir. Have you seen the statement written by Mr McMahon?'

'No. What of it?'

'I believe that what he has written may bring into doubt his loyalty to His Majesty.'

'That is a very serious charge, Hoppner.'

'I do appreciate that, sir. Hence my bringing the

matter to your attention. It may be that I have put an incorrect interpretation on the statement but surely a man who admits to fighting for the Irish rebels and who knows Marshal Bernadotte should be questioned further before we trust him with such a secret mission.'

'It may well be too late. Show me.'

Hoppner passed the papers over. Rolleston scanned the four pages.

'Who has read this?'

'The Foreign Secretary. His initials are on the file cover.'

'Anyone else?'

'It seems not. Perhaps it was initialled by mistake?'

Rolleston rubbed his chin. 'Leave this with me.'

'Of course, sir.' Hoppner turned to leave.

'Not a word to anyone. You understand?'

'Yes, sir.'

Hoppner returned to his desk and sat. His mind raced. Had he misunderstood McMahon's statement? Was there more to it than met the eye? Was he correct having brought it to Mr Rolleston? At least he was sure he had done the right thing. Perhaps there were greater games being played out, games beyond his comprehension? He tried to concentrate on his work in hand, but his mind kept returning to the man McMahon and his motives. Whichever way he looked at it, there was a whiff of treachery in the air.

28

Number 12 Krayenkamp, Central Hamburg, July 1808

Marquet's men had continued the search for the priest across the city but without success. The inhabitants continued sullen in their evasion of any questions. If the priest had been seen, no one would admit such to the hated gendarmes. Marquet had heard of the cynical joke circulating that Marshal Bernadotte had listened to the city leaders' protests and ordered General Dupas to reduce the number of dishes to be produced by the city for his supper table every evening from thirty-six to eighteen! Even the offer of substantial rewards to informants had no effect. The priest had simply disappeared or more likely, he reasoned, the man purporting to be a priest had changed his identity. Whoever he was, the man must speak excellent German to make his way across the country apparently alone. But surely not completely alone. He must have help: assistance with money and travel. Where would this come from? The answer must be the merchant smuggling fraternity and the banks that were so obviously supporting the contraband trade and, no doubt, opposition to the Emperor across Europe. The Parish bank had been closely investigated as it was rumoured that the bank acted as the Rothschild's agent in northern Germany. Father and son Parish had been arrested two years ago but nothing had come of the investigation; no doubt the local police had been prevented by Paris. What about another English bank, Thornton and Power? But then he remembered Colonel Maupont's words warning him off those lines of investigation. Frustration welled up once again.

There was a knock on the door. 'Come.' A gendarme entered, saluted and presented a letter. Marquet gave a peremptory wave in acknowledgement, dismissed the gendarme and studied the letter. It was from Colville on Heligoland who reported that it seemed that another agent had arrived on the packet boat from Harwich. He had seen that man talking to the Foreign Office officer and "Der Consul". Colville had by now established a number of contacts among the dockers. One of these had informed Colville that the man from London was due to sail to Tonningen in Denmark in three days' time. Marquet looked back to the top of the report. The date was two days ago. Given a day's sailing time from the island, the agent could be expected to land in Denmark tomorrow evening. He looked at the map. Tonningen was a day's ride from Hamburg. If he moved quickly, he could prepare a warm reception for this Englishman.

There was more from Colville. He was alarmed that a net was closing around him. He had been summoned to appear before the colonel of the garrison of the island. Colville believed that the reason for his presence on Heligoland had stood up. However, as he was about to leave, the lieutenant sitting beside the colonel told him that this meeting was by no means the end of the matter. Further investigation would continue.

Marquet sat back. To lose Colville would be disappointing, but these were the risks that the man took. He was, after all, being amply rewarded. He coded a reply: "take care".

He then wrote a note to Colonel Maupont. Explaining his plans, Marquet asked him to inform the Danes and secure the permissions. These were probably not necessary but should be gained to ensure Danish cooperation. He was sure that, after the bombardment and occupation of Copenhagen, the Danes would be keen to keep a captured British agent for themselves. Marquet had to ensure that he was first to interrogate the man.

He went to the door, opened it and shouted for the sergeant. Arrangements would be made for an immediate departure. He would take a troop of ten gendarmes commanded by the reliable corporal. As a precaution, he noted the French units stationed in Denmark and the names of their commanding officers. He might need local assistance. As he left his room, he was given a note. It was from his colleague in Lübeck. There had been a disturbance. Drunk French cavalrymen had attempted to accost a German lady. A certain Herr Rorauer had intervened. Marquet put the note on top of other papers to be read and filed. No importance.

Two hours later, fully equipped, Marquet and the troops rode out of the city's north-western gate and began the journey north.

29

Hotel Postgarten, Nyborg

Enrique Jose O'Donnell lay awake. He just could not get to sleep. The noise coming from down the corridor was intolerable: grunts, giggles and bouncing springs. Had it been anyone else, he would have charged down the corridor and hammered on the door. Since hearing that Marshal Bernadotte had recommended to the Emperor that he should be awarded the Grand Cross of the *Légion d'honneur*, the Marquis de La Romana, general commanding the Division Del Norte, had been in excellent spirits all evening. The celebrations had carried on well into the night when the general had announced that the Emperor intended to award pay rises to all the officers of the division. It was hardly surprising that the marquis had summoned his mistress to his room to finish the night properly. Even though O'Donnell was the general's trusted aide-de-camp, to interrupt was hardly appropriate.

As he stared at the ceiling, O'Donnell reflected on the past eighteen months. He had been enjoying celebrating the New Year with his family in San Sebastian when he was summoned to join the marquis to help form the Division of the North. The marquis had been instructed by Minister Godoy to form a division that should comprise some of the best troops in the Spanish Army. Godoy wanted to impress on Napoleon his commitment to the treaty of alliance.

When they marched out of Spain across France, O'Donnell was proud of the men he led. Entering Germany, they had been joined by further battalions that had marched from Spanish-controlled Italy forming a formidable force of fourteen battalions of foot and five regiments of cavalry. The division had performed well during the successful siege of Stralsund impressing the overall commander, Marshal Guillaume Brune. After wintering in and around Glückstadt, in the spring they had marched into Denmark presumably to prepare for an invasion of Sweden. Then nothing; it appeared that the Emperor's mind was focused elsewhere. Marshal Bernadotte issued orders that the division be spread across Denmark and intermingled with French, Dutch and Danish troops.

The marquis had protested to Bernadotte. Despite the close relationship between La Romana and the marshal, his objections were ignored. The orders had come from Napoleon himself. There was no option but to obey. Worse followed. The 4,000 men of the Asturias and Guadalajara regiments now stationed near Roskilde on the island of

Zealand were to be commanded by a Frenchman, General Fririon. The Algarve, Infante, Rey and Zamora regiments were stationed in Aarhus, Frederica and Randers on Jutland under the marquis's deputy General Kindelan. The 1st Regiment of Catalonia was stationed on Langeland while the remainder of the division, some 4,500 troops of the Princesa, 1st of Barcelona, Almanza and Villaviciosa regiments were on Funen, close to Nyborg. All around the Spanish troops were large contingents of French, Danish or Dutch troops. It seemed to O'Donnell that these troops had been deliberately positioned to spy on the Spanish.

To add to the disquiet, the delivery of mail from home had ceased. Initially, the staff had thought that this disruption was purely a logistical issue but as the weeks passed without letters there was increasing concern across all ranks. Then a Spanish officer had managed to avoid the French police and make his way to Nyborg. He had been sent by Madrid to find out why there had been no response to the fourteen official letters sent from Madrid. It was from this officer that they had learned of the French seizure of Barcelona, Figueras and Pamplona. With his home city of San Sebastian being close to the French border and to the north of Pamplona, O'Donnell was anxious for his family's safety.

What was going on at home? The French were supposedly allies. The withholding of mail, the capture of such important towns and cities close to the French border and the posting of the division into small units across Denmark under close supervision, hardly seemed to be the actions of friends. Had the award to the general and the pay rise for the officers been a sop to keep the Spanish officers quiet? The marquis had discussed the events with his senior staff. General Kindelan had argued that Napoleon was most likely helping the King to rid himself of the hated minister Godoy and impose much needed reforms across the country. Surely, he suggested it was time for Spain to model itself on the French constitution and abolish the ancient conservative ways so favoured by the landed aristocracy and the Church? It was time, he said, to adopt laws similar to the *Code Napoléon.*

Kindelan's views caused much disquiet. The marquis forbade him to discuss them outside the senior group of officers. Should these ideas become known to the padres accompanying the division and thence to the soldiery, he predicted a violent reaction such was the hold that the Church had on most private soldiers.

At least the cacophony down the corridor had stopped. O'Donnell turned over and tried to sleep. His mind was buzzing. He turned the facts over. Kindelan might be right. There was a considerable pro-French faction who could have persuaded the King to act. But to allow the seizure of these towns? Surely not. He attempted to look at the situation from Napoleon's perspective. The Emperor was master of Europe. Which countries were not under his complete control? Britain, of course. If he could transport the *Grande Armée* across the Channel, he would have no difficulty sweeping the puny English Army aside. He would be in London in days. However, the Royal Navy controlled the seas. Ever since Trafalgar, the British fleet dominated the oceans around Europe from the Mediterranean to the Baltic. The seizure of the Danish fleet just a few months ago demonstrated how ruthlessly efficient that organisation was. It was true that Napoleon was apparently building more ships in Antwerp but these new vessels would be no match especially when it came to manning them. No, he thought, the Emperor had tried in 1804 but had given up. Smashing Austrian, Prussian or Russian armies on land was his forte. Whatever his faults, he was a brilliant general.

So who else? Prussia and Austria had been crushed. All the Italian states were in his thrall. The Ottoman Empire stretched into the Balkans but represented no threat. After Tilsit, Russia was now an ally and could, if attacked, retreat into the vast hinterland to the east. Sweden was a minor irritation. He imagined that, at Tilsit, Napoleon would have persuaded the Tsar to attack that country through Finland. Leaving Spain, a country ruled by the Bourbons. Ever since his youth in Corsica, Napoleon seemed to have a pathological hatred of that family whether they ruled in France, Italy or Spain. Kindelan was wrong, he reasoned. Napoleon was planning to oust the Bourbons. Once he controlled Spain, no Bourbon would be allowed to remain on the throne, neither the King, Ferdinand nor any of his siblings. The capture of Barcelona, Figueras and Pamplona was a foretaste of what was to come: invasion and conquest.

Finally sleep came.

At breakfast, the coffee was insipid. How much he longed for chocolate. The marquis emerged followed by the valet Martin. La Romana looked none the worse from his night-time frolics. After the normal pleasantries were exchanged, O'Donnell was keen to discuss the news from Spain. He wanted to talk through the ideas he had propounded during the small hours. Not in the hearing, though, of the French valet who was surely a spy. Another example of how closely the French were watching the general and his staff. O'Donnell had suggested that the marquis sack the valet but La Romana overruled him. It was better to have the spy where they could see him. Removing him would lead to a replacement who might be less visible.

La Romana dismissed Martin. As he sipped his coffee, he listened to O'Donnell's exposition. Once O'Donnell had finished, the marquis leant back in his chair and was quiet for some time. What was he, La Romana, doing here? The fact was he was stuck in a small Danish town on garrison duty. Napoleon's focus had moved away from an invasion of Sweden. The prospect of any action seemed increasingly remote. How he wished he could be back home in Valencia enjoying the delights of a Spanish summer. He imagined sitting in his library, windows wide open, sipping a glass of chilled wine while delving into one of his prized books. His library was, after all, the envy of his peers. Or perhaps he would be debating a Hebrew text with one of his former professors at Salamanca University. But no, his life was set from the day he was born. Even at the tender age of ten, he had been sent from home in Palma to Trinity College in Lyon, the premier college in Europe. After naval cadetship and university, he saw action in the navy against the British in the retaking of Minorca. At the war's end, he was able to devote himself to building his library before duty called again with diplomatic missions in Vienna and Berlin. More active service followed in America before he transferred to the army in the war against the French Convention. Promotion followed quickly. By the time he retired in 1795, he was a lieutenant-general. Called to arms again in 1802, Romana became captain-general of Catalonia and finally general director of the engineers with a place on the High War Council.

It had been an honour to be asked by the King to lead the Division del Norte. After all, the division was made up of some of the best troops in the kingdom. Before leaving Spain, he had managed to counter the appointment of General O'Farrill as his deputy. O'Farrill was a known French sympathiser with dubious loyalty to the King and Prime Minister Godoy. A political victory that was short-lived, he could not prevent the appointment of another pro-French general, Kindelan. At least Kindelan was out of the way in Jutland. He, La Romana, meanwhile, was now stuck 2,500 kilometres away from Madrid with no chance of influencing events.

Back to O'Donnell's summary, the news from Spain was indeed alarming. He could perhaps tolerate the dismissal of Godoy and a move towards a more liberal constitution. Maybe even the replacement of the King with his popular son, Ferdinand. That would be a temporary sop to the liberals. With the help of the Catholic Church with its powerful hold over the general populace, the nobility could soon restore the status quo. But an invasion followed by the usurping of the rightful king by a puppet controlled by Napoleon, that was something he could never bear. The thought of a Bonaparte on the throne – never!

The marquis looked up at O'Donnell. He was fortunate to have such an able and loyal aide.

'Well, Jose, from what we know, your analysis is, I'm sure, correct. The question is what are we going to do about it? Let's look at our situation.'

La Romana walked to his office. O'Donnell followed. A framed map of Denmark was on the wall. Small flags were pinned to the map representing each of the division's battalions and regiments.

'The division is spread all over Denmark. There are six battalions on Zealand, mainly based around the old royal residence of Roskilde and they are commanded by our French friend, Fririon. Three regiments of cavalry and three battalions of infantry are spread all over Jutland in and around Frederica, Arhuus and to the north, Randers, commanded by Juan Kindelan. We have four battalions of infantry and two cavalry regiments here on Funen and finally a battalion on Langeland to the south of us. All well and good. But now let's mark what I shall call our jailers.

'In Zealand, our 4,000 men are watched by the main Danish army of observation against Sweden. Our 4,500 troops here in Funen are spread all over the island in small detachments closely supervised by 3,000 Danes in Odense in the island's centre. On Langeland, our men are mixed up with a company of French grenadiers and about 800 Danes. Finally, in Jutland our men are watched by a brigade of Dutch light cavalry and some Danish infantry. We can hardly march back to Spain!

'I shall request a meeting with Marshal Bernadotte. I get on well with him. He might give us more up-to-date news and, in any case, we may discover what the Emperor means to do with us. Our men will not tolerate being kept away from their families purely for garrison duty.'

'Very good, sir.'

30
The Safe House, Hamburg

Back at the safe house, Robertson found it difficult to shake off the vision of the gendarme. He did his best to describe the uniform to his host: white jacket and red waistcoat. Perhaps that might help identify his pursuer. Enquiries would be made. Concentrating on planning for the journey to Nyborg was near impossible. His mind kept returning to the gendarme and that briefest of eye contact. The threat reminded him of childhood in the Highlands watching falcons hovering over their prey.

He told himself to look forward, be positive, focus on the future. At least the Spanish officer had given him the key: a reason for the marquis and his staff to agree to meet him. Rorauer would become a merchant selling chocolate and cigars; a reason for travelling into Denmark.

Mr Parish was sure that merchants would be keen to engage Herr Rorauer as a commission salesman prepared to travel at his own risk to sell to a potential market of officers commanding 15,000 troops greedy for chocolate and cigars. Mr Parish had moved fast. Introductions had been made, meetings with two wholesalers had taken place, terms agreed and samples of the best Havana cigars and blocks of chocolate had been procured, and addresses of fellow merchants based in Lübeck and Kiel. As he sipped a cup of the sample chocolate in the morning room, a servant entered.

'There is a gentleman to see you, sir.'

Immediately he was on his guard. Who knew he was here? There was nothing for it.

'Show him in.'

'Herr Burkmeyer,' the servant announced.

Burkmeyer bowed. 'I have a note from Heligoland.' He gave Robertson a letter.

It was from MacKenzie. Before he had a chance to thank the man, he had turned on his heels and left.

'One of our friends,' said the servant.

Robertson retired to his room and began deciphering the message. He was amused at MacKenzie's Latin. It was something he would have expected from a fourteen-year-old schoolboy, but it sufficed. The letter brought him up to date with developments in Spain, knowledge key for his meeting with La Romana. Events had moved with pace.

Since the slaughter of 2 May in Madrid, eight days later King Ferdinand had been forced to sign a final letter of abdication. Word spread rapidly across Spain. Orvieto in the north was the first city to rise in rebellion on 24 May led by the Marquis de Santa Cruz, followed two days later by Seville in the south-west. Now it appeared that regions from the north sweeping round in a crescent to Valencia on the south coast were in open rebellion against French rule. Emissaries from Orvieto had arrived in London on 7 June to ask for assistance. Andalusians had bombarded and captured the French fleet in Cadiz. Napoleon had summoned forty-seven Spanish worthies to Bayonne to agree a new constitution and pronounce his brother, Joseph, King of Spain and the Indies. News that would surely help persuade the marquis to accept the British offer.

As he coded a short note to MacKenzie explaining that he was about to travel north, he decided not to include any reference to the route he would take. If the gendarme officer was any good at his job, he might already have taken steps to intercept mail. Breaking the code would take time but he reasoned there was no real need for MacKenzie to know.

He had already decided not to take the direct route through Schleswig but to take the coach to Lübeck. From there he might be able to take a ferry across the Baltic to the Danish island of Loland and on to Nyborg. Should this not be an option, he could travel to Kiel, on to Flensburg and take the Assens ferry to Funen. After a final visit to Mr Parish for funds and to the town hall to have his passport stamped for Lübeck, he thanked his hosts, bade farewell and climbed the steps into the coach for Lübeck.

As the coach bounced and swayed towards the city, the "Queen" of the Hanseatic League, Robertson fell into conversation with a young mother who was returning to her home city from a visit to relatives in Hamburg. She held a baby in her arms. Robertson commented how well behaved the baby was given the conditions in the coach.

'Thank you,' she said. 'This is Anna. She is lucky to be here at all.'

'How is that? She looks a healthy young girl.'

'Eighteen months ago,' she told him, 'Lübeck had been occupied by retreating Prussian troops. The chasing French Army bombarded the city. Our house was hit but we stayed where we were because I was about to give birth. The next day, the Prussians fled the city, immediately followed by French soldiers who broke down our front door and began to ransack the house. Fearing rape, I rushed out of the house and felt my waters break. I shouted for help. Women gathered round me shielding me from the gaze of all the people and soldiers in the market place and Anna was born. And here she is.'

'Wonderful, praise be to God.'

The coach pulled into an inn for a change of horses. Robertson helped the lady down. As he escorted her to the inn, he saw French chargers tied to the rail. Cavalry or gendarme horses? Cavalrymen poured out of the door, obviously very drunk. The lady grabbed Robertson's arm. A lance-corporal seemed to be the leader of the bunch.

'The answer to our prayers, lads. As the landlord can't give us girls, I'm sure this *Fräulein* will oblige us.' He swayed towards Robertson. Schnapps-flavoured spit spattered Robertson's face.

'Out of my way, Kraut.'

The lady screamed. 'What's he saying?'

As the corporal lunged, Robertson stuck out a boot. The Frenchman tripped, crashing face down on the cobbles. Robertson pushed the lady behind him.

'Back to the coach.' The mood of the remaining bunch changed. One man began to draw his sabre. A shout from the balcony above.

'Stop, you bastards.' Robertson looked up. An officer had a drawn pistol trained on the bunch. 'Back off.' A sergeant appeared, musket in hand. The men slunk away. The corporal made it to his knees, his face covered with blood. A crowd gathered. The officer came down the stairs.

'I will deal with you later.' Turning to Robertson, he said, 'Do you speak French, sir?'

'I do.'

'Then please accept my apologies and give them to the lady.'

'I will, of course.'

'What is your name?'

'Adam Rorauer.'

'And the lady?'

'I have not had the opportunity to make her acquaintance.' The lady was still grasping Robertson's arm. He could feel her shaking, the baby still clasped in her other arm. Robertson whispered to her.

'Frau Heidi Muller.' He repeated her name to the officer.

'Then my humble apologies, Madame Muller.' He bowed and turned to deal with the drunks. The coachman shouted that he was ready to leave. Robertson helped Frau Muller up into the coach. She placed the baby back in its cot, sat next to Robertson and buried her face into his chest. He put his arm around her as her breasts heaved with sobs. His waistcoat was soon soaked with her tears.

By the time the coach had settled back on the Lübeck road, its swaying motion lulled Frau Muller to sleep. Robertson felt a mix of pride in being able to protect a vulnerable young lady and the tenderness he sensed as he wrapped his arm around her. He realised that, apart from his mother, he had never hugged a grown woman. It was a strange and disconcerting experience.

A wheel of the coach crashed into a pothole. The baby began to cry. Frau Muller was instantly awake. As she found herself in Robertson's arms, she looked mortified. She pulled herself away from him.

'I am so sorry, sir. But thank you for saving us.'

'We had a lucky escape.' Frau Muller turned to look after her baby. He thought about the ramifications of the incident. The soldiers would be punished. Would a report reach the gendarmerie? If so, it was a pity that he had given his name to the officer. But he had no choice. It was surely unlikely that any connection would be made between a monk and Adam Rorauer.

The coach pulled into the Lübeck station. Frau Muller pulled down the window and looked out.

'Frans!' Turning to Robertson, she said, 'My husband.' Herr Muller ran to the coach, opened the door, took the baby from his wife and helped her down to the ground. She threw her arms around his neck, bursting into tears. Robertson climbed down and reached up as the coachman handed down his portmanteaus. Frau Muller began whispering in her husband's ear, pointing at Robertson.

Frans Muller looked astonished. He walked to Robertson, extending his hand.

'From the bottom of my heart, thank you, sir. Thank you for what you have done for my wife and child. May I ask where you are staying while you are in Lübeck?'

'A hotel,' he replied.

'Then can we repay you in a small way by offering our hospitality? Our house still shows the signs of the bombardment, but it is comfortable. We do not have any French soldiers billeted on us at the moment.'

'Thank you. That is most generous. I would be delighted as long as my stay will not cause you trouble.' *Another safe house, without the need to sign a hotel's register.*

The next day Herr Muller took him to the warehouse of one of the merchants associated with his Hamburg employers. Introductions made, Robertson was asked what his plans were. When he told the merchant that it was his intention to travel as far as Copenhagen, it was as if Robertson had lost his mind.

'Do you realise that the British naval ships are swarming all over the Baltic? There is nothing that would tempt me to take such a risk.'

Robertson smiled. 'But the potential profits are handsome indeed! I have a visa for Denmark.'

He returned to the warehouse and thanked the merchant. He would follow the travel advice given; travel to Kiel where the Danish King had a palace. From there, he was advised to take a ferry to one of the Danish islands and on to Funen.

At Kiel's gates, Robertson was asked where he had

come from, the purpose of his visit – the usual questions. His passport was not inspected or stamped. He made his way to the quay. Asking about, he learnt that there was a merchant schooner moored in the river bound for the small island of Aroe to the south of Funen. A crewman told him that the master was in a quayside café.

'There.'

Robertson followed the pointed finger. The master was drinking coffee, a schnapps chaser by the side of his cup. The price to take Robertson to Aroe was treble what he had been told to expect.

'These are dangerous times, my friend.' He had no choice but to accept, thankful that Mr Parish had been generous. He was given a cot in the mate's cabin, stowed his cases, climbed back on deck in time to watch the schooner cast off and set sail down the Kiel Fjord towards the Baltic. The schooner creaked and groaned, drawing Robertson's eyes to the rotting timbers.

At the mouth of the fjord and under the guns of a substantial fort, the master halted and ordered drop anchor. Robertson asked why they had stopped.

'We wait until dusk until the English have left for the day.'

They waited until the sun began to dip to the west. The anchor was raised, the breeze filling the hoisted sails as the vessel nosed into the Baltic. Robertson went below, climbed into the cot and drifted off to sleep. In what seemed like minutes, he woke to hear shouts. He ran up the stairs.

The master shouted 'It's an English cutter. We must

run for it.' He saw a burst of light coming from the east. A chain shot shredded the mainsail. The sail became limp. The vessel immediately slowed.

'Too late. Lower the sails or we'll be sunk.' Another ball splashed into the water short of the bows. The schooner wallowed in the water. He saw the cutter emerge from the eastern gloom and came alongside, marines aiming muskets at the master and his crew. An English voice shouted through a megaphone.

'We will board to inspect your papers and cargo.' So, this was the British blockade in action. *It would be bizarre if his mission came to an end if he was arrested by his own side.* Robertson looked at the panicked master.

'I doubt the British commander will speak German. Do you have French?'

The master shook his head.

'I have reasonable French; perhaps I can translate?'

'Please.'

A sub-lieutenant leading the boarding party clambered up onto the poop deck. He addressed the master in anglicised French.

'Papers, Captain.' Robertson stepped forward.

Using French with a Bavarian accent, he said, 'The captain has no French and asks me to translate.'

'Very well. I require his papers. He is to tell me what he is transporting.'

A three-way conversation began. It was a mixed cargo, the master explained: kitchenware, crockery, wine, reams of paper and other hardware. The sub-lieutenant read through the proffered manifest.

'Take three men and check, Mr Mate.' Looking around the schooner's rotting timbers, he shouted across to the cutter. 'God's death, no prize money here. She's in a desperate condition.'

Robertson debated if he should take the opportunity to send a message to MacKenzie but discarded the idea. He needed to keep his cover in place. A shout in English from below.

'Gunpowder, sir, disguised in wine barrels.'

The sub-lieutenant motioned the marines to aim their muskets at the master and his mate.

'Well, this is very serious, Captain. I am sanctioned to sink all smugglers. Vessel, cargo and crew.' Robertson translated. The master turned ashen. Robertson had to think fast or his whole mission would be over. He would only reveal his true identity as a matter of last resort. He looked at the Englishman.

'Sir, the captain and his men are only trying to make a living in these dangerous times. I am sure that he was forced to smuggle the gunpowder. Why not confiscate his cargo and let them return to port? It will be the merchant who will suffer the loss not these poor sailors. If you sink their vessel, they will have no way of earning a living to support their families. The word will surely spread across all of the Baltic ports, that the Royal Navy has no fight with merchant seamen but does with those who smuggle to her enemies. Surely that message will be a powerful deterrent?'

The officer paused. 'A cogent argument and well put. Let me discuss the matter with my commander. Looking at the rotting timbers, this would not make much as a prize.'

Twenty minutes later, the sub-lieutenant was back on the poop deck.

'Your argument has won the day, Herr Rorauer.' The English sailors began emptying the hold. It seemed that the cargo was much more valuable than the ancient vessel.

At dawn the next day, the empty vessel made its way back up the Kiel Fjord. Robertson did not want to be present when awkward questioning began when the ship arrived in Kiel. He asked to be transferred to a passing wherry. The master was effusive in his thanks. Robertson hadn't the heart to ask for his money back.

An hour later he was breakfasting in Kiel. As he ate, another salesman asked if he could sit at his table. Cold meats, bread, cheese and jam arrived. Robertson took the opportunity to ask advice of the best way to travel to Funen.

'Probably best across the Little Belt to Assens.' Robertson remembered studying the map.

'And worth avoiding the poste-chaise system – too many stops, too many inspections if you get my drift.'

'What do you suggest?'

'Common practice to rent a coach and horse from local farmers. Cheaper too. Works well.'

Robertson liked the idea of informality and, particularly, fewer inspections. He finished breakfast, paid and thanked his fellow salesman. The innkeeper ordered a carriage.

By nightfall he was eating a simple supper in a farmhouse near Schleswig. The next morning the farmer drove to the small port of Arosund. At the post office, he coded a letter to MacKenzie to be sent via Scheller.

Wishing to avoid likely inspections on the regular ferry to Funen he found a quiet cove. A fishing boat was moored close enough for Robertson to hail the skipper. The skipper spoke German with a broad Schleswig dialect making conversation all but impossible. A fee of one gold dollar to take him to Funen was finally agreed. Luggage stowed, they sailed first to the little island of Aro and then the two-hour journey across the Little Belt to Assens. As they left Aro, Robertson attempted to engage the skipper. Any intelligence could prove valuable. But either the man did not want to talk or more likely he simply did not understand Robertson's Bavarian German. He gave up and turned to survey the low-lying islands to the north and Funen gradually coming closer. Apart from the slap of the waves on the hull, silence.

A tap on his shoulder; the skipper offered Robertson bread and sausage. A small flagon was placed on the boards by his feet. The skipper indicated that he should clamp his feet to hold the bottle steady. As the smack moved further into the Little Belt, the sea began to develop more of a swell. The breeze stiffened. The skipper returned to the tiller, untied it and resumed his morose attitude.

As he chewed on the sausage, Robertson's mind drifted back to that day in September when he took his vows. Was it really thirty years ago that he had begun his surrender to the mercy and grace that comes from God, committing to the rules of St Benedict: stability, fidelity and obedience to monastic life? What would life have been like if he had led an ordinary life? His mind wandered to Frau Muller and the softness of a lady's touch.

Robertson needed liquid to wash down the dry bread and fatty sausage. He reached down, lifted the flagon, took out the cork stopper, put the flagon to his lips and drew a mouthful. As soon as the liquid began travelling down his throat, he spat. Firewater. He had drunk plenty of schnapps in his time, but this – he turned to see the skipper smiling. Next time, just a sip.

Turning to face the bows once again, now he had time to think, here was the conundrum. How could he resolve his current mission with the vows he had taken those years ago? Here he was, a spy in disguise, supposedly happy to lie and cheat to ensure the success of his mission. Whatever it took to protect the seminary and ultimately his Faith.

He did not hear the skipper approach. Another tap on the shoulder. Robertson looked up. The skipper was pointing. The low outline of the island was now close.

Funen at last.

31
Hotel Godewind, Tonningen

Marquet and his men had ridden hard. He estimated that they could cover the 130 kilometres in around seven hours. They might just reach Tonningen in time to meet the ship carrying the English agent from Heligoland. To be on the quayside as it docked – Marquet would savour the moment!

The change of horses in the old town of Itzhoe had gone well. They pushed on and reached the outskirts of Heide. It hardly looked much more than a village. A detachment of what looked like Danish cavalry approached and blocked the road. Not for the first time, Marquet pulled out his identification papers and authority to travel. A Danish major emerged from the melee of horses and raised his hand. Marquet turned to his German-speaking corporal.

'Come with me.' He urged his horse on to meet the

major. He asked the corporal if he knew which unit the Danes belonged to.

'I don't recognise their uniform. They are probably local militia, sir.'

Marquet inwardly groaned. No doubt the major would be full of his own importance, guaranteed to cause trouble and more importantly, delay. He rode up to the major, saluted and with the corporal translating explained his mission.

'We are on urgent state business going to Tonningen to arrest a British spy,' and then he instantly regretted telling the major the purpose of his mission.

The major replied, 'Thank you, Captain. Tonningen comes under my jurisdiction. If there are any arrests to be made, it is I who shall make them.'

Marquet bit his lip. As predicted, a jobsworth who would do everything by the book.

'Major, we have ridden from Hamburg and must reach Tonningen in the next two hours to meet the ship that we believe is carrying this man. We must leave immediately, with or without you and your men.'

'That is impossible, Captain. You must come to Heide so that I can properly inspect your papers and confirm your authority.'

'Major, you do not seem to understand the urgency. We must leave now. Surely you can complete the paperwork once we reach Tonningen?'

'Captain, you are in Denmark now. We have rules that must be obeyed. You must come with me.'

Marquet fumed in silence. He toyed with the idea

of shooting the major and blasting his way through the major's men. They were just amateurs. At the slightest threat of ball and blade, they would surely turn and run. While that might ensure that they were able to reach the town in time, the consequences of shooting an ally would prove awkward. While he could be sure of Colonel Maupont's backing, the wider ramifications were just not worth risking.

'Very well, Major, but may I ask you to exercise the utmost urgency.'

Two hours later, Marquet and his men rode out of Heide accompanied by a troop of the militia. Exactly as he predicted, the major made a great show of inspecting Marquet's documentation, some of which was in French. The major refused to allow Marquet's corporal to interpret. Instead, he sent for the schoolmaster. The schoolmaster refused to stop his lesson – more delay. Finally, the major was satisfied. Marquet asked if the major would accompany him to Tonningen to witness the arrest. No, the major replied. He and his wife were hosting a dinner party, and he must return home to prepare. Marquet bit his lip again.

The ride to Tonningen was painfully slow. The militia men were incompetent horsemen on poor quality nags. Finally, they reached the town, found the head of police who took them to the harbourmaster. The vessel had docked well over four hours ago. The policeman had personally inspected the passengers' passports. All were in order.

'Who were they?' demanded Marquet.

There were only three. Two locals who had been visiting relatives on Heligoland and a German traveller. He must be the agent.

With the corporal translating, Marquet demanded 'Tell me about him.'

'He was about thirty years old, slim, tall with light brown hair. I thought his accent was rather odd. He certainly didn't come from northern Germany. It was as if German was not his first language.'

'Why do you say that?'

'He seemed to stumble over words.'

'Did you ask him what his business was or where he was going?'

'I did. He was rather diffident. That was when he struggled over the language. But he did say that his business took him north into Jutland.'

'Did he say where?'

'Aarhus.'

'How far is that?'

'About 250 kilometres.'

'How was he going to travel?'

'He hired a four-wheeled carriage with two horses. It seemed that he had plenty of money.'

'Where would he change horses?'

'Flensburg, Haderslev and Fredericia.'

To travel in such an expensive manner was more evidence that this man was more than just a merchant. Marquet was sure he was on to a professional British spy.

The interviews of the vessel's captain and first mate provided nothing. Marquet was reminded of the surly, uncommunicative Neuwerk residents. These two were the same. He had the distinct impression that the harbourmaster and policeman were too familiar with the sailors: part of the smuggling network? No matter, he had the agent in his sights. That could wait until the morning. He penned a report to Maupont. Tomorrow he would continue the journey north.

Two days of hard riding brought Marquet and his troop to Fredericia. Travelling in Danish-speaking country necessitated a local to smooth his path. Fortunately, Colonel Terry of the 23rd Regiment of Dragoons based in Haderslev provided fresh horses and a Danish militiaman, who spoke Danish and German; not ideal but a necessity. The policeman in Tonningen had been right. The Englishman had changed horses as predicted. He had moved fast. Marquet felt sure that he must be catching up. After all, the agent couldn't know he was being chased. They came to the coaching inn. Marquet, the corporal and the Dane entered.

The innkeeper was beside himself with excitement. Just two hours ago, a German merchant had arrived, entered the bar and asked to change horses. The merchant then began a conversation with a group of Spanish officers who had been enjoying a drink. The innkeeper thought they might have been speaking French. Out of nothing, a fracas. The merchant was pinioned and marched from the inn.

Marquet asked if the innkeeper knew what the argument had been about. The man shook his head. He did not understand the language. Now the agent was in Spanish hands, more complication. He consulted the notes he had taken to check if there was a French unit based locally. The 19th Regiment of Infantry of the Line was based in the town, Colonel Benoit Regis-Manet commanding. The innkeeper informed him that the regiment's headquarters were in the town's fort.

Thirty minutes later, Marquet was saluting Colonel Regis-Manet. The colonel invited Marquet to sit and take a glass of wine. It galled him to note that the colonel was probably ten years younger than him, such were the penalties of noble birth and the consequential slow or zero promotion prospects in the new France.

'How can I help, Captain?'

Marquet explained his mission, the journey and finally the news that the agent had been captured by Spanish officers.

'Do you know why he was arrested?'

'No, sir.'

'Well, we had better find out.' He summoned his adjutant and instructed him to find the Spanish liaison officer attached to the 19th Regiment. While they waited for the Spaniard, the colonel explained that the nearest Spanish troops were the Guadalajara Regiment based in Skanderborg, four hours to the north. The officers in the coaching inn were probably returning from a liaison meeting with the commander-in-chief based on the island of Funen.

'Colonel, I cannot stress enough how important the capture of this agent will be.'

'Then we will stop the Spaniards and their prisoner immediately.'

The Spanish liaison officer was instructed.

'Take a troop of my gendarmes with you. When you have your man, bring him here. The fort has an ideal suite of dungeons. Good hunting.'

Marquet saluted, gathered his troop and with the Spaniard by his side, galloped out of the town. His luck changed. Outside the village of Egeskov, there were the Spanish officers making gentle progress. They rode up to the group. In the middle, hands tied behind his back, was his quarry.

Marquet saluted. The senior officer was a lieutenant-colonel. Through the liaison officer, he introduced himself.

'Colonel, may I congratulate you on the capture of this man. May I ask why you have arrested him?'

The colonel replied in excellent French. 'Captain, I am Don Antonio Retana of the Guadalajara Regiment. Why are you interested in this man?'

Marquet thought quickly. He had heard that the Spanish officer class could be arrogant and haughty. He would have to proceed with care. The colonel might easily take offence. If that happened and an argument ensued, to obtain the transfer of the spy would become nigh on impossible.

'Colonel, I am here at the command of Marshal Bernadotte, the Prince of Ponte Corvo. We have strong reason to believe that this man is an English spy and an enemy of the state. He landed in Tonningen yesterday from Heligoland. There is no doubt that his mission is to foment rebellion among the Emperor's subjects. The marshal instructs that all spies are to be taken to Hamburg for investigation.'

Silence. Retana looked up at the cloudless sky, then focused on his prisoner. The man said nothing but shook his head, wide eyes as if pleading not to be handed over to the French. Retana turned to Marquet.

'Captain, I am an admirer of revolutionary France. Spain needs to modernise. What has been achieved in France is remarkable. We should do well to follow. If this man is a danger to France, you should interrogate him. To answer your question: the man approached us and asked to be taken to General La Romana. I asked him why he wished to see the general. He said that what he had to say was for the general's ears only. I then told him that my superior was General Kindelan and that he could speak with him. The man refused, insisting that he must talk with La Romana and him alone. I and my colleagues found this suspicious. We therefore arrested him and would have taken him to General Kindelan. Please take him off my hands. His luggage is with my corporal.'

It appeared that the prisoner understood Retana's French. His shoulders slumped, his head dropped, chin resting on his chest. Marquet looked at the prisoner – a perfect illustration of resigned guilt.

'Thank you, Colonel. I am delighted to assist. It is good that such close allies cooperate so closely. May I ask, was the luggage inspected?'

The colonel called one of his officers and spoke to him in Spanish.

'The luggage was inspected. My captain intended to make a closer examination when we arrive at headquarters.'

'Were any letters found, sir?'

The colonel spoke to the captain again who shook his head. He snapped his fingers. The tied man was brought forward to Marquet's men. A corporal handed over the man's luggage.

'Thank you, Colonel. I shall report this example of cooperation to my colonel who will, I'm sure, bring it to the marshal's notice. Bidding you a safe journey.' He called to his men to come to attention and present arms, saluted the colonel and wheeled away to begin the journey south.

Marquet could feel the exhilaration course though his veins. He had his man, or at least one of them.

An hour later, Marquet was sitting in Colonel Regis-Manet's office, a glass of cognac in his hand. The spy was languishing in one of the dungeons in the bowels of the fort. Despite repeated questioning and physical persuasion, he had remained silent. Not a word of protest. Had he been innocent, he would surely have protested. He had been stripped. Every item of his clothing had been minutely examined for concealed paper. His suit was taken apart; collars, cuffs, lapels, every possible hiding place was examined. Nothing was found. The man's clothes were now unwearable. He was given a redundant uniform of a private of the 19th Regiment to preserve his dignity.

An initial examination of the luggage had revealed a small leather bag containing a large number of gold francs. Currency for a merchant or to pay the expenses of a spy? The other items, clothing and the accoutrements of a traveller did not seem to be out of the ordinary. Where, therefore were the man's passport and identification papers? He must have hidden them before talking to the

Spaniards in the inn. Marquet had taken ten of his men and returned to the inn. The welcome from the innkeeper now assumed the surly attitude that seemed to be common practice. Had the man given him anything? Had he seen the man hide anything; a briefcase, for example? The innkeeper had not. Marquet had ordered one of his men to find the innkeeper's wife and servants. Once assembled, the same questions were put to each, one at a time and singly. No one had seen anything. A thorough search had been made of the inn without success. Some gentle hauling of the innkeeper's arm behind and up his back produced howls of pain from the innkeeper and copious tears from his wife and the female servants. Again, nothing.

Marquet sipped a cognac. He asked the colonel.

'May I avail myself and my men of your hospitality tonight? We will then return to Hamburg with our captive. I will then hand him over to our specialist interrogators.'

'Of course, Captain. I shall look forward to your company at dinner when we can talk about more pleasant matters. I shudder to think what your friends in Hamburg have in store for your prisoner.'

'That is exactly what I had in mind, my dear Colonel. If you will excuse me, I would like to tell our prisoner what lies in store for him. May I fill my glass and take one for the spy? You never know, a more friendly approach may produce the desired result.'

'Help yourself. Until dinner.'

A sergeant led the way down to the dungeon. Tar torches belched out black smoke above yellow flames. Marquet raised his elbow across his mouth but failed to prevent the toxins hitting the back of his throat. From the ceiling, there were constant drips of tar-laden water which splattered his coat. He shouted to the corporal following.

'For God's sake, keep napkins over the glasses.'

'Yes, sir.'

The air cleared as the three reached the dungeon but changed to a stench emanating from the cells. Marquet put his hand up to cover his mouth and nose. A mix of excrement, urine, damp and rat droppings assailed him. He gagged.

'Open the cell.'

The jailer emerged from the shadows and opened the spy hatch, shouting 'Stand back, vermin.' He slid the bolts and opened the oak door. The stench wafting from the cell was much, much worse. Marquet gagged again.

'Cognac.' The corporal uncovered one of the glasses. Marquet took a pull. Better.

The jailer led the way into the cell, his torch lighting the pitch-black. No window. Not even a grille to allow in fresh air. The prisoner was sitting on the stone floor, knees drawn up to his chest, arms wrapped round his shins. The private's uniform was already filthy. Despite the gloom, Marquet could see that the cell was bare, not a stick of furniture. The smell coming from a leather bucket in a corner showed that it had already been used. The prisoner's face was a mass of scratches and bruises. From its angle, it looked as though one of his little fingers was broken. He did not look up as Marquet entered. The jailer grabbed the prisoner's chin forcing his head upwards. The back of his head smashed against the cell wall. A grunt from the man.

The jailer hissed, 'Look at the captain, vermin.' It seemed the man had difficulty in focusing.

'Enough. Get him to his feet. Take him out of the cell and find him a chair.' The jailer looked surprised but did as he was ordered. The man had to be supported and dragged to a chair in the dungeon's hall. He slumped, arms hanging down, chin on chest.

'Give him some cognac,' Marquet ordered. The jailor wrenched back the prisoner's head and forced his mouth open. The corporal poured the liquor down the man's throat. He had a violent coughing fit. The cognac seemed to have revived him.

'More.' Marquet watched as the corporal administered more liquor. The prisoner raised his head and looked at Marquet. Was there thanks in the dull eyes?

Marquet pulled up another chair, sat and waited. Nothing from the prisoner.

'Mr English Spy, for that is what you are. You may think that silence will buy you time. But time for what? Rescue? Impossible. You may think that what you have experienced down here has been, how shall I describe it, uncomfortable? Let me tell you that I have seen the results of our interrogators in Hamburg; long, lingering pain inflicted so many different ways, ways you would never imagine. It is an art form, believe me. And the results: a thousand times worse than today. What is most impressive is their ability to keep their subjects alive so that they can start all over again. They have their subjects begging to be put to death. But that will not happen because after Hamburg, you will be taken to Paris. The experts in Paris regard their colleagues in Hamburg as bumbling amateurs.'

Marquet waited for what he had told the man to sink in. The prisoner's head slumped onto his chest.

'More cognac.' The process was repeated. The man's eyes met Marquet's.

Marquet smiled. 'Good, I can see that you are beginning to understand the hopelessness of your situation. There really is no need to put yourself through any more of this unpleasantness. Answer a few questions and I can promise you a future. Let us start with your name.'

No reaction.

'More cognac?'

No reaction. The man's chin slumped back onto his chest.

'Oh dear. Well, I'll be kind. A minute should be long enough to help you make up your mind.' Marquet reached for his pocket watch.

'One minute from now.' Marquet stood, went over to the corporal and took a sip from his cognac glass.

Silence. The seconds ticked away. Marquet looked at the sergeant who raised his eyebrows with a look of resignation. Marquet shrugged his shoulders. 'Ten seconds, nine, eight... three, two, one. Right, throw him back in the cell, but...' looking at the jailer, '...don't touch him. I want him ready for our friends in Hamburg.'

The jailor yanked the man out of his chair, dragging him back into the cell. The smell became even worse. Marquet noted a brown stain on the back of the prisoner's trousers. He turned to walk back up the stairs. Time for a change and dinner.

'Captain.' The voice came from the cell, weak. Marquet turned. Louder now. 'Captain.' He walked back to the cell.

'Yes, Mr English Spy?'

'I am Irish.' The man's French had a strange accent. It sounded slightly Breton to Marquet. He turned to the jailor.

'Put him back on the chair.'

The jailor spat at Marquet. 'Make your bloody mind up.'

Marquet exploded. 'One more word from you and I'll have you in a punishment battalion within the hour.' The jailor's eyes burned with hatred. He grabbed the Irishman by the shoulders, dragged him and threw him on the chair.

The Irishman raised his head. 'I will talk but only to you alone, Captain.'

'Leave us,' Marquet ordered. The dungeon cleared. 'You have one more minute.'

The man looked straight at Marquet.

'I am Charles McMahon. I am an Irish patriot. I was able to convince the British that I was a reliable agent. I was carrying letters from the British Government to General La Romana. The letters offered to transport the general and his troops on British naval ships back to Spain or any other destination the general might choose.'

Marquet was stunned. It took time for the implications of what this McMahon had said to sink in. First, he needed some proof.

'Where are the letters?'

'I hid them in the roof thatch of the inn's privy before I spoke with the Spanish – just in case things went wrong. As it turned out, they did.' McMahon gave a wry smile.

'Where exactly?' McMahon told him. Marquet shouted for the corporal and the jailor.

'Corporal, take three men and recover the letters.' Looking down at McMahon, he said, 'Tell the corporal exactly where to find the letters.' McMahon did so.

'And you, jailor, clean our guest up, bandage his hand, give him more clothes, water and something to eat, put him in a clean cell with table, chair and a cot. Give him paper, pen and a candle. Then lock the door.' Marquet looked at McMahon.

'As for you, Mr Spy, we'll see if these letters exist and, if they do, whether the contents are what you tell me. God help you if they do not. While we wait for the letters, you will spend the rest of the evening writing down the instructions that the British gave to you and from whom you received them. Understood?'

A nod.

Marquet climbed the stairs. Outside he took gulps of fresh air. Why had the man not come clean in the first place? He could have avoided all the pain. Very strange.

32
The Foreign Office, July 1808

Hoppner was standing in front of Mr Rolleston's desk. The senior clerk looked up.

'Hoppner, the Cabinet has approved the Foreign Secretary's proposal. We will now commence planning how to transport the Marquis de La Romana and his troops from Denmark. You will be our liaison with the Admiralty, the War Office and the Transport Board.'

'Yes, sir.' It would be fascinating to listen to the planning of a naval operation. He was reminded of the success of the operation to Copenhagen just eleven months before. He had heard that the navy had transported nearly 27,000 troops to Denmark in August and brought them home safely together with most of the ships of the Danish Navy and stores valued at £320,000.

'May I ask why plans are to be put in place now when we do not know if the marquis will agree to accept our offer or indeed if his troops will obey him?'

'With the commitment to transport General Wellesley's forces to Portugal, there is a shortage of available transport ships. It will take time to hire, equip and position them for the voyage across the North Sea. As to La Romana, you may know that two deputies of the Junta of Asturia have escaped from Spain and have arrived in London. It was their letters to the marquis that McMahon was carrying. They were accompanied by a Spanish naval officer. It is planned that he should accompany our fleet to liaise with the Spanish troops once La Romana has assented.'

Hoppner was tempted to ask what would happen if the marquis continued to refuse the offer but thought better of it. A tongue lashing was the likely result.

'Walk up to the Admiralty and ask for Henry Temple, Viscount Palmerston. He's only twenty-four so two years your senior. In the year he's been the civil commissioner to the Admiralty, he has made a good impression and is already marked out for greater things. Temple will look after you and guide you through the politicking that will, no doubt, go on between these three departments. It will be an education.' Rolleston laughed. 'Oh, and by the way, he's a Harrow man, not Eton, I'm afraid.'

Rolleston waved Hoppner out. As he left, Hoppner turned.

'And McMahon, sir?'

'I wondered how long it would take you to ask. As I suspected, we were too late to stop him. He had already left Heligoland for Tonningen. What vetting there was seems to have failed.'

Hoppner smiled to himself. *When the man at the top*

says something is true, then all his minions agree it must be.

'Is he a suspect?'

'We do not know but our friends in the Alien Office have increased their surveillance of the French royalist emigré community. Word may have been sent of McMahon's departure. Enough of them swear loyalty to the French Crown but, either by compulsion or by desire, spy for France.'

'Compulsion?'

'Imagine the pressure put on them by their families in France – threats, imprisonment and ultimately execution.'

'But how do they send their information?'

'In one of the Kent ports, an Alien Office inspector had the responsibility of checking the papers and passports of all entrants to the port. Through sources in Paris, our friends in the Alien Office discovered that the inspector was allowing French agents into the country and sanctioning secret messages to be sent from French agents based in England back to France. He was paid 11,000 francs for his services. He was arrested. He was "persuaded" to work for us. He is closely controlled, allowing us knowledge of French agents arriving in England and to read all secret correspondence being sent to Paris. It is probable that if McMahon is working for Paris, French agents based in London will notify the minister of police, Fouche, of his journey to Denmark.'

'Surely we cannot take the risk that McMahon may be working for Paris?'

'It is certainly a difficult call. However, we must protect

our secret sources. In any case, it is possible that French counter-intelligence may not believe McMahon. They may regard him as an English agent sent to stir up trouble between La Romana and his French allies. However, McMahon's statement raises doubts about his veracity. Our friends in the Alien Office are checking their records for evidence of his links to the United Ireland movement. Given the history goes back ten years, it may well take time.'

'And if the evidence condemns McMahon, will it not be too late?'

'Then our friends in Hamburg can provide Marshal Bernadotte with enough evidence to sow doubt about McMahon's allegiances.'

Hoppner shuddered. 'If so, his chances of survival are miniscule.'

'Spying is a dirty business.'

'And the Reverend Robertson?'

'No news.'

'God help him.'

33

Assens, on the West Coast of Funen

As the small town of Assens came in view, the skipper pulled the tiller taking the boat away from the harbour aiming for a deserted beach to the north of the town. Alarmed, Robertson shouted. 'No, no, take me to the harbour!'

He pointed towards the town quay. He wanted to be landed where all passengers arrived. To be spotted landing on a deserted beach would instantly create suspicion, as would the walk into the town carrying luggage. Normality was required to maintain his guise as a bona fide merchant. To arrive on a fishing boat at the quayside might be regarded strangely.

The skipper shook his head. '*Nein.*' Robertson did his best to persuade him to change direction. More money changed hands. The skipper swung the tiller round back towards Assens. He insisted that Robertson hide under a tarpaulin until the boat was tucked under the quayside wall.

Once the boat had been tied, the skipper uncovered him. He looked round. The harbour was deserted. Robertson climbed the steps up to the quay. Two townsmen told him that the Postgarten was the only hotel in Assens. Directions were easy. As he made his way up the main street, he passed a large group of locals walking determinedly. It seemed like a demonstration. Such was the size of the crowd, Robertson had to pull into a doorway. Another man was doing the same. Robertson asked him what was happening.

The man pointed. 'You see the lady in the middle of the crowd, the one being comforted?'

Robertson nodded.

'She is Peter Willemoes's mother. Her husband is the one comforting her. They have just been to the mayor's office to protest at the government's refusal to move their son's grave from Odden on Zealand back to his birthplace, here in Assens. They are now marching to the church to ask for the minister's support.'

From the man's tone, it was obvious that this Peter Willemoes had been some sort of celebrity. He would have to structure his next question carefully.

'I have only just arrived in Assens and have been travelling extensively. It is most remiss, but who was Peter Willemoes?'

The man turned in astonishment. 'You have never heard of our naval hero? He was a celebrity throughout Denmark and northern Germany. Where have you been?'

It was a look of genuine amazement not of suspicion. Relieved, Robertson explained that he had been in Bavaria.

'That explains it. Willemoes distinguished himself commanding a floating battery during the battle of Copenhagen seven years ago. He was only seventeen. He became a celebrity with ladies of the Court in Copenhagen copying his curly hair. Four months ago, he was serving on our last battleship when it was cornered by a much superior British force and driven on to a sandbar at Zealand Point. Poor Willemoes was shot through the head and died in the arms of his second in command.' The man spat. 'The bastard British have driven us into the arms of the bloody French. Now we have French, Dutch and even Spanish troops camped all over Denmark. Who pays for their board and lodging? We do. When we try to trade with the rest of the world, our ships are stopped, boarded by the British and our goods confiscated. Truly we are stuck between a rock and a hard place.'

Avoid becoming embroiled in politics, a messy and possibly dangerous path.

'A tragedy for the family. Will the government accede to his parents' demands?'

'Who knows? Maybe they can apply pressure on the King through the local nobility? But he has his hands full.'

The crowd had moved off to the church. Robertson thanked the man and resumed his walk to the hotel. He stopped, bent to adjust a boot, turned. The man had gone. If he needed any further evidence of how the British were regarded, here was a stark warning. Remember, he was a German salesman looking for business.

He found the hotel, walls painted primrose, and entered. On signing the register, the innkeeper told him that he must produce his passport to the officer commanding the local yeomanry. He pointed. The officer was sitting drinking coffee. Robertson handed his passport for inspection.

The officer looked up. 'But where is the entry stamp when you arrived in Denmark? All passports must be stamped at the border.'

He'd always been quick thinking. 'It is not my fault if the customs officers do not ask me for my passport. It was probably because I had taken a short route to avoid unnecessary expense.'

The officer shrugged. 'Typical of the slapdash attitude of some of our people.'

Robertson sensed an opportunity to divert the conversation away from his passport.

'From your accent, you don't seem to be Danish?'

'I'm Hanoverian but have been serving in the Danish Army for some time. Have you travelled from Hanover?'

'Indeed, I have.'

'Then pull up a chair, have a coffee and tell me the news of home.'

Robertson spent a convivial half an hour with the officer, glad that being seen with the officer helped build his acceptance. His passport was duly validated. He returned to the innkeeper and talked through his catalogue. The innkeeper wrote out orders for wine and cigars. Just the evidence that he needed to prove that he was a travelling salesman.

Robertson asked: 'I would like to try my luck with the Spanish troops camped locally. How have you found them since they were posted here?'

The innkeeper smiled and looked up at Robertson: 'When they first arrived, we were all terrified and our women and children fled. We barricaded ourselves in our cellars. They were a terrifying sight, columns of men with dark skin and hair and black eyes that contrasted with the whiteness of their teeth. They were magnificent but nothing like the French troops we had seen. Rumours abounded that they were cannibals!

'But as we have become used to them, we have grown friendly with them. Some of the Spaniards have learnt a few words of German, so we are able to converse. They show great fondness to our children and have helped our community in many ways. On Sundays, we admire the reverence with which the Spaniards hold solemn Mass. As there is no Catholic church, the service is held outside and conducted by a regimental chaplain assisted by choirboys, the officers and their wives in their finery, the women adorned with mantillas. The men form around a temporary altar, kneeling bareheaded with their muskets in their right hands. The sound of the regimental band playing completes a magnificent spectacle.

'When they are off duty, they play cards, cook the wildlife they have caught and smoke. And do they smoke. I hardly see any of them without a cigarette in the corner of his mouth.

'We shall be sorry to see them go, despite the contribution we have to make to the cost of accommodating them.'

The innkeeper leaned towards Robertson and whispered, 'Unlike their supposed allies, the French. Did you hear what happened at Flensburg a couple of weeks ago?'

Robertson shook his head. The innkeeper continued in a whisper.

'French troops camped nearby came into the town and got drunk. Their behaviour was disgusting particularly to the women. The mayor called out the guard to drive the French out. The guard was no match for the French veterans. Many of our men were killed and wounded. It was only with the arrival of French officers accompanied by a large detachment of military police, that peace was restored.'

He made a gesture. Robertson thought he was about to spit. He looked around the inn at the other guests. None seemed to be taking an interest in their conversation. It just seemed from the innkeeper's demeanour that there might be an informer lurking. He ate supper early and retired to his room.

At breakfast the next morning, he saw that one of the dining room tables was occupied by an elderly officer and his staff. He watched and listened as they finished breakfast and lit cigars and cigarettes: Spanish.

Robertson made his way to their table. Addressing the elderly officer in French, he said, 'Sir, can you assist me? I am Adam Rorauer, a merchant from Hamburg. I am a purveyor of the finest cigars, chocolate and wine. I have heard that you and your colleagues in the Division del Norte are very short of cigars and chocolate. I wonder if you would be interested?'

The elderly officer looked up at Robertson. '*Que?*'

Another of the officers spoke. 'The colonel is rather deaf. You will have to speak up. Just a minute.' The officer rose and moved to the colonel's side. He bent to what was the colonel's good ear and spoke in Spanish. The colonel nodded. The officer retrieved the colonel's ear trumpet. A conversation could begin.

Robertson explained how he could possibly make the colonel's life more tolerable. The colonel began to ramble.

'My name is San Roman, I command the second battalion of the Princess Regiment of the Line and report to the regiment's commander, Colonel Conde de San Romain. My troops are stationed across south-west Funen with the other battalions based around Nyborg, Kerteminde and Middelfart. There is another battalion of infantry from the Barcelona Regiment stationed around Svenborg and dragoons, artillery and a company of sappers also on Funen.'

Why the colonel was giving a mere merchant this information, Robertson had no idea. *Keep quiet, listen.* He just hoped he would be able to remember for a report to MacKenzie.

The colonel continued, listing the troops stationed on Jutland, Zealand and the island of Langeland. He then suddenly changed tack.

'Of course, when we left Spain and Italy, we were over 18,000 strong. But now with desertion, fatigue and illness we are only 15,000 and surrounded by Danish and French troops. Here on Funen, they are headquartered in Odense. I am tired, sick of the cold climate and strange food. We all wish to see our homeland again. What makes matters worse is we have no news from home. We used to receive regular mail from our families and newspapers to keep up with events at home. The French seem to have intercepted all correspondence.'

His fellow officers nodded in agreement. Perhaps the old man would finally arrive at the point of his ramble.

'Therefore, Herr Rorauer, you most certainly can make our lives a little more tolerable by supplying us with chocolate and cigars, reminders of home. At least we are all better paid here than at home, courtesy of our French colleagues. Before you visit our other camps, I suggest that you make yourself known to the general.'

'The general?'

'His Excellency the Marquis de La Romana. You will find him and his staff at the hotel Postgarten in Nyborg. Now we must attend to our duties. My adjutant will provide you with our orders.'

The colonel made his way out of the dining room. As he reached the door, he turned.

'A thought: before you arrive at Nyborg, my good friend, Colonel Borellas of the Barcelona Regiment, is a lover of fine cigars. He has his headquarters at Svendborg, slightly further than the direct road to Nyborg. You will, I'm sure, do good business with the colonel and his fellow officers. I'll write you a letter of introduction.'

'Thank you, Colonel.'

Robertson watched the officers leave the dining room. As soon as they had left, he returned to his room. He wrote out the list of all the Spanish dispositions that he could remember and coded another letter to MacKenzie. The Postgarten in Nyborg was the hotel recommended by his hosts just a few days ago. But what to do about the colonel's request that he should detour to Svendborg?

He went downstairs. The adjutant's order was on the desk. Writing out as fair copy, he addressed the order to the merchant in Hamburg and gave it together with the letter for MacKenzie addressed to the Hamburg post office, to the innkeeper for posting. He then asked about the respective journey times to Nyborg via Ringe or Svendborg.

The innkeeper fired a quizzical look at Robertson.

'But the most direct route to Nyborg is to go through Odense. The roads are much better. Why do you want the discomfort?' The innkeeper paused. 'Perhaps it's because you wish to avoid the French?'

Robertson could have kicked himself. Why on earth had he invited suspicion once again? He decided to ignore the question.

'Colonel San Roman has suggested I divert to Colonel Borellas in Svendborg. He has given me a letter of introduction. I can hardly miss such a profitable opportunity! How much longer will my journey take?'

The innkeeper smiled. 'A morning's journey direct but a full day via Svendborg. By the time you've done your business with Colonel Borellas, you'll have to stay the night there.'

Robertson thanked the innkeeper. Best to stay on friendly terms. He weighed up the options. The next time the colonel and Borellas met, they were sure to talk about cigars. They would both find it very strange if Rorauer had not followed up the letter of introduction. What salesman of any quality would turn down such a gold-plated opportunity – more than strange, it would be downright suspicious. It would cost him a valuable day, maybe two. There was no alternative. He would have to divert to Svendborg. Time to pack. He made it to the foot of the staircase.

'*Señor.*' Robertson turned. A young Spanish lieutenant approached him. The Spaniard had been one of the officers sitting at Colonel San Roman's table. Robertson had noted that he was wearing a different uniform to the others, but with the same swarthy complexion. All the Spaniards seemed to have the same facial hair style: neatly trimmed sideburns stretching well below the cheekbones, pencil moustache but clean-shaven chin.

'*Señor*, I am Lieutenant Antonio Fabregues of the Catalunya Regiment based on Langeland.' Fabregues's French was just intelligible. 'I am here to liaise with the colonel's staff.' Robertson's senses heightened, immediately on his guard. What now?

'We junior officers are starved of information. Can you please spare a few minutes of your valuable time to give me a picture of what is happening in the world beyond this small part of Denmark?'

Robertson looked at the young man. There seemed to be nothing more than innocent enquiry in his eyes. Best to take him at face value. Remember, the news he should give must be from a German perspective.

'I shall be leaving for Svendborg shortly, but let's take coffee.'

Fabregues peppered Robertson with questions. What was happening in Germany? What would Napoleon do next? Would he order the invasion of Sweden? Would the British intervene? And, it seemed as though Fabregues was holding back tears, what was happening in Spain and his home city, Barcelona?'

Robertson kept his answers as vague as he could, repeating what he had read in German and French newspapers. Fabregues's questions kept coming. Robertson put his hands up.

'Lieutenant, much as I would like to, I really cannot help you further. I am simply a merchant. Anything else I tell you would be pure speculation.' *As is most of what I've told you already*, he thought.

Fabregues looked at him.

'But Herr Rorauer, I can tell that you are very intelligent. You have travelled extensively. You know so much more than I do. But I have taken up too much of your time, thank you, sir.' He stood up. Robertson shook his extended hand. Another note to himself; *watch what you say.*

34

Cesar Rainville's Hotel, Altona, North of Hamburg

Marquet was enjoying a postprandial cognac with Colonel Regis-Manet when the corporal knocked, entered and saluted.

'We have them, Captain. They were cleverly hidden. Had we not known exactly where to look we would never have found them. Here are the letters and a passport.' He handed them to Marquet.

'Well done, Corporal. Extra cognac for you and your men.'

'Thank you, sir.' The corporal saluted, turned and left. Colonel Regis-Manet clapped.

'Congratulations, Captain – what a coup.'

Marquet studied the letters. The British Government seals were intact. They looked genuine. He opened the passport. This also looked authentic. It was issued in Hanover to a Fritz Murphy, a German/Irish travelling salesman. Very clever; the reader would understand the very Irish accent when McMahon was speaking French and presumably German. He returned to the letters. They were addressed to His Excellency General the Marquis de La Romana. What next? The letters would be written in Spanish. Marquet had very limited understanding of the language.

As if pre-empting Marquet's thoughts, Regis-Manet asked, 'Perhaps my Spanish liaison officer can help with the translation?'

Marquet fingered the letters. 'Thank you, Colonel. If our spy is to be believed, the contents are so sensitive that they should only be read by our people. I will take the letters to Altona where the Spanish speakers on the Prince's staff can read them.'

'A good point, Captain.'

***

The next morning, the sergeant presented McMahon's testimony. Marquet briefly scanned the pages. They were nearly illegible.

'He said that it was virtually impossible to write with a broken finger.' Marquet nodded. Perhaps the spy shouldn't have been treated so roughly.

'Have him properly cleaned up. Give him decent clothes and breakfast. Hire a closed carriage and have two men sit with him on the journey to Hamburg. If the men are asked who the prisoner is, they can tell the local people that he is an English spy. It will do them good to see what happens to enemy agents.'

The sergeant smiled and saluted. 'Yes, sir.'

As they journeyed south, Marquet debated how best to treat McMahon. By the time his retinue had arrived at the night's stop, he had made up his mind. He would take supper with the spy. He told the landlord he would take supper in his room. He would have a guest.

McMahon was brought to his room. Marquet debated whether he should have a guard in the room but decided that privacy was more important. He ordered the sergeant to station a gendarme outside the door, just in case the man turned violent.

'Now, Mr English Spy, sit down.'

McMahon interrupted. 'I told you. I am Irish. I hate the English.' The way the words spat out of the spy's mouth had the ring of truthfulness. Supper arrived. McMahon demolished his plateful. Marquet took more time of his food.

'So tell me, Mr Irish Spy, who gave you the instructions to take the letters to General La Romana?'

'Foreign minister George Canning.'

'Personally?' Marquet was incredulous but did his best to disguise his surprise. He took another mouthful.

'Yes, in the presence of the senior British Foreign Office official, Mr Hammond.' Silence as Marquet chewed.

'And tell me, how do the British come to trust you to carry such vital letters?'

'Because they believe that I have carried out other missions for them in the past.'

'And you have?'

'Yes, but nothing that would seriously damage the

Irish cause. I had to prove myself to them so that I would be entrusted with a vital mission such as this one.'

'Why didn't you tell us this before we began to hurt you?'

'I had hoped to escape and deliver the letters to La Romana, then let the general take the bait and expose him as the traitor he is.'

'How do you know that he would have accepted the British offer?'

'There were delegates of the Spanish juntas in London who briefed the British. They were sure that La Romana would align with the Spanish rebels.'

Marquet took another mouthful. How was he going to manage this bombshell? He watched McMahon take a sip of wine. His story was so incredible that it might just be true. On the other hand, if he turned out to be a charlatan, Marquet would become the laughing stock of Bernadotte's army. He rang the bell. A waiter entered. He ordered dessert.

'While we wait, tell me a little about yourself.'

'By all means.' McMahon told Marquet of his upbringing, the beginnings of his loathing of the English, his fighting for the Irish cause in the war for independence and his escape to France. The potted history struck Marquet as too glib, as if he had rehearsed the story many times before so that it came out word perfect. Perhaps the same words as he had trotted out to the foreign minister, Canning?

McMahon continued. 'After the failed uprising in Ireland, I fled to France where relatives introduced me to

Monsieur Talleyrand, the foreign minister. Talleyrand in turn presented me to General Bernadotte, then minister of war. Bernadotte had served in the *Regiment Royal de la Marine* which was commanded by another of my relatives. While in Hamburg some years later, I met secretary Schtick who took me to Bernadotte's headquarters in Hanover.'

'You know the Prince of Ponte Corvo?'

McMahon's "Oh, yes" came out in a matter-of-fact tone.

'We have kept in contact through his secretary, Schtick.'

Dessert was served. Again, McMahon wolfed down the pudding. Marquet took his time. This was now frankly becoming surreal. So ridiculous to be true? He would need time to collect his thoughts.

'Well Mr Irishman, I have enjoyed our discussion. We will have to validate your story. My Spanish-speaking colleagues will interpret those letters. This will take some time. Meanwhile, you understand that you will remain a prisoner until the truth has been established.'

'It is all true, Captain.'

Marquet's normally reliable policeman's nose had failed him. He just didn't know if he could believe some or all of this man's story.

***

As the journey to Hamburg continued the next morning, a French courier galloped into view.

'Captain Marquet?'

'Yes.'

The courier saluted. 'I have an urgent message from

Colonel Maupont. You are to come to Rainville's Hotel immediately.' The courier handed a note to Marquet. He recognised Maupont's writing. The note simply read: *Report to me immediately.*

Two hours later, covered in dust, he arrived at Bernadotte's headquarters. Handing the reins of his mount to the courier, he did what he could to shake off the dust. Up the stairs, into the hall, he was met by Maupont's adjutant who showed him to the colonel's room.

Maupont was sitting at his desk. He looked up as Marquet entered and saluted.

'Ah, Marquet, a good journey, I trust, though looking at the state of you, rather rushed.'

'Yes, sir, and successful, I hope.'

'Explain.'

Marquet handed the letters to Maupont who summoned his adjutant. Looking at Marquet, he said, 'They look real enough.'

'As I thought.'

Maupont turned to the adjutant. 'Ensure that these are opened with extreme care and have them translated immediately.'

'Yes, sir.'

When they were alone, Maupont asked, 'So you believe that this man, McMahon, is an Irish patriot masquerading as an English agent?'

'Whoever he is, his story is so outrageous it might be true.'

'Your report matches the reason for your summons here. Read this.'

Marquet read the letter. It was from the commissioner general of police in Antwerp, Jean-François Bellemare, addressed to the Prince of Ponte Corvo – Bernadotte. The commissioner informed Bernadotte that he had received intelligence from England that the British might make an attempt to remove some or all of the Spanish troops under the command of the Marquis de La Romana. The letter continued: it seemed that the marquis was sympathetic to British policy and was suspected of being anti-French. Judging by the high opinion with which he was held in London, Bellemare suggested that the marquis be kept under close observation and precautions taken to keep the Spanish troops well out of reach of any British task force sent to remove them.

Marquet looked up at Maupont. 'How sure are we of this intelligence?'

'Bellemare has proved correct many times before. He would not be in post if Monsieur Fouche doubted the accuracy of his information. Some of the royalists so feted by the English are not what they seem!'

Marquet smiled. 'So, McMahon is telling the truth?'

'That is certainly a possibility. Have you had any news from your man on Heligoland?'

'No, unless there is a letter from him waiting for me at my house in Hamburg. In his last message, Colville warned that security on the island had been stepped up. He was having to be even more vigilant. He asked for yet more money for the extra risks he was taking. You can imagine my reply!'

Maupont shook his head. 'Now is not the time to

demotivate Monsieur Colville. Offer him whatever he wants. If the English are preparing an operation, we must have information from all possible sources.'

Marquet bit his lip, but he could see that Maupont was right.

Maupont continued. 'What about your informant in La Romana's headquarters? He's a valet, is he not?'

'Yes, sir. All his recent reports have contained nothing outside the trivial. I will ensure that he is told to be extra vigilant.'

'Do so.' Maupont moved to dismiss Marquet.

Before he could do so, Marquet asked, 'What actions is the Prince planning to counter La Romana's possible defection?'

'A good question. You should know that the Prince likes the marquis. The Prince was born and brought up in the Basque country and has an affection for those on the other side of the Pyrenees. He finds it difficult to believe that the marquis would contemplate such treason. However, we on his staff have persuaded him to take this threat seriously. What McMahon has told you just reinforces this view. The marquis will be ordered to gather all his troops and swear an oath of loyalty to His Majesty King Joseph. That is all of them from the simple private to the marquis himself and in full view of our troops. What do you think will be the reaction of La Romana, his staff, officers and men?'

Marquet paused. 'When the marquis left Spain, King Carlos was on the throne with his son, Ferdinand, heir apparent. Carlos was the king who appointed La Romana and to whom he surely owes his loyalty. Now he is being ordered to swear allegiance to a new king, a Frenchman and surely someone he would see as a usurper.'

'Exactly my point, Marquet. Yes, there may be some of La Romana's fellow officers who admire what the Revolution has achieved and the success of the Emperor, the marquis's deputy General Kindelan for one. However, the vast majority of the Spaniards are proud of their country and loyal to their former king, whatever his weaknesses. You must not forget the power of the Catholic Church and the hold it has on its people. Spaniards are deeply religious and superstitious. Once the news of a new king gets out to the rank and file of the Division del Norte, you can be sure that the priests attached to each regiment will do everything in their power to turn the troops against King Joseph and all he stands for. Remember that Joseph's brother, the Emperor, has done what he can to dismember the Church in France. Imagine the outrage in Spain when the Pope was forced to attend Napoleon's coronation and had to stand by as the Emperor placed the crown on his own head!

'You are right. We have deprived them of news from home and letters from their loved ones. To force the Spaniards to swear loyalty to Joseph will alienate them further and drive them into the arms of the British. I doubt that the Prince can be persuaded to cancel the oath-taking ceremonies, so keep these views to yourself, otherwise we will both find ourselves in the Hamburg dungeon. Chase Colville on Heligoland – he should have heard or seen something. Does the valet need any more persuasion? He must be told to be even more observant of La Romana and his staff.

'We can remind him that his son's fate is in his hands. A suggestion that the boy might be shipped to work in a labour battalion on a disease-infected island in the Caribbean would probably heighten his motivation.'

Maupont stood and made to dismiss Marquet. 'While you are chasing your informants, I will see if General Kindelan can also keep us cognisant of La Romana's intentions. By the way, were you able to discover the whereabouts of the priest you chased into Hamburg?'

'No, Colonel, it is most frustrating. He has disappeared. My men are still searching the city but my guess is that he has left. Whoever he is, I doubt he will still be dressed as a priest.'

'Could he be the same man that Colville saw leaving Heligoland? In which case, could he now be on his way to Nyborg to meet La Romana?'

'He could. We should instruct the commander of our troops on Funen to keep watch and instruct our Danish allies to check the passports of all men entering and travelling through Denmark.' *A needle in a haystack*, thought Marquet, *but they might be lucky.*

'Now, what about McMahon?'

'He is on his way to Hamburg's prison. He will be given a decent room and treated well. The interrogators will tell him to write out everything he has told me, but this time in minutest detail. We want his full history – Ireland, France, England, Germany with all his contacts, especially those in London and in Heligoland – everything. Once he has finished, we can let him sweat while we check his facts. Then, after a week or two so that he will have forgotten what he wrote, he will be asked to repeat the exercise. We will then check the two drafts for accuracy. Any discrepancies will be probed by the interrogators. If necessary, the process will be repeated. We should then have the definitive truth.'

'So you don't believe him?'

'Bellamere's warning helps, but you know the scheming British. He could be a double or even a triple agent. Maybe he's just in it for the money? He talks a good story.'

'I will talk to Secretary Schtick. Proceed.'

'Yes, Colonel.' Marquet saluted.

Maupont gave a gesture of a salute that was more a wave of dismissal.

35
The Foreign Office, July 1808

In the past weeks Hoppner had represented the Foreign Office at meetings in the Admiralty and at the Transport Office in Dorset Court off Cannon Row. Viscount Palmerston, or as he was now able to call him, Harry Temple, had been welcoming and instructive. Hoppner was initially jealous of Palmerston. It seemed that here was another example of a well-connected aristocrat gaining accelerated promotion ahead of those equally able but low-born public servants. He had to remind himself that it was possible to rise to the top without the privilege of birth; Mr Canning was a case in point.

As he watched Temple navigate through inter-departmental bickering and infighting between the Admiralty, the Transport Office, the War Office and the Treasury, he became increasingly impressed with Temple's ability to manoeuvre the various players to his advantage.

The Admiralty had sent secret instructions to Admiral Saumarez commanding the powerful Baltic fleet to make initial plans for the extraction of the Spanish troops. On board his flagship, *HMS Victory*, Saumarez had meetings with his deputy, Rear Admiral Keats, instructing Keats to increase close patrolling of the Danish islands despite the ever-present irritant of Danish gunboats. The gunboats were no match for most of the navy's ships, but their ability to navigate in shallow waters was a constant threat to sloops and other smaller patrolling vessels.

Saumarez's fleet did not possess the capacity to transport as many as 18,000 troops. Merchant transports would have to be chartered. A familiar process – Hoppner thought back to Cathcart's amphibious operation to occupy Copenhagen just ten months ago requiring the transport of 27,000 troops and the less happy evacuation of the same general's 26,000 troops from Cuxhaven in February the previous year.

Captain Rupert George and his secretary, Alexander M'Cleay, of the Transport Office reported that there was capacity but that the cost of chartering would be significantly higher than normal. Temple had asked why and was told that the Transport Office already had two operations running: Sir John Moore's troops now off the coast of Sweden and Sir Arthur Wellesley's planned campaign to land in Portugal. Hoppner was able to contribute. From what he had read in despatches from Edward Thornton, the King's minister in Sweden, it was unlikely given the mercurial nature of King Gustav IV Adolf of Sweden, that Moore's troops would ever be given permission to land. Even less so, once the news of Sir John's escape from Stockholm had arrived in London. It was rumoured that he had evaded arrest by the King's guards by disguising himself as a peasant. If General Moore and his men were to return home, would the transports become available for the Spanish troops? Hoppner had been gratified by how well this suggestion was received, even by Captain Hamilton of the Navy Board who Hoppner had heard muttering that this would at least stop pouring even more money into the pockets of the likes of Mr Henley of Wapping. Temple told Hoppner that Henley was a substantial ship owner and coal merchant whose broad-beamed, shallow-draft coal vessels were much sought after for transporting troops. His ships' ability to sail close to the shore was particularly valued, hence they commanded a premium price in normal times. Now, with demand at peak levels, the "blood-sucker" was able to demand exorbitant prices.

Hoppner listened as the minutiae of the planning continued. Where were the Spanish located? What were the docking arrangements? Were there cavalry in the division and if so were the horses to be shipped? Questions and many more that required answers for a successful operation.

Finally, Hoppner returned to the papers that had arrived on his desk. They had come from Mr Canning's office and were from Heligoland. The first pile was reports from Mr Nicholas dating from May and June. Many of the letters contained reports from Mr Nicholas's extensive intelligence network across Germany. Hoppner made notes of those that were relevant to the Spanish troops in Denmark:

9 May: the arrest of Mr Himber, His Majesty's agent in Hanover. Evidence that the French were tightening their grip on Northern Germany.

27 May: reporting that the French had 150,000 troops in Spain with a further 50,000 in reserve. Bernadotte had established a forward headquarters in Haderslev on Jutland, possibly part of the treaty with Denmark, French troops were also stationed on the islands of Lolland and Falster.

9 June: Nicholas acknowledges Mr Canning's instruction to land Robertson on the banks of the Elbe or as close as possible. He then encloses a letter from Robertson describing the danger of attempting to land from the Elbe with so much enemy activity. Nicholas confirms that he has instructed the friends in Hamburg to make £500 available for Robertson and that he has given Robertson a bill for £100.

24 June: French troops have entered Frederickstadt and Tonningen.

Hoppner read this with alarm. Tonningen was to be the landing port for McMahon.

He then turned to MacKenzie's letters to Mr Canning.

They reported Robertson's and MacKenzie's arrival on Heligoland on 7 June and that the 27,000 Spanish had been moved into Denmark – *surely an exaggerated number*, thought Hoppner. Twenty-four thousand French troops now occupied much of Schleswig making it impossibly dangerous for Robertson to be landed on the Danish coast. He read through the aborted journey to Neuwerk and the second attempt: a journey to Bremen.

Mackenzie's next letter dated 15 June acknowledged Canning's despatch No.2. He confirmed that he had written to Robertson informing him of the arrival in London on 8 June of the two Spanish deputies, Vicomte Mattoroya and Don Andrea de Cartega, both surely known to La Romana. The deputies were from Galicia and confirmed that war had been declared on France by the majority of Spanish provinces: Leon, Aragon, Old Castile, Valencia and Andalucia. Mackenzie had found it necessary to ask Herr Burkmeyer to carry his letter to Robertson. If this failed, he would have to rely on Mr Nicholas's secret channels.

The next report, Mackenzie enclosed a letter from Robertson reporting that Robertson had arrived in Hamburg on 19 June and had left for Holstein on the twenty-first. Hoppner exhaled. The agent was on his way.

Robertson also suggested that in the event of his failing in his mission, that Mr Canning should ask an Alexander Reid of the New York Coffee House to attempt to contact the Spanish. This Reid was also a Spanish linguist and reported to Her Majesty's Government on the state of the Continent. Hoppner had never heard of this

Reid and wondered how Robertson had come to know of an American coffee merchant? He paused to search his memory. Perhaps this Reid was a cover name for none other than Robertson's fellow monk at the Scottish monastery in Ratisbon, Alexander Horn. Horn continued to provide valuable intelligence from Bavaria and Austria.

36
Hotel Postgarten, Nyborg

Jose O'Donnell was talking to de la Cadena, the auditor of the army. A bellow came from La Romana's morning room.

'Colonel, in here immediately.' O'Donnell looked at Cadena, raising his eyebrows. The general had been in a foul mood since breakfast. It now seemed that he might be ready to explode. O'Donnell knocked and entered. La Romana was stomping up and down from one end of the room to the other. He threw a copy of *Le Moniteur* on the floor. 'What do you make of this?'

O'Donnell picked up the newspaper. Normally its contents were a source of jokes among the Spanish officers who knew it as purely the outlet for French government propaganda. He scanned the *Moniteur*. It claimed that King Carlos and his son, Ferdinand, had both renounced the throne of Spain.

O'Donnell looked at La Romana. 'General, this is just the usual rubbish.'

Romana went to his desk, picked up another paper and threw it at O'Donnell who managed to catch the single-page news-sheet.

'But, General, this is another British ploy to unsettle our men.' If that was its aim, with the general worked up, the propaganda had worked triumphantly.

'Read it.'

'I've already seen it, General.'

'Then you know that it confirms the report in *Le Moniteur*.'

'Yes, sir.'

'So, do we believe the British report that there was a massacre in Madrid? Both papers confirm that Joseph Bonaparte is now King of Spain, so I think we must.'

'But this is old news, General.'

'Well, this isn't.' La Romana threw a letter at O'Donnell. The weighted seal hit O'Donnell in the chest. He closed his hands around Bernadotte's seal. 'Read that.'

O'Donnell unfolded the crumpled letter and read. The parliament in Madrid, the Cortes, had recognised Joseph as king and had sworn loyalty to him. La Romana was commanded to swear fealty to the new king and to ensure that all the soldiers under his command did the same. O'Donnell looked up at La Romana who exploded.

'Well, Colonel, what do you think of that?' Before O'Donnell had a chance to answer, La Romana continued. 'I, the Marquesa de La Romana and my descendants have served and fought for the King of Spain for generations.

Now I am expected to swear loyalty to an upstart Corsican. That's not all; how am I to persuade my soldiers to obey a Frenchman – a Frenchman, for God's sake – who wants to destroy the Catholic Church?' La Romana's eyes blazed, the veins in his temples pulsed purple. 'Well, Colonel, how?'

O'Donnell had seen the general angry before, but never in such a rage. 'General, let me read the letter again.'

La Romana paced up and down while he studied the text again. Each of the units of the Division del Norte was ordered to swear loyalty. The general was to confirm to the Prince that all had done so. The text continued. The wording of the oath was to be devised by La Romana's staff.

'General, we may have a way out. We can word the oath so that we swear to the figurehead that is the king not the man himself. De la Cadena is excellent with wording. May I discuss it with him and produce a suitably vague wording that will not offend you or the men?'

'Do it.'

37
Number 12 Krayenkamp, Central Hamburg, July 1808

Colonel Maupont's note arrived. The marshal's secretary, Schtick, confirmed the man had been known to Bernadotte and to the secretary. If it was the same man, he was Irish and was known as McMahon. He had offered his services but had since disappeared. The letters McMahon carried were judged to be genuine but had been sent to Paris for Fouché's experts to inspect and validate. They confirmed what McMahon had told Marquet. The British Government offered the Marquis de La Romana and his troops passage on the British Navy to Spain, South America or wherever the marquis wished to go.

Marquet summoned a corporal. He was to take three men and ride immediately to Odense and make contact with Lejeune, the valet Martin's handler. The handler was instructed to meet Martin urgently and to put further pressure on him for anything that indicated a change in La Romana's routine. Had there been any unusual visitors to the Hotel Postgarten? Martin was to be reminded of the precarious position his son was in.

Marquet mused if there were indications of another British agent. Was it possible that the priest who had disappeared in Hamburg was one? Would the British employ a middle-aged Catholic on such a mission? It seemed unlikely, though the fact that he was a Roman Catholic would find favour with the Spanish. It was frustrating that the priest had simply disappeared. Most likely he had assumed another persona. Equally annoying, there had been nothing from Colville on Heligoland. He pushed his disappointment from his mind. The report was urgent. All French commanders in Denmark must be alerted to the possibility of a Spanish defection.

38

Assens, on the Island of Funen

Robertson woke with the July sun already beaming through his bedroom window. He washed, dressed and packed his portmanteau, carefully folding his pocket crucifix and tucking it into the secret compartment in his case. The crucifix was designed to double as a penknife. Anyone searching his luggage would assume that the knife was just that.

As Adam Rorauer, he made his way downstairs, bade the innkeeper good morning, entered the dining room and was served breakfast of bread, cold meat, cheese and coffee. Two of the Spanish officers were already breakfasting.

'Good morning.'

'And to you, Mr Merchant.'

The two were as friendly as they had been last night.

'I am travelling to Svendborg with the colonel's letter

of introduction to Colonel Borellas and then on to Nyborg to see if I can obtain a meeting with the Marquis de La Romana. If your colonel is correct, I hope to take many orders from the general and his staff and from the colonel and his subordinates.'

'I'm sure you will have a profitable visit. Sensible to avoid Odense. There are French troops stationed in the town and camped outside it. It would be best to avoid being mixed up with them whoever you are.'

Robertson cast an eye at the Spaniards. 'Do you think they might cause me trouble?'

'You never know. They might ask from where you receive your supplies and assume that they came from smugglers.'

'A fair point indeed.'

'I suggest you travel eastwards but keeping well south. First to Eberrup, on to Haarby, Espe and to Svendborg; the journey will take most of the day. Our colleagues of the Barcelona Regiment are stationed in many of the villages across the south-west of Funen. They will be able to tell you where Colonel Borellas is located if he's not at his headquarters.'

Robertson thanked the Spaniards, finished breakfast and asked the innkeeper to arrange a carriage to take him to Svendborg. His luggage was collected from his room. He paid, thanked the innkeeper for his hospitality, and walked to the waiting carriage. The driver stowed his portmanteaus and attempted to help his passenger up into the carriage. Robertson jested, 'I may look old, but I can still manage the steps, thank you.'

The driver laughed, climbed into his seat and tapped the lead horse's rump gently with his whip. Robertson sat back and began to enjoy the rolling green countryside, rather like Heythrop, he mused. Minutes later, he heard galloping hooves and a shout.

'Stop! Stop.' He turned to see a rider covered in dust, charging after them. Was the rider in uniform? He couldn't tell but there was some colour under the dust. The carriage driver pulled the reins. The rider drew up as the carriage stopped. He was wearing the hotel's uniform. He was, thankfully, a young stable lad that Robertson had seen at the hotel. Breathlessly, the lad proffered a letter.

'Thank goodness I caught up with you. This arrived just after you left.'

'Thank you, young man.' Relieved, he handed over some coins. The letter was postmarked Hamburg, from MacKenzie. The lad wheeled his horse round and set off for the hotel. The contents were surely important. He could not decode the letter while the carriage was travelling along the uneven road. He told the driver to wait while he decoded and read the letter.

MacKenzie wrote that he was about to leave Heligoland for Gothenburg in Sweden where he would be closer to Funen to arrange to collect Robertson after the meeting with La Romana. He suggested a possible pickup point once Robertson had completed his mission: the beach to the east of Nyborg.

Spanish deputies had arrived from Galicia bringing news that the provinces of Leon, Aragon, Old Castile, Valencia and Andalusia had declared war against France.

Robertson pondered on the implications; surely this would make the proposal he was to give to La Romana more persuasive. There was a scribbled footnote, uncoded.

C has sent another if R falls. M. Meaning? C must be Canning. "Another" was surely another agent if he failed, was captured or worse. He wasn't sure how to take this news. He remembered that Canning hadn't taken to him; perhaps this was a slur, but looking from the Foreign Secretary's perspective, it would be prudent to have a backup. Whatever the sensible answer, his pride was stung. It was now imperative that he reached La Romana first. He wanted the glory. He pondered telling the driver to take him direct to Nyborg but then discounted the idea. Stick to the plan. Keep his cover in place but move on as quickly as possible.

Frustratingly as the Spaniards had predicted, at Espe Robertson was stopped by some units of the Barcelona Regiment. He was taken to see the local commander, a captain. He produced the letter of introduction. The captain told Robertson that Colonel Borellas had been invited to have dinner and spend the night at Egeskov Castle that evening. The captain felt sure that the colonel would give him some time, especially if he had cigars for the colonel to try. Business was transacted with the captain and his brother officers. He was not allowed to continue his journey until he had been entertained. More delay, but surely unavoidable.

His hosts flooded him with questions about the wider world. The officers had read the *Moniteur*, the official French newspaper. It was clear that they mistrusted what they read. They also had read some English newspapers which had been smuggled ashore from the patrolling British naval ships. These had told of the events in Spain, the massacre of 2 May and Carlos's and Ferdinand's renunciation of the throne. This news horrified the Spaniards who pressed Robertson for what he could add. Remembering he was just a merchant, Robertson explained what he had read in the Hamburg press.

Lunch over, the captain suggested that Robertson should travel the short distance to Egeskov and await the arrival of Colonel Borellas. There might also be the opportunity to do business with the castle's butler. Besides, the castle was on a more direct route to Nyborg. Robertson thanked the captain and instructed his driver to make for the castle. The driver spoke some German. Robertson asked what was so special about Egeskov Castle.

'You'll see! It is owned by Caroline Agnes Raben who is one of the largest landowners on Funen. Her son lives in Hvendholm, near Faaborg.'

Half an hour later, the driver pulled up at the gatehouse. He was told that Colonel Borellas had already arrived. The gate was opened. They made their way down the drive through trees into parkland to reveal a large brick castle surrounded by a moat and lake. The driver was right: the castle was a magnificent building in the Renaissance style.

As they made their way towards the castle, Robertson spotted the colonel walking with another officer in the garden. Here was an opportunity to introduce himself. He might also obtain an introduction to General La Romana.

He ordered the driver to stop, climbed down from the chaise, walked over to the colonel, removed his hat, bowed and presented his letter of introduction. Colonel Borellas nodded and read the letter.

'So, Herr Rorauer, you are a purveyor of fine cigars?'

'Indeed, sir, and chocolate. Is it possible that both are in short supply? Perhaps the colonel would like to sample a cigar?' He opened his portmanteau and proffered a cigar. Turning to the other officer, he said, 'And one for you?' The officers unwrapped the cigars and took the match Robertson offered. He waited as both men smoked. It was clear that they were enjoying the experience.

'Well, this is an excellent cigar. Cuban?'

Robertson nodded.

'Then how are you able to source them, unless they are smuggled?'

Here was a question on which he had been briefed in Hamburg.

'The cigars and also chocolate are shipped into Spain avoiding the British blockade. They are then shipped to Genoa and on through Germany to our warehouse in Hamburg.'

Borellas raised his eyebrows, turned and smiled at his fellow officer. All three knew the reality – smuggled most likely on British ships. But the colonel had the reassurance he required.

'Well, Herr Rorauer, your cigars are excellent. If your chocolate is of similar quality, I shall place an order with you for both.'

Robertson thanked the colonel. Quantities were

agreed. Shipment would be made to the colonel's headquarters at Svendborg.

'Colonel, my next stop is Nyborg where I am hoping to meet the Marquis de La Romana. I wonder if you would be kind enough to give me a letter of introduction to His Excellency?'

'By all means.' They walked to the colonel's room in the guest block. Fifteen minutes later Robertson climbed up into the chaise ready for the drive to Nyborg. He had the letter. With luck that would give him the opportunity to meet La Romana.

39
Hotel Postgarten, Nyborg

It was not until the evening that Robertson reached Nyborg, a neat town with a fortified harbour and substantial moat. As the chaise made its way towards the town, he had been able to see British frigates and gunboats blockading the Great Belt between Funen and Zealand. Troops of what looked like the local yeomanry patrolled the walls and ramparts that surrounded the town. At the gate on the landward side of the town, his passport was inspected. He was allowed through on payment of a small fee. The gate was more like a large two-storey house with a pitched roof. Windows indicated what Robertson guessed was accommodation for the guards. His driver slapped the reins on the horse's rump. Moving forward, they entered the long tunnel through the middle of the gate. The horse stopped, refusing to move, seemingly scared of the brick arch and walls. The driver cursed and got down from the chaise. Robertson followed suit. Both led the horse through the tunnel. He had sympathy with the horse. The gate was certainly imposing, even daunting.

They remounted the chaise, passing by terraced houses. To his right, he saw what looked like a bastion. The V-shaped walls reminded him of the Vauban-designed fortifications he had seen in eastern France. Cannon pointed to the north and south. The largest looked as big as a thirty-six-pounder, big enough to fire a ball a mile.

The road to the centre of the town sloped gently downhill. To his left, Robertson looked at the pink brick walls of Nyborg Castle with its circular tower incorporated into its southern gable end. The style reminded him of Blair Castle at home and more recently Egeskov Castle. South of the castle was what appeared to be a lake, though Robertson wondered if this was a continuation of the town's system of moats. Even though it was evening, the town seemed busy. They passed an officer addressing a platoon of fifteen men who were stood to attention. All were dressed in grey uniforms. There was considerable grumbling coming from the ranks. A corporal shouted in Danish. The grumbling stopped. Robertson asked his driver who these men were.

'They are the men of the night watch who must patrol the town from eight in the evening until daybreak to keep the town secure and to police for fires. They are all townspeople. They've all finished a full day's work and now have to miss a night's sleep patrolling the walls and the streets. It's the same in all towns in the country. They all try and make excuses why they cannot appear. There's a fine if they're found out.'

'No wonder they are grumbling!'

'I heard that back in April, our Spanish friends were so cold in one of their billets that they built up a fire large enough to cause the chimney to catch. The fire police were quickly on scene. A repetition of the disastrous fire eleven years ago was prevented. Nearly 150 houses were destroyed then.'

The carriage pulled up outside the hotel with its honey-coloured walls. The landlord was at the reception. Robertson asked for a room.

'I am afraid, sir, that my hotel is completely full. Every room is taken by General La Romana and his staff.'

'But your hotel was specially recommended to me. Please let me stay. I will pay whatever you ask.'

'All the rooms are occupied. The only option is to put a bed in my dressing room.'

Robertson accepted the landlord's offer immediately. This would make him less visible to any prying eyes. He was shown to the quarters which were two separate rooms: perfectly adequate. He ordered supper and a good bottle of wine, asking the landlord to join him in a glass or two. The conversation flowed easily. It seemed that the marquis's needs were well looked after. With two chefs, two valets and a collection of liverymen, he was well provided for. The marquis "was a man of affable manners and much beloved". The landlord explained that the letter of introduction from Colonel Borellas would be given to one of the valets. He was sure that would result in gaining access to the general and most likely result in orders from the general himself and many of his fellow officers. Robertson asked why the town looked so busy.

'Normally we have around 2,000 residents and a garrison of 300 to 500 based in the castle. But now we are on a wartime footing, the garrison is now 1,000 men. Then the Spanish arrived on 23 March, nearly 900 of them! Since then, every room, attic and cellar in the town is full. Then we have to feed them to the tune of forty shillings per man per day and a lot more for the officers. Our bakers are producing 500 pounds of rye bread and the butchers 1,500 pounds of beef every day.'

Robertson wondered, 'Everyone must be working hard. But business must be good?'

'It really is. Then there have been all the improvements to the walls and ramparts. Lots of work for our builders and labourers. Good times for the town despite the crowding.'

'And how have the townspeople taken to the Spanish?'

The landlord laughed.

'Initially, everyone was apprehensive. Communication was a real problem. But over the months, things have settled down. Some of their habits are strange but overall, I'd say they have fitted in. Their discipline has been excellent, unlike the French – such arrogance – they think they rule the world.'

'Perhaps they do.'

The next morning, he awoke to find that the landlord had already left the rooms. He quickly reached into his portmanteau, took out and assembled the crucifix, kissed it, mouthed a silent prayer and crossed himself. Today was the day that the weeks of planning and travel had led up to. He pushed all doubt from his mind and focused on the task ahead. He knew what had to be done.

After breakfast, Robertson wrote a note in French requesting a private interview with "His Excellency, the Commander in Chief". He wished to show His Excellency samples of what he had to sell and to ask permission of His Excellency to visit the other units in his command. He also enclosed Borellas's letter. The landlord had explained that one of the valets was French. Robertson specifically sought him out. The valet was cleaning boots.

'Your name?'

'Martin, *monsieur.*' The valet turned to look at Robertson. The right eye focused on him. The left seemed to be looking at the tin of polish. He had seen the affliction before. One of the novices at his monastery was diagnosed with… what was it called? He remembered: Amblyopia. He looked in the good eye.

'I wish to request a meeting with His Excellency, the Marquis.' Robertson handed the valet a folded note. He had specifically not sealed the note, suspecting that had he done so, the valet might suspect something more than a simple request for a meeting. Martin took the note. Robertson was sure that the valet would read it as soon as he was out of sight.

He did not wait long. 'His Excellency will see you now.'

Robertson tucked a box of cigars under one arm, picked up a selection of chocolate and followed the valet upstairs. Martin seemed agitated. Perhaps, Robertson thought, the valet found it strange that the audience had been granted so promptly. After all, this man was no more than a salesman. He was taken into an elegant morning room. A number of staff officers sat, aides-de-camp to the general, no doubt. They eyed Robertson from head to toe and then looked at each other. Robertson found this scrutiny unsettling and embarrassing which increased as he was ushered into the adjoining room.

The Marquis de La Romana was slim, short in stature with a swarthy complexion typical of southern Europeans. His hair was short with a neatly trimmed beard. But it was the marquis's eyes that drew Robertson in; it was as if the general's gaze penetrated right into his soul. The marquis exuded an air of dignity and cool reflection, distant at first but with none of the hauteur that Robertson had experienced in his dealings with other Spaniards.

The marquis dismissed the valet. The door closed behind him. They were alone. The moment he had rehearsed so often had arrived.

Robertson had intended to speak French. Remembering the marquis's extensive education, he chose Latin, less chance that prying ears would understand. He began.

'*Señor, vides ante te peregrinum venientem animam suam in manibus tuis ponere* – *Señor*, you see before you a stranger who comes to put his life in your hands.'

He stopped, waiting for a reaction.

The Marquis de La Romana moved slowly, now upright in his chair, elbows on the table, hands clasped under his chin. He glared at Robertson. Silence. His eyes seemed to be reaching into the depths of the priest's mind. Finally, he said, '*Perge* – go on.'

'I am a Catholic priest, chosen, perhaps partly on that account, for the mission that I am about to explain. We thought that you would be more likely to trust the word of a Catholic clergyman. I am here to meet Your Excellency on the instructions of the English Government. Let me say at once, I have no papers whatsoever to give you so that, in the event of my arrest, you would not be compromised. Moreover, I ask for nothing in writing from you. My message is purely verbal. I ask that your answer should be the same.'

No reaction. La Romana continued to glare.

'All that I can offer by way of credentials is the knowledge I have of a meeting you had with Mr Frere, who you will remember was our ambassador in Spain. He asked me to remind Your Excellency of the first time he had the pleasure of dining with you at Toledo. After dinner, the two of you withdrew together to the library. In the library, there was a picture displayed in a cabinet. The painting was by Anton Rafael Mengs and depicted St Peter and St John at the gates of the temple.'

'Quite true.' The glare turned more into a smile.

'Would Your Excellency recognise Mr Frere's handwriting?'

'I probably would.'

Robertson reached into his waistcoat pocket and produced a small fragment of paper. It was part of a memorandum that he had received from Mr Frere. The marquis recognised the handwriting instantly. At least now an element of his credibility as a British Government agent had been established. He continued.

'Mr Frere assures me that I should find the general a man of the strictest honour and highest principle and an enemy of French tyranny and oppression.'

The glare returned.

'Six weeks ago, two deputies arrived in London from Galicia. They confirmed that the provinces of Leon, Aragon, Old Castile, Valencia and Andalusia had declared war on France.'

Robertson waited for the effect of this news to sink in. Nothing, not even a glimmer of a reaction. The glare continued.

'The message I am charged to deliver you, Your Excellency, is that England is ready to convey you and the troops under your command to any country you name. We ask nothing of you in return. There is no pressure for you to fight for us. You can act as you see right and proper. We simply wish to give you the power to extricate yourself from your present position. Our transports will be ready to obey your orders and meet you at any point of the coast that you nominate. You may choose South America or Canada, England or Spain as your destination. We are ready to forward your instructions or views whatever they may be. Should you wish for a formal treaty, the British government has authorised Mr MacKenzie to conclude one with you. He is currently en route to Gothenburg and will draw up the terms with whichever officer you choose to deputise on your behalf.

'Further, we will not dictate to the Spanish nation the course it should pursue. If you choose to resist the invading French, we are ready to cooperate with you with all our might. Our cavalry has never been better mounted nor our artillery more effective and powerful.'

Robertson had delivered his message uninterrupted. He paused. The general remained silent. Robertson was now alarmed. Was the general so weak that he would attempt to curry favour with the French and hand the agent over to Bernadotte as proof of his loyalty? He was now seriously worried. He tried to stop himself rubbing his sweaty palms on his trousers and decided on an aggressive approach.

'General, should I be concerned that my confidence will be betrayed by a Spanish cavalier?'

Again, the marquis said nothing. He put the tips of his fingers together. Speaking slowly at last, he said, 'Sir, you have nothing to fear from me. But have you mentioned your errand to anyone else since you arrived on the Continent?'

'I have, *Señor*, but only out of necessity. Our Foreign Office were not sure where you were stationed. They thought that you were based in Glückstadt on the River Elbe. When I arrived in Hamburg, I made my way to a hospital which was caring for some of your officers. There I met a Spanish priest who I swore to secrecy. He introduced me to one of your injured officers. The officer assured me that he would sooner die than reveal the fact that I had been enquiring of your whereabouts. It was he that told me that your troops had been moved into Denmark.'

The marquis persisted. 'I ask you again are these the only people in whom you have confided?'

'I remember one other. I had presented a letter of

credit to him. As soon as I asked where you were based, he guessed the reason for my mission.'

'I am sorry for that.' The marquis glared once again at Robertson.

'So am I, my lord, especially as you view this knowledge in such light. However, you will be relieved to hear that this person enjoys the confidence of our Foreign Office, otherwise I would not have referred to him. I know that he has too much property at stake both in Germany and in England to be compromised. I would have a strong reason to complain if he had refused to forward any letter I had written to you and left in his safe keeping should my journey to Nyborg fail. Can you please tell me, Your Excellency, has any other agent from the British Government reached you before me?'

Once again the marquis glared at Robertson who hoped that the general had not taken offence.

'Be assured, there is no truth in his assertion. If such papers had been distributed among my troops, such news would not escape my notice. Yours is the first and only communication of this kind that has reached me either from England or from Spain. One of my officers has recently returned from Spain. He told me of the events of 2 May and of the abdication of the King and Prince Ferdinand but travelled before any declaration of war.'

'Well then, General, may I ask you for an answer to the offer, at least in principle? I have the means of forwarding your response to Mr MacKenzie and on to London.'

'An answer – what, now? Surely you do not intend to leave immediately?'

'Certainly not, my lord, though I was in great danger throughout my journey here and remain at the same risk.'

'Then we shall meet again.'

'Whenever Your Excellency pleases. I have a larger choice of excellent cigars and chocolate which can be the pretext for another interview.'

The meeting was over. Robertson made his way to the hotel's lobby. The landlord was behind the reception desk and called him over and gave him a letter addressed to Herr Rorauer which had been sent from Hamburg. Robertson recognised MacKenzie's writing.

Back in the landlord's room, he locked the door, sat and decoded the letter. MacKenzie was now in Gothenburg to be closer to Nyborg and would board a Royal Navy ship, sail to Funen and meet Robertson on the coast at an agreed time and place. A skiff would land to ferry him to MacKenzie's ship. He instructed Robertson to reply where and when he would be able to make it to the coast to the east of Nyborg or, failing that, he was to make his way to the west coast of Funen to a point on the Little Belt a little above the narrow passage between Funen and the town of Kolding on Jutland. Robertson smiled: an escape route. He memorised the letter and put a match to it. As he watched the letter burn, he realised that he would have to wait at least another two weeks before he could be rescued; that being the minimum time that it would take for his reply to reach MacKenzie in Gothenburg. He had no time to lose. It was time to understand the geography of his surroundings, select a suitable landing spot for the skiff and write, code and post his reply.

It did not take him long to walk round the town. Turning left from the hotel's entrance, he turned left again with a church on his right, past the half-timbered town hall and on to Nyborg Castle, still showing signs where cannon balls had struck the walls during the wars with Sweden over 150 years before. Once a royal palace, it looked as though the building was now just a shell used for storage, not a barracks as he had been told. Robertson continued down to the harbour which gave access to Nyborg Fjord and on to the Great Belt and to the Baltic. The harbour was a hive of activity with fishing boats vying for quay space with merchant ships. Here too were two Danish naval vessels. He wandered past them doing his best to assess their size and armaments without seeming interested. Robertson had heard from Mr Nicholas on Heligoland that while the ocean-going Danish Navy had effectively ceased to exist after the capture of Copenhagen the year before, there were many smaller ships which caused smaller British warships and unprotected merchantmen much trouble.

He strolled past the larger ship, a brig, he thought. None of the sailors on board seemed to take any notice of him. Counting his paces, he estimated it to be around eighty feet long. At a rough count, from what he could see, it was armed with sixteen or more guns. Walking past the stern, he saw the ship's name, *Fama*. Carrying on along the quayside, the second warship was smaller, perhaps a cutter. He counted guns on the side of the ship that was moored along the quayside. Allowing for guns on the bow and stern, the cutter was probably armed with twelve guns. Past the stern, he caught sight of the name: *Salorman*.

Robertson returned to the town. With Danish naval vessels in Nyborg harbour, a pickup by a skiff from a Royal Naval warship in the fjord was out of the question. He would have to look further afield. MacKenzie's preferred location was to the east of the town. He walked to the east gate, explained to the Danish soldiers on guard that he needed exercise and some sea air and asked them how far it was to the beach. Half an hour later, he arrived at the gently sloping sandy beach. The sea was flat calm. Even with the naked eye, he could see the pennants of the patrolling Royal Navy ships. There was a small wooden jetty. He looked around for a landmark easily identified from the sea. Trees lined the shore edge. Directly behind the pier stood a large oak. It was much taller than any of its neighbours. He looked up and down the beach. There were no other trees of a similar height. He would instruct MacKenzie to look for the oak and then the jetty: an excellent pick-up point. Looking further up the beach, he saw a group of soldiers walking towards him. Time to move.

Robertson walked back to the town, thanking the guards as he went through the east gate. Up the steps into the hotel lobby, the French valet, Martin, was waiting for him. The man with the cigars had been spotted by one of the Spanish officers who was looking out from an upstairs window. Martin told him that the general wished to see him again. He followed Martin upstairs to the main salon. The room was full of the general's staff officers. The atmosphere was very different from that of the first interview. Robertson was greeted by smiling faces. It was difficult to disguise his elation. He wondered what had changed the general's mind from suspicion and mistrust to acceptance of the truth of the mission. It seemed that he was not now regarded as a French stool pigeon.

Back in the marquis's office, he decided to take advantage of the positive mood. He came straight to the point.

'I presume, General, that I shall now have the honour of your reply?'

'Sir, before I decide on your proposition, I should tell you that we are utterly ignorant of what is going on in Spain. We have been without letters from home for a full year. We know no more than the French choose to tell us by reading newspapers such as the *Moniteur* which we do not trust. One article reported the death of King George III on 4 June.'

'I can confirm, Your Excellency, you are correct in doubting such fabrications. I left London on 8 June to the sound of church bells ringing out across the capital to celebrate His Majesty's birthday. Let me provide more detail about what I know about events in Spain. The insurrection has already begun in Galicia and the Asturias. A deputation has already arrived in London to ask for assistance from our government. You may know Don Andres Angel de la Vega Infanzon and Don Jose Maria Queipo de Llano, Conde de Toreno?'

'Indeed I do. I know both well. They are men held in the highest regard in Spain.'

'So much the better. Then you can say if they are men of honour and have Spain's best interests at heart.'

'I can and do.'

'Therefore, you as commander-in-chief of the Spanish forces in Denmark will be of the same mind as such men?'

La Romana skirted the question. 'They would have us believe that there was universal celebration at the arrival of Joseph in Madrid. We hardly credit such a story. Now, Marshal Bernadotte requires us all to swear loyalty to Joseph. I fail to see what I can do. My troops are spread all over Denmark and are closely monitored by French, Danish and Dutch troops. As well as here, I have men in Zealand, Langeland, Jutland and others in Schleswig. Had your navy not blocked the Great Belt, we might all have been in Zealand. That would have given some opportunity to do something.'

'If it is not too late, I am sure that our government will act on the slightest indication that you give and leave your passage to Zealand unobstructed.'

'That would win us great prestige, but is now impractical. I have two infantry regiments on Zealand, the Asturias and Guadalajara. That is well over 3,200 men. However, they are surrounded by General Friant's French troops and well over 10,000 Danes. It is simply not feasible for the men here to sail to Zealand or for the troops there to escape here. They would be cut down.'

'Well, *Señor*, if you cannot rescue all, at least rescue those you can.'

There was a knock on the door. The general's tone changed instantly. Easing effortlessly into French: 'And where do you say these cigars are made?' And then to the door, 'Come.'

The door opened. It was the French valet, Martin.

Robertson turned, glanced at the valet and then back at the general. 'These are the finest quality cigars from Cuba, Your Excellency. Please try one.'

The general put his hand up and looked at the valet. 'Why are you here, Martin?' La Romana's tone made it patently clear how irritated he was.

'I thought that Your Excellency and your guest might like some coffee or perhaps some chocolate?'

The general looked at Robertson. 'Herr Rorauer?'

'Chocolate please, Your Excellency.'

'And one for me. Now leave us.'

The valet bowed and left, closing the door behind him. The general stood, made his way silently to the door, put his hand on the knob and in one motion tore the door open. Nothing. He checked the hall beyond, closed the door and sat again. Back to Latin: 'We are surrounded by spies. Martin is the most concerning because he has access to our rooms. I could sack him, but he would be replaced by another. It's better to manage what we know. But that takes a degree of care. What a game!' The marquis smiled. 'Now, where were we? Ah yes, if we did manage to escape, what can we in Spain do against the might of the French? Yes, England remains free but even England is not exempt from danger while so much discontent exists in Ireland while your government refuses to grant Catholics equal rights. That part of your country is vulnerable to invasion and rebellion. If Britain falls, who then shall stand against Napoleon?'

'General, as to the state of Ireland, I am well qualified

to answer. I have recently returned from Ireland. I was working for the chief secretary of the Irish Office, Sir Arthur Wellesley. He instructed me to tour the country to gauge the state of feeling of the populace. While there is ongoing resentment of the British and especially English and Scottish settlers who have made their home in Ireland, unless the French mount a serious invasion of Ireland, I believe the populace will be quiescent. With the Royal Navy's command of the seas, a French invasion seems most unlikely.

'I have also listened to the debates in both Houses of Parliament on Catholic emancipation. As a Catholic, I must agree with Your Excellency that the delay in passing this measure is unjust and its passing would no doubt strengthen our common cause. After all, many English equate the Scottish invasion of 1745 with Catholicism. But much has been done for the benefit of Catholics during the reign of His Majesty, King George III. Catholics are not ungrateful for the progress made. I am sure that emancipation will be granted in the fullness of time. Any insurrectionary movement would retard that process. Any service we as Catholics can render to the government would accelerate it.

'At present, we have nothing to fear either from rebellion at home or invasion from abroad. Our major difficulty is the disgraceful spinelessness and passive submission of other countries.'

The marquis exploded with frustration. 'But the rest of Europe does nothing!'

Robertson felt he was making progress. He felt that his points were striking home.

'Your Excellency, over the last ten years, I have travelled extensively in Europe. Throughout many parts of Europe, people are indignant at being restrained by their rulers, by kings, princes, dukes and margraves unworthy of the positions that they hold. They preserve a shadowy semblance of royal dignity for themselves and their families. They are content to sacrifice their honour and the welfare of their subjects to accept their condition of vassals.'

Pausing, Robertson lost his train of thought briefly. He began again, but now back in French.

'Meanwhile, a mistaken sentiment of loyalty paralyses their subjects, even when handed over to a foreign dictator.' Romana looked at him, eyebrows raised.

There was another knock on the door. The valet entered immediately without being given permission. Back in French, Robertson simply switched subject.

'Have you tried Filipino cigars, General? We acquire these from our Dutch suppliers who ship them with spices from Java and Sumatra.'

The valet placed the cups of chocolate on the table.

'We have nearly run out of chocolate, Your Excellency. Perhaps this gentleman will be able to replenish our store?'

'We are discussing cigars, Martin. I will ask the gentleman to meet the quartermaster to see if he can help with supplies of chocolate. Now leave us and make sure the door is firmly closed.'

Once they were alone again, the marquis continued. 'Even if he was listening at the door, I doubt he would have picked up anything significant. I admit though, I have not tested his Latin! Go on, sir.'

Robertson collected his thoughts. 'Spain is still at liberty to act for itself. Your kings have been deposed. Europe can now look to you to be an example to take on Napoleon. Who knows what Spain's resistance might produce? As we speak Austria is gathering allies to strike against the dictator. If you instruct me, I will travel to Austria to meet the Archduke Charles to tell him of your sentiments. I will suggest that it is his duty and in his best interests that he should now rule Spain. Now that the Bourbons have been deposed, he as a Hapsburg has the right to assume control.'

The marquis sat back in his chair. There was silence as he thought. 'It would be best if a regent was appointed immediately, ideally with royal blood. He should be assisted by a council to help him govern the country. Everything should be done to prevent Napoleon from attacking our American colonies or indeed, Spain's other dependencies.' Another pause. 'I will also define the number of troops that we will require to occupy Minorca and the other Balearic islands.'

Robertson was elated. The tone in which the general now spoke seemed to indicate that he would indeed agree with the British proposals.

'General, with the Royal Navy in command of the ocean, I have the fullest confidence that Spain's American possessions can be protected from the French. In time, we should be able to wrest the whole of Spain from Napoleon's grasp.'

The marquis stood. 'I need more time to consider your offer. If I decide to accept, I shall need time to brief my officers, and collect and prepare my troops for embarkation. I will not commit myself to anything, nor will I put anything in writing. However, you can give me your address in Hamburg but that does not mean that you can expect to hear from me. The risk is too great.'

'I understand, Your Excellency. My handler, Mr Mackenzie, is in Gothenburg to be closer to Nyborg. I shall write a coded letter to him to tell him of your intentions and to make plans to collect me from a beach near here. He can then make arrangements to contact you.'

'You should be able to avoid the Danish militia who patrol the shoreline. How long will it take to get a letter to him? Can you be sure that the code in the letter cannot be broken?'

'There is an express service from here to Hamburg and an efficient smuggling route from there to Heligoland. From the island by fast sloop to Gothenburg, Mr Mackenzie should receive the letter in around ten to twelve days. As to security, I use a one-off code that cannot be broken without the key. The message to MacKenzie will be disguised within my orders for cigars and chocolate!'

'That will give me time to brief my officers and make plans, should I decide to proceed.' La Romana walked towards the door pulling it open abruptly. There was no one kneeling with an ear to the keyhole. The interview was over.

Robertson returned to his shared room, relieved to be alone. An hour later, he made his way to the post office, making a great show to the postmaster and other staff and customers.

'Urgent orders of cigars and chocolate for His Excellency the Marquis. Please send this letter express to Hamburg.' In among references to Havana and Java, was a coded message to MacKenzie. In it, Robertson expressed his belief that the marquis would accept Canning's proposal. He also nominated a date and the location when he could be collected from the beach.

40

Hotel Postgarten, Nyborg, July 1808

Robertson retired to bed tired but satisfied with the progress he had made, the room with a low ceiling under the eaves in a strange way comforting. Closing the door, he knelt at his bedside and whispered the Compline prayers. He was asleep as soon as his head reached the pillow. Deep sleep and dreams followed. One dream was unsettling. He imagined that he held Frau Muller in his arms. The dream changed. He couldn't breathe. It was as if he was being suffocated. There was a tonsured head leaning over him. Was he still dreaming? He opened his eyes. His nose was being pinched.

'Get up.' The fingers released his nose. His eyes focused on what he slowly recognised as a Dominican friar.

'We need to ask you some questions. Come with us, but quietly.' Robertson looked over the monk's shoulder and saw a Spanish officer he recognised from the second meeting with Roman. He sat up, rubbed his eyes, now wide awake and alert. He stood, wrapped a cloak over his shoulders and followed the two men. His mind cleared of sleep as the officer led the way to the cellar with the friar behind Robertson. They entered a storeroom which looked more like a cell. His mouth dried, fear welling up.

'Sit down. I am Colonel O'Donnell and this is our senior chaplain, Francisco de Alvarado. You understand that we must be sure that you are who you say you are.' In the back of his mind, Robertson had expected an interrogation. For a change he had nothing to hide. The initial shock dissipated.

'Of course.'

De Alvarado began, the questions all in Latin. 'Be aware that I am a member of the Inquisition. You told the general that you are a Catholic priest.'

'I have nothing to fear from the Inquisition.'

'What is your name?'

He decided to keep to his religious name. 'I am Father Gallus.'

'When were you ordained?'

'Thirty years ago.'

'Where?'

'At the Scottish Benedictine monastery in Ratisbon in Bavaria.'

'You are a Benedictine?'

'I am.'

'You are Scottish?'

'I am.'

De Alvarado's questions became more aggressive. 'But the Benedictines are a contemplative order, how can you work for the British Government and maintain your adherence to the rules of Saint Benedict?'

'I have the blessing of my abbot.'

'Who is he?'

'Arbuthnot.'

De Alvarado changed tack. 'What are the rules of Saint Benedict?' Robertson always had an ability to "read" people. This Spaniard was a bully. He wondered how much was behind the bombast.

'Where do you want me to start? Shall I take the seventh rule as an example? The seventh rule concerns humility. Within that rule, there are twelve steps. Would you like me to list them?'

The friar was beginning to lose his temper; another change. 'Have you published any work?'

'I have: a new edition of John Austen's prayer book. I also worked on translating the Mass into English.'

'Sacrilege! The Church cannot allow God's word to be read by mere commoners. Its true meaning must be for the clergy to interpret.'

Robertson was beginning to enjoy himself. 'What, in Latin? It was originally written in Aramaic.'

O'Donnell butted into the argument. 'Enough. Does this man talk as a Benedictine?'

De Alvarado nodded.

The colonel continued, now speaking French. 'Tell me how you arrived here?'

'That is secret, but I can tell you that my instructions

were given to me by George Canning himself.' He described the meetings with Wellesley and Canning. The questions went on for another hour. Robertson answered some, refusing others. His refusal did not seem to antagonise O'Donnell who stood.

'I believe we can all retire to bed. I bid you goodnight, Father.'

'What is left of it.'

***

'You're late this morning, Herr Rorauer. There isn't much breakfast left.'

'I had a rather disturbed night, my host. Please bring me what you have.' As he ate, Spanish officers came and went. There was no sign of O'Donnell or De Alvarado. He presumed he had passed the inquisition. He told the landlord that he would take a walk around the town, not far, should La Romana summon him.

He walked past the town hall and saw the castellated brick west wing of the Church of Our Lady. He would probably never become used to the strange style of Nordic churches. He had an urge to pray, walked up the steps and entered. He would never enjoy the stark interior of Lutheran churches now lacking the glory of Catholic decoration as this once had. The church was empty. Not wanting to be disturbed, he tucked himself away in a side chapel and began to pray.

'You're late, Martin.' Robertson saw a French corporal followed by the general's valet walking up the aisle. The two men entered the side chapel next to Robertson's. He couldn't be seen but could hear.

He heard Martin's voice. 'I couldn't get away, Corporal.'

'If you want your son to avoid further punishment, be on time. Your report, now.'

'Yes Corporal Lejeune. Two matters of interest: I heard one of the Spanish officers shout that he would never swear an oath of allegiance to that usurper Joseph Bonaparte. The other is odd. The general had a visit from a German salesman peddling chocolate and cigars.'

Robertson strained to hear.

Lejeune spoke. 'What of it?'

'The general made it very clear to me that he wanted to talk to the salesman in private. Why so if the talk was just about cigars?'

'Perhaps the salesman was dealing in contraband and did not want you to hear?'

'But then the salesman said something about a foreign dictator. How can that be anything to do with chocolate?'

'Did you find out the salesman's name?'

'Adam Rorauer, from Hamburg.'

'I will inform Captain Marquet. In the meantime, keep a note of any changes in routine, any secret meetings and if this man Rorauer reappears. Until we meet again.'

'Yes, Corporal.' Robertson heard the two walk down the nave and the clunk of the oak doors closing. As he finished praying, an idea began to form. Perhaps he could use the valet to feed disinformation through to Captain Marquet? To have the policeman, if that is what he was, running off on a wild goose chase was deliciously appealing. In the meantime, he had time on his hands. There was nothing more he could do to influence the marquis. Nor could he apply pressure to speed up the general's decision-making; that was likely to be counter-productive. It would seem strange to his host, the landlord and, more seriously to the valet, if he remained in the hotel kicking his heels. The solution came: to everyone outside the marquis's inner circle, he was a merchant. It was time to take more orders. He left the church and walked back to the hotel. As he arrived in the hall, the general's aide-de-camp, Major O'Donnell, came down the main staircase.

'Major, may I have a word in private? Perhaps you could tell the general what I witnessed in the church?'

O'Donnell walked into the empty dining room. 'Well?' Robertson told him about Martin's meeting with Lejeune and of his misinformation idea.

The Spaniard smiled. 'Thank you, Herr Rorauer. As we suspected. We will just have to be even more vigilant. I'll discuss your idea with the general. It would be satisfying to watch it develop.'

'There is one other matter.'

Two hours later, he was armed with permission to visit the other Spanish units on Funen, the First Princessa and the division's artillery unit in the north, the Second Princessa in the north-west, his friend the colonel of the Third Princessa around Assens, and the Barcelona and Villaviciosa regiments in the south of the island. There might even be time to cross to the small island of Langeland and show his wares to the officers of the Catalunya Regiment. For those such as the valet who took an interest in him, this would be an opportunity to demonstrate the veracity of his cover. The journey would also give him a chance for intelligence gathering and to come up with a plan for the goose chase – a nice solution.

41

Hotel Excellent, Lübeck

Ten days had passed since Marquet had delivered his report to Colonel Maupont. He had stressed the urgency and the need for rapid action, but nothing. Finally, a courier arrived summoning him to Lübeck. Lübeck? He was mystified. The town was way out of his area of jurisdiction. He asked the sergeant who kept his ear close to the ground on all matters of rumour, true or not. Apparently, it was common knowledge; the Prince of Ponte Corvo was taking the waters at the fashionable resort of Scharbeutz on the Baltic coast. It seemed that most of his staff were following the Prince's example. After all, July was the best month to enjoy the delights of the Baltic summer. The temperature was hardly up to the standards of Pau, the Prince's home town, but pleasant nevertheless.

Marquet and a two-man escort had ridden the seventy

kilometres to Lübeck where he had been ordered to stay. Another day wasted. When he arrived at the hotel, he was in a foul temper. He dashed off a note to Maupont saying that he had arrived and demanded that the innkeeper deliver the letter immediately. When he was told that it would take at least an hour to locate a courier, by making to draw his sword he made it clear to the innkeeper that an hour was unacceptable. Twenty minutes later the courier was leaving the hotel.

There was nothing to be done but wait. Marquet was shown to the best room in the hotel. His men were billeted in an attic room. At least he would hope to enjoy supper with perhaps more than one glass of wine. His temper was not improved when the waiter explained that there was no wine, just beer. The innkeeper was called. The waiter sent out for the best wine in Lübeck. There was no French wine to be had. Any decent French wine had been requisitioned and sent to Scharbeutz. However, Marquet was pleasantly surprised by the sparkling Elbtal-Sekt followed by Goldreisling, memories of visits to Alsace.

The next morning, Marquet made his way to Scharbeutz. Colonel Maupont was billeted with a family whose house was close to the luxurious hotel taken by Bernadotte and his generals. Marquet found the colonel sitting at a table in the garden sipping a black coffee. He was told to pull up a chair. He sat. The colonel's eyes were bloodshot.

'It was after four that I finally got to bed this morning. The Prince insisted that everyone stayed until he was ready to leave.'

'Yesterday was not the birthday of the Emperor or any of his brothers so what was the reason for the celebration?'

'You will recall that in June last year, the Prince was shot in the head. Last night was to commemorate the anniversary of his recovery.'

'Ah.'

'I have discussed your report with the Prince's chief of staff. He spoke with the marshal himself. We are to increase surveillance of La Romana and his staff, but are not to take further active measures.'

Marquet was amazed.

'But, Colonel, we now have proof from two different sources that the British will do their utmost to persuade La Romana to defect. The man McMahon confirms the report from chief of police, Bellemare. McMahon is the second agent sent to La Romana. For all we know, the first spy may already be in contact with the Spaniards. Surely, we should take immediate action to squash any attempt?'

'Exactly the point I made to the chief of staff, Marquet. The Prince sees things differently. First, the sending of two agents is most probably a British ruse to sow dissent among us and our allies. You know how much the English have used disinformation to destabilise the Empire. Even if this first spy managed to meet La Romana, the likelihood that his story would be believed is miniscule. The Prince is convinced that the marquis is a man of honour and would do nothing to put his troops at risk, surrounded as he is by General de Brigade Fririon's men and Dutch and Danish troops. The Prince has asked the marquis to organise parades of all his troops so that they can all swear loyalty to the new King of Spain. This will tie him and his troops closer to the Empire.'

'Won't that do exactly the opposite? Even the most ardent supporters of modernisation will surely find it difficult to understand why Carlos and his son have been replaced. When the news of the events of 2 May seeps out, as it inevitably will, the reaction will surely be violently anti-French. Then the Spaniards will understand why we have blocked all news and mail from Spain for the past months. They will have every reason to believe what is written in the newspapers the British have been feeding them for the past months.'

'Then we must be forewarned of any revolt. I recall that the marquis's deputy, General Kindelan, is an enthusiast of the Revolution and all the measures the Emperor has taken to modernise France. In which case, he should be a supporter of King Joseph and will warn us of any planned rebellion.'

'Indeed, but he is based in Jutland with limited contact with La Romana in Nyborg. The marquis knows Kindelan's sentiments and would surely keep any such planning hidden from him.'

'Enough "yes buts".' Irritated, Maupont had had enough of Marquet's pushing back. 'The Prince has ordered Major Franco, the commander of his personal guard, to travel to Nyborg. There he will present the marquis with the insignia of *Commandeur de la Légion d'honneur* and a superb pair of pistols in recognition of the high esteem in which he is held. The marquis's deputy, General Kindelan, will become an *Officier de la Légion d'honneur*.

'Franco will also deliver orders forbidding any contact with the British and also copies of the new Spanish constitution approved by the junta and King Joseph. The orders will require La Romana to visit his troops wearing his *Légion d'honneur*. He is instructed to assemble each of the units. The same will apply to Kindelan and the colonels of the Guadalajara and Asturias regiments on Zealand. You, Captain Marquet, are ordered to travel to Denmark with Major Franco. You ensure that Franco carries out his orders. You will also brief the French, Dutch and Danish units you pass through to give them the intelligence you have gathered on possible Spanish intentions to rebel. You will also have the opportunity to search for the British agent. Here are your orders.'

As Maupont slid the letter over the table, Marquet could see Bernadotte's seal on the cover. He might be able to argue with the colonel and possibly change his mind, but this was a direct order from the marshal and that was that.

'I don't know Major Franco; he sounds Spanish.'

'He is. He and his men are the elite of the Zamora Regiment and form one of the Prince's guard units. He is well regarded in the Prince's circles. The Prince has every confidence in Franco's support of our new regime in Spain.'

'That sounds as if you have your doubts.'

'My dear Captain, that is what I am paid for. Deep down, what if Major Franco is a closet Bourbon and wants Ferdinand back on the throne? You are to go with him to ensure the Prince's orders are carried out. There must be no backsliding.'

'And what do these orders command?'

'As I have said. That all the troops of the Spanish division swear loyalty to King Joseph. The Prince considers the form of words for the oath the Spanish submitted too open to, shall we say, interpretation? The words that the Prince's adjutant has devised leave no doubt as to their meaning.'

Marquet paused. This was taking him away from his counter-intelligence role. But then maybe it was not. Back to the questions he had.

'And the agent, McMahon, what of him?'

'He will be sent to Paris. As our Irish friend has recent knowledge of Mr Canning and his colleagues, Monsieur Fouche's interrogators wish to understand more of the English Foreign Office and its intelligence network. Should he not be able to provide satisfactory information, or he is found to be a triple agent and in truth still spying for the British, I rather suspect that Madame Guillotine will have another customer.'

The meeting was over.

As he made his way back to his hotel, Marquet was already planning the journey. It would take him into Jutland, Funen, Zealand and even on to the small island of Langeland to the south-east of Funen. Days of hard riding to come.

42

Gothenburg, July 1808

MacKenzie was both frustrated and concerned. He had been in Gothenburg for over a week. He was the guest of the British consul, John Smith. Mr Smith had been appointed four years previously. He briefed MacKenzie on the sensitivities of Swedish politics. Though Sweden and Britain were allied, the erratic behaviour of King Gustavus dictated the utmost sensitivity. General Sir John Moore commanded 10,000 British troops cooped up in 200 transports off the coast of Gothenburg. He had travelled to Stockholm to consult with the King. Moore's orders were to support the Swedes in their fight with Russia. Now Gustavus insisted that Moore should add his troops to the Swedish Army units in the south, invade Zealand and capture Copenhagen. When the general pointed out that there were well over 40,000 enemy troops defending Zealand making any invasion suicidal, the King lost his temper and ordered Moore's arrest. The general disguised himself as a peasant and escaped Stockholm. Four days later, he arrived in Gothenburg. It was Mr Smith who had organised a ship's boat to take Moore to Admiral Saumarez's flagship, *HMS Victory*. A dishevelled Sir John had arrived on board in the middle of a party much to the amusement of the guests, local dignitaries and the naval officers who were always looking after an opportunity to have a joke at the junior service's expense.

As he had time to kill while waiting for news from Robertson or McMahon or preferably both, he asked Mr Smith for the full story of Sir John's escape. As Smith rambled on, MacKenzie's mind drifted back to his mission. He had agreed with Mr Nicholas on Heligoland that any letters from the two agents should be decoded and copied, the original to be sent by packet to London and the copy by the fastest means to him in Gothenburg. There were many possible reasons for the silence: arrest, their letters had gone astray, the smuggling routes between the mainland and Heligoland might be compromised or simply the time it took to locate the Spanish general. There was nothing to be done but wait, exasperating as it was.

The consul was still in full flow when a servant knocked on the door, entered and gave Mr Smith a letter.

'Sir, this arrived by courier who is awaiting a reply.'

The consul examined the outside of the letter.

'For you, Mackenzie,' and to the servant. 'Give the courier some refreshment while we study the contents.' He handed the letter to MacKenzie. He immediately recognised Mr Nicholas's handwriting. Inside was a note from the consul on Heligoland which simply read *Progress*. Another letter was tucked inside the first. On the cover was Robertson's neat writing. MacKenzie excused himself and made his way to his bedroom. Fifty minutes later, the decoding was complete and a report written for Mr Canning. It was the news he had been hoping for. Robertson had met La Romana. A further meeting was promised. The monk was positive.

When he returned to the morning room, he could not wipe the smile from his face. The consul was too experienced a diplomat to ask MacKenzie about the contents of the letter.

'Good news, I trust?'

'Positive, Mr Smith.'

The consul summoned the servant with instructions to the courier that MacKenzie's report should be delivered to the Harwich-bound packet. With a fair wind, the report should be with Mr Canning within three days.

MacKenzie thanked Mr Smith and continued, 'I wish to collect my agent from a beach location close to Nyborg in a week's time. Can you suggest the best method?'

Smith was silent for some time. He walked to the window and gazed over the Gota Alv river. Turning to MacKenzie, he said, 'I suggest you make your way to Helsingborg and meet my colleague, Charles Fenwick. Mr Fenwick was formerly consul in Elsinore before taking up his consular duties in Helsingborg. He knows the area intimately. More importantly, he has a network of merchants and fishermen who keep him informed and, no doubt, perform more confidential missions for him, if you get my drift?'

MacKenzie did.

'Mr Fenwick will make the arrangements to get you to your rendezvous in the most appropriate manner.'

43

The Church of Our Lady, Nyborg

Marquet found Major Franco at Scharbeutz. He was not looking forward to the journey to Nyborg. Four days hard riding, however comfortable his saddle might be.

Franco was standing by one of the Prince of Ponte Corvo's carriages.

'We will travel in style, Captain, and with an escort.' As Marquet climbed up into the carriage and sat on the soft leather seat, Franco joined him.

'The Prince wants to create the right impression. He does not care about our comfort. He does not wish to risk damaging such expensive gifts.'

Franco and Marquet's first appointment was with La Romana's deputy, General Kindelan. They travelled via Kiel, into Jutland and on to the general's headquarters in Aarhus. On behalf of the Emperor, and following Bernadotte's instructions, Franco presented Kindelan with the *Légion*

D'honneur and a pair of magnificent pistols. He then presented Bernadotte's order. There would be no changing of the wording of the oath this time. No more words that might be subject to interpretation or to give an excuse to backslide. The order instructed both Kindelan and La Romana to assemble each regiment of the Division del Norte in full parade dress. Each colonel would be commanded to read the words of the oath to King Joseph to all the assembled troops. Every man would then shout out the oath. Each officer would then sign a copy of the oath. Copies of these documents would be collected and sent to Bernadotte's headquarters.

Marquet had asked Franco if he expected trouble, or worse, mutiny. Franco was obviously worried. General Kindelan though seemed to show his loyalty to the new master of Spain. The general confirmed what Franco had told Marquet. His troops were very conservative. They would listen to and believe what their priests would tell them. The priests almost certainly knew of Napoleon's hatred of the Catholic Church. A Bonaparte brother on the throne would surely lead to the weakening of the Church's power. The priests would be passionately against any change. It would certainly be difficult but what the Prince had ordered would be done.

Three days later, Marquet and Franco arrived in Nyborg. The journey had been pleasant. Franco had been surprisingly good company. They had stopped at French garrisons en route. At Odense, Marquet sought out Corporal Lejeune instructing him to arrange a meeting with the valet, Martin. Time to press the man for news on the British spy.

Franco went to make arrangements to meet the marquis. Marquet found Lejeune outside the church. Martin arrived a few minutes later. The three sat on pews in a quiet side chapel under a large wooden plaque dedicated to a Johann Friis. The bright colours and gold of the plaque contrasted with the rest of the church's starkness, apart from other memorial plaques, bare walls devoid of decoration. It struck Marquet how different this was from the highly decorated churches at home. Martin had hardly begun when there was a slight cough behind them. Marquet turned to see a man – the priest? The priest began in very broken French, 'I am the vicar, Christopher Nyholm, can I help you gentlemen?'

Marquet thought quickly. How best to get rid of this interruption? Truth or near to it was the best option.

'Ah, *Monsieur le Cure*, we are the bearer of news for the valet Martin. I hope that we can use the peace and dignity of your church?'

The vicar smiled. 'Of course. I shall be in the sacristy if you need me.'

'Thank you, Father.'

As soon as they were alone, Marquet told Martin to repeat what he had told Lejeune. As he spoke, his hands trembled, eyes darting in different directions. It was as if the man was desperate to please, terrified he might invent anything to satisfy his interrogators. There was no point being heavy-handed. Marquet took the gentle approach.

'You have done well, Martin.' Marquet put his arm around the valet's shoulders.

'Thank you, Captain.'

'Now what did you say the merchant's name was?'

'Adam Rorauer.'

'What did he look like? How old was he?'

'He was short, rather stocky, probably in his mid-forties.'

That was the same description of the priest Marquet had glimpsed in Hamburg.

'When the man Rorauer spoke with the general, what language did he use?'

'French and I thought I heard him speaking Latin as I have heard in church.'

'And when Rorauer first arrived at the hotel, what language did he use?'

'German. The hotel manager remarked that he seemed to have a Bavarian accent.'

Marquet was intrigued. A merchant who was fluent in three languages including Latin – most unusual.

'And where is the merchant now?'

'He has left Nyborg to travel round Funen to visit the other Spanish regiments looking for more business. He was given a letter of introduction by Colonel O'Donnell, the general's aide-de-camp.'

'Will he return to Nyborg?'

'I don't know, Captain.'

Lejeune made to strike Martin. The valet's eyes, working in different directions, leapt. Marquet restrained Lejeune.

'No need for that, Corporal. Martin has served us well and will continue to do so, will you not?'

Martin again looked terrified. 'Yes, Captain, of course.'

'Continue the good work. I will see what can be done to make your son's conditions a little better.'

'Thank you, Captain.' The man stood and bowed.

As they watched Martin walk away from the church, Lejeune turned to Marquet.

'You were rather gentle on him, sir?'

'Sometimes a softer approach achieves the required result, Corporal. He will do anything for us now. We can always resort to more persuasive techniques should we need to. Martin knows that only too well.'

Lejeune did not look convinced. He saluted and left to make his way back to Odense. Marquet walked back to the hotel to find Franco. It was time to talk with the man Rorauer. Ideally, he would simply have the merchant arrested and taken back to Hamburg in chains. However, he was in Denmark with the Danish police and army nominally upholding Danish law. Marquet had no proof that the man had broken any local law. There was also the difficulty of arresting a man who was so obviously well liked by the marquis. It would certainly not help the already sour relations between the Spanish and French if the merchant who was to supply some of the luxuries so missed by La Romana and his officers was arrested. And certainly not when the marquis and his troops were being ordered to swear oaths of allegiance to King Joseph. No, he would have to engineer a meeting with this man and see if he really was who he claimed to be.

44

Hotel Postgarten, Nyborg

Marquet joined Franco in the dining room of the hotel. The meeting with the general was arranged for 2 p.m. Time for lunch. Marquet summoned the waiter and asked to see the innkeeper. The innkeeper told him that this was the only hotel and was completely full as were all the other spare rooms in the town. He even had to give up his dressing room to a visiting German merchant. He could arrange comfortable rooms with a relative in the nearby village of Vindinge.

Marquet looked up at the innkeeper. 'Would the merchant be Herr Rorauer?'

'It is indeed. Do you know Herr Rorauer?'

Marquet avoided the question. 'Where is Herr Rorauer now?'

'He is visiting the other Spanish regiments stationed on Funen. He told me that he would return in four or five days.' *Time enough to carry out Bernadotte's orders before grilling this man, Rorauer.*

Just before 2 p.m. Franco and Marquet climbed the stairs to the morning room. The Marquis de La Romana sat while his staff officers stood beside him. Franco made a great show of presenting the *Légion D'honneur* to the marquis. Marquet thought that the general was hardly effusive in his thanks for the award despite the 2,000 francs that came with it. He did appear delighted at the pair of pistols. The marquis then read Bernadotte's order. His face drained of colour. He looked up at Franco and then to Marquet.

'I will discuss these orders with my staff. You will leave us – now.'

Franco and Marquet saluted. Marquet followed Franco out of the hotel.

Franco turned to Marquet. 'Trouble.'

'You suspect that the general will disobey the order?'

'No, he has no choice but to comply, surrounded as he is. But the bond of trust between the two of them has been broken. La Romana is a proud Spaniard. He will not forget or forgive.'

Marquet nodded. This would be a test of Franco's loyalty. Where were his true ties? No doubt, to Spain. Time to warn the French commanders in Denmark. First General Fririon on Zealand while Franco delivered the Prince's orders to the commanders of the Asturias and Guadalajara regiments. He ordered a boat to take him across the Great Belt to Zealand and packed. A stable hand gave him a leg up on to his horse. He squeezed his horse's withers and at a gentle walk, made his way up the slope past the castle to the land gate.

45
Svendborg, Funen

Robertson had finished his discussions with the officers of the Villaviciosa Regiment. With the Barcelona Regiment to visit on the road back to Nyborg, there had even been time to cross the small sea channel to the island of Langeland and take orders from the officers of the Catalunya Regiment. He was rather taken with his alter ego, that of the merchant Adam Rorauer. His tour of Funen had been a success. Armed with the introduction from Major O'Donnell, at all the Spanish bases he had met with nothing but welcome and excellent hospitality. Such was the volume of business he had received, he mused that in another life he would have made a successful salesman. But of course, as a persuader of a different type, that was what he had been for the last twenty years. He smiled to himself remembering the successes he had had: the visit to Paris five years ago, persuading the French-Scottish general on Napoleon's staff to intervene and prevent the closure of his monastery as all other Catholic institutions were being shut. And the simpler, but no less satisfying pleasure of watching novices he had recruited in Scotland developing into committed and valuable members of the Benedictine community. Had he finally put behind him the nagging sense of failure that his life had not progressed to the level of responsibility he had once dreamed of? He hoped he had. Now it was time to add to those happy memories by convincing La Romana to take up the British offer; back to Nyborg for a final meeting for what he hoped might be the summit of his career.

As he sat back in his open carriage, he heard hooves behind him. He turned to see two Spanish officers cantering up. As the two men reached him, he recognised one. It was Lieutenant Fabregues who he had met in Assens. He ordered the driver to stop.

'Lieutenant Fabregues, good to see you again. Where are you going?'

'Herr Rorauer, a pleasure. This is my friend and colleague, Lieutenant Carreras. We are on our way to deliver the regiment's status report to headquarters.'

Carreras saluted. Robertson thought for a moment.

'Please join me in my carriage for the journey to Nyborg. It will be more comfortable. I would enjoy your company. Your horses can be tied to the back.'

Fabregues and Carreras looked at each other. 'Thank you, sir. We would be delighted.'

Their conversation during the drive was so wide-ranging that Robertson had to remind himself of his cover. The two young lieutenants even had him speaking a few words of Spanish. They reached Nyborg's landward entrance. Danish militiamen with three Spanish guards stopped the carriage. Robertson handed over his passport and paid the entrance tax. Fabregues and Carreras were waved through. The Danish corporal recognised Robertson and handed back his passport. The driver flapped the reins on to the horses' rumps but immediately pulled back to stop the carriage. Robertson looked up. An officer had entered the other end of the gate's tunnel. As the man emerged from the tunnel's gloom, he could see the white button jacket with green piping and a scarlet waistcoat visible underneath. Robertson had seen the uniform before, at the Hamburg gate. The thought of a hovering falcon shot through his mind once again.

'French military police. He's an officer. They're bastards.' Fabregues nearly spat the words out. The Frenchman rode up to the carriage, looked at the two Spaniards and then at the portly figure of Robertson. His eyes widened in recognition.

'*Mon dieu*, you!' His hand reached down to his saddle holster. Fabregues put his hand to cover his pistol and shouted to the Spanish guards on the gate.

'Cover him.' Two raised and cocked their muskets.

Fabregues shouted at the Frenchman. 'Who are you? Why do you want to draw your weapon on us?'

'I am Captain Marquet of the Gendarmerie of the Imperial Guard. The man sitting next to you is a British spy. He must be arrested and questioned.' Robertson sat bolt upright. Fabregues tuned to him.

'The captain is mistaken.' Looking up at Marquet, he said, 'Captain, you are wrong, this is Herr Adam Rorauer, a merchant from Hamburg and a friend of Spain.' Marquet's face reddened.

'It is you who is being tricked.' He then shouted, 'He is an English spy, believe me.'

'How do you know? What's his name if it isn't Adam Rorauer?'

'I have been tracking him for weeks. I don't know his name. That is why I must take him in for questioning to find out.' Marquet's voice became higher pitched as his exasperation grew. Fabregues turned to Carreras.

'Well, Lieutenant, it comes to a pretty pass when even the illustrious Gendarmerie of the Imperial Guard can't catch one man and don't even know his name!' Carreras and Fabregues burst into laughter. Robertson thought it would be best if he did so as well.

Marquet screamed, 'You stupid ignorant Spanish yokels, I am telling you that this man is a British spy. Hand him over to me!'

Fabregues's face darkened. He drew and cocked his pistol. 'Captain, you have ten seconds to leave before I shoot you.' He raised the pistol to point at Marquet's chest. Marquet's face turned from red to white. His eyes burnt with a mixture of fury and revenge. He wheeled his horse round and turned once more to look at Robertson.

'We will meet again, Mr English Spy.' He dug his heels into the horse's flanks. The horse whinnied and moved straight into a gallop across the bridge over the moat and away.

46
Roskilde, Zealland

'Where have you been? Not chasing your English spy again? You really need to concentrate on the task in hand.'

Marquet had nothing to say to Major Franco. He had pushed his horse to the limit to make the rendezvous with the small Danish gunboat moored at the easterly end of the Knudshoved peninsula, the closest point between Funen and Zealand. He was still fuming. To think he had the Englishman in his grasp only to be stopped by a Spanish lieutenant. If it ever got out, he would be a laughing stock. He resolved to kill the Spanish lieutenant on sight if he ever saw him again. As for the Englishman… The only positive from the debacle was that he now knew what his quarry looked like close up.

He heard the Danish skipper shout. 'Captain, you must board now.' He clambered on board the gunboat. As dusk turned to darkness, the sixteen rowers eased the boat into the Great Belt.

'What about the British Navy?' Franco asked the skipper. A gob of chewing tobacco from the skipper's mouth hit the water.

'They may have hundred-gun battleships but that counts for nothing in the shallows of the Baltic and with our knowledge of the coast. We are Vikings!'

As the boat slid through the calm water, Marquet closed his eyes. Franco was right. He must do his duty. Delivery of Bernadotte's orders to General Fririon was all important. But he found it impossible to put the sight of the fat Englishman out of his mind. *Merde!*

The skipper eased the gunboat into Korsor Fjord. Marquet and Franco collected horses and rode into Roskilde. As they made their way through the town's gates into a square, they were spotted by a large group of Spanish soldiers. Franco leant over to Marquet. 'They are from the Asturias Regiment.' The soldiers surrounded the two men.

There was a shout from within the crowd.

'What news from home, Major?' Franco looked flustered.

'Yes, come on, Major, tell us the news from Spain,' called another voice. In seconds, all the men were bellowing, 'What news, what of the King?' A crescendo of shouts swept across the square.

As the soldiers began to jostle Franco's and Marquet's horses, the major turned white.

'Come on, Major, what's so difficult to tell us news of home?'

Franco made to kick his horse to escape the crowd. Two soldiers grabbed the horse's reins, ripping them out of Franco's hands. Others pinned his legs to the saddle.

Marquet made to pull his pistols from their holsters.

'None of that, you bloody Frenchie.' Marquet felt a bayonet in the small of his back. He held his arms up.

Shouts grew louder from all sides.

A staff sergeant pushed his way forward.

One of the soldiers holding the reins shouted, 'The sergeant is going to let the major speak.' The crowd grew quiet.

The sergeant looked up at Franco.

'Now, Major, you have to understand, like you, these men have been away from Spain for over a year but unlike you, they have had no news from home. They have heard rumours of rebellion at home. Some of them have read the news-sheets that the British leave on the beaches. They talk of a revolution in Madrid being bloodily put down by French troops. They say that the King, minister Godoy and the King's son, Ferdinand, are prisoners in France. Is this true? Now come down off your horse, Major, and tell us the news.'

Franco looked at Marquet as if appealing for help. With a bayonet in his back, there was nothing Marquet could do. He looked round the square for any French troops – none.

The sergeant looked up at Franco. 'Now, Major, what is the problem? Surely, it cannot be too difficult for one Spaniard to give your fellow countrymen the news?'

Marquet was disgusted with Franco. Why didn't he just

invent a plausible story to satisfy these oafs? They could then make their way to safety. He would then organise suitable punishment for such a mutiny. Line a few of them up against a wall *"pour encourager les autres"*.

It was too late.

The sergeant turned to the crowd. 'Well, men, it seems as though the major has something to hide. Shall we bring him down to our level?'

As if in unison a shout went up. 'Down!'

In a flash, hands extracted Franco's left foot from the stirrup. His calf and the sole of his boot were grasped and violently pushed upwards forcing the major out of his saddle. He crashed head first onto the cobbles, his right foot trapped in the other stirrup. Cheers went up.

Marquet again tensed to move but felt the point of the bayonet piercing his coat. 'One more move will be your last,' came a hiss from behind him. He relaxed back into his saddle, hands well away from his pistols.

Franco's right shoulder and cheek rested on the cobbles. His right foot was still caught in the stirrup. The sergeant put his hands on his waist.

'Well, lads, while the major makes up his mind whether to bring us the news or not, shall we have a look at what treasures he has in his saddle bags?'

Another shout of approval.

Hands unbuckled the saddle bags. Papers were handed to the sergeant.

A hush descended as the sergeant read. Finishing, he looked up. His face flushed. 'My French may not be the best, but even I can understand these orders from Marshal

Bernadotte to General Fririon. They instruct the general to command the colonels of the Asturias and Guadalajara regiments to assemble all their troops in full dress to stand behind their colours and swear allegiance and loyalty to their new king, King Joseph.'

A pause.

The sergeant now shouted, 'The new king, King Joseph Bonaparte!' Summoning as much mucus as he could from the back of his throat, he spat on Franco's face.

'Traitor.'

It did not take long for the enormity of Bernadotte's orders to sink in.

From the heart of the crowd, a voice shouted 'Never!' Soon he was joined by the whole chorus. The shouts of 'Never, never!' echoed around the square.

From behind Marquet the familiar and threatening voice spat 'And let's send this bastard Frenchman to where he belongs.' Marquet tensed for the point of the bayonet to pierce his skin.

A shot rang out. The Spanish soldiers quietened and turned to the source of the shot. Colonel Dellevielleuze of the Asturias emerged from the corner of the square. He was accompanied by his personal guard in full fighting order. The guard cleared a path for the colonel to reach Franco and Marquet. Franco's foot was released from the stirrup. The major crumpled to the ground but was then hauled to his feet. Unsteadily he dusted himself down. The staff sergeant saluted.

'My Colonel, these officers have brought orders for us to swear loyalty to Joseph Bonaparte, the new King of Spain.'

Dellevielleuze was visibly shocked. Turning to Franco, he asked, 'Is this true, Major?'

Franco nodded.

The colonel turned to the sergeant. 'Tell the men to return to their quarters while I question the major. I must understand exactly what orders he has brought. I will then talk with my staff. Your officers will return with my orders for you. Do you understand, Sergeant?'

'Yes, my Colonel.' He shouted a command. The men began to move.

Dellevielleuze looked at Marquet. 'And who are you, Captain, and what is your role in this outrage?'

It was Franco who answered. 'This is Captain Marquet of the Prince of Ponte Corvo's staff. I am Major Franco of the Prince's personal guard.'

The colonel looked with disgust at the crumpled state of Franco's uniform. 'We leave for my headquarters before they change their minds.'

At his headquarters, Dellevielleuze was briefed by Franco. He then called his officers together. They would instruct the troops under each command that the oath they would take was no different to that taken by the marquis himself and all the other men under his command. This, the colonel hoped, would put an end to the disquiet. By late afternoon, he had received reports from all his officers. The report of the order to take the oath had spread like wildfire. The mood was ugly and mutinous. The colonel issued orders. Anyone found on the streets of Roskilde after regimental prayers would be shot.

An hour later, there was a knock on the door. One of

his personal guards entered and reported that a mass of the colonel's troops had armed themselves and were advancing on his headquarters. Was it time to face them or run to where they could find protection and reinforcements? They ran to General Fririon's headquarters in a castle close to the town.

The French guards saw the general and opened the stout oak doors to let them in. Fririon bent over, hands on his knees. In between gasps for air, he whooped, 'Sound the alarm. Bolt the doors. Immediately!'

The doors crashed closed, iron bolts sliding into place. Fririon had caught more breath. 'How many Spaniards are involved in the mutiny?'

Marquet answered. 'Five hundred, maybe more.'

'I have no more than seventy troops which are quartered all over the town. If the Spaniards are in the murderous mood you say they are, it will be impossible to stop them. Upstairs, quickly.'

As they reached the first floor, looking out of the window, they could see the horde gathering in the castle's forecourt. Two of Dellevielleuze's officers made it to the castle entrance. Marquet could just about hear their voices shouting above the hubbub as they pleaded with their men to desist and return to their barracks. The enraged troops were adamant. There would be no swearing of an oath to a French upstart. Marquet then saw two blue uniforms: French officers dashing for safety. Too late, both were spotted and engulfed. Swords and knives were raised: 'Death to the French'; 'Death to Bonaparte. Death to traitors and usurpers'; 'Long live King Ferdinand!' A cheer went up. Marquet feared the worst.

Dellevieulleuze opened the doors of a first-floor balcony. He bellowed for quiet so that he could be heard. The noise below him began to subside.

'The order to take the oath has been revoked.'

His words seemed to have an effect. Marquet was impressed but then was too late to stop General Fririon stepping onto the balcony. Seeing a hated Frenchman appear could only mean one thing. The colonel was being forced to lie to them. The Spaniards erupted in fury. The shouts began again but even louder. Marquet pulled the general back out of view. He was about to shout "imbecile" in Fririon's ear but thought better of it. Window glass shattered. The colonel screamed. Blood streamed down his face. A rock thrown from the crowd below caught him on the cheekbone. An aide caught him as he slumped to the floor.

Fririon took no notice of the colonel.

'It's us, the French, they want. If we don't make a run for it, they'll tear us apart. Come with me.' Marquet and the other officers followed Fririon into a back room. They all stopped for a moment to catch their breath. A young lieutenant put his hand up.

'Sir, there are Danish uniforms in a storeroom downstairs. The red coats should confuse the mob long enough for us to get away.'

'Good, show me.' They ran down the back stairs. The lieutenant wrenched open the storeroom door. Uniforms hung on a rack. Fririon shouted 'Coats and shakos only, no time for trousers.' Marquet ripped off his coat. He realised that he had been wearing it for over twenty hours non-stop. No time for tiredness. As the others struggled into the ill-fitting jackets, he opened a cupboard: a stack of muskets.

'General, let's line up in platoon order with these muskets shouldered.'

'Good idea, Captain.' They made their way to a rear entrance. Marquet slid the door bolts back as quietly as he could, opened the door ajar and peered into the courtyard.

'Clear.'

'Move, now,' Fririon ordered. Marquet opened the door fully. The eight emerged into the sunlight.

'Form up.' The general took front right. As he took position to Fririon's left, Marquet felt beads of sweat pour down the small of his back. The shako was too small and perched precariously on top of his head.

'Shoulder arms,' ordered Fririon. The eight shouldered their muskets.

Marquet hissed, 'General, you cannot speak French. We are supposed to be Danes.' Fririon swore.

'How is your Danish, Captain?'

'I'll use German. That should confuse them. *Marz!*' As the platoon moved, a group of Spaniards ran into the courtyard. Thirty or more, Marquet guessed. The leading Spaniards rushed up to the platoon. A corporal shouted at Marquet what sounded like "French?" Marquet shrugged his shoulders. The Spaniard swore. Marquet tried to smile and shrugged his shoulders again. A shout from another Spaniard. He had seen the open back door to the castle. He ran towards the door followed by the others, shouting triumphantly.

Marquet ordered, '*Marz!*' Then in French hissed, 'Keep your discipline. Heads front.' The platoon marched off away from the castle towards the town's outskirts. They rounded a corner and saw a group of French soldiers milling around, seemingly unsure of what was happening. Fririon stepped forward. A lance-corporal recognised the general. His mouth dropped open. He snapped to attention and saluted.

'Don't ask, Soldier. Where are the stables? We must ride to Copenhagen immediately.'

'Follow me, sir.'

Two hours later, Fririon and Marquet were sitting with the French ambassador. A message had been sent to the King of Denmark requesting help to put down the mutiny. Marquet was found a hotel room. A bath was brought and filled. He stripped off and realised he stank. He used a mirror to inspect the puncture in his back. No damage done. He lowered himself into the hot water. Tiredness washed over him. He luxuriated as his muscles relaxed. Next: sleep followed by the return to Nyborg. The interview with Mr Rorauer was calling him.

47
Hotel Postgarten, Nyborg

Relief coursed through Robertson's veins as he arrived back at the hotel. He thanked Fabregues and Carreras, watched them leave to deliver their report and went to his room. Perhaps La Romana had made up his mind? He would ask Major O'Donnell for another interview with the general. As he sat on the bed, there was a knock on the door. It was the landlord. He gave Robertson a letter, postmarked Hamburg, in MacKenzie's handwriting. At last, were these the instructions for his means of escape? He thanked the landlord and waited for him to leave so that he could begin decoding the letter.

The landlord looked at him. 'Herr Rorauer, you should know that a French officer has been asking about you.' The same one or were there more than one gendarme looking for him?

No need to tell the landlord about the altercation at the town gate.

'What sort of French officer? I mean, do you know his unit?'

'Not exactly but I asked some of our Spanish friends. His name is Captain Marquet. He is a military policeman. It appears he is one of the officers responsible for counter-intelligence operations in north Germany. He was here with a Spanish officer, a Major Franco. I overheard some of the marquis's officers say that Franco had delivered orders from Marshal Bernadotte to La Romana instructing him to assemble the soldiers in his command. He and all his men are to swear loyalty to King Joseph.'

'Where is this Marquet now?'

'It appears he left to deliver the same order to the Spanish troops on Zealand.'

'Is he coming back here?'

'I don't know, but if he will be returning to Germany, it must be likely.'

'Thank you, my friend.'

'You should also know that the mood among the Spanish officers has completely changed since they received these orders.'

'In what way?'

'All the humour has left them and they are thoroughly depressed. But I also sense pent-up anger.'

Robertson thanked the landlord again. He stretched out on his bed. So just one policeman; it was fortunate that he had not returned to Nyborg a day or so earlier. It was time to conclude discussions with the marquis. Then he must leave Denmark as soon as possible. There was one positive. Surely La Romana and his officers would resent being ordered to swear fealty to a Frenchman and to a king who was Bonaparte's brother.

He decoded the letter. MacKenzie was now in Sweden. He wrote that a cutter would be off the place Robertson had suggested at twilight for three consecutive evenings commencing the day after tomorrow – good.

At supper time, Robertson walked downstairs. As he reached the bottom of the staircase, the marquis and some of his staff officers were about to climb the stairs. Maybe he would be summoned now. As they passed each other, La Romana looked at him, paused and then walked quickly up the stairs. His heart sank.

A day passed. Robertson kept to his room as much as possible. He attempted to keep busy by writing out the lists of orders he had received but found it impossible to keep his mind off the ever-squeezing time frame. Would the general call him before Captain Marquet returned?

After a fitful night's sleep, Robertson woke, prayed and dressed. Only then did he see a note pushed under the door. *His Excellency will see you at 8 a.m. today.* It must have been pushed under the door in the early hours. He'd heard nothing. He breakfasted early and took a stroll around the town to calm himself. He was outside the marquis's quarters in plenty of time. At exactly eight, O'Donnell ushered him into the general's room.

La Romana smiled. 'I have fully weighed up what you have said. I have also consulted with a number of my officers in whom I have absolute confidence. I can tell you that I have decided to accept your government's proposal.'

'I am delighted, Your Excellency.'

'You will know that my regiments are spread all over the Danish islands and mainland. If we are going to be transported home, I will have to concentrate as many as possible in one place. You will also know that all the troops in my command have been ordered to swear an oath of loyalty to King Joseph.'

'Yes, Your Excellency.'

'I have written to Marshal Bernadotte suggesting that once the oaths have been taken, he should come here to inspect and review the whole Division del Norte to demonstrate the loyalty to the new king. The marshal has agreed but has not agreed a date. I therefore have the chance to concentrate my troops.'

'A brilliant strategy, Your Excellency.'

'You should report my decision to your handlers. In the meantime, I shall instruct one of my officers to make contact with your naval colleagues. Once we strike, we will have little time to make our escape before Bernadotte reacts. If he is able to gather his troops, we will be outnumbered by three to one at least. Surrender or massacre would be the alternatives.'

Robertson nodded. The plan carried huge risk.

The marquis continued, 'You have been here too long. It is time that you left. Any further delay will excite suspicion and risk the whole operation.'

Too true, Robertson thought.

La Romana continued. 'Thank you for the valuable service you have rendered to me, the men under my command and to Spain. This is a time of imminent risk, but if it pleases God to allow me to return to my country,

I will on all occasions bear testimony to the admirable manner in which you executed your commission. Look after yourself and good luck on your journey home. Now go.'

Robertson bowed and left the general's room. Elated at his success, he returned to his room and coded two messages to MacKenzie; one addressed to Helsingborg and the second to Heligoland. He also coded a further letter for Mr Canning sent via Mr Nicholas. All the messages would go via the usual route to Hamburg and onwards. He made his way to the post office, and smiled as he handed them over to the postmaster, mixed up nicely with the orders for chocolate and cigars.

'More orders for our Spanish friends. Please send them by express; my customers cannot wait!'

'Of course.'

Back in his room, he packed and then rested. There would be time for a good supper before the town's gates were closed and he had to make his way to the agreed meeting point on the beach. Managing to suppress his excitement, he slept.

Waking refreshed, he finished his packing, paid for his room, finished a good supper, bade the landlord farewell and slipped out of the hotel. Through the gate and by a circuitous route he arrived at the beach. Two hours to wait until twilight.

48
Roskilde, Zealand

Marquet was fuming. He had implored General Fririon to let him travel back to Nyborg to interview the merchant, Rorauer. Fririon assured him that his efforts during the mutiny would not go unrecognised but told him in no uncertain terms that he was required to help restore order among the Spanish troops on Zealand. When that tack did not work, Marquet suggested that he should return to Funen and then move to Jutland to warn other locally based French commanders. Finally, he should report to the Prince of Ponte Corvo. Again, he was rebuffed. Messages had already been sent and in any case, Marquet's skills as a counter-intelligence officer were required in Zealand. What made the refusal even more galling was the realisation that Fririon was only three years older than he was. The general had risen through the ranks of the

revolutionary army and was not a son of the nobility –
how the world had changed.

The mutiny had been quashed as quickly as it had
started. There were to be summary courts martial for the
ring leaders. The soldiers were to be split into small groups
and cantoned in villages across the island. Communication
between the Spaniards was to be kept to a minimum. Being
dragged away from what he saw as his real objective was
intensely frustrating. But he now had interrogation work
to do. It would be unpleasant, but these mutineers needed
to be taught a lesson. The consequences of mutiny would
be published throughout the *Grande Armée* and across
the Empire. Perhaps his role would become known in
influential circles and have a positive impact on his career?
However much he tried he could not get the picture of the
stout spy out of his mind.

49

The Beach at Teglvaeksskoven on the Great Belt

Robertson just hoped that the sailors would spot him in the gloom. To keep himself amused he looked for interesting pebbles and shells. The time passed. The collection grew. Then he spotted it. The cutter was sailing directly for him. He drew a handkerchief and waved it. A noise came from the dunes behind him. He turned. A musket was pointing at Robertson's chest. He looked up. A Danish militiaman; what did those blue eyes indicate? Fear, incomprehension, resolve? Was the musket cocked? The cutter was 300, maybe 400 metres away, way too far for a shot at the man, even if they knew what was happening. Time to brazen it out.

'Well, I must congratulate you on your vigilance especially when the enemy is so close.' Robertson turned, pointing towards the British ship. The cutter was still too far away to help.

He smiled at the Dane. 'Can you tell me the best way to get across the Belt without being captured by the British?' The man eyed him with suspicion.

In broken German, he said, 'You could ask Lars who fishes these waters. He has several boats.'

'Where does he live?'

The Dane pointed to a cottage further down the beach.

'Thank you.' Robertson walked towards the cottage. This would buy some time for the cutter to reach the beach. The door of the cottage opened. The fisherman emerged. Before Robertson could say anything, the militiaman was joined by six of his colleagues. Bayonets were lowered at his stomach. The odds for escape to the cutter vanished.

The older of the Danes pushed his bayonet more firmly into Robertson's ample midriff.

'And who the hell are you? What are you doing here?'

No time for weakness now.

Robertson smiled at the man. 'I am a merchant.'

The Dane interrupted. 'Where is your passport?'

'Here.' Robertson reached into his jacket. The bayonet prodded harder.

'Show me.' He reached out over the rifle. The passport was in German. 'It is no good.' Robertson realised that none of them could read. 'What is wrong with it?'

'It is no good.' This time louder. The bayonet was forced harder. He wondered how long the coat fabric would withstand the point.

'Have a look at it again. Look, it has the arms of your king.'

'It is no good. Where have you come from?'

'Nyborg.'

'Then we will take you back there.'

Robertson reckoned that the cutter must have reached the beach. He was sure that the sight of armed sailors or marines would scare the Danes off. 'I need to go back the way I came, I don't want to get lost.'

'We will show you the way. Come now.'

A crowd had gathered to watch the spectacle. The militiamen made no attempt to stop the locals from jostling him. It was clear that they were sure that a spy or criminal had been captured. A young girl pushed her way through the melee to have a closer look at this villain. Robertson held out his hand in a show of friendship. The girl grabbed his hand, bent down and bit hard. As she let go, he could see blood. He was unable to hide the pain.

'My god, ouch!' came out in English. *What have I done?* But the crowd was too busy cheering to hear.

It seemed the militiamen did not know what to do with him. He was taken to a local tavern, given a glass of brandy and questioned again. He gave the same answers. The men looked at each other, unsure. He was then marched on to a larger village. Here they found their sergeant. The older of the group reported to their superior, handing over Robertson's passport, all eager for praise for the capture of the prisoner. The sergeant led Robertson into his house.

'How on earth did you manage to get caught by these clods?' He spoke in excellent German. Robertson thought he could detect a Hanoverian accent, widely regarded as the language's most prized.

'With bayonets prodding me, I had little choice!'

The sergeant carefully looked through the passport, and he looked at Robertson.

'There's nothing wrong with your passport. It is all in order. Why did they arrest you?'

'None of them can read.'

'Sadly, there is nothing I can do to rectify their mistake. I have no authority to release anyone who has been arrested.'

'So, what are you going to do with me?'

It was obvious that the cutter would have given up looking for him as dusk was closing in.

'I must take you to Nyborg.'

'That is where I have been staying these past days, at the Hotel Postgarten.'

'But that hotel is the most expensive in the town and only for gentlemen.'

'I have spent plenty of time with the gentlemen at the hotel. As a gentleman and a merchant, it would be embarrassing to be marched into the town like a criminal. Can I ask that you take me on your own? I am an old man, unarmed. I have this walking stick which I will throw away if it alarms you.'

'Agreed. Keep the stick. It is best that we go to my colonel's country house. It's not far to walk. He has the authority to release you.'

They found the colonel playing skittles with friends. Despite the interruption, the colonel was polite. He also validated the passport.

'I am indeed sorry that my men have caused you so much trouble. They are ignorant and cannot read German.

But I trust you will understand that with so many enemies, they are suspicious of strangers.'

'Of course.'

'Then you are free to go. My sergeant will escort you back to the hotel.'

'Thank you, Colonel. Your men were only doing their duty. They are a credit to you guarding the coast so diligently.'

Walking back to the hotel, Robertson cursed his luck, but then smiled to himself. Things had been going too well. Back to reality, he realised that any chance of a rescue by sea had evaporated. Whatever he chose next, the priority had to be to leave Funen.

The landlord was surprised that his guest had returned. He seemed happy with Robertson's explanation, but there was something in the look he gave that was a cause for concern. At least he had the confidence of the militia colonel to fall back on if the landlord's suspicion materialised. There was also La Romana but that would surely be a last resort.

Lying on the newly made-up bed, he considered his position. He had been lucky. The militiamen could well have shot him. That the sergeant was a Hanoverian was fortunate. That the colonel has taken his story at face value was a relief. Better still, it seemed that Marquet, the French military policeman, had not reappeared. Perhaps he was still on Zealand? Escape across the Great Belt to Sweden was now surely out of the question. To try again with the militia prowling the beach was just too risky. Another message to MacKenzie would take at least ten days to receive an answer. No, the Great Belt route was finished. There was nothing for it but to retrace his steps, return to the safe house in Hamburg and be smuggled back to Heligoland. He still had enough money to afford the quickest transport. What really concerned him was the Frenchman knew what he looked like and that he was a German merchant. Once he was clear of Funen, it would be time to dispense with Adam Rorauer, the German merchant who has been so successful selling his chocolate and cigars. It was time to assume another identity. Jan Petersen would emerge once he had reached Haderslev on the mainland.

50

Mr Fenwick's house, Helsingborg

MacKenzie's journey to Helsingborg had taken nearly three days along bumpy roads. The Swedes, he thought, could benefit from the technology used to build the turnpikes in England. Mr Smith had been right, Fenwick was a model of helpfulness and knowledge. A skipper was contacted, gold changed hands. MacKenzie was able to watch from the mole as the vessel slid into the darkness to begin its journey around the north of Zealand down into the Great Belt to the appointed beach near Nyborg.

Fenwick had assured him that the captain had run many covert missions over the past three years. Indeed, the captain had provided valuable information in advance of the British invasion of Copenhagen the previous year. Of course, there would be danger from aggressive Danish gunboats that operated from inlets around Zealand but with the Royal Navy's presence, as long as he kept well away from the coast until he reached Nyborg, the journey should be straightforward. MacKenzie found waiting was a painful business.

Six days later, a messenger brought news that the cutter had been sighted. Fenwick and MacKenzie were on the quayside as the vessel came alongside. No sign of Robertson on deck. Perhaps he was below? The captain shouted, 'He was captured by the Danish militia.'

MacKenzie's heart sank. His mouth dried up.

Once ashore, the captain explained what he had seen. Yes, it had been nearly dark but there was no doubt, it was Robertson being led away by soldiers in red. MacKenzie's mind filled with nightmarish thoughts: had the monk been jailed, tortured or worse, handed over to the French? What of the discussions with La Romana? Fenwick advised him to delay writing to Mr Canning until the next day when the shock of failure had subsided. For failure it was.

51

The Transport Office, Dorset Court, Cannon Row, Westminster

Hoppner was sitting in on another meeting presided over by Captain George, the chairman of the Transport Office. Sitting to his right was Mr M'Cleay, the secretary. They looked down the table at a group of officers from the Admiralty and the War Office. Since Mr Canning had persuaded the Cabinet to approve the rescue of the Spanish troops in Denmark, Captain George and his staff had been severely over-worked. Not only had the office to provide tonnage to carry Sir Arthur Wellesley's troops to Spain but also to collect troops from Cork. At the end of June, the office had contracted 652 ships from the merchant marine. Now this had risen to over 820 vessels. Surely, Hoppner thought, no other country had the capacity to provide what the Transport Office was delivering. For the Danish operation thirty-four troop ships and five store ships were assembling in Portsmouth, the Downs, the Nore, Harwich and Yarmouth.

Hoppner listened as the technicalities of equipping the fleet were hammered out: how the convoy would assemble and sail to Denmark; what protection would be given to protect the convoy from French frigates, Danish gunboats and even roving privateers. It was then that Mr Barrow, the second secretary of the Admiralty turned to Hoppner.

Without looking at Captain George, he said, 'If I may, Mr Chairman, I would like to ask our representative from the Foreign Office whether contact has been made with the Marquis de La Romana?'

Captain George nodded.

All eyes turned to Hoppner. This was the question that he hoped would not be asked, or more specifically the follow-up. Hoppner had checked with Mr Hammond for advice on how best to answer. He attempted to look confident.

'Yes, sir. One of our confidential agents has had two meetings with the marquis. We have also had reports from other sources which indicate that there is considerable disquiet within the Spanish division now that the news of the rebellion in Spain has become known. As you know, the Royal Navy has delivered many copies of news-sheets around the beaches of the Danish islands. These have detailed reports of 2 May uprising and the violence that was used by the French to suppress the revolt.'

He was interrupted.

Mr Barrow looked at him. 'This is all well and good, Mr Hoppner. You have obviously been well trained by your masters in the Foreign Office. Obfuscation may work well in diplomatic circles, but you are among friends here. Will you kindly answer the question?'

Hoppner flushed. 'The question, sir?'

Clearly irritated, Mr Barrow spoke very slowly. 'The question, sir, is simple. Has the marquis agreed to His Majesty's Government's proposal to transport him and his division out of Denmark? Yes or no?'

'Not exactly.'

'Typical! More muddying of the waters. What do you mean by "not exactly"?'

Hoppner swallowed.

'The last report we had from the confidential agent stated that the agent was confident that the marquis would agree to our proposals but that he wanted more time to consider them. A third meeting was planned but we do not know if that meeting took place or if it did, the outcome.'

There was silence.

Captain George then looked at Hoppner. 'Your lords and masters wish us to despatch over forty vessels to Denmark on your agent's confidence that the marquis will agree? Quite apart from the risk involved, have you any idea of the cost to my lords and masters at the Treasury?'

'No, sir.'

'Mr M'Cleay will inform you after this meeting.'

Hoppner hoped that now was the time to push back. 'Thank you, sir. The decision to proceed with the expedition was made by the Cabinet as a whole.'

'That may be so but perhaps the members of the Cabinet were unaware that the marquis had not actually agreed to the proposal? Gentlemen, I suggest that we report back to our respective masters and ask for clarification. Agreed?'

Heads nodded.

Walking back to the Foreign Office, Hoppner reasoned that there was nothing else he could have done. That the mission might be postponed could well incur the wrath of Mr Hammond who would not enjoy informing the Foreign Secretary. On the other hand, Captain George did have a point. What if La Romana turned down the offer? The Admiralty would have to abort the expedition. Hoppner did not want to calculate the military and political consequences quite apart from the reputational damage. Britain would be a laughing stock. Robertson's third meeting must have surely taken place – where was his report?

52

Mr Fenwick's House, Helsingborg

At breakfast, MacKenzie and Fenwick were discussing the reports Fenwick had received from his informants in Denmark. It seemed that there were rumblings of discontent within some Spanish units. It appeared that Bernadotte himself was due to travel to Nyborg to inspect the whole division. Did that mean that the Spanish general was concentrating all his regiments on Funen? Was this significant?

A knock. Mr Fenwick's clerk entered the morning room and gave MacKenzie a letter. It was from Heligoland. MacKenzie excused himself, went to his room and decoded the letter. Mr Nicholas had received the news of Robertson's third meeting with the marquis. La Romana agreed to take up the government's offer. MacKenzie could have cheered. There was a postscript. Mr Nicholas had received an unconfirmed report from one of the Hamburg watchers. A carriage carrying what was described as a British spy had been seen entering Hamburg's prison. It was rumoured that the man was actually Irish. He was to be questioned before being taken to Paris for "rigorous" interrogation. This surely could only be McMahon. Everything now rested on Robertson's shoulders.

Back in the morning room, he told Fenwick the news of La Romana's acceptance. No need to talk about McMahon.

'Bravo!'

Mr Nicholas had already reported the news to Mr Canning. Instructions were to be sent to admiral Saumarez to assist La Romana. A Spanish envoy would travel on the sloop carrying the message to the admiral.

'Congratulations, MacKenzie, a splendid coup. You should celebrate.'

'Not yet. Not until I have news that Robertson is safe.'

53
The Foreign Office, July 1808

Since the meeting at the Transport Office, Hoppner had done his best to keep his head down. Word had got out. There were the usual snide remarks from some of his more senior colleagues. Were they jealous of the role that he had been given? He just needed to keep a low profile until some other crisis occupied the office chit-chat.

He was buried in a mountain of reports from across Germany and Austria. He was keen to read about the early reaction of Napoleon's erstwhile opponents to the news of the Spanish defeat of a French army at Baylen, south of Madrid. Eighteen thousand French troops had been forced to surrender. The news would surely stun all Europe. The invincible *Grand Armée* beaten! Though with no ambassador in Russia, Austria or Prussia, it would be difficult to broadcast news except through informal channels. No doubt the French would do everything they could to suppress or obfuscate the truth. He wondered if it would be possible to provide the Marquis de La Romana with the news. That would surely help him make the decision to accept the government's offer.

Hoppner made a note to himself. At his next meeting with Mr Hammond, he would suggest that funds should be provided through Mr Nicholas on Heligoland to be distributed through his network to print leaflets locally publicising the results of the battle. He tried to remember when a French army had been so comprehensively beaten. Thinking of the various agents across Germany, Prussia, Bavaria and Austria reminded him of Alexander Horn, another monk based at the Scottish seminary at Ratisbon. Horn had provided much valuable intelligence, so much so that he had been forced to escape from the monastery and was now constantly on the move in Bavaria and Austria. He paused writing. Horn was a colleague of the Reverend Robertson.

There was a tap on his shoulder. Hoppner looked up. It was the librarian.

'Dreaming, Hoppner?'

'Concentrating, Mr Ancell.'

'Mr Hammond wants to see you immediately.'

His heart sank. A reprimand following the debacle at the Transport Office was no doubt on the way and no time to prepare a defence.

He knocked on the door to Mr Hammond's office.

'Come.'

'You wish to see me, sir.'

Mr Hammond waved at a chair. Not what Hoppner expected. If he was in for a roasting, he would have been made to stand. He sat.

'Well, young Hoppner. I have news from Heligoland. Mr Nicholas has received Reverend Robertson's letter following his third meeting with La Romana. The marquis has accepted our offer.'

'That is excellent news indeed.' The tension that had built up inside him evaporated.

Hammond raised his hand. 'We must now plan the next stage. You are aware that there are Spanish emissaries in London. They are from the juntas who oppose Napoleon. These deputies have requested any support we can give. We have asked that one of their party becomes the liaison officer with the marquis and his staff. You are to ask your Admiralty friend, Palmerston, to issue instructions to transport the chosen officer to Admiral Saumarez's fleet in the Baltic.'

'Yes, sir. Do we know who the Spaniards have chosen?'

'I understand that it is to be a naval lieutenant who has recently arrived in London from Seville with messages for the deputies: a certain Don Rafael Lobo y Campo. Here also is a note from Mr Canning to the lords of the Admiralty requesting that Their Lordships order the commanding officer in the Sound and Belt to open communications with the Spanish Army, with a view to their embarkation and I quote "placing them in a state of security until transports for their reception can be sent from hence to convoy them to Spain".'

Hoppner bowed and took the note. 'Is the commanding officer Rear Admiral Keats?'

'It is.' That meant that the government was acting immediately on the success of Robertson's mission. Hoppner was delighted for the monk.

'Can I ask, do we know if Robertson is safe?'

'We do not know. There has been nothing since his letter.'

'And McMahon?'

'Nothing certain. Though Mr Nicholas's contacts report that a special prisoner was to be delivered from Hamburg to Paris. The joke going round was he was to be for Monsieur Fouché's delectation.'

'Delectation?'

'Interrogation and all that goes with it.'

Hoppner felt cold. His imagination began to stir but he then remembered the doubts he had about McMahon. The man had managed to talk himself into Mr Canning's confidence. Who would dare question the Foreign Secretary's decision to believe McMahon? Perhaps he could do the same with Monsieur Fouché, if he had the opportunity to meet him away from his torturers.

He looked at Mr Hammond. 'Is there anything we can do for Mr Robertson?'

'No, we don't even know where he is. He knew the risks. We must let him rely on his own wits. They have served him well thus far.'

Hoppner knew that Mr Hammond was right. The monk was on his own.

'Sir, the Spanish victory over the French has surely come at a fortunate moment. La Romana will probably not have heard the news. If we can brief Señor Lobo, one of his first tasks must be to ensure that the marquis has cause to celebrate.'

'Excellent, Hoppner. Add this to the discussion with Palmerston.'

***

Hoppner stood in the outer waiting room of perhaps the most fashionable club in London. Here, gentlemen and lady members of the "Ton", those "Exquisites" of the highest strata of London, would gather. Admission was by voucher, given only to those who met the approval of a select committee of highly influential and exclusive ladies known as the Lady Patronesses of Almack's.

Hoppner had sent a note to Palmerston at the Admiralty. A reply told him that the young civil commissioner had already left. If urgent, he could be found in the Almack's. From the Foreign Office, he took a back entrance, walked across St James's Park, crossed the Mall, up St James's before turning right into King Street. At Almack's, the doorman summoned a footman. A butler asked him the purpose of his visit.

'I have an urgent message for Viscount Palmerston.'

Hoppner had not seen an exquisitely dressed young man who shouted, 'You mean Lord Cupid. He won't appreciate having to let go of one of the beauties he has his arm round.' The dandy laughed and disappeared. The comment seemed to confirm the rumours. Perhaps Temple was a ladies' man.

As if to confirm the gossip, Henry Temple swept through double doors with a true beauty on his arm.

'Hoppner, I trust you are not about to spoil my evening with business. May I present Emily, Lady Cowper?'

He knew of the famed beauty. Was she one of the Patronesses of Almack's?

Hoppner bowed. Lady Cowper nodded. 'Are you taking the viscount away from me? The evening has only just started.'

'I regret so, my lady. I have messages from Mr Canning that cannot wait.'

Palmerston escorted Lady Cowper back into the inner sanctum and reappeared. He led Hoppner into an anteroom.

'Well?'

Hoppner explained.

'That finishes my evening, blast it.'

54

The Landporten Gate, Nyborg

This was the day Robertson would begin the long journey home. He remembered the advice he had been given to avoid Odense with the many French military camps located in and around the town. He therefore decided not to retrace his steps through Assens. While he had been on Langeland, he had heard that there was a ferry from the east coast of the island to the nearby island of Lolland. There was another ferry from Lolland back to mainland Germany. The route from Langeland had the added advantage that he might have the opportunity to find a patrolling Royal Navy ship.

At breakfast, he asked the waiter to call for the landlord. When the waiter returned, he was told that the landlord was taking instructions from the marquis's valet and would come as soon as he could. The waiter smiled as he put his index finger to his left eye, moving the finger to the left. Robertson ignored the gesture, an obvious reference to the valet's eyesight. He had nearly finished eating by the time the landlord arrived.

'Ah, there you are, my host. I shall be leaving this morning. Please prepare my bill and hire me a carriage.' The landlord gave what he thought was a strange look and hurried away. He returned to his room and packed. A boy came to the room to collect his portmanteaus and gave Robertson the bill. The boy told him that the landlord had been called away. He paid, walked down the stairs, climbed into the waiting carriage and gave instructions to the driver. The carriage moved off, up the incline past the castle, on through the town to the land gate. Entering the forty-metre tunnel with sunlight flooding through the distant exit, Robertson felt a sense of relief. He sat back, some of the constant tension dissipating.

'Halt!' Danish militiamen emerged from doors in the tunnel walls, muskets aimed at his chest. A sergeant walked up to the side of the carriage.

'Get down. You are under arrest.'

Robertson stood up. 'What am I accused of?'

'I am to escort you to the castle where you will answer questions.'

He repeated, this time louder, 'Why am I being arrested?'

'My orders are to take you to the castle. Now get down or shall we use force?' Robertson looked round again at the muskets, all with bayonets fixed. Against eight in a confined space, he had no chance. He stepped down.

'Take his luggage.' A private hauled the portmanteaus

from the coach. Two of the militiamen took the lead, two more positioned themselves either side, but just behind Robertson. The sergeant and the other three followed. No chance of making a run for it even if he was quick enough. The group emerged into the sunlight walking down the slope towards the castle. Townsfolk gaped, pointing at Robertson and whispering to each other. As they neared the castle's entrance, he saw La Romana and O'Donnell walking towards them. La Romana stopped, staring at Robertson.

'What's happening, Herr Rorauer?'

Robertson stopped. 'Under arrest, Your Excellency.'

He felt the sharp prod of a bayonet in the small of his back. The sergeant shouted 'March, prisoner.' He was pushed through the entrance of the brick castle. Inside, hidden from onlookers' gaze, the militiamen used musket butts to force him down the stairs to the dungeon. A cell door was opened. A butt caught him between the shoulder blades. He pitched in, tripped, crashing against the far wall. As he slumped to the floor, the sergeant shouted 'Be ready to talk, Spy.' The door slammed shut. Bolts slid in place.

55
Rudkobing, Langeland, August 1808

After siesta, Teniente Antonio Fabregues and his batman walked from Colonel Dionisio Vives's office to the quayside of Rudkobing, the main town on Langeland. The commander of the first regiment of Catalunya had selected him to deliver letters to General Fririon on Zealand. The hope was that the summer afternoon haze on the still water would make it difficult for the watchers on the Royal Navy's ships patrolling the Great Belt to spot the small Danish cutter. Talking with Danish naval officers, he understood that the British would not sail their smaller vessels too close to the shore for fear of attack by Danish gunboats. There had been great celebration back in June when the Danes had ambushed and captured *HMS Seagull*. This brig was now being rebuilt and would become part of the Danish Navy. However, once in open waters, the gunboats were outgunned by larger British vessels. With luck and a fair wind, the journey would take around six hours with a mix of sail and oar.

Fabregues had had enough. The officer who had called him a "*tas de merde*" all but confirmed that it was French policy that had stopped the mail being delivered, not, as he did his best to assure his "children", the inefficient postal service from Spain. Then having to defend the poor German merchant in Nyborg from the gendarme. Next came the instruction that he must tell his men that there was a new king, Joseph Bonaparte. Fabregues had difficulty supressing the grumbling. Then, before the monthly Mass, Colonel Vives had explained to his officers that General La Romana had instructed the division that all the troops must swear an oath of loyalty to the flag of Spain rather than to the new king himself. Some of Fabregues's colleagues argued that it was tantamount to doing exactly that. Vives let the discussion continue before ordering "enough". The men assembled. Hearty cheers erupted as the flag was raised. It was strangely embarrassing, even deceitful that they had got away with pulling the wool over the men's eyes. It left a foul taste. But now his colonel told his officers of orders that had arrived from the Prince of Ponte Corvo himself. Every man of the division was to swear loyalty to Joseph while the colonel held a bible. Every officer was ordered to sign the oath while holding the Bible. Finally, the colonel was instructed to confirm in writing that the orders had been obeyed. To Fabregues, this was confirmation that Spain was no longer a partner ally, but now was subservient to France – a slave of the hated French. Never – never!

His order from the colonel was the opportunity he had been waiting for. It was time to get home. If there was a British ship in sight during the journey, he would take control of the cutter and order the skipper to make for the British vessel. He wasn't quite sure what would happen after that, but he must take action. As they approached the quayside, he stopped, pulled his batman aside and whispered instructions. Cloaks covered their weapons as the two men clambered onto the Danish cutter. The skipper ordered "cast off".

The first part of the journey sailing up the channel between Langeland and Funen was relatively risk free. Three hours later, well clear of the northern tip of Langeland, they were in the open sea. To make the cutter a smaller target for any prowling English ship, the eight sailors took down the sails and began to row. Fabregues looked around; nothing. Forty minutes later, he saw what he wanted: a ship of the line, a British battleship, flying the White Ensign. He prodded his batman. The batman nodded. Both men pulled out and cocked their weapons, two pistols for Fabregues and a blunderbuss for the batman. Three guns covered the rowers. Bewildered, the sailors stopped rowing. Fabregues raised his pistol aiming at the forehead of the nearest sailor. The Danish he had picked up over the past months would now be useful.

Fabgregues shouted '*Ro*', gesturing that they should row towards the British ship. The sailors looked at each other, unsure what to do next.

'*Du er ikke i fare. Ro.*' No danger he assured them. The

sailors turned and saw the British ship. The oldest turned back, glaring at Fabregues.

'*Nej.*' No. The sailor stood then bent to reach for the boat hook. Fabregues levelled his pistol at the man.

'Cover the others.' The batman raised the blunderbuss to his shoulder. The sailor's hand reached the boat hook all the time fixing Fabregues's eyes with his.

Fabregues shook his head. The sailor stared at him, then lunged for the boat hook. Fabregues pulled the trigger of the pistol in his right hand. An explosion, a puff of smoke and the sailor collapsed backwards into the well of the boat. He clutched his shoulder. Blood began to ooze from his torn shirt and between his fingers. The pain then hit. He screamed.

Fabregues waved the pistol. The nearest of the man's crew should help the screaming wreck.

Fabregues shouted at the other sailors. '*Raekke!*' The men grabbed their oars. To the batman, 'Watch them.' The batman nodded. Fabregues stood, picked up a piece of white cloth and waved.

A boat was already being lowered from the British ship. Keeping a check on the Danes, he watched as the British boat made its way towards them. As it drew close, Royal Marines in red uniforms aimed muskets. The midshipman commanding shouted in French.

'*Posez vos armes.*'

Fabregues and the batman lowered their weapons. He shouted back '*Nous voulons nous rendre.*' And held his arms up.

The midshipman shouted back. 'You two Spaniards

come with us.' The British boat came alongside. Fabregues and his batman took the proffered hands and jumped aboard. Two marines climbed into the cutter and searched the Danish boat. After a few minutes;

'No weapons.'

'All right, come back on board.' The marines transferred back.

'Cast the Danes away. They're no good to us,' the midshipman ordered. Boathooks pushed the cutter away. The Danes picked up their oars and made for Langeland.

'Back to *Edgar*.' The sailors picked up the oars and pulled for the battleship.

'Your pistols, Lieutenant. You may keep your sword.' Fabregues presented the butts of his handguns to the midshipman. The batman was relieved of his blunderbuss.

Sailors held the boat close to the ladder. As he climbed up the side of the seventy-four-gun battleship, Fabregues was astonished at its size. He reached the main deck and looked up. Three masts disappeared into the sky.

'Take his man below. This way, Lieutenant.' He followed the midshipman to the poop deck of *HMS Edgar* as his batman was marched down into the bowels of the ship. Perhaps he would be made to surrender this to the ship's captain. Fabregues assumed that it was the captain who stood on the deck surrounded by his senior officers. Two marines stood by, muskets with bayonets ready.

The midshipman stood to attention and saluted.

'Sir, may I present Lieutenant Antonio Fabregues of the Catalonia Regiment of the Division of the North of the Spanish Army. He has come from Langeland.'

The captain nodded. The midshipman turned to Fabregues and spoke in French.

'Lieutenant Fabregues, I have the honour to present Captain MacNamara of *His Majesty's Ship Edgar.*'

Fabregues snapped to attention and saluted. The captain nodded and addressed the Spaniard in French. 'Well, Lieutenant, at ease.' Fabregues relaxed, spread his feet wide and waited. 'What brings you on board one of His Majesty's ships?'

'Sir, I wish to return to Spain and fight against the imposter king, Joseph.'

'And how do you believe that we can help you?'

'By helping me and my men to return to Spain; after all, the British Navy rules the waves.'

MacNamara let out a belly laugh joined by his fellow officers. 'A bold statement.' Turning to his audience, the captain raised his voice. 'And do we agree with our Spanish guest that the navy rules the waves?'

A roar erupted around the ship, 'Huzzar!'

'Now, young Lieutenant, what assurances do I have that you are who you say you are and not one of Boney's lackeys, by that I mean a spy?'

The colour drained from Fabregues's face. Was it a combination of the perceived insult or the fear of the consequences of being accused of espionage? His native reaction would have been outrage and a demand of satisfaction. A duel, ridiculous, he had to put up with what came next. Sweat poured. Be practical. Be calculating. What was needed was bait.

'Sir, despite the French efforts to keep news from

Spain from us, we have heard of the massacre of 2 May, the abdication of the King and Ferdinand. Now we are being forced to swear allegiance to the usurper Joseph Bonaparte. I and many of my fellow Spaniards find this intolerable. I have been sent by the French commander on Langeland to deliver orders from Marshal Bernadotte to General Fririon on Zealand.' Fabregues patted the small knapsack attached to his belt.

'I took the opportunity to commandeer the boat and instruct the Danish rowers to make for your ship with the express purpose of handing these orders over to you.'

A pause while MacNamara stared at Fabregues. 'Well then, Lieutenant, we had better have a look at the marshal's orders. Mr Midshipman, kindly relieve our Spanish friend of his correspondence.'

Two hours later, Fabregues was escorted to Captain MacNamara's stateroom. He had been fed. Such was his hunger that he had wolfed the mess down. The taste was foul. Coupled with the rolling of the ship, he deposited the contents of his stomach into a bucket positioned beside his stool.

MacNamara looked at Fabregues. 'A little grey around the gills, I see, Lieutenant. Since we last spoke, matters have moved on apace. You are to be moved to Rear Admiral Keats's ship immediately. Take him away.'

Another hour, another boat and Fabregues found himself on the deck of *HMS Superb*, also a seventy-four-gun ship of the line. The English had been formal and polite, but he had no idea if he was believed. A marine officer pointed to the poop deck. He climbed the steps.

'Lieutenant, may I present Rear Admiral Keats?'

Fabregues stood to attention and saluted.

'At ease, now tell me how you come to be here.'

He explained.

'And how many French troops are based on Langeland?'

'Perhaps a hundred. There are over 1,100 Spanish soldiers on the island. But also, many Danish troops under the command of the Count Alrenfeldt.'

'And on Funen?'

'I believe that the French are based in and around Odense. We have units spread all around the island. Our commander-in-chief is headquartered in Nyborg.'

'That confirms what we already know, Lieutenant.' The admiral turned to one of his officers. 'Summon Lieutenant Lobo.' And back to Fabregues. 'Lieutenant Lobo is a representative of the deputies of the Junta of Seville who are in London. He has letters for General La Romana.'

Fabregues was astonished. Another Spaniard on board. His presence confirmed the rumours that spread among the officers on Langeland. The opposition to the French in Spain was widespread. A Spanish naval lieutenant emerged from the deck below.

The officer saluted Keats who turned to Fabregues. 'Lieutenant, may I introduce you to Lieutenant Rafael Lobo?' Fabregues saluted Lobo. Beaming, he shook his hand. Keats continued, 'I suggest that you two become acquainted and that Lieutenant Lobo gives you the news from Spain. We will then discuss how best to communicate with General La Romana.'

Lobo took Fabregues aside. For the next hour,

381

he explained the events since the spring, answering Fabregues's questions as he could; that the rumours they had heard were true, Joseph was King of Spain. The same midshipman instructed both men to follow him to Keats's quarters. Entering, both saluted and were instructed to sit at the far end of the dining table. Keats turned to them.

'I can give you news just received from Spain. A battle took place at Bailen in Jaen province two weeks ago. The Spanish Army was victorious. There were many thousands of French prisoners.'

Lobo and Fabregues leapt to their feet embracing each other. Keats slapped his hand on the table. 'Enough; and before you ask any questions, I have no further information. A defeat of a French army is news indeed. Now to work: how can we evacuate the general and his troops?'

56

Roskilde, Zealand

Marquet sat on his bed. Another long day of interrogation, the necessity of courts marshal – though these were just a formality – and executions. General Fririon insisted that formal procedures were strictly adhered to. They had to be seen to be delivering justice, not just to the Spanish but also to their Danish allies. Consequently, the process was taking much longer than he anticipated. Marquet thumped the bed frame in frustration. General Fririon had refused to let him travel back to Funen once again.

If the Spanish troops on Zealand had mutinied, surely it was likely that the same might happen on the other islands and particularly on Funen where General La Romana was based. The British spy had met the marquis on more than one occasion. More than one discussion surely indicated that the general might be receptive to whatever plan the

British were hatching. It was essential that he arrested and captured the German merchant, Rorauer. For he was surely the spy. He had pleaded and cajoled but to no effect. Marquet was to remain on Zealand until all the courts marshal and executions were complete.

Enough of anger, think through the problem, work round it. He moved to his desk. A full report to Colonel Maupont might work. Maupont had the ear of the Prince of Ponte Corvo. Fririon could be ordered to release Maupont back to Funen. He began to write. A knock on the door.

'Come in.'

A private from the telegraph unit entered and saluted.

'Well, what is it?' Marquet could hardly hide his irritation from being interrupted.

'My captain thought you should see this.'

Marquet took the proffered note. 'Dismissed.' A salute and the private was gone. Marquet read the note. It came from Lejeune. He had received a message from the valet, Martin. Rorauer had been arrested by the Danes. Surely Fririon could no longer object.

57
Nyborg Castle

Robertson sat on the stone floor. The cell was empty, no chair or bed. He would have liked to rest his back against the wall but the bruising from the musket butt was too painful. The most comfortable position was to sit with his knees up to his chest and wrap his arms around his legs. Stretching his back gave some relief. He began thinking about how he had ended up here. If the gendarme, Marquet, was involved, he would now be in a French prison. Marquet was nowhere to be seen. Had he been betrayed? Was one of La Romana's staff officers responsible? Surely not. Then he remembered being told of the valet talking with the landlord. That could well be the answer. After Copenhagen, Danish hatred towards the English was still visceral. If the valet had suggested that he, Rorauer, was a spy, the landlord may well have spoken to the authorities; a possibility. Apart from his crucifix, there was nothing incriminating in his luggage. If the Danes worked out the disguise, he was sure he could explain why he had a concealed crucifix. When the questioning began, he would brazen it out.

Hours slipped by. Looking through the small, barred window at the top of the wall, he judged that the afternoon was slipping into evening. He heard footsteps, the bolts being slid back. The door opened. The sergeant stepped into the cell.

'Time to answer questions, Mr Spy. Pick him up.' Two militiamen grabbed his arms, yanking him upright. He gasped as the pain shot through his back. His knees crumpled. The Danes took his weight and hauled him through the cell door and up two flights of stairs. The sergeant knocked on a heavy oak door.

'Enter.'

'The prisoner, General.'

'Bring him in and tie him to that chair.' Robertson was dragged across the panelled room and thrown into a large armchair. He winced as the bruises hit the back of the heavy oak chair. His forearms were tied to the chair's arms. He looked up as the general came across the room to him. The Dane was elderly, probably well over seventy.

'I am General Baron Guldencrone. I am the district commander. What is your name?'

'Adam Rorauer.'

'No, no, your real name.'

'That is the name my parents gave me.'

'Where were you born?'

'In a village in Bavaria. You would not have heard of it.'

Robertson hated having to tell outright lies. It went against everything he had been taught. But this was a matter of necessity, as Abbot Arbuthnot had said: for the greater good.

'When?'

'1758. I shall be fifty years old in October.' It was easiest to stick to the truth whenever possible.

As the questioning went on, he began to realise that Guldencrone was old in mind as well as body. Smiling at the general, despite the pain, he decided to take the offensive.

'Sir, on what charges am I being held?'

'That you are an English spy.'

'What evidence do you have?' The general looked flustered. 'Have you found anything in my luggage?' Guldencrone looked at the sergeant who shook his head. 'So, who told you that I was this so-called English spy?'

'A respected member of the Nyborg community.'

'And who told him? Was it by any chance a French valet?' The general flushed. Robertson was beginning to enjoy himself. 'Have you questioned the valet?' Another question found its mark. It was obvious that Martin had not been interrogated. 'Is it possible that he wishes to stir up trouble to suit his own agenda?' Guldencrone was looking increasingly uncomfortable. 'So I, a respected German merchant here to do legitimate business, have been locked up on the word of a mere valet? You should know that I have taken orders from the Marquis de La Romana personally. Perhaps you should ask him?'

The general thumped the table. 'Enough. Take him

away but lock him in the dining room. Give him something to eat and make sure he is comfortable.' He looked back at Robertson. 'I will investigate further.' Turning to the sergeant, he said, 'Go.'

Robertson smiled to himself. A small but important victory.

58
Rudkobing, Langeland, August 1808

Sitting in the stern of *HMS Edgar*'s pinnace, Fabregues patted his pocket to check that the letters he was to deliver to the general were safe. One letter was from Admiral Keats, the other from Lobo. He could hardly contain his excitement. To think he was the one to break the news that the regiment was to be rescued by the British.

The sun was setting. The pinnace glided up on to the beach on the small island of Tasinge. Fabregues and his batman made their way forward and climbed over the bow. The water was only ankle deep. He made his way up the beach, turned, waved to the midshipman and started for the ferry to Rudkoping. As they approached the ferry, Fabregues heard Spanish voices. One he recognised. It was Sargento-mayor Ambrosio de la Quadra, deputy to the commander of the Spanish troops on Langeland.

Fabregues saluted. Before Quadra had returned his salute, Fabregues's words tumbled from his mouth.

'I have just come from Admiral Keats's ship. The British will take us home.'

He reached into his pocket. 'Here are letters for General La Romana from the admiral and the Spanish emissary, Lobo, who is on board the flagship.' Before he had a chance to gather his breath and continue, Quadra raised his hand.

'Stop there, Lieutenant, calm down. Give me a proper report.' They climbed on the ferry. Three French soldiers sat in the stern talking among themselves. Far enough away not to hear Fabregues relating the events.

The ferry docked. Neither saw the French soldiers disembark and walk to a troop of French dragoons. A dragoon sergeant rode up to Fabregues as he and Quadra stood on the quayside.

'The corporal here,' pointing at one of the soldiers who had been on the ferry, 'tells me that he and his men watched you disembark from an English cutter. Colonel Gauthier will want to hear what you were doing – conspiring with the enemy, were you? Do we need to use a little persuasion to loosen the tongue, before we put you up against a wall?'

Before Fabregues could say anything, Quadra stepped forward.

'Sergeant, do you know who I am?'

'You are Major Quadra.'

'Is that the way you speak to a senior officer? Salute and say "Sir"!'

The sergeant was taken aback. He saluted.

'Sir, these men watched this man and his servant land from a boat crewed by English sailors. When he had landed, they saw him turn and wave to the British as they rowed away. What is a Spanish officer doing consorting with the enemy?'

'This is a very serious allegation, Sergeant. The lieutenant reports to me. I will question him. He will face the full rigour of Spanish military law if he is found to have been conspiring with the enemy.'

'No, sir, the lieutenant is under arrest. He comes with us to be questioned by Colonel Gauthier.' The sergeant pulled a pistol from its saddle holster. His left hand pulled back the hammer. The dragoons either side of the sergeant followed suit.

Quadra realised that his bluff had been called. Standing beneath the dragoons, armed only with a sword, he was in no position to put up a fight. If he did, there would only be one result. It might be a hero's death but what would be achieved? And he had the letters which must reach the general.

'Hardly the way to treat an ally, Sergeant. Where will you take the lieutenant?'

The sergeant smirked; he had won, beaten a Spanish aristocrat. 'He will be placed in the jail in Rudkobing,' with a pause, 'Sir.' It was as if he spat the word out.

Quadra turned to Fabregues, now speaking Spanish. 'You will have to go with them.' Fabregues looked resigned and nodded. Then looking up to the Frenchman, he said, 'I shall visit the jail to make sure that the lieutenant is being properly treated.'

'That is your privilege, sir. Bring up a spare horse for the lieutenant.' Fabregues mounted. The troop saluted Quadra, wheeled and trotted towards the town.

Quadra swore under his breath. He promised himself the sergeant would pay. Woe betide a member of the peasantry if he crossed a member of the Spanish aristocracy. But first, how to free Fabregues?

59

Roskilde, Zealand

The delicious thought of interrogating the English spy as soon as he made it back to Nyborg had faded. He hoped he was wrong, but the more he thought about it, the more he doubted that the man Rorauer would still be in custody in Nyborg. It was unlikely that the Danish militia would find anything incriminating on a professional spy. Those amateurs wouldn't know what to look for. What would they do with him? Send him to Copenhagen? Possible. Release him through lack of evidence? More likely. It was essential that the French had him, not the Danes. Properly questioned, the spy would reveal a mine of information about his mission and wider British intelligence activity.

Marquet finished his report. With luck Maupont might receive it in three or four days depending on where he was. How long would it take for Maupont to have an interview with the Prince? And that assumed that both were in the same location. More time wasted.

Then he remembered: the optical telegraph. He had heard that the Danes had begun to build a network which would use semaphore to send messages from the north of the country all the way to Kiel. If the Danish system worked as well as the French Chappe system, messages could be sent in a matter of minutes. He had seen messages being sent from Paris to Venice and back again in under an hour. With luck he could send a message to all the French garrisons across Denmark to alert them of the presence of a British spy.

He left his room, walked across the town to where a tower was being built. A Danish engineering officer was supervising the construction. A short conversation was all that Marquet needed to add to his sense of frustration. Work had only begun in the spring. It would not be until the end of the year or more likely early next that the network would be completed. He swore.

Time to confront General Fririon again. Time to do away with the niceties of rank. The general had to understand that it was critical to warn all French, Dutch and Danish troops of the activity of this English spy. Should their allies arrest the man, it was to be made clear that he was an enemy of the Empire and as such must immediately be handed over to French authority. After the frustration of the past weeks, the thought of the spy being ministered to by Fouché's interrogators was rather appealing.

Back in his room, Marquet drafted the message. Short

and to the point, but how should he describe the priest-cum-merchant? He had seen Rorauer sitting in the carriage. Height? Maybe one metre seventy. Build? Portly... no, the man looked fitter... stocky was better. Age? Mid-forties, probably. At least a brief description would give the police something to go on. Which military and civil police units should he particularly warn? If the spy was to be picked up by the British Navy, it would be impossible to guess where the rendezvous point would be on the long Danish coastline. But what if the man was to retrace his steps? That was certainly a possibility, particularly if he was running short of funds. So, specific warnings should be sent to Hamburg, Dresden and Cuxhaven. Perhaps a message should also be sent to Heligoland? Marquet discounted this idea. Nothing had been heard from Colville for weeks. It was best to assume that he had been captured. Any message to him would most probably be intercepted. The spy's escape plans would then be changed.

An hour later, Marquet was sitting with fellow officers sipping cognac. The meeting with Fririon could not have been easier. His message had been sent to the Prince's chief of staff and to Colonel Maupont. Fririon agreed that Bernadotte should be asked to authorise the message. It would reach all French and allied units across Denmark and northern Germany within two days. Once the message had arrived in Hamburg, the French optical telegraph would relay the news to Paris. In a matter of hours, it would be in Monsieur Fouché's hands, surely promising for Marquet's prospects.

60
Rudkobing, Langeland, August 1808

Sargento-mayor Ambrosio de la Quadra reached Rudkobing's modest town hall which doubled as the police station. He recognised the two French soldiers guarding the entrance. Quadra was followed by a private from his escort. The private carried a tray covered with a cloth.

Both guards saluted Quadra.

'Where is your sergeant?'

'He is eating his supper, Señor Major.'

'And Colonel Gauthier and his fellow officers?'

'Dining with Count Ahlefeldt at Tranekaer Castle.' Quadra had also had the pleasure of dining at the castle. The count owned Langeland and was a fine host. Gauthier would be out of the way long enough for Quadra's needs.

'I wish to see Lieutenant Fabregues. To check that he is being properly looked after and to give him some food.'

The sergeant was sent for. Quadra repeated his demand. 'Of course, sir.' The sergeant led Quadra and his private to the cell, unlocked the door and let the two Spaniards into the cell.

To one of his men, he said, 'Stay outside.' The door closed and was locked.

Fabregues leapt to his feet, saluting. Quadra put a finger to his lips. He then raised his voice.

'Lieutenant, you seem to be well treated. I have brought you something to eat. Private, show the lieutenant what you have brought.'

The private laid the tray on the prison cot, taking off the cloth.

'But where is the wine, Soldier? A Spanish officer cannot eat without wine.' Quadra thumped on the cell door. The door was unlocked. The French guard entered.

Quadra pointed to the private. 'This imbecile has forgotten the lieutenant's wine. Go down the street to the Spanish mess and ask for some. Here is my authority; the mess staff will understand.' He wrote a note, passing it to the soldier. The man looked flummoxed.

'Well, get on with it, man. The food is getting cold.' The Frenchman saluted and turned to leave.

'Haven't you forgotten something?'

The man looked at Quadra, baffled.

'Hadn't you better lock us in while you fetch the wine?'

He saluted, left the cell, slammed the door shut and turned the key. Fabregues turned to see the private already undressing. Of course. He began to strip. The private was a similar build. They swapped clothes.

Minutes later the key turned in the lock. The French guard entered. He looked round. The lieutenant was sitting on the cot, head bent, already eating.

'Now open and pour the wine for the lieutenant, Private.' Fabregues took the wine from the Frenchman, used the corkscrew on the tray and poured the wine. The lieutenant nodded.

Quadra looked at the Frenchman. 'Lieutenant Fabregues is obviously hungry. We will leave him to his supper. Come, Private.' The guard saluted, leading the way out of the cell. At the main door, Quadra turned to the soldier. The man saluted again.

'Soldier, you have done well. I shall tell Colonel Gauthier when I next see him.' The man came to attention, back ramrod straight. He was beaming. Quadra gave a cursory salute in return, turned and was followed by Fabregues doing his best to keep his face shrouded.

Back in the Spanish officer's mess, Fabregues was profuse in his thanks to Quadra.

'How did you manage to persuade the private to take my place?'

'Simple, I told him that it was his duty and that you were in the middle of a top-secret mission for the general. I also told him that he would be well rewarded.'

'But won't the French take action against him?'

'I think that we can make it clear to Colonel Gauthier that he is not in a position to punish the private. What will his one hundred dragoons do when confronted by 1,200 Spanish troops?' Fabregues wanted to ask more questions. Quadra raised his hand.

'You, Lieutenant, have work to do. You will take the letters from Señor Lobo and the British Admiral to the general in Nyborg. You will leave immediately. Lieutenant Carreras will go with you. The general will be found at the Hotel Postgarten. Carreras has orders for the Villaviciosa and Barcelona regiments to provide you with fresh horses. Now go.'

Fabregues was delighted that his friend Don Felix de la Carreras was with him. Taking the ferry across to Tasinge, they rode as hard as they could across the island, on to Vindeby and on to Funen, pushing themselves and their horses to the limit.

61

Hotel Postgarten, Nyborg, the Night of 6 and 7 August

Colonel Jose O'Donnell lay on his bed, hands cupping the back of his head. At least there was quiet. He had finally managed to persuade the marquis to let him move to one of the ground-floor rooms. He'd had some good nights' sleep. Tonight would not be one of them. He closed his eyes. What a few days.

La Romana and he had ridden to Svendborg to watch the Barcelona Regiment's oath-taking ceremony using Cadena's form of words. What a wonderful sight it was to see the regiment's 1,200 men formed up in an open square; the men in blue jackets with yellow collars set off with white cross-chest belts. A drum roll sounded the arrival of the flag party marching into the centre of the square. The sergeant-major shouted 'Attention! Present arms.'

As one, 1,200 muskets were brought upright in front

of each man. Officers raised their swords to the vertical. The band struck up. Regimental flags decked with battle honours won over the years of the unit's illustrious history were followed by the national flag carried by a tall, young sub-lieutenant. With General La Romana watching, the colonel and senior officers followed. The chaplain carried the elaborately decorated regimental bible. O'Donnell's chest swelled. He choked with pride and emotion. The men carrying the regiment's flags surrounded the national flag carrier. The regiment's flags were lowered in deference. Colonel the Baron of Armendariz, marched to the national flag, took a corner and kissed it. Still holding the flag with his other hand on the Bible, he shouted 'The regiment will take the oath of allegiance.' There was silence.

A corporal left his place in the line, marched to the general, saluted and, pointing to the national flag, said: 'My company does not swear to Joseph or to anyone else, but to that flag, for when we get to Spain, we shall see who it represents.' A wave of whispers and mumbles swept through the ranks. La Romana looked at the corporal.

'You are being ordered to swear allegiance to the flag. Is that so difficult?'

'No, General.' He saluted La Romana, turned and took his place back in the line. The colonel repeated the order. A desultory viva voce drifted up and down the soldiers as the officers tried to encourage a more enthusiastic response. Some men spat. The fusillade that followed was so sporadic that it reminded O'Donnell of raw recruits. As the smoke from the muskets cleared, the band struck up the "Melancholia", music used when an execution was to be carried out.

La Romana and O'Donnell rode back to Nyborg in silence, shaken by what they had witnessed. On their return to the hotel, letters from the colonels of the Infante and Princessa were waiting, reporting similar protests. The news that Kindelan, his staff and the three battalions of the Zamora Regiment based in Fredericia had taken the oath without objection caused little surprise. O'Donnell knew only too well that the general regarded Kindelan's loyalty as suspect. News arrived that the King's and Algarve regiments had followed suit.

The next morning, the official orders from King Joseph arrived from Bernadotte. These confirmed the oaths were to be taken again. This time in front of each regiment, the officers were commanded to swear "fidelity and obedience to King Joseph Napoleon". All the soldiers were then to shout their acclamation with a viva voce to the King followed by three closed fusillade discharges. The commanding officer was ordered to record each regiment's oath-swearing and sign the record in confirmation.

More pressure was applied when the general was told that the orders had been sent direct to La Romana's deputy, General Kindelan, on Schleswig and to Colonel Dellevielleuze commanding the Spanish troops on Zealand, contrary to military command protocol and a slight to the marquis. Intelligence then emerged that King Frederick of Denmark had written to his commanders that Danish troops had a duty to intervene on behalf of the French should the Spanish troops be reluctant to take the oath.

Finally, the news of the mutiny on Zealand had arrived. It seemed to O'Donnell that the general had an impossible choice. La Romana had asked O'Donnell if he agreed that now was the time to tell the staff officers outside his core team about the meetings with the British agent. There had, after all, to be some glimmer of hope. It was good of him to consult his chief of staff, but O'Donnell knew that the general had already made his mind up.

Before the staff meeting, the valet had been sent on an errand. Once the morning room was secure, surrounded by his most trusted officers, La Romana summarised their position. They were alone. However much the new regime was loathed, the temptation to take action against the French and her Danish and Dutch allies without outside help was impractical, surrounded as they were by superior forces. Even if they managed to concentrate the division in one location, the march back to Spain would take at least three months. It was also clear that some officers of the division were supporters of the French. O'Donnell knew to whom La Romana was referring. There was silence.

La Romana described the meetings with the British agent. When he described the British offer, only Deputy Chief of Staff Vera raised concern, asking if this man could really be trusted. O'Donnell remembered that Vera had lost a brother at the Battle of Trafalgar. Understandably, it was difficult for Vera to see the English as anything else but enemies. To have them as trusted allies required a leap of faith for all of them. The general explained that the agent was a Benedictine monk who was well connected at high levels in the British Government. That he was a Catholic priest seemed to satisfy Vera.

The general listened as his staff expressed their views. O'Donnell knew this ploy. Let them have their say, then he would tell them what was to be done. It was unlikely that anything they said would make any difference to his decision. The discussion began to ramble. La Romana put his hand up and the room went quiet. All eyes were on the general.

'Like our men, I remain loyal to King Ferdinand. I cannot accept a French imposter. It is our duty to lead our men back to Holy Spain to fight for the rightful king. Even if we accept Joseph as King, most of our common soldiers will not. They will revolt, just as has happened in Zealand. We will be powerless to prevent them. There will be bloodshed. The revolts will be quashed. The leaders of the mutiny – for that is how the French will regard it – will be executed, the remainder imprisoned. And we officers? Almost certainly we will be regarded as rebels for failing to prevent the mutinies. Result? Firing squad for you and Madame La Guillotine for me.'

La Romana looked round at his officers. All nodded.

'We will wait for news from the British. Meanwhile, I have written to the Prince of Ponte Corvo. As you know I have built up a good relationship with Marshal Bernadotte over these past months. He knows of the mutiny in Roskilde. I have told him that many of my other soldiers feel the same way as those on Zealand. To ensure compliance with the usurper Joseph's order to take the new version of the oath, I have proposed that the regiments of the division shall concentrate on Funen. Once assembled, the Prince himself can attend the oath-taking ceremony which should take place on the Emperor's birthday, 15 August.'

Silence, as his staff digested the consequences of what they had been told.

The general continued, 'Now that they have mutinied, I doubt that the Asturias and Guadalajara regiments on Zealand will be allowed to move to Funen, but the troops on Jutland could well be permitted to make the journey. With the El Infante, El Rey, Algarve and Zamora regiments joining us here on Funen, we will have over 10,000 troops on the island. We will outnumber the French and Danes locally, giving us power to act as we wish while we await the British.'

Again, silence. The officers looked at each other, then turned to La Romana. 'Bravo!' echoed round the morning room. A way out. A glimmer of hope.

The meeting broke up. La Romana beckoned O'Donnell. Once they were in the study, the general lit a cigar.

'Well?'

O'Donnell smiled. 'It's risky but it's the best chance we have. Do you think that Bernadotte will agree?'

'A birthday parade for Napoleon will appeal to him. Though his wife is a Bonaparte, I doubt that the Emperor has yet forgiven him for his lack of action at Jena and Auerstadt. Anyone else but a relation to Bonaparte would have been court-martialled. As well as the good relationship that I have built up with him, remember before Bourrienne became consul, he was Napoleon's secretary. There is surely no doubt that our consul is reporting on the Prince's performance to the Emperor and the Prince knows it. Bourrienne will also have reported on my behaviour and loyalty. He may even have told Napoleon about the many evenings that I spent at the consul's house in Hamburg and even joked about my inability to stay awake when partnering Madame Bourrienne at after-dinner whist. I'm sure that would have been the cause of much mirth as it was with Monsieur Bourrienne. And I have been given the *Légion d'honneur*, that would not have been awarded if there was any doubt of my trustworthiness. On the balance of probability, Bernadotte will agree.

'Oh and one other matter, we should do what we can to persuade the Danes to release our British friend.'

As he lay on his bed, O'Donnell hoped that the general was right. However, the risks were immense. *Now clear the mind and get some sleep.*

62

Nyborg, the Night of 6 and 7 August

Four hours later, Fabregues and Carreras tied their sweat-covered horses to a tree growing not far from the moat surrounding the town. A full moon illuminated the north-western earthen ramparts roughly equidistant from the Kronprinsens and Dronningens bastions. Carreras had been to the town on a number of occasions. The town gates were closed at nine every evening. Danish militia patrolled the town, its walls and ramparts throughout the night. He had remembered that there were workers' boats tied up on the moat at various points.

Their journey from Rudkobing, ferry to Tasinge, and changes of horses at Svendborg and Hesselager, had worked as well as they could have hoped. Now came danger. Fabregues and Carreras slid down the moat's bank, keeping as low as possible. Even with the moonlight, hopefully they would be difficult to spot from either bastion. Carreras had seen that there was an inwards curve in the embankment. Once they had rowed across the moat, the curve should shield them from detection until they reached the top of the grass-covered earth rampart. At the water's edge, a small rowing boat was moored, its painter line secured to the bank with a wooden spike. Carreras pulled the boat towards the bank. Fabregues boarded quickly followed by his friend. Carreras sat on the centre thwart, keeping crouched, unshipped the oars and placed them in the rollocks. Fabregues sat on the bottom boards, keeping his head below the gunwale. There was complete silence. It was only forty, maybe fifty, metres across the moat. Carreras lowered the oars into the depth and pulled. The boat eased through the water. As he lifted the oars out of the water for the next stroke, the noise dripping from the oars seemed to reverberate across the moat. He eased the oars back into the water, pulled again, lifting the oars free once again. Two more strokes were enough. The boat bumped into the bank under the rampart. Fabregues looked up and around: clear. Carreras moored the boat. Both men disembarked, beginning the scramble up the steep sides of the rampart. Fabregues patted his pocket. The letters were still safe. As they reached the top, both checked the path running towards the two bastions – nothing. Standing, glancing each way again, they sprinted across the path and down the town-side rampart. At the base they came to rows of single-storey terraced cottages. They had discussed how they would act once they had made it to the town itself. To attempt to creep along the side streets to the Hotel Postgarten would invite suspicion if they were spotted. No, better to walk in the open; after all, Spaniards were popular allies of the Danes, at least for the time being.

Brushing down their uniforms, they looked presentable enough in the moonlight. Past rows of cottages, alongside the imposing brick wall of the castle, returning the salute of the Danish duty guard, they came to the main square.

'*Standse.*' A shout from what looked like the town hall. They stopped.

A troop of Danish militiamen dressed in grey uniforms with white buttons marched across the square. Fabregues counted sixteen men and the officer who had shouted. Fabregues and Carreras returned the officer's salute.

'*Holz*,' said the officer, pointing a finger to his chest. Holz began to speak. In the past months Carreras had managed to pick up a little Danish. In the main, he found the language quite unintelligible. Holz finished. Carreras only understood one word, a name that sounded like Klaumann. To reply in Spanish was pointless. He tried his limited German.

'We have an urgent message for the General La Romana,' he said, pointing at Fabregues's pocket. One of Holz's men marched to the officer's side. He spoke to Holz. The officer nodded, pointing across the square towards the hotel. Holz spoke to his man. The man nodded.

'We are the fire police. We patrol Nyborg every night to watch out for fire.'

Carreras nodded and explained to Fabregues. Holz smiled, saluted and led his men away. As they watched the fire watch troop disappear, Fabregues let out a sigh of relief. They reached the hotel. Steel gates across the main entrance were bolted shut. A side door was also locked.

'What now?'

'Try the windows.'

The ground-floor windows were out of reach.

63
Hotel Postgarten, Nyborg, the Night of
6 and 7 August

O'Donnell finally managed to drift off to sleep. What seemed a few minutes later, he heard noises from the window. Barely awake, he sat up in bed. The curtains parted. There was just enough light to see first one man entering the room closely followed by another. O'Donnell reached to the bedside table, felt for the handle of his pistol and drew the gun to him. Before he could cock the pistol, the first man whispered.

'Sir, I am Lieutenant Fabregues of the Catalunya Regiment. This is Lieutenant Carreras. We are here to deliver urgent letters to His Excellency the Marquis de La Romana.'

Wide awake, heart pumping, O'Donnell cocked the pistol. Spanish spoken at least.

'On your knees, both of you.' If they were the enemy, at

least one of them would meet their maker before the other could launch himself at O'Donnell.

They knelt. In the gloom the uniforms looked right.

'Down, palms on the floor.' Obedience. Now at least there was little chance that an attack could be launched. O'Donnell lit a candle. Did the Catalunya uniform have yellow or blue collars? These men's were yellow. They looked correct. He sat back on his bed, the pistol trained on the man Fabregues.

'Now, tell me again, slowly. Who are you, where have you come from and why are you here?'

Fabregues repeated their names, ranks and regiment. 'We have come from Langeland as instructed by Major Quadra. I have recently been on board the English flagship. I met Vice-Admiral Keats and Señor Lobo, an emissary from the juntas in Spain. Both have given me letters for the general. May I ask, sir, who are you?'

O'Donnell ignored the question. 'Tell me how this came about.' Fabregues told his story. As he spoke, O'Donnell became sure that he was being told the truth. It was the language used. Words particular to Catalonia slipped out. The description just sounded right. If he was a spy or something else, he was a remarkable actor. Fabregues finished. O'Donnell recalled hearing the name recently. Wasn't he the officer who had been involved in the fracas with the French gendarme at the town gate?

'Gentlemen, you can now stand up. Sit if you wish.' Stiffly they got to their feet.

'I am Colonel Jose O'Donnell, ADC to His Excellency the General.' Both men snapped to attention. 'At ease, let me have a look at the letters.' Fabregues undid the button on his jacket, reached into the pocket and handed over the letters. Both were still sealed.

'Do you know what is in the letters?'

'Not exactly. They were both sealed before I was given them. Señor Lobo said that his letter was a message from the government in Seville who oppose the French. Admiral Keats's contains an offer to return our troops to Spain. It's incredible.'

O'Donnell could see that Fabregues was bursting with excitement. 'Come with me.' He grabbed a cloak, throwing it across his shoulders, and led the young officers along the passageway, up the stairs to the marquis's quarters. A member of La Romana's personal guard blocked the door. O'Donnell instructed the guard.

'And make sure that you tell the general that it is most urgent.' A salute as the guard opened the door. A few minutes later the guard emerged.

'His Excellency asks for you, Colonel. The two lieutenants are to wait.'

O'Donnell knocked on the door.

'Come.'

He went in. Minutes passed. Fabregues sighed. More delay. The guard reappeared with another man in the same uniform. Another member of La Romana's elite private guard, Fabregues presumed. The second guard disappeared down the corridor. The first resumed his position in front of the door.

64
Hotel Postgarten, Nyborg, the Night of
6 and 7 August

The valet Martin was half awake. At the other side of
the garret room he shared, the French chef's snoring
had woken him up. Over the past months he had become
used to the snoring. He normally slept through the noise.
It was when the chef had attacked the cooking brandy that
the snoring became unbearable.

He lay back in the hope that the cook would turn over.
He hoped that Lejeune had been able to pass on the fact
to Captain Marquet that it was he, Martin, who had been
instrumental in securing the arrest of Rorauer. That surely
would be the deciding factor in persuading the captain to
order the release of his son. The more he thought about
it, the more pleased with himself he became. Who would
expect him, a mere valet, to sow the idea that Rorauer was
in fact an English spy? And the landlord had swallowed

the bait hook, line and sinker. He smiled to himself; a real Judas!

The cook's snoring became even louder. Martin leant over the side of his cot, reached down and felt for a shoe. As he did so, the door burst open. Four Spanish soldiers filled the room. The chef continued snoring.

Two Spaniards advanced to the end of Martin's cot, uncovered the blanket exposing Martin's feet. Each man grabbed an ankle, yanking Martin off the end of the bed. His nightshirt rode up exposing his nakedness. His head smashed onto the floorboards. As he lost consciousness, all he heard was a volley of abuse and the word "spy" as a globule of tobacco spit hit his cheek.

Sometime later, groggily Martin came to. The back of his head ached. He was still in his nightshirt. He lay on a stone floor. Some light fed through a small, barred window. Looking around, he recognised the surroundings: a small storage cellar in the basement of the hotel. He was on his own. Unsteadily, he made it to his feet. The door was bolted from the outside. A Spanish voice on the other side murmured.

'You'll soon be meeting your Maker, you squint-eyed French spy. Not a moment too soon.'

Martin slunk back. How had they found out? He wet himself.

65

Hotel Postgarten, Nyborg, the Night of
6 and 7 August

In what seemed like an age to Fabregues, the colonel came out of La Romana's rooms.

'You, Fabregues, are to tell the general exactly what you told me. Follow me. Carreras, wait here.' Fabregues followed O'Donnell back into the room.

The marquis was sitting in his dressing gown. The letters from the admiral and Lobo lay open on the table at his side. Fabregues saluted.

'At ease. You have had a busy twenty-four hours, Lieutenant. Now tell me your story.' He repeated what he had told the colonel. Then came the questions. One after the other, each from different directions, each seeming to seek confirmation to an answer that he had given to three, four or more questions previously. It was as if he was being peppered by grapeshot on both flanks. Finally, the interrogation stopped. Fabregues was drained.

The general looked at Fabregues. 'I have finished with you, Lieutenant. Leave and send in Carreras. I hope for your sake that he will corroborate your story.'

Back in the corridor, he told Carreras to go in. Drained, all the euphoria dissipated, he slumped in a chair. At first, he felt a wave of disappointment. He had expected to be congratulated for bringing such vital information. But slowly the realisation dawned of the momentous decisions the general would have to make. How was he to get his troops to the British ships, scattered as the troops were all over Denmark? What would be the reaction of the French, their Danish allies and the Dutch troops who were to have made up the force to invade Sweden? Surely Bernadotte would see his former allies as traitors with all the fury of betrayal. To prevent massacres, how would the general disguise his intentions and ensure that his troops were safely boarded before the French could react?

The door opened. Colonel O'Donnell was followed by Carreras. O'Donnell smiled at Fabregues.

'Lucky for you that your friend's story matched yours. Now both of you have something to eat and then get some rest. I expect the general will need you. I must assemble the staff.'

66

Hotel Postgarten, Nyborg, Morning of 7 August 1808

Fabregues was slumped in a chair, in a deep sleep. Someone began shaking his shoulder. He opened his eyes. It was his friend Felix Carreras.

'The general has summoned us.'

Fabregues stood up, stretched and looked at his watch; not even four hours' sleep. He followed one of La Romana's bodyguards and Carreras upstairs to the general's morning room. The guard knocked on the door, entered and returned to the two lieutenants showing them into the room. Cigar smoke filled the chamber. Carreras coughed. Colonel O'Donnell ordered the windows to be opened. As the smoke cleared, Fabregues could see that the room was full of what he presumed was the general's staff. Some were still in dressing gowns as was La Romana. All were unshaven. It was clear that they had worked through the night. Seated to one side were three artillery officers. Fabregues knew that men from that regiment specialised on tasks of extreme difficulty.

It was Colonel O'Donnell who addressed them.

'Lieutenants, you should know that the general has decided to accept the British offer to transport as many of the troops of the division back to Spain.'

Fabregues blurted out, 'Wonderful news.' O'Donnell cut him short.

'There will be plenty of time to celebrate once our mission is completed. Now, listen carefully.' Fabregues flushed. O'Donnell continued.

Pointing at the artillery officers, he said, 'Captain Lamor, Lieutenant Bentardes and Sub-Lieutenant Zacares will carry orders to the commanders of the Infante, Rey, Algarve and Zamora regiments instructing them to march to the nearest ports, Snoghoj, Fredericia, Aarhus and Randers. There they are to negotiate transports, or seize them if necessary, sail to Funen and make for Nyborg. They are to leave their horses and mules behind. This will not be a coordinated mission. As soon as each regiment is ready to march, they should do so. Should they come across Danish or French troops, they are to say that the regiments have been summoned to Funen to take part in the mass swearing of the oath of loyalty to King Joseph and to parade as a division for the Emperor's birthday.

'We have a significant superiority over the Danish and French troops here on Funen. We will take control of Nyborg for a short time while our men are shipped to

Langeland which is more easily defended. From there, we hope that the British can take us home.

'You two have been selected to act as our liaison officers with the British. As you are known to the British, I have asked Admiral Keats that you remain with him throughout the evacuation.'

O'Donnell turned to Carreras. 'We understand that you, Lieutenant, are a powerful swimmer.'

Fabregues couldn't stop himself. 'He is the best swimmer in Spain!'

'Quiet. You, Carreras, will swim out to the nearest British ship patrolling south of Nyborg Fjord. The terrain on Cape Knudshoved should afford you plenty of cover from any Danish foot patrols and gunboats. You will ask the captain to take you to the admiral's ship and ensure the letters are delivered to him in person. The letters are written in French. Fabregues, you will watch Carreras' progress. We assume the British will return Carreras to the same beach. You will be taken to the admiral's flagship. Carreras, you will return here and be ready for further swims. Understood?'

The two young lieutenants looked at each other, came to attention and saluted. 'Yes, sir!'

'Well, get on with it.' When Fabregues and Carreras and the three artillery officer messengers had left, La Romana looked round at his staff. O'Donnell thought his face looked even more haggard. His skin was grey through the stubble. It was only seven thirty in the morning but it felt like midnight.

There was a knock on the door. 'Come.'

One of La Romana's guards entered. 'Sir, Monsieur Villate has returned. He awaits your reply to the Prince of Ponte Corvo.' In the excitement of the last few hours, O'Donnell had forgotten that Bernadotte's ADC had delivered another letter detailing the way that the oath of loyalty should be carried out. A reply had been demanded by return.

Romana looked up at the guard. 'Tell Monsieur Villate that I admire his promptness.' Turning to his senior secretary, Estanisloa Sanchez, he asked, 'Is the fair copy of my letter finished?' Sanchez nodded. 'Then tell Monsieur Villate that I shall be ready to receive him in my study in ten minutes.' O'Donnell realised that while he was asleep, the general must have been working with Sanchez to compose a suitable reply. Perhaps it was this that had made La Romana so receptive to the British offer?

La Romana stood. His staff followed suit. 'Gentlemen, once Monsieur Villate is on his way back to Rensborg, it will be time to discuss our deception plans. It is not just the French that we must put off the scent, our Danish hosts must also believe in our continuing acquiescence. Let me have your ideas while we eat a rather early lunch. Then we might allow ourselves a short siesta.'

As his staff officers left, La Romana turned to O'Donnell. 'Time for you to pay a visit to the castle.'

67
Nyborg Castle, 7 August

What should he have done? Since he had woken, Robertson's mind was full of "what ifs". How had he managed to land up here in the castle? All right, the dining room with a cot bed was better than the stone floor of the cell. It seemed that Guldencrone's word was good. Despite being a prisoner, he had been reasonably looked after. When he had been moved, he realised that he had not bathed or changed clothes for hours – he stank worse than his guards. As a novice, it had been drummed into him that "cleanliness was Godliness". He'd insisted that a bath be brought, and his clothes be taken for washing. There was no objection. However, when he asked for a change from his portmanteaus, he was firmly told that these were still being inspected. A woollen nightshirt was given to cover his portly modesty after he had bathed.

He wandered over to the window looking over the

town. There seemed to be some commotion around the hotel. Frustratingly, he couldn't see the building itself. He did not really take in what he was looking at. His mind was in turmoil. What should he have done differently? For the umpteenth time he circuited the room. How he missed the calming influence of his crucifix. Another lap of the room ended at the window. In frustration, he slapped his palm on the frame. Then he saw the Cross. There were many – all crosses in the lead in the leaded lights of the window. He sunk to his knees. It only took moments to clear his head. He always found it extraordinary what prayer could do. He stood now resolved to hold a firm line when the next interrogation began. The Danes had no evidence, and, in any case, he had established psychological superiority over Guldencrone. Adam Rorauer he was and would remain.

He heard the door being unlocked. The guard was followed by a servant carrying a breakfast tray. The food looked more appetising than previously.

'Good morning, Herr Rorauer, your breakfast.' The tone had changed completely. 'The general will be with you once he has finished his breakfast.' The servant laid out the food. Both Danes left. Robertson noted that the door had not been locked. He had just finished eating when Guldencrone entered followed by the servant carrying Robertson's cases.

'I trust you slept well. An unfortunate misunderstanding, Herr Rorauer. You are free to leave.' Guldencrone attempted an embarrassed smile.

Robertson decided that there was nothing to be gained by complaining about his treatment.

'Of course, General. These things happen in these difficult times.' He returned the smile and bowed.

Outside the castle entrance, he was surprised to see Colonel O'Donnell and asked, 'Did you have a hand in my release?'

O'Donnell smiled. 'Let's say that the ancient general was made aware of his error. Now, please come with me, the marquis wishes to see you. They walked down the gentle slope skirting the moat. As he entered the hotel, the landlord saw him.

'Herr Rorauer, what can I say? Such a regrettable error.' His face flushed. Robertson did not have time to reply. O'Donnell pushed him up the stairs.

'Please, time is short.' As they arrived at La Romana's morning room, he noticed that the ever-present valet was nowhere to be seen. The colonel ushered him in and shut the door. La Romana, still in his dressing gown and unshaven, looked up from his desk.

'Ah, Father, I hope you were not too mistreated?'

Robertson shook his head. 'Thank you, Your Excellency, for securing my release.'

La Romana waved his hand as if to dismiss the subject. 'Father, I have to request that you carry out one more task before you begin your journey home. Let me explain.' Robertson listened intently as the general explained his plan.

'You can see that there is little chance of rescuing the men on Zealand. With luck, we can move those on Jutland to Funen. However, I have grave doubts that Colonel Yebra of the Asturias will respond to my orders. He will need to be persuaded. I would like you to do the convincing. You will have to travel to Horsens on Jutland where the Asturias are located. If you are successful, you will be able to journey back to Funen on one of the seized vessels. By that time, we will be in control of Nyborg. You will be able to travel home on one of your navy's ships.' La Romana paused.

'If Yebra refuses, then it is unlikely you will be able to return to Funen before we leave. You would have to retrace your steps back through Jutland to Hamburg and home. I quite accept you may wish to remain here and wait for the Royal Navy.'

Robertson was quiet. The sensible course would be to stay in Nyborg. After all, he had done his duty and fulfilled Canning's order. But didn't he have the moral obligation to do all he could to help his rescuers? What a decision to have to make.

'Your Excellency, may I have a little time before I answer?'

'You may, but time is pressing.'

68

HMS Edgar: Third Rate Seventy-four Guns.
North of Langeland, 3 p.m., 7 August 1808

A shout came from the topgallant, 'The cutter is signalling. Nor-nor-west!' The officers on the poop deck lifted their telescopes focusing on the ship's cutter. A sailor in the stern of the cutter used hand signals. The officer on the cutter had his eye to his telescope.

'They've picked up a swimmer.'

'Signal the cutter to return. Summon the captain.'

Half an hour later, the midshipman commanding the cutter was on the quarterdeck. Beside him was the swimmer, now wrapped in a blanket, shivering. The midshipman saluted Captain James MacNamara.

'I think he's a Spaniard, sir. My French is not very good but he says that he has letters from General La Romana for the admiral.'

'Where were you when you spotted him?'

'Just over a half a league south of Cape Knudshoved, sir. If he set out from there, he must have been in the water for nearly an hour. He had a waterproof pack strapped to his back.'

'Get him some flip, but with plenty of rum.'

MacNamara turned to the swimmer. In French, he said, 'Well, sir, I am Robert MacNamara, Captain of *His Majesty's Ship Edgar* at your service. To whom do we owe the honour of such an unexpected visit?'

Lieutenant Felix Carreras introduced himself and explained. Five minutes later, MacNamara asked, 'How long will it take to get to signalling distance of the *Superb*?'

'About an hour, sir.'

'Well, let's make way with full sail.'

Bosuns' whistles rang out. Sailors scurried up the rigging. The speed the men climbed seemed extraordinary to Carreras. His eyes were transfixed looking at one sailor. The man had no shirt. His back was a mass of deep scars, stripes of red wheals contrasting with the tan of what was left of his unbroken skin. The man disappeared among the sails. The midshipman was alongside him proffering a mug.

'What is this?' Carreras asked.

'It's flip. It will warm you up.' Carreras took the mug, sipped. He recognised the rum but what was the rest? The midshipman smiled. 'It's rum and beer with plenty of sugar.' The taste was foul but at least it was having the desired effect. He was beginning to thaw out.

'What happened to that sailor I saw climbing the rigging? His back was a mass of scars.'

'Ah, he was one of the lucky ones. He only received 200 lashes. The captain of the main top, Henry Chesterfield, was given 700 lashes and the bosun's mate, John Rowlands, had 300.'

'What did they do to deserve such a punishment?'

'They mutinied last March.'

Carreras had heard the British naval discipline was severe, but 700 lashes? The midshipman smiled; it was as if he knew what Carreras was thinking.

'Mutiny besmirches the honour of the ship and the ship's company. Captain MacNamara will do all in his power to defend the honour of those under his command. Did you know that he fought a duel with the owner after his dog had been attacked by another?'

Carreras had heard of some strange British traits, but to fight a duel over a dog, that was surely stretching credibility too far.

69

Nyborg Castle, the Afternoon of 7 August

Following the note that had been sent requesting a meeting, O'Donnell walked from the hotel the short distance to Nyborg Castle, headquarters of General Baron Guldencrone, the commander of the Danish garrison. Villate had left with a letter from La Romana addressed to Bernadotte. The letter confirmed the plans to bring the regiments on Jutland to Funen. There, the whole division would take the oath of loyalty in the manner the Prince had instructed. A troop of Spanish cavalrymen accompanied Villate's escort to ensure the aide stayed clear of the messengers sent to the units on Jutland.

Another letter was carried by a junior aide to be delivered to General Fririon on Zealand. This letter apologised for the mutiny and for the death of Fririon's aide. The junior aide also carried secret orders for the commanders of the two Spanish regiments on Zealand,

Dellevielleuze and Martorell. The orders spelt out La Romana's intention to return to Spain on British ships. They instructed the commanders to seize the port of Korsor on the south coast of Zealand from where the regiments could be transported. O'Donnell had questioned La Romana if it was sensible to send the secret orders when the state of the two regiments was unknown. The general had agreed but decided that the risk was worth taking. He would do everything in his power to bring the whole division back to Spain. At least the aide would be able to bring back up-to-date news from Zealand. O'Donnell suggested that watch should be kept on the main body of French troops on Zealand in southern Jutland. Agreed: another artillery officer, Captain Jose Guerrero, was despatched to Haddeslev. What else could be done? All things considered, they had covered the obvious contingencies.

When he had first seen the brick-built castle, O'Donnell was dismissive. With its clay tiled roof, the castle looked more like a manor house. Only the lack of windows on the ground floor gave any idea that it was a fortress. Unless the castle had secrets, it would not survive bombardment for more than minutes. At the gatehouse, he presented his credentials. The reception by the elderly Guldencrone could not have been more friendly. The two men reminisced on the various evenings they had spent together over the past months.

O'Donnell changed the subject. 'I'm glad that you were able to release the merchant Rorauer, General. We would certainly miss his cigars and chocolate.'

'There was no evidence that he was an English spy. The landlord of the hotel was rather taken in by the valet.'

'Martin has been dealt with.'

'Now, Colonel, the reason for your visit?'

'General, you are aware of the difficulty we have persuading our men to take the oath of loyalty to the new King of Spain.'

The general interjected. 'I note, Colonel, that you do not describe the new king as "our king".'

'After so many years under Bourbon leadership, a Bonaparte king is something all patriots will struggle to become used to.'

'I understand. We too mourn the loss of our late king, but at least our new King Frederik is not unstable; mentally, I mean.'

'Yes, indeed. If I may continue?' Guldencrone stretched out both arms, palms upwards. 'The Marquis de La Romana has suggested to the Prince of Ponte Corvo that all the men of the division should be gathered here on Funen to celebrate the Emperor's birthday and swear the oath of loyalty.'

'Including the regiments based on Jutland?'

'Yes, you know of the trouble we have had convincing the men even without the Prince's new form of words. If the whole division is gathered together, we should be able to impose our will.'

'And what about the men who mutinied on Zealand?' O'Donnell stared at Guldencrone. The reports that he had simply mentioned that there had been trouble from the assembled Asturias and Guadalajara regiments when the men were ordered to swear. The Dane using the word mutiny implied something much more serious. No doubt he would soon hear more when he received replies to the secret letters sent to the two regimental colonels. What reports had Guldencrone had? Time to bluff.

'We understand that the leaders have been arrested and the remainder are quiescent.'

'Only after General Fririon called for help from the King in Copenhagen. You know that Fririon's aide was killed during the uprising?'

O'Donnell tried to hide the shock he felt. 'I am sorry. Then it is better that both regiments are moved here to be under the close supervision of the marquis.'

Guldencrone looked hard at O'Donnell. 'I doubt that will be allowed. His Majesty flew into a rage on hearing of the mutiny – on Danish soil!' This comment implied that overwhelming force had been used to quell the mutiny. If the two regiments were surrounded by, what was it, 40,000 Danish and French troops? There was little chance of capturing Korsor or being taking off Zealand by the British.

The general was still talking. 'So let's look at the practicalities. Who do you expect to feed? Maybe 6,000 mouths?'

'The men will all come as if on campaign with rations for five days. We will not impose on your people any more than we are already doing.'

Guldencrone sat back in his chair. 'If the King grants permission, where would the troops assemble and when would the units from Jutland arrive?'

'The flat land to the east of the town is the best location and away from Nyborg itself. The troops will need to arrive in the next few days in time for the ceremony on the fifteenth, the day of the Emperor's birthday.'

'Thank you, Colonel. I will write to the King asking for instructions. I should have a reply in the next two days or so.' The interview was over. As he made his way back to the Postgarten, O'Donnell was relieved that he had bought some time. It had been a debate whether to tell Guldencrone at all. But on balance, he thought that this meeting would set the Dane's mind at rest. He could relax until he had a reply from the King. By which time it would be too late. Lying to the old man was distasteful but necessary.

70

Horsens, Jutland, Evening, 7 August

Of course, Robertson had agreed to La Romana's request. If he could use his powers of persuasion to convince Colonel Yebra to lead his troops to Funen, then there would be 500 more cavalrymen to fight Napoleon. He owed it to La Romana for rescuing him from the Danes and, despite the risk, the excitement that pumped adrenalin through his body was addictive.

He and Captain Bentardes took a fast carriage, with changes of horses, a quick ferry across the Little Belt to Fredericia and another carriage ride, and they arrived at the Algarve's headquarters at Bygholm Manor as the sun was setting. The guard told them that the colonel had already retired for the night. They were shown into the hall while the officer of the watch was summoned.

A young lieutenant emerged. It looked to Robertson that he had just woken up. Buttoning his jacket and yawning, he asked Bentardes how he could help at this late hour.

'Salute when you are in the presence of a senior officer!' The lieutenant produced a half-hearted gesture of a salute.

'We have come from Nyborg with urgent orders from General La Romana. Go and wake Colonel Yebra.'

'That will be difficult, sir.'

'Why?'

'It was the colonel's birthday yesterday. There was a celebration.'

'What of it?'

'The colonel indulged. He was carried to bed.'

'I don't care what condition he was in, go and wake him.'

'I am forbidden to do that. Only his adjutant, Captain Rivas, is allowed to wake him.'

Bentardes exploded. 'Well, wake Rivas – now!'

The lieutenant looked embarrassed. 'Captain Rivas is otherwise engaged.'

'What do you mean?'

'He has company.'

'I don't care if he is entertaining the Queen of Sheba, fetch him now.'

The lieutenant turned and ran up the stairs. Ten minutes later he was back, followed by a furious-looking Rivas wearing nothing but a cloak. Robertson couldn't hide his smile.

'I am Captain Rivas. The lieutenant has explained why you are here. This can all wait until the morning. Besides, there is no chance you will get any sense from the colonel tonight. Until the morning, goodnight, gentlemen.' Rivas turned on his heels heading back upstairs. The lieutenant shrugged. Robertson turned to Bentardes.

'There's nothing more we can do this evening, Captain. I suggest we find some supper and a bed.'

Bentardes nodded.

After a night in a nearby inn, they returned the next morning. As they waited in the hall, Rivas emerged from a side room. A French officer followed. Considering that Rivas had had a busy night, Robertson thought that he looked reasonably bright.

Rivas scowled at Bentardes. 'The colonel is still not awake. I'm sure he will be with us shortly. This is our liaison officer with our French friends, Lieutenant Moreau. He has come to warn us there is a British spy masquerading as a German merchant in the area. What did you say his name was?'

Moreau took out his notebook. 'Albrecht Rosauer. The intelligence came from the Prince's headquarters.' Robertson bowed his head, attempting not to show his face, sweat trickling down from his armpits. He was compromised. Luckily, the name had been transposed incorrectly but Rosauer was much too close for comfort.

Rivas asked, 'Do you have a description?' Moreau read from his notebook. The depiction was accurate. Robertson was unimpressed to be described as "*gros*" – fat. Who had seen him at close quarters as Adam Rorauer? Martin the valet? Unlikely that he would send a message, but of course, the gendarme, Marquet. But he was in Zealand. If he had sent a despatch, how had it been circulated so quickly? He couldn't remember if Bentardes had given his name to the lieutenant last night. It had not been used this morning.

Bentardes butted in. 'We will keep a close watch for this man. I think we shall take a turn around the grounds while we wait for the colonel to come down. Come, my friend.' He took Robertson's arm.

Rivas waved. 'I'll send word when he appears.' Bentardes led Robertson out into the fresh air. As soon as they were well away from the manor house, Robertson looked round to check that they were out of earshot.

'Thank you, Captain.'

'You must leave now, Father. I will talk with the colonel.' Robertson knew he was right. 'It's too dangerous for you to return to Funen. Take the carriage; I can borrow a horse. Do you have another disguise?'

'Yes.'

Bentardes gave him a smile that was tinged with sadness.

'Good luck, Father.' He turned and walked back to the manor house. Robertson trudged back to the waiting carriage. News of what would be seen as the Spanish troops' mutiny would be common knowledge in a matter of hours. French, Danish and Dutch troops would block routes to Funen. All hope of a quick return home on a navy ship had seemingly vanished. The only option now was a return to Hamburg and with the smugglers' help, a boat to Heligoland. Best to stay clear of the eastern side of Jutland to avoid inspection.

He climbed into the carriage. The driver demanded an exorbitant sum to take him south-west to Ribe.

'You'll be paid when we arrive. There'll be a bonus if you can make it by nightfall.'

From the look on the driver's face, he wondered if he could trust the man not to hand him over to the Danish police. Hopefully, greed would overcome any pangs of duty. As the carriage moved off, he sat back, realising how exhausted he was. On his own once again, he needed time to recuperate and plan.

71

Cape Knudshoved, Funen, Evening, 7 August

Fabregues hid in the undergrowth set back from the beach. The morning, then afternoon came and went. A patrol of Danish militia walked past and he ducked down, watching the squad disappear. Finally, Carreras emerged from the gentle waves. Fabregues checked. The beach was clear. He ran towards his friend. They sprinted up the sand into the bushes. As Carreras dried himself, Fabregues asked, 'I never saw the boat which dropped you. How far have you swum?'

'Far enough! Now listen. I have letters for the general. You are to wait here until dusk when the British will collect you. You are to act as liaison officer on Admiral Keats's flagship. I will ride to Nyborg and will return here in the morning with the general's reply to the admiral's letters. If it is safe the British can pick me up from the beach, if not, more swimming.'

'So the British have accepted La Romana's plan?'

'They have.'

Carreras dressed, bade his friend adieu and slipped away for Nyborg.

***

Fabregues stood with Señor Lobo on the quarterdeck of *HMS Superb*. It had not been until the late afternoon that he had been collected from the beach. The same Danish patrol had marched past his hiding place, returning to their homes, no doubt. He had spotted the boat's signal light and had returned by waving his white shirt. Minutes later he was up to his waist in the sea with strong arms reaching under his shoulders, hauling him aboard. On board *Superb*, a Lieutenant Robert Harvey was assigned to look after him.

How he loathed waiting. As the time passed, questions bounced around his head. Had Carreras made it safely back to Nyborg? What would the general decide now that the British had arrived? Where was Carreras now? A cutter and pinnace patrolled closer to the shore, telescopes scouring the beach. Fabregues had warned of militia patrols. Late in the morning Danish gunboats were spotted but driven off. He told Lieutenant Harvey that he was sure Carreras would not wait to be collected off the beach. He would swim. Harvey pointed out the difficulty of spotting a swimmer even in the calm sea conditions in summer.

A shout came from above. Fabregues followed

Harvey's gaze up the mast to the highest sail on the ship and a platform, the crosstrees.

'Signal from the pinnace. They have him.'

As Carreras emerged onto the deck, Fabregues embraced his friend and escorted him to the admiral. A salute, the waterproof pouch handed over and Carreras despatched below to eat and rest. He would be swimming again.

More waiting. Two hours later, Admiral Keats and his staff emerged on deck. Harvey was sent to collect Carreras. What had the British decided? Carreras followed Lieutenant Harvey on to the quarterdeck. He smiled nervously at Fabregues and Lobo. Keats turned to the Spaniards.

'Well, *señors*, tomorrow is the day.' The waterproof pouch was strapped to Carreras' bare back. Turning to Harvey, Keats said, 'Lieutenant, you will go with the pinnace and signal as soon as Carreras is clear of the beach and on his way to Nyborg.'

'Sir!' Harvey snapped to attention and saluted.

Harvey and Carreras disappeared down the steps to the waiting pinnace. Fabregues waved and mouthed "*buene suerte*" to his friend.

Keats looked at Fabregues and Lobo: 'Your leader has rather jumped the gun. Our Transport Office has hired thirty-nine vessels that are en route. However, they will not arrive in the Baltic for some time. There has been pressure on the Transport Office's requisitioning skills in the past weeks. Ships are required for Sir Arthur Wellesley's expedition at exactly the same time as those for your men.

We understand that there are a good selection of vessels in Nyborg harbour. Have you been there, Lieutenant?'

'To Nyborg harbour? Yes, sir. Close by, it was full of all sorts of ships.'

'That at least could be a temporary solution.'

72

Roskilde, Zealand, Morning 8 August

Marquet was enjoying another coffee in the officers' mess when two guards entered. Sandwiched in between them was a Spanish lieutenant. The lead guard saluted.

'This officer has a letter for General Fririon. We found him on the road from Korsor.'

The Spaniard stepped forward. His French was tolerable. 'I have come from Nyborg. The letter is from General La Romana.'

Marquet pointed at another officer. 'This is the general's adjutant. He will deliver the letter. Now sit down. If you have travelled overnight, you must be ready for coffee or is chocolate more to your liking?'

'Coffee please, I must try to keep awake.'

'What does the marquis have to say to the general, or is it secret?'

'No, the letter regrets the recent events in Roskilde and the death of the aide, Marabail.'

'I see.' Why would La Romana have sent this officer on a mission to personally deliver the letter when normal channels worked perfectly well. Of course, that would have taken longer but why risk capture by the British for such a formality? Was there another agenda?

Marquet had his answer immediately.

The Spaniard asked, 'Can you tell me where I can find the colonels Dellevielleuze and Martorell?' These were the commanders of the Asturias and Guadalajara regiments.

Marquet guessed, 'If you have letters for them, I can instruct one of our couriers to deliver them. You can rest here while the colonels write their replies.'

The lieutenant flushed. 'No, no, I have to deliver them personally.'

'It really is no trouble. Let me have the letters. The couriers are completely reliable.'

The Spaniard struggled for an answer. 'These are personal letters from my general to two of his senior officers.' *But what's in them?* thought Marquet.

'Come, come, my friend, we are allies. You can trust me with the letters. A moment, your coffee is a long time coming.' Marquet rose, went over to a side table and rang a hand bell. From a drawer in the table, he produced a pistol. Covering the Spaniard, he shouted for the guard. Two soldiers burst in.

'Cover this man while I search his knapsack.' The man offered no resistance. He handed over the bag. Marquet undid the buckles, producing letters addressed to the two colonels.

'I shall take these away. Cover him.'

In his room, Marquet opened the letters. Not even coded, sloppy. Ten minutes later, he was standing in front of General Fririon.

'It seems, General, that La Romana orders his commanders on Zealand to capture the town and port of Korsor so that the British can evacuate both regiments off the island. If this is what is planned here, then it's logical to assume that he plans the same for the whole Division Del Norte.' He handed the letter to the general.

Fririon inspected the document.

'The letter is not signed. How do we know it is from La Romana himself?'

'We don't, General, but the paper bears La Romana's coat of arms.'

Fririon held his hands together as if praying. The Spanish on Zealand were neutralised. In any case, they were heavily outnumbered by Danish and French troops. But Funen was a different matter, and those on Jutland? King Frederik had only been on the Danish throne since March. From what Fririon had seen of him, he was sure that the King would take aggressive action to stamp out the revolt. Roskilde was only two hours away from the royal palace in Copenhagen. The King would have taken action by the end of the day. He wondered how much Bernadotte knew of the Spaniard's intentions. Even if the Prince had been told, would he believe the intelligence as trusting as he was of Romana? Bernadotte had to be shown the evidence.

Fririon looked up at Marquet. 'You are to take one of

the letters to the Prince of Ponte Corvo. As you have seen the results of the mutiny here, I'm sure you will be able to convince the marshal to take action. Leave immediately.'

Marquet saluted. He smiled to himself. His route would take him through Nyborg; an opportunity to track the merchant, Rorauer. Four or five hours hard riding should find him in Korsor ready for the night crossing to Funen.

73

Hotel Postgarten, Nyborg, Evening, 8 August 1808

O'Donnell also hated waiting. How long had it been since the three artillery officers had left for Jutland? Surely by now Lamor, Zacares, Bentardes and Father Gallus had made contact with the regiments on the mainland. The general's orders were clear. The commanders were to act with the utmost urgency. Other orders had been sent to the commanders of the regiments on Funen. Those in the north were to march to Nyborg while the 3rd Princesa, Barcelona and Villaviciosa were to move to Langeland.

O'Donnell heard the clatter of hooves on the stone paving. A messenger was shown in.

'A letter for the general, sir. It's from Captain Lamor on Jutland.'

Letter in hand, O'Donnell took the stairs to La Romana's quarters two at a time. The sentry knocked on the door. O'Donnell was admitted. The marquis was sitting at his desk, chair tilted back with his boots on the desk corner. He was smoking a cigar, a cup of chocolate rested in its saucer. Compared to the turmoil in O'Donnell's mind, he looked a picture of contentment.

'Ah, Colonel,' he took a draw on the cigar, 'this really is an excellent Cabanas.'

'Cabanas?'

'Hand-rolled Cuban, the name has been around for about ten years. I wonder how our English monk managed to source them?' A pause. 'I enjoyed talking with him. Let's hope he has managed to persuade old man Yebra out of his lethargy.' La Romana took his feet off the desk and sat up. 'Now who has been writing to us?'

It seemed extraordinary to O'Donnell that the marquis could remain so calm when his whole world could blow up in his face.

'A letter from Captain Lamor in Fredericia.' He handed the unopened letter. La Romana slid his letter-opener around the seal, unfolded the despatch, tipped back his chair, feet returned to the corner of his desk. Two, three minutes passed.

'Ah well, his true colours are now revealed. I'm glad we briefed the captain.' Passing the letter, O'Donnell read.

Lamor had reached General Kindelan's headquarters in Fredericia. Before meeting Kindelan, Lamor was able to brief Colonel Darcourt, the commander of the Zamora infantry regiment, and his staff on La Romana's orders. Pulling Darcourt aside, he had whispered La Romana's suspicion of Kindelan's true loyalties. Would his officers and men follow the marquis? If there was any chance to return home, we will all take it, was the reply.

Kindelan's aide-de-camp summoned Darcourt, his staff and Lamor. In Kindelan's presence, Lamor handed La Romana's orders to the general. Once read, Kindelan enthused about the plans for the evacuation, declaring them perfect in every way. He concluded with fulsome praise for the marquis before instructing Darcourt to prepare the regiment to move the next morning. Kindelan then announced that he would retire to personal quarters in Kolding to instruct the other regiments on Jutland to make their escape. Later that evening a courier was intercepted. The man carried a letter from Kindelan to Bernadotte informing the Prince of La Romana's "treachery" and that the general was about to leave for Bernadotte's headquarters in Rendsborg.

Lamor further reported that Bentardes and Zacares were on their way to contact the regiments in Horsens and Aarhus.

O'Donnell frowned. 'So Kindelan is finally confirmed as the traitor he is.'

La Romana looked up at his ADC. 'I concur, maybe his treachery will catch up with him. But for now we must assume that Bernadotte is aware of our intentions. Pray that the regiments on Jutland move quickly enough and before the French assemble enough strength to stop them. Tomorrow will be a long day.'

74
Nyborg Castle, 6 a.m., 9 August 1808

O'Donnell walked towards the main entrance of the castle. He was accompanied by one of the marquis's assistants, Julius O'Neill, and two soldiers of La Romana's personal guard. O'Neill, another Spaniard of Irish descent, had received part of his education in Denmark. There would be no misunderstanding during any translation that might be required. The interview would be conducted in French.

As they reached the entrance, O'Neill motioned the soldiers to take up position either side and behind them. The two Danish guards were barely awake. O'Neill spoke: 'The colonel must see the general immediately.'

The two men looked at each other and smirked. 'The general's orders are that he should not be disturbed until seven thirty. I suggest, Colonel, that you and your colleague come back at 9 a.m. when the general has breakfasted.'

O'Neill's face reddened. 'And I suggest that you wake him now.'

The lead guard spat. 'I don't take orders from Spaniards.'

'If you care to look over my left shoulder, you will see one of our finest marksmen has a musket pointing at your chest. Another to my right has his gun trained on your friend.' The colour drained from the man's face as he saw the musket.

Ten minutes passed before General Baron Guldencrone emerged, still dressed in his dressing gown, sleep still in the old man's eyes. O'Donnell saluted.

'General, my apologies for disturbing you so early. May I ask you to look at the flags now flying from the Dronningens and Krogens bastions?' The general wiped his eyes and stared at the nearest bastion, Dronningens. A Spanish flag flew from the rampart. He turned to look south, the same. O'Donnell continued.

'Our troops are now in control of all Nyborg's bastions. We control the gun batteries, the ramparts and therefore the town. I must ask for your complete cooperation.'

'And if I don't give it?'

'The guns on the bastion will be turned on the town. I should also tell you that if you care to climb to the top of the castle, a telescope will afford you a view of British naval forces making their way up the fjord. You know the damage thirty-two-pounder guns can inflict.'

Guldencrone stood in silence, shock written across his face. O'Donnell let the enormity of the situation sink in.

'But what of our discussion two days ago? We agreed to wait for His Majesty's instructions.'

'Matters have moved on since then. It is impossible for us to swear loyalty to the upstart Joseph. We must do all in our power to return to Spain to fight for our freedom.'

'But how?' O'Donnell was again silent. Goldencrone looked at the ground and then back at O'Donnell. 'The British will take you.'

O'Donnell smiled. 'We shall only require your cooperation for a few days, then we will be gone. Meanwhile, I ask that you talk to the town's leaders and explain the situation. Consider your position. There is no need for bloodshed. Let's meet again.'

O'Donnell saluted leaving the general to his thoughts. He watched Spanish troops marching into the town. Stage one complete, now for the British operation.

75

The Landporten Gate, Nyborg, 8 a.m.,
9 August 1808

Marquet had made good time to Korsor, though tiredness coursed through his limbs. There was time for rest and supper before the night crossing to Funen. The ferry captain had said that he would land Marquet when it was still dark so that he could return to Zealand before daybreak, avoiding British patrols.

The boat eased through the shallows allowing Marquet to jump from the bows on the sandy beach. Good to start the day without wet feet. He trotted up to the treeline, found a grass bank and laid down. He awoke with the weather changed. A stiff westerly wind blew down the Great Belt. Checking his watch, he'd been asleep for more than three hours. Angry that he had overslept, he walked through the scrub to the path leading to the town. He crossed the moat at the north gate. It was a surprise that there were no guards. Looming above him, the yellow-painted building with its pitched roof and windows looked more like a house than a gateway. The tunnel underneath stretched for forty metres, dark before the sunshine lighting up the buildings of the town beyond. Still no guards, sloppy. Into the dark, past doors on either side of the tunnel, a door behind him opened. He turned. Two soldiers emerged in white uniforms. Odd, he thought, all Danish troops wore red. Another door opened behind him. Turning again towards the town, another three white-coated soldiers appeared. Even in the gloom, Marquet could see the tanned, swarthy faces. Hardly Danish complexions; what were Spaniards doing manning one of the main gates to the town?

He shouted, 'Salute when you are in the company of an officer of the Ordinance Gendarmerie of the National Guard.' No reaction. Of course, no French. He tried his limited Spanish. Turning again, he saw muskets raised to the shoulders of the two men behind him, thumbs cocking the weapons. Marquet spun round again. Two of the other Spaniards advanced, grabbing his arms as the third removed his sword and pistol.

The third spat a globule of tobacco. Into Marquet's ear, with breath that was a combination of stale tobacco and garlic, the Spaniard shouted, '*Marzio, marche.*' Marquet felt two bayonet points in his kidneys. He was prodded through the streets of the town. Past terraced houses and the castle. More white-coated soldiers were on guard. Townspeople stopped and made way, whispering to each other. At the hotel, he was marched up the steps into the main entrance hall. The lead soldier spoke with an officer who pointed towards the cellar. Down the steps, past storerooms, a guard stood by a heavy door. The door was unlocked. Another bayonet prod thrust him into another storeroom. The door slammed shut, the key turned. He looked about. Another man emerged from the shadows. It was Martin. Before Marquet had a chance to speak, he heard gunfire from the harbour and fjord beyond.

76
HMS Brunswick, Nyborg Fjord, Tuesday, 9 August 1808

Fabregues woke to find Lieutenant Harvey pulling his leg. 'Get dressed. Orders, we are to accompany the admiral to *HMS Brunswick.*'

As he turned over, the hammock twisted. Fabregues lost his balance, collapsing in a heap on the cabin floor. He looked up at a smiling Harvey.

'*Brunswick*, why?'

'She is another "seventy-four", moored in Nyborg Fjord. The wind and currents prevent *Superb* from entering the fjord. The admiral will take his barge and command from *Brunswick*. You are needed to liaise with the general when we arrive in Nyborg. Move.'

Three hours later, the barge pulled alongside *HMS Brunswick*. The rowing crew of twenty were covered in sweat having fought against the stiff north-westerly breeze, even though now in the lee of the land. Fabregues had cheered as he saw the Spanish flag over the Slipshavn battery. Surely that meant that the town was captured.

At anchor close by were two smaller ships. Harvey pointed out *HMS Hound* and another sloop, *HMS Kite*. Fabregues asked if there was any difference between the two.

'*Kite* has carronades, deadly in close combat. *Hound* is a bomb vessel, armed with mortars, just in case of any trouble from the town.'

'Let's hope that will not be necessary. Nyborg would be reduced to rubble in no time.'

The two men followed the admiral and his staff up the steps on the side of *HMS Brunswick*. As Keats reached the deck, Captain Graves saluted. Whistles rang out. They in turn saluted the captain. Fabregues looked up at the three masts soaring above him and down along the deck with rows of cannon. The ship oozed power.

The admiral's pennant was raised. Soon underway, tacking northwards towards the town, the ship was cleared for action. A shout from the topgallant platform.

'Two Danish warships moored across the harbour entrance.'

A midshipman was sent up the rigging to identify. 'A brig, probably eighteen guns and a cutter, twelve.'

Fabregues attempted to estimate the British guns ranged against these Danes. Thirty pop guns against probably close to one hundred twenty-four-pounders and carronades. Brave but futile. He watched as the British officers talked. Harvey was summoned, briefed, saluted and came over to Fabregues.

'We are to take the barge, land close to the town, find your general, give him a letter from the admiral and take another letter to the town's governor. Then, we are ordered to the harbour under a flag of truce to tell the two Danish captains of the hopelessness of their position. They and their crews will be given safe passage once they have handed their ships over to us. The last thing the admiral wants is bloodshed.' This was what Fabregues craved – to be at the heart of the action.

It took Fabregues, Harvey and an escorting squad of marines forty-five minutes to march from their landing place at Avernakke, south of the town, to the Hotel Postgarten. Once inside the town, residents lined the street. A few murmured hisses, an occasional spit, but on the ground, not directed at the marines. There was no trouble. In the hotel, they were welcomed by Colonel O'Donnell who introduced Harvey to the marquis. La Romana and O'Donnell retired to read Keats's letter. O'Neill was despatched to deliver the admiral's letter to the governor and to order him to join the parley group to persuade the two Danish captains to surrender.

The marquis and O'Donnell reappeared at the same time that O'Neill returned from the castle. O'Neill saluted.

'Guldencrone refuses point blank to demean himself talking to lowly sailors.' Fabregues watched O'Donnell's face colour.

'Doesn't he realise that he would be saving the lives of his compatriots?'

'He does, sir, but still refuses. He could not in all honour order a fellow Dane to capitulate.'

There was silence.

'Enough.' La Romana looked around the group. 'We cannot wait on that man's arrogance. You, O'Neill, will go with Lieutenant Harvey and Fabregues to act as interpreter. Now go and good luck.'

The three walked down to the quayside, the marines marching behind them. Fabregues carried a large white flag. A skiff was commandeered. Four marines took the oars. They rowed out towards the two Danish ships moored across the entrance to Nyborg harbour.

The midshipman had been correct. The larger ship was an armed brig. Fabregues counted eight guns along the port side, double that and add guns on the bow and stern: eighteen. As they closed, the ship's name became visible – *Fama*. The other was a cutter, *Salorman*, probably twelve guns. As they approached, he could see muskets aiming at the skiff. Some of the crew were loading a swivel gun.

Harvey stood in the bows of the skiff as Fabregues waved the white flag. 'We have come to parley.' An order was barked from the poop deck of the *Fama*. The muskets were withdrawn. An officer appeared at the gunwale and shouted down to the skiff. His French was just understandable.

'I am Lieutenant Rasch commanding His Majesty's brig *Fama*. How may I help you, gentlemen?'

'Lieutenant Harvey of *HMS Superb* and two Spanish officers of the Division of the North, O'Neill and Fabregues.'

'I see the Spanish are now allied with their enemies at Trafalgar.' Harvey ignored the barb.

'Lieutenant, we are here to parley with you. May we come aboard?' Rasch beckoned them.

A ladder was let down the ship's side. Harvey ordered the marines to "stand off". The three climbed on deck. Fabregues looked around. The *Fama* was closed for action.

Salutes exchanged, Rasch looked at the Englishman and the two Spaniards. 'Well, gentlemen, I repeat, how may I help you?'

Harvey gestured at O'Neill. 'Señor O'Neill was educated in Denmark. He will translate, should the need arise.' Rasch was silent. Fabregues attempted to read the man. Was he offended? Scared, of course. But maybe he was realising the enormity of the decisions that he would have to take not just for him but for his men?

'Once again, how may I help you?'

Harvey began. 'Lieutenant, I am commanded by Sir Richard Keats, the admiral commanding this task force, to ask you to remove your ships from blockading the entrance to Nyborg harbour and to take no offensive action against the British and Spanish forces. You will know that the Spanish forces now control the town and its batteries. Señor O'Neill has a letter for you from General La Romana which guarantees safe passage for you and your men.' O'Neill passed the letter to the Dane. Rasch did not open the letter.

Harvey continued. 'What you may not know is the strength of the British naval force gathered in the fjord. This force comprises a seventy-four-gun ship of the line supported by other ships armed with carronades and bombs – mortars. The admiral wishes to avoid any unnecessary bloodshed but will take steps to ensure that his orders are carried out. With the forces ranged against you, you know that there can be only one outcome should you not comply.'

Rasch remained silent as if seeking the best form of words to compose his reply. 'Sir, ever since the treacherous action in Copenhagen last year, Denmark has been at war with Britain. Now it would appear that our supposed allies, the Spanish, have also turned to treachery. I swore an oath to defend His Majesty King Frederik and all his subjects. This I will continue to do until my last breath.'

'And your men?'

'They will obey my orders.'

Fabregues understood Rasch's predicament. He had been commanded to defend Nyborg. Despite the hopelessness of his position, he would remain at his post. It was a matter of honour. In the same situation, would he, Fabregues, do the same? He hoped so.

It was Harvey's turn again. 'Sir, I appeal to you, not for yourself, but think of your men and their families. If you continue to refuse, there will only be one outcome – blood. Let us withdraw while you consult with Captain Rosennorn of the *Salorman*.'

'I appreciate your concern, sir. You may return, but my response will be the same.' Rasch saluted. The three returned his salute and turned back towards the ladder.

As the skiff moved away from the *Fama*, Fabregues asked Harvey, 'Were you not being too lenient on the Dane?'

'We must use every ruse we have to persuade Rasch to surrender. Besides, as the transport ships to carry you back to Spain will not arrive for some time, we need every ship we can lay our hands on. To wreck or sink *Fama* and *Salorman* would be very careless.'

Always another agenda with these British, thought Fabregues.

They returned to the hotel. Harvey asked that the marquis should leave the suppression of the two ships to the British Navy. La Romana nodded his agreement.

'Lieutenant, I am still hopeful that my regiments on Jutland will arrive on Funen in the next two days. We therefore have time before we need to leave Nyborg. Take a letter to the admiral asking him to delay any action against the Danish vessels to give time for the pressure to build on the captain.' The marquis turned to O'Donnell.

'It is time, Colonel, for you and O'Neill to call on the governor once again. You will instruct him to write to Captain Rasch and order him to surrender. If Rasch does not, I shall order the batteries to be turned on the town before firing on his ships. Make sure the governor understands.'

77

Nyborg Castle, Tuesday, 9 August 1808

O'Donnell and O'Neill returned the salute of the Spanish soldiers now on guard at the entrance to the castle. The officer commanding told them that Guldencrone was compliant and had continued to direct the town's affairs, albeit reluctantly. He showed them up the stairs and into the main hall. The governor was sent for and glowered at O'Donnell on arriving into the room.

O'Donnell dispensed with any niceties. 'Baron, Captain Rasch has refused our generous terms of safe passage for him and his men. He must be made to see sense. General La Romana insists that you now must write to Rasch, commanding him to obey.'

'Colonel, even if I was minded to write to the captain, what would you have me say that would impel him to obey?'

'That is simple. You will give him a direct order. Should

he not agree, it will not just be the British Navy's guns that will be trained on the town but also the guns of your own batteries. I do not need to tell you the damage they would do at such short range.'

Guldencrone blanched.

O'Donnell continued. 'Sir, we do not wish to confront Denmark. However, you should be in no doubt that we are determined to return to Spain. If you and your countrymen stand in our way, we will take whatever action is required even at the expense of the people of Nyborg who, up until now, have been hospitable to us.'

No reply. Silence in the hall. It was as if both men knew that the next to speak would lose. Rapping on the door. A guard appeared.

Saluting, he said, 'Colonel, sir, a messenger from Jutland has arrived.'

O'Donnell turned back to Guldencrone. 'I will return in the morning to collect your letter.'

Outside the castle, O'Donnell saw Captain Bentardes. Covered in dust, sweating, Bentardes saluted. 'Sir, have you heard from Zacares? He should have got to you two hours ago to bring news of the regiments on Jutland?'

'No sign of him. What news? Come with me to the general. Tell me as we walk.'

'The Zamora Regiment seized boats around Fredericia and has already landed on Funen to march here. El Rey and El Infante have captured vessels local to Randers and Aarhus and are, I believe, sailing round the north of Funen. They should land close to Nyborg.'

'And the Algarve? And Father Gallus?'

'That is why I did not travel with Zacares. After I had said goodbye to the Father, I returned to find Colonel Yebra. I gave him the general's orders, but he dithered. The Danes got wind of what was happening and warned the main French and Danish forces that were marching up from the south. Neither Yebra nor Lieutenant Colonel Carbonell would act. I managed to persuade Captain Costa to gather the men of the regiment together and march to the coast. Too late. They were surrounded by the much superior French and Danish forces.'

'I have met Costa. Isn't he a French exile?'

'Yes, sir. He and the French Colonel Biaunte talked. Biaunte assured Costa that their action would be regarded as nothing more than a seduction attempt by the British. As such they would not be regarded as enemies. Costa rode back to his men explaining that he only was to blame. The troops shouted back "We are all equally guilty!" Costa rode back up to Biaunte, offered him his sabre, leant over his saddle and embraced the colonel.

'Biaunte shouted "*Gardes vos armes!*" Before anyone had a chance to react, Costa pulled a pistol from its holster and putting it to his forehead, the émigré blew his brains out.'

'My god!'

'The French and Danes raised their weapons. Given the strength of the French and Danish forces, I would guess that the men of the Algarve had no other alternative but to surrender. While those watching were numbed by what they had seen, I took the opportunity to escape. I turned my horse. In seconds he was in a full gallop, musket balls pinging all around me.'

'You've had a lucky escape, Bentardes. Well done. And Father Gallus?'

'By the time I had left Yebra to find Costa, the Father's carriage had gone.'

78

HMS Edgar, Evening, Tuesday, 9 August 1808

Harvey and Fabregues were back on board *HMS Edgar*. In their absence, Captain MacNamara had already put plans in place to take both vessels. The action would take place at dusk. *Hound*, *Kite* and *Minx* would surround *Fama* and *Salorman*. Grapeshot would be used to rake the decks before "cutting out" boarding parties would attack the bows and sterns while the Danish were sheltering from the grape broadsides and covered in smoke. The ships would be taken with minimal damage.

Harvey stepped forward saluting the captain. 'May I have the honour to command one of the boarding parties?'

MacNamara turned to the admiral who nodded. 'You may.' Fabregues had just about understood what the English were talking about.

'May I join Lieutenant Harvey, sir?'

'That is not my decision, but if Harvey would like to take you, I have no objection.'

Harvey smiled. 'Agreed.'

The two boarding parties were selected, a combination of sailors and marines. All had been trained in this vicious form of hand-to-hand combat. Weapons were chosen; grenades, pistols, cutlasses and boarding axes. Given the likely close quarters of the fighting, pikes and muskets with bayonets were rejected. The men clambered down into a cutter and a pinnace. Both boats pushed off. The row towards the Danish vessels began. Harvey and Fabregues's party took the cutter. Their target would be the *Fama*.

The strong north-westerly breeze continued to blow as the *Hound*, *Kite* and *Minx* tacked their way towards the harbour entrance. Both Danish ships opened fire. Seconds later, the twenty-four-pounder guns of *HMS Edgar* responded. Chain shot ripped through the rigging sending spars, sails and rope crashing onto the decks. Deck guns were soon silenced well before they were able to range on the approaching British ships. The *Minx*'s carronades opened up. Grapeshot scoured the decks of the *Fama* forcing the crews to take cover. Despite the wind, smoke covered both ships. The shooting from the *Fama* and *Salorman* became sporadic.

As the cutter approached, Fabregues watched with admiration as Harvey directed the boatswain to make for the *Fama*'s bows. They would attack from underneath the bowsprit. The rigging was perfect for clambering. Oars muffled, the cutter slipped past the anchor chain easing gently under the bows, unseen by those above. Suddenly, the British guns ceased firing. At that signal, Harvey began the climb to the deck, soon followed and overtaken by the nimble seamen, hungry for prize money.

Fabregues was the last to reach the deck. Shouts and screams mingled with explosions from grenades and pistols as the two crews fought hand to hand. Blood already spattered the deck. He pulled a pistol from his belt and drew the cutlass he had been given; so much heavier than his sword. He saw Harvey run towards a Danish officer. The Dane pulled a pistol, cocked it and fired just as Harvey reached a sword's length from him. Harvey staggered, fell to his knees and collapsed face down on the deck. Fabregues cocked his pistol, extended his arm, took aim and fired. The ball found its mark in the Dane's shoulder. The man screamed with pain falling against the ship's wheel. A shout went out from another Danish sailor. It was all over. The Danes disengaged and laid down their weapons.

Fabregues surveyed the carnage. Harvey lay motionless, obviously dead. Two British sailors nursed wounds. Of the enemy, seven were dead and thirteen wounded. The smoke had cleared. There was enough light to see that the *Salorman* had also struck her colours. A sailor and a marine knelt by Harvey's body. The marine shook his head. Tears welled in Fabregues's eyes. Then the shock hit. He vomited.

79

HMS Superb – Tuesday, 23 August 1808

O'Donnell rested his forearms on the gunwale of the battleship as the convoy sailed northwards up the Great Belt. He watched Fabregues and Carreras chat excitedly about the prospect of being home again. Passing Nyborg, there had been some sporadic gunfire from the Cape Knudshoved battery. The shot landed well short. As he looked down the lines of the British ships each with its following transports, he was reminded of swans with lines of cygnets obediently following. Fifty-seven sloops and other vessels had been found in Nyborg harbour. Requisitioned, they had been made sea-ready to transport the Spanish troops. The transports en route from England would not now delay the evacuation. Each vessel was painted with a letter and number on the bow and stern. The letter represented the mother ship – S for *Superb* and 1, 2 and onwards for the number of the vessel attached to the "mother ship".

Thank goodness the weather was fair. He worried about the men packed into the small vessels with little room to move and nowhere to lie down at night. Anything more than a slight sea would soak the soldiers making the journey even more miserable. But then to improvise transport for over 9,000 soldiers and around 240 wives and children was a miraculous achievement.

O'Donnell was in a strange mood; looking forward to reaching the safety of Gothenburg and the onward journey home. The anticipation of being in Spain again was tinged with apprehension of the fighting to come on home soil. His mind then switched back as he reflected on the past two weeks.

He had seen Fabregues soon after the crews of the *Fama* and *Salorman* had surrendered. The man's blood-spattered hands were still shaking. Fabregues looked at O'Donnell, face gaunt, white as if he had seen a ghost. Perhaps he had. Was it the first time, O'Donnell had asked. Fabregues nodded – classic symptoms of shock. He would get over it.

As soon as the fighting in the harbour had finished, the British admiral Keats had come ashore to meet the marquis. Agreement was swiftly reached that the island of Langeland would provide security from French and Danish troops who would surely concentrate on Funen. The British commandeered the vessels moored in Nyborg harbour. Their sailors made the vessels ready for the embarkation of the Spanish troops. Petty officers were put in command of each vessel. Sails and rigging were inspected and repaired. Each ship was fumigated. Water and rations were loaded. O'Donnell doubted if any other navy could ready the convoy with such speed and efficiency. But then the British were well practised at such combined operations. Instructions were sent to the units based elsewhere on Funen – Assens and Faaborg to move to Langeland.

He remembered the relief when the units that had escaped from Jutland had arrived in Nyborg. Some had made the hazardous journey by sea around the top of Funen in an assortment of craft seized from the Danes. Over 1,800 men had managed to evade the enemy who was by now thoroughly alerted. It was just a matter of time before Bernadotte would be able to move enough strength on to Funen to prevent the escape. What enjoyment he had showing La Romana the first of the leaflets that appeared. Written by Marshal Bernadotte, the leaflet exhorted the Spanish soldiers to remain. The men would *carry everywhere the shame of disgrace and dishonour.* The British, the paper continued, would *conduct you to Canada or the Indies where you would forever groan under the oppression of the yoke of England* and finished, *Soldiers, those among you whom this Proclamation will reach before you embark are bound to remain on the spot where you are… I take you under my protection and offer to send everyone who wishes it to your families.* The leaflets had no effect on the soldiers who read them. O'Donnell had even seen one of the wives using the paper to light a cooking stove.

Inevitably, there had been despair. He would never forget the day when a delegation of the Almansa cavalry regiment arrived at the hotel. With frantic preparation work for the evacuation, he was irritated when an aide interrupted him.

'Yes, what is it now?'

'Lieutenant Colonel Becar, Major Combay and three captains from the Almansa to see you, sir.'

'My god, don't they know how busy we are? What do they want?'

'It's about their horses.'

'They know the general's orders.'

'Yes, sir, but they hope you might be able to arrange for them to see the general. They believe they will be able to change his mind.' O'Donnell knew there was no chance of that. He was now so distracted from his work. He stood.

'All right, all right, I'll see them. Where are they?'

'In the dining room, sir.' Still irritated, O'Donnell followed the aide downstairs and into the dining room. As he entered, the five cavalrymen, immaculate in their light green uniforms, stood and saluted. O'Donnell returned their salute. The aide formally introduced Becar.

'Teniente Coronel Don Miguel Becar.' O'Donnell had previously met Becar.

'Good to see you again, Colonel, how can I help?'

Becar's passion came through his voice 'We must see the general. We must save our horses. They cannot be shot.'

'Colonel, you know that the general loves horses. When he gave the order, he fully appreciated how difficult it will be for cavalry regiments to comply. But you must.'

'But, Colonel, you just do not understand. In the Almansa, we have some of the finest horses in all Spain.'

'I do understand. You have seen the size of the boats in the harbour. There will only just be room for all our men not forgetting the women and children. Nor is there space on the British naval ships. And if they are left here? The French will seize them; the best for their cavalry and the rest as pack horses. You must see there is no other way. They must be shot.'

Combay stepped forward. 'Sir, I am Sargento Mayor don Francisco Combay.'

'Yes, Major.'

'Sir, please come to the window.' O'Donnell followed Combay who pointed through the open window. Tethered just outside was the most magnificent horse O'Donnell had ever seen. Standing perhaps sixteen and half hands, jet black, long mane beautifully combed and tail nearly reaching the ground, it was an Andalusian stallion.

'Isn't he magnificent? He is a Cartujano, the finest strain of Andalucians.'

'He is a wonderful specimen, Combay, but the general's orders must be followed.'

Combay fell to his knees, tears streaming down his cheeks.

'Colonel, I beg you. I raised him myself. He is my life.'

'Major, this demeans you. Get to your feet.' O'Donnell turned to Becar. 'I am truly sorry.' He turned away and left.

When the Almansa arrived to be loaded into the transports, O'Donnell noticed that Becar, Combay and other officers were riding old nags that looked more like farm than cavalry horses. He had no time to investigate. Later at a dinner that the general gave for the regimental commanders, O'Donnell happened to be sitting next to Colonel Becar.

'Ah, Colonel, I have been meaning to ask. The horses you were riding before you boarded the transport vessels did not seem to be much like cavalry horses?'

'You have eagle eyes, Colonel, we hoped you wouldn't notice.'

'What happened to the Spanish horses?'

Becar smiled. 'Let's just say that some local farmers will now have the best breeding stock in Europe.' O'Donnell saw that La Romana had heard the conversation. His orders had been deliberately disobeyed. The general's face flushed dark red, his jaw tightened. He picked up his napkin, began to twist then tried to pull it apart. The room went silent. O'Donnell thought he would explode. Then suddenly, as if a pressure valve had been released, La Romana's mouth cracked into a wide smile. He began laughing.

'Bravo, Colonel Becar!'

***

La Romana wrote to the Danish King asking that the men from Asturias and Guadalajara captured after the Roskilde mutiny be released. The King ignored the request, perceiving La Romana's actions as traitorous. The marquis was delighted when 150 men managed to escape from Zealand across the Belt to Langeland.

On 11 August, the evacuation to Langeland began. By the weekend, there were over 9,000 Spanish soldiers, wives and followers camped on the island. Ominously, French units were spotted in Tasinge, just across the narrow straight. Danish gunboat activity increased. Three soldiers from the Villaviciosa Regiment guarding the west coast of Langeland were killed by cannon fire.

Up to this time, relations with the island's governor, Count Frederik Ahlefeldt, had been cordial. Now with the French so close, Ahlefeldt had to be treated as a potential threat. Two thousand Spaniards surrounded his residence at Tranekjaer. Brigadier San Roman informed the governor of the French presence and demanded the surrender of all Danish guns and artillery on the island. Ahlefeldt complied within the twenty-four hours demanded. Despite his submission, the count still managed to distribute more pamphlets with proclamations from Bernadotte and Kindelan. The latter assured the Spaniards that he still loved them like his own sons and promised that if they returned to Flensborg, he would grant them permission to return to Spain.

Advised by the British that the transport and supply ships were still many days away, La Romana's quartermaster general gathered stores for the journey. On 18 August alone, he paid cash for 200 cattle, 600 tons of rye, 200 tons of peas, 800 pounds of lard and some beer. All the stores were distributed around the convoy's vessels.

The next day, word spread like wildfire throughout the division. The commander of the British Baltic fleet had arrived on *HMS Victory*. As the 104-gun first rate moored off Spodsberg, O'Donnell was in awe of its size when compared to the nearby seventy-fours. Perhaps twenty-five per cent larger, the ship radiated power. Was this the ship that led the British fleet at the Battle of Trafalgar against the combined Franco Spanish not even three years earlier?

Instructions arrived from the marquis; he was to wear full dress uniform and accompany La Romana to meet Admiral Saumarez on board *HMS Victory*. As the general, O'Donnell and the rest of his entourage arrived at the quayside, they saw all the British ships flying the Spanish flag from their top masts. What a sight! A twenty-four-gun salute then thundered from the British ships saluting the marquis. How proud he was to be a Spanish patriot. To think, over two thirds of the troops that had arrived in Hamburg in 1807 were now on their way home to fight against the Corsican and all he stood for.

His mind wandered again. It had only been a few weeks since the odd little Scotsman had arrived and had been the catalyst for what had happened. O'Donnell hoped the man was safe.

80

Ribe, Jutland, August 1808

After two nights in Ribe's Weis Stue inn, Robertson felt less tired. On the journey from Horsens, they had been waved through by Danish and French patrols, seemingly intent on moving east towards Funen. He was still shocked that the news that Adam Rorauer was a wanted British spy had been spread so far and fast. He had to assume all authorities in Denmark and northern Germany had arrest warrants for him. Rorauer had to disappear. In the privacy of the enclosed coach, he was able to extricate the passport and other proofs for his new identity hidden in between the lining of his portmanteau. Herr Petersen was a commercial traveller in wines and spirits. Rather too close to Rorauer's job, but that would satisfy any questions about his south German accent. It would be natural for the wine wholesalers of the Mosel and Palatinate to employ a local. At a stop for a change of horses, he went to the privy and burnt everything related to Rorauer. As he hoped, the payment and bonus ensured the coach driver delivered him to Ribe without question. Though when he handed over the coins, the driver had given him a quizzical look, hopefully just in amazement at the amount he had just been paid.

Ribe had been a lucky choice. There were no French units based nearby. He had spotted a few Danish militiamen, but as he strolled around the small town, he had not been regarded as suspicious. He had flattered the innkeeper about the charm of his old inn and impressed him with his knowledge of wine. An apology for having run out of samples was accepted without question, such had been the success of this visit to Denmark. He promised to return with a full selection on his next trip. Turning the legend of his new personality into reality was progressing well.

As he entered the dining room for breakfast, he noticed a framed map of Jutland and Schleswig on the wall. It had probably been there all the time, but he had been too tired to notice. He wandered over. He began to study the map. Well to the south of Ribe, he spotted the coastal town of Tonning. Where had he heard the name being discussed – the Foreign Office or was it with Mr Nicholas? There to the far left of the map was a tiny dot. He peered closer. Heligoland. An idea began to formulate; could he pay a fisherman to take him from Tonning?

He never heard the innkeeper come up behind.

'There's no business out there. Heligoland was captured by the British last year.' Robertson did his best to disguise his surprise.

'I'd heard. I was looking just out of interest. But tell me, I've not been to Tonning. Rumour has it that the town is thriving. I might add it to my schedule on my next visit.'

The innkeeper looked at him. 'You're nearly correct, Herr Petersen. It was a great centre for smuggling from Britain. There would have been lots of business there for you, but sadly the French put a stop to that. A real shame.'

'Oh well, thank you for putting me in the picture.' That really was a shame. The end of that idea. Now he would have to make his way back to Hamburg.

'I shall be leaving after breakfast. Can you prepare my bill and organise a carriage to take me south?'

'Of course, Herr Petersen.'

On his own once more, he looked at the map again. At the mouth of the River Elbe was the village of Brunsbüttel. Maybe another possibility for escape?

Three days later, keeping to the west coast to avoid Bernadotte's Danish headquarters in Rensborg, he arrived in Brunsbüttel. He paid the driver and took a room in a quayside inn. Walking up the quay, he passed French customs officers inspecting a group of fishermen's papers. More disappointment, no chance of paying one of them for a ride to Heligoland. He returned to the inn. Apart from a group of uniformed Danes sitting at a table drinking, the bar was empty. As he sat sipping coffee, one of the sitting Danes rose. He towered over Robertson.

'Passport.'

Robertson handed over the document. The man gave it a cursory look.

'Not good.'

Not again; another Danish official who could not read. The strain of the past weeks boiled over.

'You and your stupid men haven't a clue what you are looking at. This passport was approved by a colonel of the militia just days ago.' He snatched the passport back and went to his room, opened the door and slammed it behind him. The Dane had not reacted.

Minutes later the door burst open. The Dane's bulk filled the door frame. He pointed at Robertson's portmanteau.

'Open.'

Robertson did so. The Dane proceeded to inspect every item in the case. Finally, he found a cylindrical shape wrapped in paper.

'What's this?'

The Dane unwrapped Robertson's shaving brush, threw it down and flattened out the paper. He looked elated but soon realised that it was part of a letter written in German detailing an old order for wine. This too was thrown onto the pile of clothes. Robertson smiled to himself: it had been worth taking the time to ensure that there was nothing written or otherwise to link him to England.

The Dane turned and left the room. The door slammed behind him.

Minutes passed. Another rap on the door of his room. He opened the door. This time a Danish officer faced him, the huge militiaman behind him.

'Passport.'

Robertson realised that once again he had little choice.

He handed the passport over again. The officer left with the passport. He now felt exposed and apprehension began to turn to fear. Without the correct documentation, he would be arrested. He lay on his bed, waiting.

Two hours later the officer returned.

'My apologies, Herr Petersen. Here is your passport, perfectly in order. I have stamped it accordingly. The man was just doing his duty. Everyone in my squad is keen to catch this middle-aged English spy, especially as there is such a large reward for his capture. If I may say, you are middle-aged and German!'

Robertson laughed. 'Indeed, I am, but not an English spy.' Scottish, he smiled to himself. The Dane turned to leave.

'Perhaps you can suggest the best way to journey to Hamburg?'

'There is a good ferry service up the Elbe. Much less uncomfortable than the road.'

81

Cesar Rainville's Hotel, Altona, North of Hamburg, 24 August 1808

Ever since his release from the cellar in the hotel, Marquet had turned over in his mind to see if he could have done anything differently to prevent the disaster. Fortunately, the Danish authorities had tight control on the press. The fact that some 9,000 Spaniards had escaped was only known to locals in Funen, though word would surely leak out. The more he thought about it, the more convinced he became that there was little he could have done. Had he not been stuck on Zealand for those crucial days, things might have been different. And as if a spider at the centre of its web, the catalyst was the English spy. If the thought of catching the man had been an intermittent itch before, now it had become a constant rash.

Marquet sat across Maupont's desk waiting for the colonel to finish reading his report. Finally, Maupont looked up.

'A rather unpleasant experience being incarcerated in a cellar and especially with only a servant for company.' Marquet did not want to be reminded of the days locked up with the valet especially as he began to smell worse, but then so probably did Marquet himself.

'Poor Martin looked as if he was about to have a heart attack at any moment. His nerves are so frayed that he will never be any use as a soldier. I have written to his commanding officer requesting that he should be discharged. He was a useful spy who did his best. Can you ask the Prince to order his son's release?'

'If you think Martin has done his duty.'

'I do.'

'Very well.' Maupont returned to Marquet's report. 'You maintain that there were a number of opportunities to prevent the Spanish escape but you do not specify what those were. Why not?'

'For the simplest reason that to commit the truth to writing would send me and probably, you, my Colonel, to Madame La Guillotine.'

'Explain.'

Marquet put his finger to his ears and made to wiggle them. 'Shall we take a turn around the garden?'

Maupont nodded and moved to the French doors. As soon as they were well clear of the building, he turned and faced Marquet.

'Well?'

Marquet looked around. They were in the open, clear from prying eyes.

'The failure came from the very top. The Prince trusted

La Romana and believed everything the Spaniard told him right until it was too late. That is why my report is suitably vague in apportioning blame. It appears that the Prince continues to have the Emperor's confidence. Therefore, I suggest that my report is suitably filed before anyone decides to look for more junior scapegoats.' Marquet pointed at his chest and then at Maupont.

'I expect I can find a convenient bottom drawer. Let's move on. You suggest that you should pursue this English spy. How sure are you that he has not escaped back to England?'

'I'm not. However, a Lieutenant Moreau reported that a man answering his description was seen in Horsens. The whole area on eastern Jutland was flooded with troops moving to Funen. It is very unlikely that he will have been able to get back there in time to board a British ship. What are his choices? The heightened police and customs activity all along the coast will have made it difficult for anyone to have been smuggled to Heligoland. If he has not broken through our coastal blockade, with Denmark so anti-British, his only choice will be to go south using the networks that we know the British have across Germany. To follow him will give us the opportunity to break up these groups and disrupt the intelligence going back to London. But first, I plan to break the sources of the spy's funds, starting with Parish's bank here in Hamburg.'

The colonel was quiet. They had moved well away from the house. The view over the Elbe was delightful in the afternoon sunlight. Maupont looked around. They were still alone.

'Maybe I should explain again. We arrested John Parish months ago on suspicion of helping the British but were ordered by Paris to release him immediately. It seems that his brothers had been helpful in organising transactions with the American Government – perhaps you remember the sale of Louisiana? You will have to stay well clear of that organisation. However, I will recommend the rest of your plan to the Prince and to Paris. You want revenge.'

'I do.'

'Well then, gather your thoughts and report back to me.'

'I will.' Marquet saluted. He was reminded of that bon mot – "revenge is a dish best served cold".

82

Cesar Rainville's Hotel, Altona, North of Hamburg, 25 August 1808

Marquet returned to the hotel the next day. He was ushered into Maupont's office.

The colonel leant back in his chair, hands behind his head. He looked out of the window of his office. Sitting opposite him, Marquet thought that Maupont would like to be elsewhere.

'So, Marquet, what about the English spy?'

'We know the alias Adam Rorauer acting as a merchant. No doubt there were other aliases. If you remember, I told you about the priest. How about if the two are one and the same? I would have liked to question the other spy in more detail. Is there any news from Paris about the man McMahon's interrogation there?'

'I haven't heard anything.'

Marquet continued, ignoring the disinterested

comment. 'In any case, it was probably likely that the two were operating independently of each other.

'It was a Catholic priest I caught a glimpse of. It makes sense to employ a Catholic priest to talk to the highly religious Spanish. Now, assuming the spy's escape route across the North Sea has been blocked, where would he find refuge? Not eastwards until he reached Poland. South in Germany would be my guess. Bavaria is largely Catholic but allied to France. Safety within the general populous is unlikely. Perhaps there is an organisation in Germany that is pro-British?

'I have concentrated my research on the presence of British Catholic priests and monks in Germany. Many of the institutions have been closed down. One remains in operation; the Benedictine monastery in Ratisbon. This appears to be staffed largely by Scots. More interesting, one of the monks, a man named Horn, has been found to be in regular contact with British agents in Austria. It is suspected that Horn also has direct contact with the government in London. Such is the respect the monks have in elite circles in the Bavarian Government, that attempts to arrest Horn have been prevented. However, it has been made clear that the monk is a marked man. Horn has got the message and fled, it is assumed to Austria.'

Marquet waited for Maupont to comment. He was confident that he would be given the authority to travel to Ratisbon and continue to track the spy to his lair.

'Excellent work, Marquet. But it will be someone else who will pursue this man.'

'What do you mean?'

Maupont pushed a letter across his desk. 'Congratulations. You are to travel to Kassel to become the secretary to the War Ministry of the Kingdom of Westphalia. You will have regular access to King Jerome, the Emperor's brother. You have been angling for promotion. Now you have it.'

Marquet sat back in his chair trying to grasp the implications of this news. It grated that he would now not be able to conclude business with the spy. But as the news sank in, Maupont was right, promotion it was and what a promotion.

The door opened and was flung back on its hinges. It crashed against the wall. Six gendarmes in Imperial Guard uniforms marched in taking positions all round Maupont's office. They were followed by a general de brigade. Marquet spun round. He did not know the gendarmes but instantly recognised the imposing figure of Etienne Radet. Marquet had met the general once before and knew of his fearsome reputation. Maupont leapt from his chair and began to open his mouth to speak.

Radet shouted, 'Quiet! You are under arrest.'

Surprised, Maupont quickly gathered himself. Looking at Marquet, a hint of sadness mixed with his smile.

'Well, I suppose the captain deserves the punishment that is coming. We cannot tolerate failure, can we, General?' Marquet's face drained of colour. He swallowed. Perhaps he should have seen this moment coming. Too late now.

It was Radet's turn to smile. 'You have it wrong, Colonel, it is you who is under arrest.' Gesturing to the gendarmes, he ordered, 'Take him.' Maupont slumped back into his chair. Two gendarmes shouldered their muskets and grabbed Maupont's arms, yanking him upright. The chair tipped back, crashing to the floor. Shock and horror were written over Maupont's face. It was his turn to turn white.

He shouted, 'There must be some mistake! Does Bernadotte know about this? Who gave the order?'

'The order, Colonel, came from the Emperor himself. As you rightly say, we cannot tolerate failure. Now take him away.' Maupont's legs gave way. The gendarmes held him up. He was hauled from the room. The other four gendarmes followed.

Radet turned to Marquet. 'Now, Captain, close the door.' Marquet did as he was ordered. 'I should congratulate you, you are now Major Marquet. You will not take up your new role in Westphalia for six months. Your task is now to find and arrest the English spy who has caused so much embarrassment. You reported that he is probably still in Germany. Well, find him.'

Marquet's mind was in turmoil. He began to speak. Radet put his hand up.

'Listen. You will have a troop of six gendarmes. You can choose the best. You will also have this.' Radet produced a letter from his case. 'This commands that you are given any assistance and funds you require across the Empire. All must obey, from humble soldier to the most senior general. Look who has signed the letter.'

Marquet read. He saw the signature of Napoleon himself. The Emperor's seal was attached to the letter.

'This makes you the second most powerful man in

Europe. Now do the Emperor's bidding. Good hunting.' Before Marquet could ask any questions, Radet opened the door and was gone.

He walked over to the window of Maupont's office and looked across the manicured gardens with the view down to the Elbe in the distance, water shimmering in the late summer sunlight, remembering the strolls he and Maupont had had. Why the colonel and not him? As he had said in his report, the fault lay right at the top, with Bernadotte, but Napoleon would never order the arrest of a member of his family. There had to be a scapegoat. The scapegoat had to be reasonably senior. Maupont was the obvious choice. And him, Marquet? He might be the second most powerful man in the Empire for the moment. But fail and he would certainly follow Maupont.

What now? First, assemble a team. A lieutenant and five men. Corporal Lejeune could lead the men. He would ponder the choice of second in command. Then, he would use his new powers to order the tightening of control of the coast to prevent any escape to Heligoland and plan how to close the net. And order a new uniform to suit his new status as a major of the Gendarmerie of the Imperial Guard.

He walked to Maupont's desk, pulled the chair upright, sat, found paper and pen. He looked up at the elegant, plastered ceiling, thinking. He then began to jot notes. Who would be in his team? That came easily. Closing escape routes, he would order (a delicious thought!) General Dupas to double army patrols in and around Hamburg. The same order to Pyonnier's customs officers.

The local police would be ordered to commence house-to-house searches in the city and surrounding towns and villages.

On the next sheet, Marquet wrote a description of the man he had seen at the gate in Nyborg. That would be printed and circulated to all officers and men. Just in case there were some local policemen sympathetic to Britain, the man they were searching for would be accused of conspiracy and theft. In Marquet's mind the spy was guilty of both offences – the theft of the Spanish troops. He sat back. That would do for a start.

He stood and moved to the door. Something was wrong. Then it struck him. Where was the report that he had asked Maupont to bury? If that fell into the wrong hands, he would find himself up against a wall facing a firing squad. He went to Maupont's desk and began to empty the drawers. Nothing. Perhaps Maupont had put the report somewhere else? He started to replace all the papers. Then, out of a corner of a file, he saw a few words written in his hand. At last. He took the report to the fireplace, took a match and watched the paper burn. Thank God.

He left the office and made his way to the chief of staff's suite. General Gerard would ensure that his instructions would be carried out. As he walked, members of the headquarters staff stopped and stared at him. Word had obviously already got out. He smiled to himself. It felt good to be the second most powerful man in the Empire.

83
Hamburg, Late August 1808

Robertson's passport was checked twice on the leisurely journey upstream, once by Danish officials and again by French customs. Other passengers became surly when the French cutter pulled alongside, the French being blamed for the catastrophic decline in trade since the imposition of the hated Continental System. When the ferry docked at the Hamburg quayside, a gendarme glanced at and stamped his passport without comment.

He took a carriage to within a few minutes' walk of the safe house, sat in a window seat of a café to check that he was not being followed, before taking a circular route to the house. There seemed to be more police on the streets than he remembered on his last visit. The housekeeper was surprised to see him but let him in. He sent a coded note to the bankers, Parish & Co. He would come to the bank that afternoon to replenish his funds.

The meeting with John Parish was short. Parish, rightly, did not ask Robertson about his activities but hoped that they were successful. Robertson smiled. John Parish did not return the smile.

'I suggest that you should forget any idea of travelling home through Heligoland, at least for the time being. There has been a significant increase in French police and customs activity that has made trading activities increasingly risky. A number of our smuggler friends have been arrested. Others are understandably wary of taking to sea.'

'That tallies with what I saw on my journey south. Danish militia and gunboat activity ramped up all along the North Sea coast.'

'No doubt things will calm down but now is not a good time.'

Parish handed over the cash, making a note in a ledger. Wishing the Scotsman a safe onward journey, they shook hands.

It was only after Robertson had walked for ten minutes that he sensed he was being followed. There was nothing specific, just a sense, as if the hair on the back of his neck was standing up. He passed a bookshop, turned at the next corner, bent down as if to adjust a shoe, looked around. No one ducked out of sight. Nearly at a run, he turned back round the corner, entered the bookshop, picked up a book and made as to browse. A mirror gave a view behind him as he looked over the top of the book. Nothing, just normal pavement traffic in both directions.

Robertson waited fifteen minutes. Still nothing. A

book would give some credibility. He asked the bookseller if Goethe had published anything new. The bookseller was delighted. He had recently received new stock of the master's latest: *Faust, Part One*. A sale was made, the book wrapped. Robertson left the shop. He could not see anyone loitering. Maybe a false alarm? Just in case, he took a circuitous route back to the safe house, with plenty of doubling back. Was there anyone in familiar dress? Not that he could spot. But that sense would not go away.

Back in his room, there was a knock. The housekeeper came in.

'I am sorry to disturb you, sir, but there were two men asking for Herr Rorauer.'

As calmly as he could, Robertson thanked the housekeeper. The visitors to the safe house must be police. If the men knew of Rorauer, did they know of his Benedictine persona? Possibly. The Petersen passport was not questioned when he arrived back in the city. He thought that this identity was safe for the time being. However, a description of him was already circulating. It was time to put into action the escape plan he had developed while traveling south. Of the city gates, he guessed that the north and west would be the most on guard for any agent attempting to make a run for the North Sea coast. The lower reaches of the Elbe were also likely to be heavily patrolled on the lookout for smugglers' vessels. He would leave by the south gate and travel south-east before turning west to Bremen. He packed, paid what he owed and followed the owner down the cellar steps, past the pile of coal and along a narrow passage. They walked in silence for two, maybe three minutes. The owner's torch showed a flight of stairs. Robertson climbed to the top. The door led out onto a narrow passageway. Empty. As he walked towards the main street, he could hear women screaming at each other. Other voices joined in. Robertson smiled: the housekeeper and one of the servant girls putting on just the show the owner had promised. Any watchers would be distracted.

At the southern gate, he was waved through, no questions asked. He hired a gig to take him to Bergedorf, south-east of the city and on to Zollenspieker. Luck was on his side. The ferry was on the quayside. No one in pursuit. Thirty minutes later, the gig paid, his ticket purchased, Robertson watched the riverbank as the ferry made its way across the Elbe to Hoopte. Though he was now back in Lower Saxony, he was not asked for his passport when he stepped down from the ferry. Another gig took him the short ride to Winsen, an inn and a night's rest before the next stage of his journey in the morning. He was now two hours' ride south of Hamburg. His passport had not been requested – possibly a modicum of safety?

84

Winsen, Late August

Robertson woke early. He ordered a carriage, breakfasted and set off from the inn just after 8 a.m. Now was the time to run for home. He had debated whether to call for help from his smuggler friend but decided that he would travel straight to Cuxhaven. There he could pay a fisherman to take him back to Heligoland. It would be expensive, but he had ample funds whatever the sailor wanted to charge.

The rutted roads on the cross-country journey combined with the dust the horses kicked up made travelling tiresome and uncomfortable. He looked forward to every halt. What a change from the turnpike from London to Harwich. That comfortable journey now seemed aeons away. Finally, they reached the small town of Stade, an old Hanseatic town linked by canal to the River Elbe. At the Hotel Stadthaven, the driver disappeared to make arrangements to change horses. Robertson dusted himself down and entered. As he sat waiting for the menu, he overheard two men at the bar. From what they were discussing it seemed that they were fishing-boat skippers. Time for some intelligence gathering. The waiter came. Robertson looked up at him, ordered and asked 'Those two gentlemen seem rather unhappy with life. Is the fishing no good?'

'It is not the fishing that they are worried about. It's the French. There seems to be a campaign all along the coast to make life difficult.'

'Why is that?'

'They want to do what they can to stamp out smuggling. It's not just their customs officers who are making a nuisance of themselves. There's been a real increase in military police patrols.' Alarm bells rang. Customs were an irritation but military police, that was another matter. Robertson thought quickly. If the two skippers were the same as the majority of fishermen, they probably were involved in illegal and very profitable activity. The risk was worth it.

'Would you ask those two gentlemen if they would join me in a glass of schnapps?' The men heard and turned, eying Robertson suspiciously.

'Why should we sit down with a stranger, even one who offers to buy us drinks?'

Robertson stood, moved to the bar and said quietly, 'I am a merchant. Perhaps we have matters of mutual interest that are worth exploring over some schnapps?' The two men looked at each other, nodded and moved to

Robertson's table. The schnapps arrived. Robertson began. His customers were increasingly unhappy. Constant shortages and the prices being asked were ridiculous. All this change in just the last few weeks. Again, the men looked at each other, still suspicious.

'Both our vessels have been boarded and searched many times in the past two weeks. But now the police bastards have come to our homes, threatening our wives and children.'

'When did this start?'

'In the last two, maybe three weeks.'

'What were they looking for, contraband?'

'No, an English agent disguised as a merchant.'

'What was this merchant supposed to be selling?'

One looked at his empty glass. Robertson waved at the waiter. 'Bring us the bottle.' He filled both glasses to the brim. Mistrust clouded both faces.

'And what do you trade in, Mr Merchant?'

'Johann Petersen, please.' He pulled out his passport. 'Wine and coffee are my business.' The men exchanged glances.

'Well, Herr Petersen, that's a relief. The man they were looking for worked in chocolate and cigars. Now what was his name?' A pause, then the man smiled. 'Of course, it was Ror something.'

The other butted in. 'Adam was his Christian name.' Robertson tried to prevent the colour draining from his face. The Rorauer identity was known out here in rural Hanover.

'And the bastards thought that this Adam... damn,

what was his surname? This Adam would make his way to Cuxhaven and then on to one of the nearby islands where the British would take him off. Neuwerk, most likely. *Prost!*' Delighted at having remembered, the two men clinked glasses. Robertson clinked the two proffered glasses.

'*Prost*,' Trying to smile.

'As they left my house, the bastards told me that I was lucky. They'd instructions from the very top to take every fisherman's and merchant's house in Cuxhaven apart. God help them.'

It was tempting to make an excuse and leave immediately. But that would be too obvious. He ordered lunch and another bottle of schnapps. By the time he had eaten, the second bottle had been finished. Robertson managed to make just one glass last. When he told his new friends that he had to be going, the two tried to persuade him to join them in a third bottle. Profuse in apologies, he managed to pay the bill and escape. Outside the driver was waiting.

'A change of plan.' He gave the driver the address of the smuggler's house in the country outside Bremen.

Another four hours being bounced from one side of the carriage to the other, they arrived. Robertson knocked. The door opened.

'What the hell are you doing here? For God's sake, go! I know what you want. There's nothing I can do for you. My house was searched just this morning. The police had a leaflet describing you. They asked if I had seen anyone answering the description. If we are found together, we'll both be shot. Now go!'

The door slammed. Robertson climbed back onto the carriage. What now? He knew that the smuggler's network was compromised at least for the time being. He would have to resort to another network that could always be relied on. 'Bremen,' he told the driver.

At Bremen's eastern gate, looking around there seemed to be no more than a usual contingent of guards. He scanned the nearby windows and possible observation points. No obvious watchers. The Petersen passport was given a cursory examination. He was waved through.

At the market square, he paid the driver off. Walking past the town hall, he looked up at the facade of the cathedral, once Catholic, now Lutheran. How the world had changed from the certainty of a united Church to the divisions of the Reformation. South and on to the High Street, he reached St John's Church. The priest was closing the building for the evening.

'How may I help you, my son?'

'I am Father Gallus.' The priest looked surprised. Robertson had rehearsed what he would say. At least some of it would have a modicum of truth. He turned from German to Latin.

'Father, I am with the Benedictine seminary in Ratisbon.'

The priest followed in Latin. 'I know of it. But how can I help?'

'I am being pursued by the French police who wish to arrest me for distributing leaflets to the Catholic community.'

'What did the leaflet say that so upset the French authorities?'

'It describes the assault on Rome in February and the danger for His Holiness the Pope. We must tell our flocks the truth, not let them be seduced by the lies in the French controlled press. We must keep the flame of Catholicism burning bright.'

'Of course we must. Do you know how far the police are behind you?'

'No, I hope with these clothes as a disguise, I have been able to stay well ahead of them'

'Come with me. You can stay with me for a day or so while I make arrangements for a safer refuge.' Relief swept through Robertson. He was now back in the bosom of his Catholic family. Three days later, Father Gallus was delivered to the home of a saddler, the head of a staunchly Catholic family. He was close to Hamburg once again.

85

Almack's Assembly Rooms, St James's, London, 22 September

Hoppner had become used to sitting in the waiting room. The porter had not waited for him to ask for Palmerston.

'I'll send someone to find His Lordship. Coffee while you wait?'

'Thank you.'

For a change, Hoppner did not have to wait long. Palmerston ordered coffee.

'I understand that General La Romana is in town?'

'Yes, Mr Canning is hoping to arrange an audience with His Majesty. What news of his troops?'

'They left their mooring off the Downs two days ago. With favourable weather, they should reach Santander in ten days or so. Reports from Admiral Keats say that the men are much happier now they are in proper transports. The journey from Langeland to Gothenburg was testing. Many of the men had to spend most of the journey stood up, so tightly were they packed on the vessels Keats had commandeered. Some men of the Catalunya Regiment were close to mutiny by the time they reached Sweden. But frankly, I am surprised that there was not more trouble during the journey or while they were waiting for the transports from England. Keats had asked the Swedes to provide transports but they wanted to charge a ridiculous amount, hence the wait while our transports arrived.'

'How many soldiers did Keats manage to rescue?'

'Well over 9,000. A well-executed plan with plenty of improvisation; textbook is what my lords of the Admiralty are calling it. It is likely that Keats will be decorated.'

'A coup indeed. Do we know how many Spaniards were left behind?'

'Maybe four or as many as five thousand. Have you heard what has happened to them?'

'Reports suggest they have been marched back to Hamburg. Presumably they will end up in prison in France.'

'What news of your agents?'

'One has disappeared, we presume captured.' Hoppner ran his finger across his throat. 'He was spotted leaving Hamburg en route, it was rumoured, for Paris. We had evidence to question his loyalties but the Foreign Secretary believed the man despite his Irish nationalist past.'

Palmerston interjected. 'So, you think he was a double agent working for the French?'

'Even a triple agent. But I'm sure of one thing.'

'What's that?'

'He had one true loyalty – McMahon was faithful to himself.'

Palmerston raised his eyebrows. Hoppner continued. 'MacKenzie heard from the monk. He was in hiding near Hamburg waiting for the opportunity to slip back to Heligoland. But we have heard from Mr Nicholas that French police activity along the coast has made any smuggling activity very risky.'

'What will he do?'

'Either wait until police activity returns to more normal levels – the French cannot do without their smuggled coffee! Or he will have to travel south, perhaps to his monastery in Ratisbon. If that is the case, it will be many months before we see him again.'

'That presumes he does not suffer the same fate as your other man.'

Hoppner swallowed. 'I do hope not. I rather liked the monk.'

'And what about you, Hoppner? Stay with the Foreign Office or follow in your father's footsteps and become an artist? I've seen your work. You have talent.'

'Thank you, my lord. I enjoy painting but I doubt I'll ever be as good as my father. No, I will carve out my own career. I shall stay where I am, despite all the foibles and frustrations.'

'I'm glad to hear it. I was at a soirée last evening. Society's talk was full of the Spanish escape. Canning was present, receiving all the plaudits for the successful operation. I heard him say that it could not have been carried out without the hard work of his people. He was fulsome in his praise for a young clerk named Hoppner, someone he thought would go far. Well done!'

Hoppner's face turned bright red.

86

Cesar Rainville's Hotel, Altona, North of Hamburg, September 1808

Marquet began to enjoy being the second most powerful man in Europe. He took over Maupont's office. It was highly unlikely that the colonel would ever be needing an office again now that the unfortunate Maupont had been taken to Paris. The colonel's fate was a constant reminder to Marquet that he had better succeed.

He recruited Bernard, the best sergeant in the gendarmerie and instructed him to find five high-calibre gendarmes. All must be literate, at least 1.8 metres tall and three must speak fluent German. For the duration of the assignment, they would be paid double the existing rate, be equipped with new uniforms, new equipment and the best horses. One at least should be a sharpshooter. If it was necessary to shoot the English spy it would be unfortunate. If circumstances dictated, Marquet wanted to be sure that he had a crack shot in his team. All would be armed with the latest version of the Charleville rifle, two Pistolet cavalry pistols and sabres.

While Bernard assembled the squad, Marquet set about ensuring that the coast and towns were so heavily guarded that the spy could not escape to Heligoland. With delicious anticipation of how they would be received, he wrote orders to Pyonnier of the customs service, Bourrienne, the consul, and General Dupas, commanding Hamburg. Patrols were to be trebled for the next two months and operated on a twenty-four-hour basis. It was not long before he heard that both Pyonnier and Bourrienne had complained bitterly to Bernadotte. The Prince of Ponte Corvo just shrugged his shoulders. Both were told to obey.

Marquet was in his office when the door was flung open. General Pierre-Louis Dupas stormed in. Long, straggly, unkempt hair reached the general's shoulders. His moustache covered his bottom lip. A man known for his bravery, "General Forward" strode up to Marquet. A mix of spittle and garlic breath hit Marquet as a torrent of expletives tumbled from the general's mouth. He made to draw his sword.

'By whose authority do you, a mere major, presume to order me, General Dupas? You nasty little bastard of the minor nobility.'

Marquet took a pace back to avoid smelling any more of the revolting breath.

'On the instruction of His Majesty the Emperor himself, General. You are to provide me with any assistance I deem necessary to fulfil my mission.'

Dupas exploded again. 'Where is this so-called authority?' Marquet went to the desk, pulled open a drawer and produced the order, ensuring that Dupas could see the Emperor's seal. The general glanced at the seal, slammed a fist on the desk and turned with a parting shout. 'We'll see about that.'

When Dupas had gone, Marquet quietly closed the door. Not a good enemy to have made, but what could he have done?

He sent for three of the finest portrait artists in Hamburg. There would be a competition to draw the man he had seen at the gate in Nyborg. The best would be rewarded handsomely. Each artist sketched as Marquet described the man and made suggestions to refine each portrait. Hours passed until the winner produced a close likeness. The sketch was sent to the premier printer. Thousands of copies were made and distributed to guards, customs officers and police. "Wanted" posters were pinned to community noticeboards and sent to all newspapers. Editors were ordered to give maximum exposure with substantial rewards for information leading to an arrest.

Marquet interviewed each of the recruits Bernard found. He was impressed with the calibre. Four of the five spoke German. Bernard assembled the men for final inspection. Marquet congratulated his team for passing the selection process.

'The man we are looking for is an English spy. He may have been spirited away to Heligoland, but I doubt it. I believe he is still here in Germany. He has used a number of aliases, one being Rorauer. However, I think he is now using another disguise. He may also be a priest of some sort, maybe a monk. He is wanted by the Emperor himself. If we are able to capture him, each of you will be rewarded. We work as a team. Now let's find this man.'

Six men shouted in unison. 'We'll find him, Major.' One put his arm up.

'Yes, what is it?'

'Does the Emperor want him dead or alive?'

'Alive, if at all possible, so that he can be questioned. But if we need to execute him, then kill him we must.' Marquet was impressed by the torrent of other questions that followed. He answered as best he could.

The next day he visited the prison. A discussion with the governor produced the required results. That afternoon, Sergeant Bernard and his squad marched to the prison. They came out with a prisoner who was covered in bruises, blood spattered across the man's torn clothes. A sign reading "the penalty for smuggling and assisting spies" hung around his neck. Crowds stared in silence as the man was dragged to a wall in the main square. Bernard lined up the squad then turned to ensure there were plenty of spectators.

'Firing squad, load, present, aim – fire!' The volley rang out across the square. The prisoner collapsed to the cobbled pavement. Blood stained the wall. Gasps from the crowd intermingled with shouts of "no". Women fainted. Children screamed. Then silence as the throng cowered as Bernard marched his men away leaving the crumpled body where it had fallen.

Back at the hotel, Bernard reported to Marquet.

'Excellent, Sergeant. That will have the desired effect. Word of the execution will spread like wildfire across the region. That should put a stop to smuggling activity for some weeks at least.'

'A question, Major; who was the prisoner?'

'A murderer. He was due to be executed in the prison anyway. I am sure we can use the same ploy again should we need to. Customs officers who turn a blind eye, for example? We could dress another condemned man in customs uniform and execute him in public. Good for morale, don't you think?'

Bernard laughed.

The combined tactic of the publicity and threat produced results. Marquet and his men had to sift through multiple fantasy sightings. However, some reports did appear to be accurate. A man answering the description had been seen leaving Hamburg's southern gates some time ago. More recently another report: a coach travelling at speed with a single passenger had nearly run a local florist off the road. The florist was questioned closely. His description seemed to be accurate. The coach was travelling south.

As he lay in bed after another exhausting day, Marquet reviewed progress in his mind. He was reasonably sure that the whole coastline was as secure as possible. Smuggling activity had virtually stopped. From the reports it did seem that his hunch was correct. The spy had not escaped and was heading south. Marquet kept returning to his target as a priest or more particularly, a monk. This was the best lead he had. Of the monasteries he had researched,

Erfurt was the closest. But Erfurt's monastery was closed, and the town was the location of the conference between Napoleon and the Tsar. It would be crawling with soldiers and police. The spy would surely give Erfurt a wide berth. No, as he had discussed with Maupont, he would travel direct to Ratisbon.

He turned over affording himself a smile. He wrote an interim report for Radet. Another target would be the bankers Parish & Co, the suspected source of the spy's funding. He delivered the report to the chief of staff. Gerard told him that Dupas had had a blazing row with Bernadotte. The Prince decided that Dupas would be placed on the retired list ostensibly because of his numerous war wounds. No more trouble on that front at least.

When he returned to his room after dinner, he found a note from Radet. He was forbidden to investigate Parish & Co. The bank's services were too valuable to the Empire. Minor discretions such as funding enemy spies were to be tolerated, though such illegal activity would be held against the Parish brothers if they ever stopped being of service. Marquet swore.

87

The Saddler's Shop, Close to Hamburg, September 1808

Robertson finished reading the *Hamburgischer Correspondent*. The newspaper carried a long report on La Romana's escape. Even the French censor could not disguise La Romana's coup. To be spirited away from under the noses of 40,000 enemies was a remarkable achievement. Robertson looked forward to reading the accounts in *The Naval Chronicle* and *London Gazette* when he returned home.

Over the last three weeks, he had sent coded messages to the contacts in the Hamburg post office and at Parish's Bank. The replies were, to say the least, discouraging. French police and custom officer activity had been raised to near emergency levels. Reports circulated that a detachment was intermittently stationed on Neuwerk. Smuggling activity into northern Germany had all but stopped. Whispered conversation talked about searches for British spies. Fishing boats were regularly stopped and searched. Merchants were regarded with suspicion and randomly questioned. It seemed that the smuggler was right. The police did have a description of him. The message was clear. Any escape through Cuxhaven carried exceptional risk.

Robertson coded a message to MacKenzie to be sent through the Hamburg post office contacts' network. Now that the news of the Spanish escape had hit the headlines across Europe, could MacKenzie ensure that the London newspapers carried news of the safe return of the agent who had helped to make La Romana's escape possible? Knowing that British newspapers were avidly read in Paris, perhaps this might reduce the counter-intelligence activity and give some chance of a less risky escape.

Time for coffee with his host. Father Gallus's offer to say Mass and hear Confession for the saddler and his family had been enthusiastically accepted. In return, the saddler used his membership of the virulently anti-French local Catholic network to provide Robertson with intelligence on French police activity. As time passed, more reports circulated about the police search for the thief. Days later, the saddler was summoned to the local police station to repair a scabbard. While he was working, he overheard officers describing their quarry. When he returned home, he told his guest what he had heard. From then on, Robertson kept his bags packed ready for a quick getaway. The saddler arranged for a reliable driver and carriage to be available at very short notice. He hoped that the police would become bored of the search so that he could escape to the coast and on to Heligoland. Meanwhile, he worked on contingency plans.

One morning, as he descended the stairs, he heard the door of the shop open. Through the bannisters he saw uniforms, uniforms he did not recognise. He was about to turn for his hiding place when one of the uniformed men spoke; Spanish. He carried on downstairs, welcoming the two Spanish officers in French. From the scowls on the Spanish faces, he realised that they assumed him to be French. One put his hand on his sword. Robertson put his hands up.

'I am English.'

The change on the men's faces was dramatic. Both embraced him, squeezing and kissing him.

'*Bueno Ingles*,' again and again. He thought he was about to be smothered. Finally released, they sat down. Coffee arrived. The three began to talk. Italian was easiest. The Spaniards had been members of Bernadotte's personal guard. As soon as news of La Romana's escape was confirmed, they were arrested and imprisoned. Being officers, both were offered parole. One of the conditions of their parole stipulated that they should give up their horses. They had come to the shop to dispose of their saddles.

Both enthused about what they knew of La Romana's escape and their desire to return home to fight against the French.

'But what about you, *bueno Ingles*, aren't you in danger? A troop of police is making house-to-house searches in the next village.'

Robertson's face drained of colour. Time to run again. He would have to implement the backup plan. Thanking the Spaniards, he spoke with the saddler. Half an hour later, he was sitting in the back of a buggy heading south. Home and safety were a long way off.

88
Erfurt, September 1808

As part of his contingency plan, Robertson wrote to the prior of the former Benedictine monastery in Erfurt, Joseph Hamilton, to ask if he could stay. The monastery had close ties with his in Ratisbon. He had met the prior on many occasions and enjoyed his company. He received a reply by return. Had Robertson not heard that Napoleon was due to hold a conference with Tsar Alexander at the end of the month? The town would be full of dignitaries and crammed with soldiers. Napoleon planned to impress the Tsar and had ordered the *Comédie-Française* to entertain the royal parties. It was even rumoured that the poet Goethe would attend. Hamilton suggested that if Robertson wished to avoid attention, he should give Erfurt a wide berth. Much as he would like to spend time with the prior, he decided to follow his advice.

Robertson said a hurried thanks and goodbye to the

saddler and his wife, and stepped up into the carriage. He instructed the driver to stay well clear of the main towns, Hanover in particular. Three days later, the driver stopped at Landgrafen to change horses. The village was on the extensive battlefield of Jena. Robertson was tired of being bounced around on the rutted roads. He told the driver that he would stretch his legs.

Whether it was some ghoulish infatuation to see the land on which there had been 36,000 casualties just two years previously or a more spiritual purpose, he just could not remember. He wandered across some of the site, still littered with the debris of battle. Perhaps he was not concentrating but he slipped and impaled his knee on a half-buried blade of a cavalry lance. With blood pouring from the wound, close to fainting from the pain, he could only half crawl back to the coach. He shouted for the driver and passed out. He woke to find the driver and a stable lad binding the wound. It was obvious that he would need proper medical attention. To continue the planned journey was impossible. The driver suggested a doctor in close by Jena could tend to his injuries. He could not think properly. Loss of blood and pain muddled him. There was a baser instinct – to get to safety. He told the driver to take him to Prior Hamilton's house in Erfurt.

The driver did his best to avoid the ruts and potholes but without success. Robertson was bounced around the carriage. His knee began to leak blood again as it throbbed with pain. At least his head had cleared somewhat. After two hours of misery, they arrived in the outskirts of the walled town. Rows of white military tents stretched across the fields in front of the walls. Flags of France and Russia flew from the towers. Crowds watched soldiers parading. There was a line of coaches, carts and foot passengers at the north-eastern gate. Messages were passed down the queue. All documents were being inspected in turn by local police, French soldiers and finally by military police. Some people were being pulled out of the line for questioning. As more traffic arrived behind, the coach was hemmed in and there was no turning back.

Finally, they arrived at the police checkpoint. The Petersen passport was inspected. Asked why he wished to enter the town, he showed the policeman his leg.

'To see a doctor.' He was waved on to the next barrier. French soldiers peered around the carriage as a corporal grabbed the passport that he held through the coach window.

'Get out of the coach.'

'I can't, I am wounded.' The corporal peered through the window and saw Robertson's bloodied knee.

'All right, you can stay there. So, you have come to see the Emperor and the Tsar?'

'No,' he repeated. 'To see a doctor to tend to my wound.'

'Where were you wounded?'

'At Landgrafen.'

'But that's on the battlefield of Jena! I fought with General Suchet, part of Lannes's corps. What a day, what a victory!' The corporal turned to his men.

'Lads, the gentleman was at Jena!' There was a cheer. 'Let him through.' The barrier was raised. Robertson realised that the NCO believed that he had taken part in the battle. The corporal took hold of the lead carriage horse's reins and led the coach to the final barrier. He shouted to a gendarme sergeant.

'Sergeant, this gentleman fought at Jena. He's injured and needs a doctor urgently. His passport is fine. Let him through, please.' The gendarme marched to the coach window, saw Robertson's bandaged knee, now soaked in blood.

'You got this at Jena?' Robertson nodded. It was true, he had sustained the wound on the battlefield.

'Anyone who was there on that glorious day deserves to have the best medical attention. Raise the barrier. Let him through.' The driver slapped the horses' rumps with the reins. Seconds later they were in Erfurt. Robertson afforded himself a smile.

The town was packed with tourists, military and locals all keen to see the Emperor and Tsar. The driver threaded his way through the crowds towards the Petersburg citadel. Robertson knew the vast monastery buildings well. As they reached the gates, a barrier blocked the entrance; the massive stone walls of the citadel loomed above them. French guards signalled the coach to stop.

A corporal shouted 'What do you want?' The driver looked scared and bemused. Robertson leant out of the window, blood oozing from the knee once again. The corporal only needed a glance to see Robertson's face was ashen. 'My god, you look terrible. Why are you here?'

Robertson croaked, 'Prior Hamilton will find a doctor for me.' He sat back into the carriage. The loss of blood was making him light-headed. The corporal looked in through the window and saw the blood-soaked knee.

'Don't you realise, this is a barracks now, not a monastery?' How the world had changed since his last visit.

'But does the prior still live in the grounds?'

'Yes, you'd better go to him and have that looked at.' The corporal waved for the barrier to be lifted. No more questions. Robertson passed out.

***

He woke. His eyes slowly focused to see Prior Hamilton leaning over him.

'Ah, there you are. At one stage, we thought we might lose you. You had lost a lot of blood. The doctor thought that he might have to remove the leg but he worked miracles; you should make a full recovery.'

Robertson looked alarmed.

'Don't worry, the Herr Doctor is a friend and completely trustworthy.' Robertson closed his eyes again, relief across his face. He tried to sit up.

'And the French?'

'The French are much too busy parading to impress the Emperor and the Tsar. You are safe at least until the congress is over. Now, rest.'

The Emperor and Tsar began their conference on 27 September. Seventeen days later, Robertson slipped out of Erfurt heading for his other home, the Scottish Benedictine seminary at Ratisbon.

89

Scottish Benedictine Abbey of St James, Ratisbon, November 1808

The journey to Ratisbon was slow and painful. Hamilton urged Robertson to leave Erfurt before the congress finished on October 14th. With his leg tightly strapped, he slipped out of the town the day before. Hamilton hired a carriage with the best available suspension. Even so, Robertson ordered the driver to make regular stops and to finish each day's travel early. It was not until the beginning of November that Abbot Arbuthnot welcomed him home.

He soon immersed himself in the routine of monastic life. Initially he had to be physically supported by brother monks to attend the hours of divine office. After so long out of practice, pre-dawn vigils were a test, but soon, being surrounded by his old friends and the sound of Gregorian chanting at Mass, his body and mind recovered. Hours of Confession and conversation with the abbot cleared his mind of most of the discretions forced upon him during the mission. He began to find peace.

***

Preparations for the journey to Ratisbon took Marquet longer than expected. He was increasingly concerned that the spy's trail would become cold. Despite the Emperor's authority, passports required to travel unimpeded through all the various German states were frustratingly slow to obtain. The more he railed against bureaucratic incompetence, the slower the process seemed to become.

When he and his squad finally set off, to ensure the trail was not missed, he had to spread the search across three different routes, slowing progress further. What should have been two weeks took a month to travel. At last, Bernard found a reliable witness south of Nuremburg on the road to Ratisbon. His hunch was looking promising. Autumn was well advanced by the time the six of them crossed the stone bridge into Ratisbon.

After Marquet had ordered Bernard to find lodging for him and his men, he checked into a central hotel. Although French influence in southern Germany was strong, since the dissolution of the Holy Roman Empire two years previously, Ratisbon was governed by the pro-French prince-primate, von Dalberg. Marquet requested a meeting with Dalberg's chief of staff to check how the land lay locally before taking any action against the monastery. The chief of staff explained that the Scottish monks were popular and the prior, Arbuthnot, as a renowned mathematician, well regarded with many powerful friends. The Emperor had been persuaded by his Scottish generals not to close the monastery but there were to be no more new novices. Marquet came away from the meeting with an idea.

He purchased a suit of civilian clothes and penned a letter to Arbuthnot. *Jacques de Norvins requests an interview. He has some advantageous news which should be of benefit to the monastery.* It was his turn to go undercover and play spy.

'So, Monsieur Norvins, what advantageous news do you have for us? We could do with it.' The seventy-year-old Charles Arbuthnot shook Marquet's hand, gesturing where in his study Marquet should sit. The abbot's rotund figure filled the black monk's habit. Marquet had received a reply to his note the same evening. At eleven the next morning, he arrived at the main gates of the monastery. A young monk showed him to Arbuthnot's quarters.

Marquet cleared his throat. 'My dear Abbot, do you know General Etienne MacDonald?' He hoped Arbuthnot would not.

'I know of him but have never met him. From a Jacobite family, I believe. His father served with Prince Charles. He and General Lauriston lobbied the then first consul to keep this abbey open.' Marquet breathed a sigh of relief. With luck that meant that the abbot did not know that the general was now out of Napoleon's favour.

'Your memory is excellent. The general wants to do anything he can to promote the Catholic cause. He believes that he may be able to use his influence with the Emperor to persuade him to overturn the decision to forbid novices joining the monastery.'

'That would be very welcome, though after the way the Pope has been treated, I am surprised. How can I help?'

'By writing to the general and asking for help. He has also asked that I have a good impression of your monastery.'

There was a knock on the study door. The door opened. Marquet turned and saw a monk also dressed in the black Benedictine habit, the hood covering his face. The monk raised his hand.

'My apologies, Father Abbot, I didn't know you had a guest.' The monk turned and left. Marquet noticed he was limping. Arbuthnot rang a bell. A young monk came in.

'Father, please give Monsieur Norvins a tour of the monastery. We need to give him a good impression for his report to his patron.'

'Of course, Father Abbot. Please come this way, *monsieur*.' Marquet was elated. Just what he wanted; an opportunity to scout the complex. As he was shown round the complex including the abbey church, Marquet asked his guide about the daily life of the monastery. By the time the tour finished, he had a plan in place. He turned to the monk.

'Thank you, that has been most informative. I will report positively to General MacDonald. Oh, and by the way, has one of your fellow monks returned from the north recently?'

'Why yes, how did you know? Father Gallus came back from doing pastoral work.'

'Father Gallus?'

'Sorry, that is his religious name. He is James Robertson.'

Marquet smiled to himself. At last.

***

At two the next morning, Marquet, back in uniform, briefed his squad. Avoiding the city's night patrols, the six men stole through the silent streets to the abbey church. They waited for the bell summoning the monks to the first service of the day, pre-dawn lauds. Marquet stationed two men to guard the main doors. As the monks began to sing the first hymn of the service, he and the other four crept in. Three covered the congregation with their muskets. As the hymn came to an end, Marquet made his way to the altar.

'My apologies for interrupting your service, Father Abbot. However, I am ordered by the Emperor to arrest one of your flock.'

Arbuthnot strode to confront Marquet in the candlelit gloom. 'This is an outrage.' Then he saw Marquet's face. 'But you are Monsieur Norvins!'

'Not *Monsieur*; Major. I will not detain you long. Father Gallus, James Robertson, step forward.' No one moved.

Marquet raised his voice. 'I said, James Robertson, come here, you are under arrest.' The monks looked around at each other. Nobody came forward. Marquet sighed.

'Well, if we must play it this way, we will. You have

muskets trained on you. I will order my men to fire.' Turning to Bernard, he said, 'Sergeant, bring me the candelabra from the altar. We will inspect the face of each and every man here.'

Arbuthnot interjected. 'There is no need for that, Major. I can assure you that Father Gallus left us yesterday. He is by now on his way to Austria. Well out of your reach.' There was a triumphant tone in the abbot's voice. 'Enough of this sacrilege, leave us.'

Marquet did his best to suppress the mixture of anger and failure.

'Sergeant, I said bring me the candelabra. We will check every face.' Ten minutes later, it was all over. No sign of Robertson. He gathered his men outside the church. Bernard turned to him, his men watching intently.

'What now, Major?'

'We go on, of course. We must complete the mission.' There was nodding. 'But first we ride to Munich. General Radet is there. One thing I've learnt is to deliver bad news before anyone else does.'

90

Alexander Horn's house, Linz, Austria, November 1808

'Your escape was pure luck?'

'It was.' Robertson was enjoying a glass of hock with his old friend and former monk, Alexander Horn, now an agent and Britain's last remaining diplomat in central Europe.

'When I came into the abbot's study, the gendarme turned and looked at me. I recognised him immediately and left before he saw me. Thank goodness I had the habit's hood over my head. After the Frenchman had left, I told the abbot who the man was. As you can imagine Arbuthnot was furious. He organised a passport for me while I hired a landau. I left Ratisbon three hours later.'

'Fortunate indeed.'

'Are you still in contact with London? If so, can I include a letter with your next despatch? I should tell MacKenzie where I am.'

'Of course, I must report that things are brewing. It won't be long before the Austrians will mobilise the forces against Napoleon and his Bavarian friends. My guess is there will be war again next year.'

'That soon?'

'I fear so. The Austrians want revenge for Austerlitz, no doubt encouraged with plenty of English gold. Now there is something you can do to help. Have you heard of Sir Arthur Wellesley's victory over the French in Portugal?'

'No, that's wonderful news. That's been kept very quiet.'

'Exactly, the pro-French press has done its best to stifle anything that would dent the *Grande Armée*'s reputation for invincibility. What if the news became public in such a city as say, Munich?'

'It would cause a sensation.'

'Exactly. I have organised for handbills to be printed in German spelling out the news. I need someone to distribute them around the city.'

'You mean me?'

'I would do it, but London has forbidden me to leave Austria. I know it's a lot to ask but you are eminently qualified. Once you have rested, it would only take two weeks. You'll have help in the city from one of my agents.' Robertson knew he would agree but looked at his friend.

'Will you give me time to mull it over?'

'Of course.'

***

Wrapped in a fur greatcoat which gave some protection from the biting winter wind, Robertson slipped into Munich. The guards gave the coach a cursory inspection missing the handbills hidden under the floor. He had decided to resurrect the Adam Rorauer identity. As a Bavarian, he was less likely to be questioned. He found the agent's house. They discussed the best locations to drop the bills for maximum effect. As darkness fell, Robertson toured the city. Avoiding police patrols, he quietly placed bundles of the handbills in hotels, inns, the opera house, outside the town hall, around the Marienplatz and in an empty coach on its way to collect guests at the royal palace. Three hours later, he returned to the agent's house. With a curfew in place, he was forced to stay the night in the city. He would leave at first light.

***

Marquet discovered that General Radet was staying at the best hotel in Munich just off the Marienplatz main square. The general was at the opera and would then attend a private dinner. He left a note requesting an interview. Ever since the disaster in Ratisbon, he had been planning what to say. Now he would have to wait another sleep-interrupted night as his mind churned through the options and with the hope that Radet had not already been told.

It was not until ten the next morning that Radet emerged. Marquet noted the general's bloodshot eyes.

'Join me for breakfast, Major.' Marquet's breakfast had been three hours ago. As he watched Radet down three cups of coffee, he realised that the general was only a few years older than him. A peasant's son becomes a general while he, nearly forty years old, with all the advantages of a good education, had only just become a major. All because of the accident of birth. How life turns out.

'That's better. Rather late last night. Now, what do think of this?' Radet pushed a crumpled handbill across the table.

'I'm sorry, sir, I don't read German.'

'Nor do I. Here's a translation.'

Marquet read the French version. 'Is this true?'

'Yes. Marshal Soult was outnumbered but even so it was a beating. At least in the truce negotiations afterwards, Soult persuaded the British to ship him and his troops with all their weapons and loot back to France! That part of the story is not in the handbill.' Radet took another sip of coffee. 'We cannot have dangerous material like this spread across the Empire. It will encourage dissent and worse. I have spoken to the Bavarians. They have no idea how these bills were distributed. The typeface is Austrian.'

It seemed to Marquet that Radet was completely focused on the handbill issue. His report on the spy's escape could be quietly forgotten.

'Sir, that would indicate that someone entered and left the city within twenty-four hours. We should be able to match the lists of strangers entering and exiting Munich yesterday and today. The Bavarians can be told to collect lists of names from each of the gates.'

'Good, Marquet.'

'And if this man entered Munich yesterday, to avoid

detection he would have waited until after dark to distribute the bills. By then, the city gates would have been closed, meaning that he must have spent the night in the city and left this morning, most likely towards Austria.'

'Excellent. The Bavarians can send light cavalry to chase the agent. And by the way, you were unlucky at Ratisbon.'

'You heard?'

Radet smiled.

It took another two hours to wade through the diplomatic niceties before the Bavarian authorities took action. It was into the afternoon before the cavalry had been despatched, the lists collected and handed over to Marquet.

He distributed the list from each gate between his men. The laborious process of matching the incoming with the exiting began. Finally:

'Sir, we have a match. An Adam Rorauer came in just before dusk and left at first light this morning. Wasn't that the name of the agent you were chasing in Denmark?'

Marquet could hardly believe his ears. Robertson. But he now had a nine-hour start. No chance of catching him before he made it to the safety of the Austrian border. *When would his luck run out?* He joined Radet for supper.

'So, General, what are your predictions for 1809?'

'There will be war with Austria by the spring. That will force your English spy to run again. Italy is too dangerous. He will be forced east and then north.'

91

Dresden, Late Spring 1809

On his return to Linz, Robertson was only able to watch Horn raising a glass to the success of the Munich mission. Gout had struck him. Horn's doctor forbade any alcohol. Some relief came from reading Austrian and German newspapers which were full of the French defeat.

His rest was cut short as Austrian army units moved through Linz to attack Bavaria. With the chaos of war imminent, now perhaps was the time to make another escape attempt. After news came through of clashes in Italy, a southern route was too risky. Horn advised Robertson to move east. He travelled first to Vienna. News arrived that the Austrians were being pushed back. Napoleon himself was approaching the Austrian capital. Robertson moved north into Bohemia and on to Saxony, heading for Dresden, a calculated risk; his passport did not cover travel in Saxony.

Reaching the hills above Dresden, he looked down on the Saxon capital. Robertson thought back to the last time he had seen the River Elbe. Hamburg seemed aeons ago. As he debated whether it was safe to attempt to enter the city, an Austrian officer accompanied by a single trooper rode up. More than just an officer – a general, accompanied by just a single trooper. Robertson stepped down from the landau.

'Sir, can I enter Dresden without a passport? Are you still in control of the city?'

'I am General Kienmayer. The French, Saxons and Poles are marching in a pincher movement. They hope to surround us. We have pulled out of the city and aim to give them another bloody nose. I expect the French under King Jerome will occupy the city. They have not arrived yet. My guess is that you will be safe if you go now.'

Kienmayer wheeled his horse and turned away before Robertson had a chance to ask more.

Such was the turmoil at the city gates that he had no trouble entering the city. It seemed that it would be the French that would occupy, not the hoped for Saxon and Polish troops. Rumour and counter rumour spread. Robertson booked into a hotel. Again, no request to show his passport. Two hours later, Jerome's troops arrived.

As he rested, there was a loud knock on the door of his room. Two local policemen entered. He was asked his name and profession.

'Adam Rorauer. I am a language teacher.' Apparently satisfied, they left. Three hours later they reappeared.

'Show us your passport.'

'I don't have one.'

'You have given us a false name. Your name is James Robertson – you are native of Scotland.' He was thunderstruck. Not for the first time, his quick wittedness saved him. Giving no indication of surprise or alarm, he turned on the two.

'What of it? I am still a language teacher.'

'But you cannot stay here.'

'That's fine. Let me have a passport and I'll be on my way.'

'We are the police. You need to go to the city hall to obtain a passport.'

'Then let me go without one.'

'That is equally impossible.'

'Ridiculous!'

'It is not ridiculous.' The words came from another voice. Robertson looked over the shoulder of one of the policemen. 'Step aside, officers.' The policemen moved. A French gendarme officer stepped into the room. Their eyes met. Recognition was instant. More gendarmes filled the corridor behind the officer.

'Well, Herr Adam Rorauer, or shall I call you by your real name? Mr James Robertson of Scotland, or better, British Spy, we have been expecting you. We have not been properly introduced. I am Major Marquet of the Gendarmerie of the Imperial Guard. You have been rather elusive.'

Robertson felt the colour drain from his face. The image of the falcon flashed across his mind. It was at the end of its stoop, wings flared, talons spread, ready for the kill. He tried to gain some composure.

'I'm not sure it is a pleasure, Major. I have been doing my best to avoid you.'

'But we have so much to talk about since our paths crossed at the gate in Nyborg.'

'How did you know that I would travel through Dresden?'

'It was an educated guess. Since you used the Rorauer name in Munich, we have circulated your description across the region with the promise of a substantial reward for your arrest, dead or alive.'

'You knew that I was responsible for distributing the handbills?'

'Yes, it was rather careless of you to continue to use the Rorauer alias.'

'And my name?'

'By subterfuge, I asked one of the monks. He was most obliging.'

Robertson knew that this day was likely to arrive. He had prepared himself but somehow never thought that it would actually happen. Now that it had, he felt strangely relieved, relaxed even.

He and Horn had talked about the consequences of being caught. He hoped for a quick demise but in his mind did his best to prepare for the questioning, the beatings, torture and the inevitable slow death. He just hoped that all those years of prayer honing his Faith would see him through before the wonder of meeting his Maker.

He looked at Marquet. 'What now?'

'I think you can guess. If you tell us what we need to know, it will not be too painful.'

There was a commotion in the passageway. Sergeant Bernard pushed into the room.

'Major, can I speak with you, in private?'

'Hardly a good time, Sergeant, but if you must.' Pointing at Robertson, he said, 'Cover him.' Pistols were aimed at Robertson's stomach. He looked round at the faces staring at him with a mixture of pleasure and awe at the success of his capture. Was this really a British spy?

Marquet followed Bernard to a quiet alcove.

'This arrived by express messenger, Major.' Bernard handed over a letter, watching intently as Marquet slipped his finger around Radet's seal.

Authority rescinded. Return immediately. Four words. At the moment of his victory, his dreams were dashed yet again. He read the words again. His eyes had not deceived him. He felt his knees buckle. He leant back on the wall for support. What now? Would he follow Maupont to the guillotine? Four words. The bile of injustice filled his throat.

'Are you all right, Major?' Bernard's concerned voice brought him back to reality.

'Orders, Sergeant, just orders.'

Marquet returned to his prisoner. 'Take him to the garden.' Two gendarmes pinioned Robertson's arms. Bernard led the way down the passageway and sets of stairs out into the hotel's walled garden. Guests and hotel staff slunk back into adjoining rooms. Silence descended waiting for the inevitable. Robertson took a last look at the blue sky. *At least it will be quick.*

'Leave us. I shall question the spy alone. I will summon you when I need you.'

Marquet took Robertson's arm, leading him to a corner of the garden hidden from sight from the hotel. They were alone. Marquet drew his pistol motioning Robertson to stand against the wall. Robertson stepped back, turning to face his executioner. Marquet raised the pistol extending his arm to avoid the smoke and recoil. Robertson was hypnotised by the muzzle of the gun, the source of his ending. He managed to close his eyes, whispering a prayer to himself.

Nothing happened.

He opened his eyes. The pistol was pointing to the ground. Marquet smiled.

'Go, go now.' He pointed to a door in the garden wall.

Robertson could not comprehend. 'Why?'

'The Revolution promised a new start for France. Now look, everything has reverted to what it was before. All that sacrifice, wasted. The injustice disgusts me. Now go.'

'Go where?'

'Go home.'

Robertson walked to the door half expecting to be shot. He pulled the door open, turned. Marquet mouthed "go". He took two paces out into the street, closing the door behind him.

A pistol shot rang out from the other side of the wall.

This book is printed on paper from sustainable sources managed under the Forest Stewardship Council (FSC) scheme.

It has been printed in the UK to reduce transportation miles and their impact upon the environment.

For every new title that Troubador publishes, we plant a tree to offset CO_2, partnering with the More Trees scheme.

For more about how Troubador offsets its environmental impact, see www.troubador.co.uk/sustainability-and-community